Sir Apropos of Nothing

SIR APROPOS of NOTHING

PETER DAVID

POCKET BOOKS

NEW YORK LONDON TORONTO SYDNEY SINGAPORE

The sale of this book without its cover is unauthorized. If you purchased this book without a cover, you should be aware that it was reported to the publisher as "unsold and destroyed." Neither the author nor the publisher has received payment for the sale of this "stripped book."

This book is a work of fiction. Names, characters, places, and incidents are products of the author's imagination or are used fictitiously. Any resemblance to actual events or locales or persons, living or dead, is entirely coincidental.

POCKET BOOKS, a division of Simon & Schuster, Inc.
1230 Avenue of the Americas, New York, NY 10020

Copyright © 2001 by Second Age, Inc.

Originally published in hardcover in 2001 by Pocket Books

All rights reserved, including the right to reproduce
this book or portions thereof in any form whatsoever.
For information address Pocket Books, 1230 Avenue
of the Americas, New York, NY 10020

ISBN: 0-7434-1234-6

First Pocket Books paperback printing July 2002

10 9 8 7 6 5 4

POCKET and colophon are registered trademarks of
Simon & Schuster, Inc.

For information regarding special discounts for bulk purchases,
please contact Simon & Schuster Special Sales at 1-800-456-6798 or
business@simonandschuster.com

Front cover illustration by Sonia Hillios

Printed in the U.S.A.

To Jo Duffy,
who was the first to believe

Acknowledgments

Apropos first stepped into my head fully formed during a Wisconsin convention called Mad Media in 1998, and would not leave until I wrote down his history. I'd like to thank early supporters of my little antihero, including Susan Ellison, Jo Duffy, Harlan Ellison (who fixed the opening paragraph), and the extremely receptive audiences at Dragon*Con in Atlanta where I first test ran sections of the book. Special thanks go to Andy Zack, who sold it, and John Ordover, who bought it; Sonia Hillios who did such a great job with the cover art; Gwen! David, who took the author photo (there, I'm covered in case they didn't fix the photo credit, which was wrong in the proofs); my daughter Shana, who read it but was skeeved by the parts with sex because her father shouldn't know about such things; Ariel, who's not old enough to read it now, but someday will be and will want to know why her name wasn't here, so here it is; and my beloved wife, Kathleen, for putting up with my neuroses.

And by the way . . . I wrote his story, but Apropos is still rattling around in my head. But that's a tale for another time.

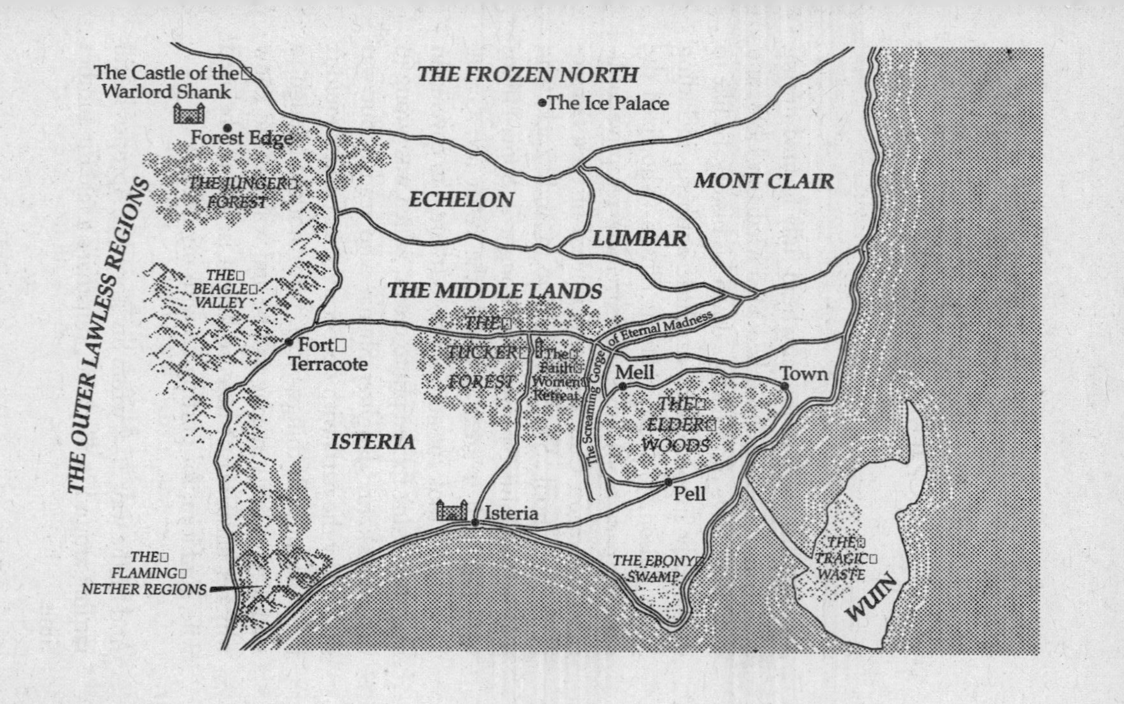

The Castle of the Warlord Shank
THE FROZEN NORTH
The Ice Palace
Forest Edge
THE JUNGER FOREST
MONT CLAIR
ECHELON
LUMBAR
THE OUTER LAWLESS REGIONS
THE BEAGLE VALLEY
THE MIDDLE LANDS
of Eternal Madness
The Screaming Gorge
Fort Terracote
THE TUCKER FOREST
The Faith Women Retreat
Mell
Town
THE ELDER WOODS
ISTERIA
Pell
Isteria
THE FLAMING NETHER REGIONS
THE EBONY SWAMP
THE TRAGIC WASTE
WUIN

Chapter 1

As I stood there with the sword in my hand, the blade dripping blood on the floor, I couldn't help but wonder if the blood belonged to my father.

The entire thing had happened so quickly that I wasn't quite sure how to react. Part of me wanted to laugh, but most of me fairly cringed at what had just occurred. I didn't do particularly well with blood. This tended to be something of a hardship for one endeavoring to become a knight, dedicated to serving good King Runcible of Isteria, a ruler who more often than not had his heart in the right place.

The recently slain knight also had his heart in the right place. This had turned out to be something of an inconvenience for him. After all, if his heart had been in the wrong place, then the sword wouldn't have pierced it through, he wouldn't be dead, and I wouldn't have been in such a fix.

I stood there stupidly in the middle of Granitz's

chambers. Like much of the rest of the castle, it was somewhat chilly . . . all the more so because I was only partly dressed and the sweat on my bare skin was feeling unconscionably clammy. There were long, elegant candles illuminating the room, giving it a rosy glow, since thick drapes had been drawn over the large windows to keep out both daylight and prying eyes. From nearby on the large and damaged four-poster bed, my lover—and the knight's wife (well, widow)—was letting out short gasps, trying to pull air into her lungs and only marginally succeeding. The tiled floor seemed to tilt under me for a moment, and I steadied myself as my mind raced, trying to determine what the hell I was going to do next.

The knight's name had been Sir Granitz of the Ebony Swamps, although he was generally referred to as "Sir Granite." The nickname had been well earned, for on the battlefield he had been indeed a sight to see. I had seen it myself, many a time . . . from a safe distance, of course, since my mother, God bless her, had not raised an idiot for a son. Understand: I did not, nor have I ever, shrunk from a fight when it was absolutely necessary. However, my definition of "absolutely necessary" wasn't precisely in keeping with that of everyone else in my immediate sphere.

For people like Granite, "absolutely necessary" included times of war, matters of honor, and similar esoterica. For me, the term "absolutely necessary" meant "self-defense." I considered war to be an utter waste of my time and energy, since most wars involved people I did not know arguing over matters I did not care about in pursuit of goals that would not have any direct impact upon me. As for honor, that was an ephemeral consideration. Honor did not feed, clothe, or protect me, and seemed to exist primarily to get otherwise inoffensive creatures into a world of trouble.

"Self-defense," however, was a consideration that I could easily comprehend. Whether it be an envious knight attacking me on horseback, an enraged dragon belching plumes of flame, or a squadron of berserker trolls swarming over the ramparts of a castle, those were instances where my own neck was at stake and I would happily hack and slash as the situation required so that I might live to see another sunrise.

I liked sunrises. They made anything seem possible.

Now, Granite . . . he was the type who would fight anywhere, anytime, at the least provocation. That is precisely the kind of attitude that gets one killed at a young age if one is not a formidable fighter. To his credit, that certainly described Granite. Well over six feet tall and built like a brick outhouse, he often found it necessary to enter a room sideways, his shoulders being too broad to be accommodated by a standard doorframe.

Sir Granite had returned most unexpectedly, at a moment that could best be described as inopportune. For at that particular point in time, I had been in the middle of opportuning myself of his wife.

As burly, as brusque, as fearsome as Granite had been, the Lady Rosalie had been the opposite. Delicate and pale, Rosalie had cast an eye that clearly fancied me in my direction. Considering that, at the time she did it, I was mucking out the stables and up to my elbows in horse manure, she clearly saw something within me not readily apparent from my surface appearance. She and old Granite had just come in from a ride; he perched upon his white charger, and she riding daintily sideways on a brown mare. She winked at me and I hurriedly wiped my hands on the nearest cloth, aware of the disheveled and frankly tatty sight I must have presented. The Lady Rosalie chose that moment to try and dismount. But her foot snagged on the stirrup and she tumbled forward, only my quick intervention preventing her from hitting the straw-covered floor. I caught her, amazed by how light she was. I'd bounced soap bubbles off my fingertips that had more substance.

For the briefest of moments, Rosalie insinuated her body against mine, mashing her breasts against my stained tunic. They were round and felt surprisingly firm beneath her riding clothes. It was not the fall that had carried her against me in that manner; she had done it deliberately with a subtle arching of her back that only I detected. Then, after the ever-so-brief gesture, she stepped back and put her hand to her throat in a fluttery manner. "Thank you, squire," she said, her voice having a most alluring musical lilt.

"Not . . . a problem, milady," I replied.

Old Granite did not seem to be the least bit supportive of my chivalric endeavors. His thick red mustache bristled and he said contemptuously, "I give you lesson after lesson, Rosalie, and still you can't so much as get off the damned horse. You shouldn't have caught her, squire. A far greater favor you'd have done her if you'd let her fall flat on her ass. It's the only way she's going to learn anything about successful mounting."

"Well . . . one of two ways," I said in a low voice, just enough for her to hear. Her cheeks colored, but not in embarrassment because she put a hand to her mouth to stifle what clearly sounded like a giggle. I grinned at her. She did not return the smile with her mouth, but it was clearly reciprocated in her eyes.

Granite smoothly jumped off his horse and thudded to the ground like a boulder. "Come, madam," he said, sticking out an elbow in a manner intended to be gallant but that instead simply appeared stiff and uncomfortable. This was not a man who was accustomed to the slightest gesture of gentility. She took his elbow and walked out with him, but glanced back at me just before they left.

From that moment, it was simply a matter of time.

I knew all about Granite. He was typical of Runcible's knights, spouting words of chivalry and justice, but doing whatever he desired behind the king's back. He made polite and politic noises to the king, but he could be as much of a brute as any common highwayman or any member of the Thugs' Guild, and he also had a string of mistresses in various towns and villages. He frequented the whores' tent, which was usually set up at the outskirts of an encampment during a campaign. More than one tart had supposedly come away from the amorous encounter with bruises to show for it when Granite was impatient with his own . . . performance. The mighty knight, you see, had a bit more trouble wielding his sword off the battlefield than on, if you catch my drift, and that difficulty translated to welts for those who couldn't easily overcome his problems.

I, however, had no such difficulties.

The Lady Rosalie, "heeding" her husband's suggestions to improve her riding abilities, took to the stables more and more frequently to get in practice time. Well . . . allegedly, that was the reason. But an intended hour of riding would end up an hour of conversing with me as I groomed and tended to the horses while she laughed and giggled and watched me perform my duties with a sort of doe-eyed fascination. I knew exactly where matters were taking us, and did absolutely nothing to deter them in their course.

One day she asked me to accompany her on a jaunt, since her husband had gone to deal with a minor uprising in the nearby city of Pell, and she was concerned lest bandits be wandering the roads. This, of course, wasn't her major concern. We rode several miles away from the good king's stables, chatting about trivialities, nonsense, and just about everything except for what really occupied our thoughts. By the lakeside, on a cool morning, nature took its course.

Let us just say that she did not ride exclusively sidesaddle.

I'm sure that I provided little more than an amusement to her, a dalliance. The obvious conclusion was that she was using me to get back at her husband, to make him jealous. But I doubt that was the case, because siccing the green-eyed monster upon Granite could only have fatal consequences. Rosalie may not have been the most polished apple to fall off the tree, but she was most definitely not suicidal. Maintaining a shroud of secrecy over our relationship heightened the likelihood of her keeping her pretty head on her shoulders. Besides, when you get down to it, isn't it the very illicitness of an affair, the forbidden nature of it, which makes it so exciting? Even pedestrian sex can be elevated to new heights when one isn't supposed to be having it.

That was probably what kept it going. Old Granite had made very clear to all and sundry that he thought very little of his wife's mental prowess. He considered her something of a twit. But twit or not, she ably concealed the existence of her tawdry little escapades (and I say that with only the fondest of recollections and greatest esteem) from this great warrior who thought himself one of the most canny and discerning of men.

Consequently, when it all came crashing down, it landed with a most pronounced thud.

The Pell situation, which started as something rather inconsequential, began to spiral out of control. Granite made a tactical error, you see. There had been a hard core of individuals utterly opposed to pouring more tax money into the king's coffers. I couldn't blame them, really. Most of the money paid in taxes didn't go into providing resources for public works, but instead either lined the pockets of key knights, or served to fund foreign wars that most of the peasants never heard of and didn't care about.

The hard core of individuals were endeavoring to organize protests, even stonewall against further taxes. The other peasants were reluctant to join with them. This came as no surprise to me. Being a peasant, I know the mind-set. One becomes so used to being downtrodden that one starts to believe that it's nature's intent that one should inhabit a low rung in society. Lack of movement is a formidable force to overcome.

The rabble-rousers called themselves the Freedom Brigade and set themselves up as enemies of the king and his policies. But they weren't enemies, really. An enemy is someone who has the capability to do you genuine harm. Calling this lot enemies was like referring to head lice as criminal masterminds. They had the ability to irritate, but they were no threat. Only one of the "Brigadiers" had any knack for rabble-rousing at all. I knew him from the old days. His name was Tacit, he was damned good-looking, and the women tended to swoon when they saw him coming. But swoon-inducers aren't necessarily great leaders of men, because men tend to mistrust other men who are that handsome. They start thinking that there's some other agenda in force, such as seeking out leadership just to get the attention and favors of the women, and perhaps they're not wrong to believe that.

Besides, Tacit wasn't the leader of the Brigadiers anyway. I don't even recall the name of the leader offhand; that's how forgettable he was. He was simply stolid and determined to change things, and wasn't particularly good at making that happen.

The truth was, the Brigadiers really just wanted to be in the favorable position enjoyed by those they were opposing, which is usually the case of protesters. If Granite had given them just a taste of the good life, the Freedom Brigade would have melted like a virgin's protests on her wedding night. One of the best ways to dispose of enemies—even perceived ones such as the

Brigadiers—is to make them over into allies and friends. When someone is not truly in a position to hurt you, that is the time to approach him or her with an air of camaraderie. Respect. Bribery. The Freedom Brigade could easily have been bought off. Hell, I suspect they could have been retooled into a formidable squad of tax collectors that would have put the king's own men to shame.

But not old Granite, oh no.

For Granite was a fighting man, you see. Put him on a field with a sword and buckler, give him a squadron behind him, point him in a direction—any direction—and say, "Kill," and watch him go at it. As a slaughtering machine, he was a thing of beauty. There was a tendency to elevate him in positions of importance and rank as a consequence. It's understandable, I suppose. Put yourself in the place of the king. You come riding up to a field after the battle is done, there are bodies strewn all over the place like clothes at a brothel, and there's one man standing there, wavering slightly, wearing tattered armor, copious amounts of blood (none of it his), and a somewhat demented smile. You would tend to think that this fellow knows what he's about. Such was the case with Granite.

Unfortunately, what the king did not realize is that just because one was skilled at one means of controlling an uprising—namely by whacking it until all of its internal organs are on the landscape—did not automatically translate into any sort of aptitude for handling other situations.

When Runcible learned of the situation in Pell, he

sent Granite, convinced that he was dispatching one of his best men to attend to it. Were Pell in the midst of full-scale riot, Granite might indeed have been just the fellow for it. But matters were still controllable. Why wade in with a broadsword when a whispering dagger would do the job?

Well, Granite used a broadsword and a half. He and his men rode in like the great damned king's own Ninth Army, stampeded through Pell, rounded up a dozen townspeople at random and threatened them with beheading if they didn't produce the names of the Freedom Brigadiers. The citizenry, who were upset about their taxes but not *that* upset, coughed up the identities like phlegm. Better to live poor than die with a few extra coins in your pocket.

Granite then rounded up the Freedom Brigade. What a great bloody row. The noise, the screaming . . . it was horrific. They captured almost all of them, and—truth to tell—the Brigadiers didn't exactly conduct themselves as heroes. Playing at being freedom fighters, criticizing the king from a distance, declaring that taxes would not be forthcoming and that the king should take his best shot at collecting them—these are all well and good in the abstract. Faced with a sword to your throat, however, your priorities tend to shift. Rhetoric takes a second chair to saving your own skin. My understanding is that they begged, pleaded for their lives. They wept, they entreated, they soiled their breeches . . . in short, they made godawful fools of themselves.

Once again, Granite could have gotten out of the entire Pell mess with a minimum of fuss and muss. Not old blockhead, no. The unmanly wailing of the Brigadiers offended Granite's sensibilities. He felt that his valuable time had been wasted rounding up such clearly unworthy foes. This set his anger all a-bubbling, and he needed an outlet for his rage. As it turned out, the only available target was the Brigadiers.

So he put the stupid bastards to the sword, every one of them. Every one except Tacit. Tacit had not been captured with the rest. They tried to take him, to be sure. But when Granite made his sweep, which dragged in the rest, Tacit had managed to fight his way through it, battling with the ferocity of a manticore when faced with death. His freedom had not come without a price. He lost half an ear and his right eye, poor bastard. He took refuge in the Elderwoods, his old stomping grounds, which he and I frequented as children. Once he'd reached there, he was a phantom. There he healed, and eventually returned to Pell with an eyepatch and a new and deadly resolve. Tossed capriciously in the crucible, he'd come through it forged into a cold and formidable enemy.

He rallied the people of Pell in a way that no others of the Brigade had managed, and he turned the entire town into an army. Every man, woman, and child rallied behind him, refusing to pay taxes and demanding the head and private parts of Granite.

Granite obliged. He brought his head, his private parts, and his sword arm—all still connected to the rest of his sculpted body—and he also brought along armored troops. They laid siege to the town, and within hours all of Pell was aflame and easily sixty percent of the populace was dead, and another twenty percent or so was dying.

Naturally this resulted in an eighty percent drop in taxes from Pell, which was what all of the to-do was about in the first place. Granite, however, had lost sight of that.

King Runcible had not.

He didn't get truly angry—he rarely did. But he informed Granite that he was not happy, no, not happy at all with the situation. Granite hemmed, hawed, made apologies, and tried to defend the extreme actions he had taken. "We shall have to think on this," Runcible said finally, which is what he always said when faced with something unpleasant. He then ordered Granite to patrol the outer borders of the kingdom.

I was present when the order was given, standing discreetly behind Sir Umbrage of the Flaming Nether Regions, the elderly knight whom it was my "fortune" to be squiring at the time. It was easy to remain out of sight behind Umbrage. He was such an uninteresting bastard that no one glanced in his direction. He would just stand there, long, skinny, white-haired, and jowly beneath his scraggly beard, leaning on his sword and nodding as if he were paying attention to what was going on.

Granite bowed, nodded, and left immediately.

I, opportunistic little creep that I was, saw my chance to have yet another toss with the Lady Rosalie. I waited until I saw Granite ride away on that great charger of his, and then went straight to the chambers that he shared with his lady.

Rosalie, bless her heart, read my mind. She was lying

there, naked and waiting. And she was holding her crystal ball.

Now, Rosalie had no knack for fortune-telling, but she fancied that she did. She obtained the large crystal from a woman purporting to be an oracle, and she would stare into the crystal ball for hours on end, trying to discern her future. Every so often she would make thoughtful pronouncements in a voice that I think she thought was great and profound. In point of fact, it just sounded like Rosalie talking oddly. I never paid any mind to it. It seemed a harmless enough diversion.

"Did you see me coming in that?" I asked teasingly.

She smiled in that odd way that she had, that made the edges of her eyes all crinkly. "In a manner of speaking," she said, and laid the crystal ball on the floor.

My tunic was off and my leggings were just descending below my knees when the door burst open. There was Granite, looking considerably larger than he had when he'd been riding off into the distance minutes before.

I caught only the briefest of glimpses, though, because the moment the door opened, I had already rolled off the bed, landing on the far side, out of view. I may not have had a good deal going for me, but my reactions had always been formidably quick. Long practice, I suppose in keeping one eye behind me at all times. I lay paralyzed on the floor. The door slamming back against the wall had covered the noise of my thudding to the ground, but I was concerned that any further movement on my part might attract his attention. Granite was a formidable warrior with a sense of hearing only marginally less sharp than his blade. I held my breath so that he didn't hear it rasping against my chest, but I was positive that he could nonetheless detect my heart slamming in my rib cage. In any event, I certainly didn't want to risk making scrabbling noises against the floor. That would tip him for sure.

Rosalie was not the brightest of things, but barely controlled panic gave wings to her moderately capable brain. Upon the door slamming open, she had automatically clutched the sheet under her chin, covering herself. "Milord!" she burst out. She certainly did not need to feign her surprise. "I . . . I . . ."

I practically heard the scowl in his voice. "What are you about?" he demanded.

"I . . . I . . ."

"Well?!"

She suddenly tossed the sheet aside, wisely letting it tumble atop me to further hide me, although—truth be told—I'm not entirely certain how effective a disguise it would have been, since piles of laundry do not generally tend to quiver in fear. "I was . . . waiting for you, milord!" she said, throwing her arms wide and no doubt looking rather enticing in her utter nudity. "Take me!"

I still held my breath, which, actually, was no great trick, because my chest was so constricted I couldn't exhale if I'd wanted to. My heart had also stopped beating, and I was fairly sure my brain was in the process of shutting down. I was hoping, praying that Granite would go for the bait. If he did, and she distracted him sufficiently, I could creep out on hands and knees while they were going at it.

"Take you where?" demanded Granite, never one to pick up on a cue.

"Here! Now!"

He had to go for it. How could he resist? Certainly I couldn't have. Then again, I wasn't a knight, at least not yet. Knights were apparently made of sterner stuff. Either that or Granite was just too block-stupid to be distracted from something confusing to him. Apparently he'd gotten a thought into his head, and the damned thing wouldn't be easily dislodged, probably because it was fairly quiet in his brain otherwise and the thought enjoyed the solitude.

"How could you have been expecting me when I didn't know I was coming back?" demanded Granite.

"I . . ." I heard her lick her lips, which were probably bone dry by that point. "I . . . anticipated . . . or hoped, at least . . . that you would return to service me once more before you left."

"I didn't. I came back to get my lucky dagger. I forgot it."

"Oh."

If Rosalie had just let that harmless little "Oh" sit there, we might well have avoided discovery. He was, after all, perfectly willing to accept that she was a nitwit. Unfortunately, because a silence ensued, Rosalie felt the need to fill it with words. "Yes. I . . . saw it over there on the wall and knew you'd be back."

Granite, unfortunately for us, was able to track the conversation. "You just said that you were hoping I'd return to service you. Now you say you knew I'd be back for the dagger."

"Yes, I . . . that is to say . . . I . . . that . . ."

There was another dead silence, and I could only imagine the blood draining from her face as her poor brain twisted itself about in confusion. I heard the door bang suddenly and prayed that he had simply exited with no further words . . . but that hope was short-lived as I heard the bolt slam into place.

Granite was no idiot. I had to give him that much. "What," I heard him rumble, "is going on?"

I thought furiously at her, as if I could project words into her brain in hopes that they would spill out of her mouth. *I am . . . tongue-tied by your presence, milord . . . I would say anything just in hopes of saying something you want to hear, milord . . . I hoped that, in your returning for your dagger, you would savage me like a wild animal, milord . . .*

Something. Anything.

"Don't . . ." There was a choked sob. "Don't hurt him, milord. . . ."

Anything but that.

I heard a roar then. I think the word *"What?!"* was in there somewhere, but it was like trying to sort out one particular scream from the howling of a hurricane. There was a quick sound of steps coming around the bed, and suddenly the sheet was yanked off me. My bare ass was still hanging out as I squinted up at Granite.

He wasn't moving. He trembled in place, seized with such fury that he could not yet budge.

I rolled to my feet, yanking my breeches up as I went. The bed was a huge four-poster affair, and I leaned against one of the thick oak bedposts, trying to compensate for my fairly useless right leg. I must have been quite the sight at that moment. At that age, I was thin and gawky. My arms were well muscled from years of hauling myself around while compensating for the lameness of my leg. My ears stuck out too much, and I didn't have normal hair so much as a thick, wild mane of red that proved annoyingly difficult to brush or style. My nose was crooked from the times in the past that it'd been broken. My best feature remained my eyes, which were a superb shade of gray, providing me with a grim and thoughtful look whenever I put my mind to it. However, I suspect at that point that he wasn't exactly concerned with admiring my orbs.

We stood there, frozen in time for half an ice age it seemed. I don't even think he quite focused on me at first, as if his brain was so overheated that he needed time to fully process the information. "I . . . know you!" he said at last. "You're Umbrage's squire! You clean out stables! You're Appletoe!"

"Apropos," I corrected him, and then mentally kicked myself. As if I wasn't in enough of a fix, I had to go and remind him of my name. Why didn't I just stick my neck out and offer to hack it through for him?

Then I realized he wasn't waiting for an invitation, as I heard the sword being drawn before I actually saw it. I took a step back, making sure to play up my limp so that I could seem as pathetic as possible.

His eyes were fixed on me, but he was clearly addressing his nude wife. "A squire? You cuckold me . . . for a squire? For a shoveler of horse manure? *For this you shame me?!*"

Rosalie was not going to be of any help. Her mouth was moving, but no sounds were coming out.

There was no point denying the actual cuckolding. I can be a dazzling liar given the right circumstances, but these were certainly not they. So I felt my only hope was to try and address the other side of the equation. "Now . . . now t . . . t . . . technically, mi . . . milord," I stammered out, "there's been no, uh, actual shaming, as it were. No one knows. You, Rosalie, me . . . that is all. And if we can agree to, uh . . . keep this among ourselves, then perhaps we can just, well . . . forget this all happened, sweep it under the carpet until . . . until . . ."

I was going to say, "Until we're all dead and gone." Unfortunately, at that moment Rosalie found her voice.

"Until you leave again," she suggested.

He swung his sword around and bellowed like a wounded boar. I tried to back up. Not only did my limp impede me, but also my feet became tangled in the sheets and I tumbled to the floor. Rosalie let out a shriek.

I considered telling him at that point that he might or might not be my father, but that statement—albeit true enough—seemed to smack so much of a desperation move that I figured it would be perceived as a ploy. So I chose to appeal to the one thing which might serve as his weak spot.

"Where's the honor in this?!" I shouted.

He was standing directly over me, his sword drawn back and over his head, ready to bring it slamming down like a butcher slaughtering a bull. This was no ordinary sword, it should be noted. The damned thing had teeth: jagged edges running down either side, particularly useful for ripping and tearing. It was also formidable for a good old-fashioned slicing. If the blow had landed, it would have cleaved me from crotch to sternum. But he froze, his mustache bristling as if acquiring a life all its own. I thought for a moment that it was going to rip itself off his lip and come at me. "Honor?" he growled. "You have my wife . . . and speak to me of your honor?"

"Your honor, milord, not mine . . . I . . . I am nothing." I spoke as quickly as I could. "I am nothing, no one . . . but that, you see . . . that's the point . . ."

"What is?" The sword, which had a far more formidable point than any points in my repertoire, hadn't moved from its rather threatening position above me.

"Well, milord, obviously . . . when my corpse turns up, and you, as a man of honor, why, you'll have to own up to your slaying of me . . . and explain why . . ."

"I have no intention of hiding it," he snarled. "Not a man in the court will deny my right as a husband!"

"No question." I felt the longer I kept it going, the more chance I had of talking him out of what was clearly his intended course. "But look at the slaughter situation."

"The . . . what?" The snarl had slightly vanished; he seemed a bit bemused.

"Look at you . . . full in your leathers, your sword in hand, rippling with power . . . and here I am, half-naked, on my back, unarmed . . . well, honestly!" I continued, as if scolding a recalcitrant child. I couldn't believe the tone of voice I was adopting. One would have thought that, in some fashion, I possessed the upper hand. "And a lowly, untitled squire with no land or privilege at that. Where is the challenge in skewering me? Where is the redemption of honor? A stain on your status as husband and man requires something more than mere butchery."

I would have felt just a bit better if the sword had wavered by so much as a centimeter. It did not. But neither did it come slamming down. "What," he asked, "did you have in mind?"

"A duel," I said quickly, not believing that I had managed to get it that far. "Tomorrow . . . you and me, facing off against one another in the proper manner. Oh, the outcome is foregone, I assure you. I'm but a squire, and lame of leg at that. You're . . . well . . . you're you . . ."

"That is very true," he said thoughtfully.

"Certainly you'll massacre me. But if we do it in the manner that I suggest, no one can look at you askance and say, 'So . . . you carved a helpless knave. Where is the challenge in that?'" I paused and then added boldly, "I'm right, milord. You know I am. A husband's honor restored. A philanderer put to rights in a way that no one can question. It is the thing to do."

I had him then. I knew that I did. I glanced at Rosalie, praying that she would keep her mouth shut and say nothing to spoil the moment. Thank the gods, her lips were tightly sealed.

In point of fact, I had no intention of battling Granite on the field of honor. The man could break a griffin in half. I wouldn't have had a chance against him; he would have driven my head so far down into my body that I would have been able to lace my boots with my teeth. Fighting him man to man would be suicide.

I intended to use the night between now and tomorrow to bundle together everything that I owned in the world—which was, admittedly, not much. Then, under cover of darkness, I would slip away. There was a wide world out there beyond the kingdom of Isteria, and I couldn't help but feel that there had to be sufficient room in it for Apropos. Granted, my flight would be an irretrievable besmirching of my honor. To hell with that. Honor did not pay bills, nor keep one warm at night. Apropos would disappear; I would take up a new identity. It wasn't as if the one that I had was all that wonderful anyway. Start a new life, learn a trade, perhaps become a knight eventually somewhere else. Who knew? Perhaps, at some point in the future, Granite and I would meet on the battlefield. We would face each other, glowering . . . and then, with any luck, I'd shoot him with an arrow from a safe distance.

All this occurred to me in a moment's time.

And then Granite said, "I don't care."

That was all the warning I had before the sword swung down toward me.

Fortunately it was warning enough as I rolled out of the way. The sword came down with such force that it clanged into the floor and bit right into the paving with that jagged edge.

Rosalie shrieked. So did I. Even as I did so, however, I lurched to my feet, pushing up with my good leg. I was still clutching the sheet in my hand, and I threw it over his head to obscure his vision. At that moment Granite struggled with his sword, trying to extricate it from its state of being temporarily immobilized, and he sent up a caterwauling that was a fearsome thing to hear. So infuriated was he that he had practically lost capacity for speech, instead generating a sort of inarticulate grunting.

Picking a general area of the sheet that seemed to represent his head, I drew back a fist and struck as hard as I could. My upper-arm strength, as noted, is somewhat formidable. I hit him on what felt like the side of his head, probably causing a profound ringing in his ears. But by that time he had a firmer grip on his sword, and he ripped it from the floor and swung it about so that it shredded the sheet, which fell to ribbons around him.

Rosalie was shrieking his name, trying to get his attention. That probably wasn't the wisest course. He seemed ready to decapitate her as soon as look at her, but at the moment he appeared more interested in getting to me. He swung again, cleaving straight down once more. Apparently he didn't have an abundance of moves, but the few he did have were devastating if they happened to connect. I lunged onto the bed, barely avoiding the sweep. Rosalie adroitly vaulted over me as I rolled toward the other side, landing on my feet but not smoothly, and stumbling back.

He came after me, his eyes wild, his face turning as red as my hair. He didn't seem in the mood to reason.

I heard a pounding at the door. The sounds of commotion had started to attract attention. The door, however, was bolted. People were calling Granite's name, asking if anything was wrong. Granite didn't bother to respond. I made a motion toward the doorway, and he leaped to intercept. He moved with the speed of a damned unicorn, cutting off my possible escape route. A sneer of contempt was curling his upper lip.

I backpedaled, headed back toward the bed. Symbolic that it should begin and end there. Rosalie had wisely vacated the bed by that point, grabbing a dressing gown from her wardrobe and tossing it over her nakedness. "Milord, stop! Stop!" she said over and over. He seemed disinclined to attend to her wishes, however.

He swung at me and I ducked again, and he hacked right through one of the bedposts. It fell into my hand, a length of wood about three feet. It was better than nothing, although not much. I gripped it firmly, waited for his next pass. It wasn't long in coming. I couldn't let it come into direct contact, because he'd just chop right through the wood as he had done a second ago. I stepped back, angling the wood, and managed to deflect the flat of his blade, preserving my makeshift cudgel for perhaps another second or so.

Granite repositioned himself, the better to get some swinging room so that he could properly bisect me. The hammering at the door became louder. Apparently others in the castle were being drawn by the sounds of . . . of whatever it was they thought they were hearing. Granite still hadn't said anything particularly useful, seized as he was in voiceless paroxysms of fury.

He took a step back, and for a moment I thought my salvation was upon me, for he stepped on the crystal ball that Rosalie had placed so delicately upon the floor. The large crystal rolled under his foot, causing Granite to stumble. I tensed, waiting. If he went down, I might have a chance to run madly for the door. I don't know how likely escape would have been in that situation; there were apparently knights crowding in on the other side, and the moment that Granite managed to find his voice, they might very well seize me bodily and hold me still so that Granite could finish the job. But I was dealing with one crisis at a time.

He went to one knee, but it was the most fleeting of pauses. Then he was on his feet once more, holding the crystal ball and glowering at it as if the thing had been sentient and tried to trip him out of spite. I made a desperate bolt for the door, but only got a short distance when he froze me with a glance. I stood paralyzed some feet away, my body sideways to him with my lame right leg facing him.

The perpetually screaming Rosalie made a grab for him from the back. He shoved her away without even looking at her, cocked his arm, and let fly with the crystal ball. It hurtled toward me at roughly chest-high level. From the size of the thing and the speed with which it was moving, it would easily have broken any bone with which it came into contact.

My next action was entirely instinctive. With my right leg useless, I pushed off with my left, driving my body weight forward. As I did so, I swung the cudgel, keeping my eye on the crystal ball.

I was nothing but fortunate that Granite had thrown the crystal ball fast and hard. If he had put any sort of spin onto the thing, causing it to move in, say, a curve, I never would have hit it. As it was, it was nothing short of miraculous that I made contact at all.

When the cudgel struck it, I felt a shudder that ran all

the way down to my elbows. The cudgel shattered when it hit the crystal ball, and the sphere rocketed right back at Granite. It struck him soundly in the forehead and bridge of the nose, before falling to the floor and rolling serenely away. I'm not sure what that damned thing was made of, but Rosalie had certainly gotten her money's worth. It seemed indestructible.

Granite stood there with an utterly stunned expression. His eyes crossed, his hands went slack . . .

. . . and his sword clattered to the ground.

"Sir Granite!" The shouting increased from the other side of the door. There was now concerted pounding against it. Perhaps those on the other side had become even more alarmed at the sudden cessation of noise.

I threw myself across the floor, skidding on my stomach, and grabbed the fallen pigsticker. If I could keep the bastard at swordpoint, I might just be able to reason with him somehow. I angled the sword upward, and was about to issue a warning to him to stay right where he was. I then realized just how profound an effect the crystal ball had had upon Granite, for the knight chose that moment to fall forward like a great tree.

Naturally he fell on the sword.

Rosalie emitted a shriek, as her husband's fine, teeth-bladed weapon suddenly appeared protruding from his back. Granite, for his own part, hadn't said anything especially useful in the past few minutes, and his record didn't change. He gave off a confused-sounding grunt. He slid down the length of his blade without having any true awareness that he had just managed to kill himself. There seemed to be a sort of blubbery surprise in his face. Having slightly broken his fall by catching himself on his elbows, he saw that I was clutching the sword's hilt. He batted me away, as if annoyed that I was handling his beloved weapon. He clutched the hilt himself then, pulled slightly, and it was at that point that he truly understood, I think, that his entire upper torso was serving as the blade's new scabbard. He managed to spit out a profanity, which is not the most noble of last words, but probably among the more common, and then he slumped over, unmoving.

There was now a repeated thud against the chamber door. Several of the knights were obviously putting their shoulders into it in an organized fashion.

"This is not going to look good," I observed. Considering the circumstances, I sounded remarkably sanguine. The truth was that I was terrified, and it was all I could do not to vomit.

Rosalie made small whimpering noises, not appearing to be of much help. I was going to have to do the thinking for both of us. Unfortunately, my brain somewhat locked up at that moment, but I forced it to unfreeze as I whispered sharply, "My tunic! Quick!" Rosalie grabbed my fallen clothing and tossed it to me. I threw it on so that I would have the appearance, at least, of propriety.

"Hide! Hide!" she urged.

"No time! Just yell what I'm yelling, and do it as loudly as you can!"

"But they'll hear you!"

"That's the point!" And without further explanation, I began bellowing, *"Don't do it, milord! You have so much to live for!"* Bless the old fool, he'd had the grace to die with his cold, dead fingers wrapped firmly around the hilt. All the more convincing for my needs as I wrapped my own fingers around his dead ones (a nauseating sensation, that) and kept calling out, "Please don't! Don't do it! They're not worth it! We need you! This isn't the way!"

Rosalie appeared clueless as to what I was about, but she went along with it. At first she spoke with clear hesitation and uncertainty, but within moments she yowled as well, "No, my darling! Don't do it! Listen to Apropos! Don't do it!" Obviously she wasn't quite clear on what it was he wasn't supposed to do, but that didn't stop her from participating with considerable gusto.

At that point, the door cracked open, the bolt shooting across the room and ricocheting off the far wall, and the knights fairly stumbled over each other to get into the room. Sir Coreolis of the Middle Lands was the first one in, with Sir Justus of the High Born directly behind him. Others were crowding in, and I could even spot my master—my alleged master, in any event—Sir Umbrage trying to get a look. There was gasping and muttering, and suddenly the words "Make way! Make way!"

They parted like priests in a fart factory as the king stepped through them to examine the situation personally. At his right elbow, as was not unusual, crouched the court jester, Odclay. They could not have been a more disparate twosome. The king, for all that I might have held Runcible in contempt, was nonetheless a regal figure with great bearing and presence. He looked somewhat like a hawk, his entire face almost pushed forward as if he was in flight and seeking out prey with his beak.

His reputation as a just and fair man, and supernaturally canny opponent, preceded him. Preceded him so much, in fact, that oftentimes he had to run to keep pace with it. His queen was a gentle, doting, and relatively inoffensive thing, and had produced for the king his sole heir (heiress, I suppose), the Princess Entipy, whom I had never met.

Odclay, on the other hand, was bent and misshapen. A few tufts of light brown hair stuck out at odd angles on his equally misshapen head, and his eyes were mismatched colors . . . and the colors kept changing. He was good for capering about and drooling every now and then. He was screamingly unfunny and therein lay the humor.

Runcible did not speak immediately. That was his way. I was never quite sure whether he did it deliberately so that he would appear great and wise as people waited for him to utter a few words (as was the general perception) or whether he was just so clueless that he never knew what the hell to say and had to strive mightily to manufacture even the most rudimentary of pronouncements.

"What . . ." he finally asked in slow, measured tones, "happened?"

Rosalie looked panic-stricken. She had been babbling about how Granite should not do it, whatever it was. But now faced with the question, she had no clue as to how to proceed. Fortunately enough, my mind was already racing. Near-panic tends to focus me.

Letting out a long sigh, clearly not wanting to be the bearer of bad news, I slumped and only at that point released the hilt. I made no endeavor to hide the fact that my hands had been on it. Only a guilty man would feel the need to hide his involvement, and I was anything but guilty. At least, that's what I had to put across.

"Sir Granitz," I began, using his more formal name rather than his popular nickname, "was devastated over the outcome of the Pell uprising."

"Go on," the king said slowly.

"Well . . . his presence here makes it obvious, doesn't it," I continued. "I mean, you, Highness, sent him on a mission . . . but yet, he has returned here. He did so because . . . because he felt that he was not . . ." I bowed my head. ". . . not worthy. Not worthy of the trust that you had put on him."

I paused then, waiting to get some measure of how this was going down. The king considered the words long and hard.

"Go on."

Clearly the king was not going to be of much help.

I decided I sounded too calm, considering the circumstances. So the next bit came out all in a rush.

"He was consumed by second-guessing what happened with Pell. Here he was asked to put down a simple uprising, and it resulted in a loss to Your Highness of tax income . . . and yet, to Granitz, that was not the worst of it. No. No, he had a side that he hid from all of you . . . hid from everyone except for the Lady Rosalie, of course. A softer side, a side that was . . . was . . . was . . ." I was stuck, and I slammed the floor with my fist to get myself going again. ". . . was distraught, yes . . . distraught over the loss of life. The women, the children of Pell, crying out, consumed in fire . . ."

"I thought he set the fire," said Coreolis in polite confusion.

"Yes! Yes, he did, he set the fire and he ordered the slaughter, but that doesn't mean that inside him, there wasn't a . . . another side, a softer side, that cried out against what he was doing. A softer side that would not let him rest. Call it a conscience if you will, call it a spark of the divine, call it guilt if you must . . . call it whatever you wish, but understand that it completely undermined and unmanned him."

"Unmanned him." The words spread like skin rot throughout the gathering.

"What were you doing here?" That was Sir Justus, and he sounded suspicious.

"Happenstance, milord. Pure happenstance. I was passing by the door and I heard what sounded like . . . sobbing. It was so high-pitched, so womanish, that I naturally assumed it to be a damsel in distress. Even a humble squire must attend to such a situation when it presents itself. That, at least, is what my good lord and master, Sir Umbrage, has taught me."

He had, in fact, taught me nothing of the kind. Nonetheless, the other knights looked at him and nodded in approval, and he took their acknowledgments with clear pride over having done his job well.

"So I entered, inquiring as to what I could possibly do to render aid . . . and discovered, to my amazement, Sir Granitz in the midst of the most terrible lamentations."

"The Granite one? Nonsense!" said a skeptical Justus.

I was not ecstatic about the way the burly knight was looking at me. "In all the years, I never heard him utter so much as one lament. Not a one."

There was murmuring assent from the others. I did not like how this was going, so I raised my voice—a chancy enough proposition, considering the circumstances I was facing—and said, "And in all those years, did 'the Granite One' ever once let down his king in the way that he recently had?"

Momentary silence fell over the room as they racked their brains trying to recall such a happenstance. Giving them time to ponder was the last thing I wanted to do, however. I limped in a circle, accentuating my bad leg, to appear all the more pathetic . . . and also, ideally, all the more helpless in the face of an uncaring and overwhelming fate. "Did it ever occur to any of you that perhaps there were softer aspects of himself that he kept hidden? Hidden deep down so that it would elude your collective notice? A heart that bled when his enemies bled, a heart that felt the pain of every loss. But his head, milords . . . his head would not allow any of you good knights to see that which he himself found so repulsive: his gentler side. Why do you think he was so formidable at war on the field, eh? Because he was accomplished at being at war with himself! Yes, milords, with himself. But this most recent, crushing indignity, this devastating failure . . . it was too much. The years of repression burst from him."

I took a moment to try and compose myself, but only a moment, because as soon as one of them even started to form a sentence, I was off again. "The instant I entered, he bolted the door to make sure that no others would follow. Overwrought and ashamed of himself, he knew he could not face you, my king, after he felt he had failed you. Nor did he feel that he could face you good sirs, knowing that this more tender side was . . . and there is no delicate way to put it, milords . . . out of control. He felt the only honor left to him was a respectable death. But I," and I clenched my fist, "did not agree. I begged him to reconsider, to think of all the carnage and slaughter that he could still inflict. There was so much death left for him to live for. But he wouldn't attend my words, milords, no, he wouldn't." I made a visible effort to keep back the tears. "With those great hands of his, those great hands that have throttled so many, he tried to drive his sword into his mighty chest." There were gasps now. I was reasonably sure I had them, but I didn't let up. My voice went up an octave, to properly project my fear and terror. It wasn't much of an acting chore. If I didn't get the job done, they'd see through this crap I was hurling at them and have me executed, most likely right on the spot. "I struggled with him, milords. As presumptuous, as doomed to failure as that may sound, I tried to stop him. I'm sorry, Sir Umbrage," I said to my master as humbly as I could. "You have taught me" (no he hadn't, see above) "to obey the wishes of a knight, whatever the circumstance. But I could not do so here. I wanted to try and save one of the king's own greats. I wanted to be . . . to be a hero, milords. To be like you." This brought nods of approval. My heart was pounding. "And then . . . and then—"

"And then . . . then it was amazing, milords!" Rosalie suddenly cried out. I felt my heart sink into my boots.

One false word out of her and the entire thing was done for. But Rosalie rose to the challenge. "My husband's strength . . . it's . . . it's legendary. But this young man, this squire, nearly matched him pound for pound, milords! He came so close, so close to saving the life of my noble husband, your noble peer. But . . . ultimately . . . he . . ." She choked on the words. "He . . . could not. My noble lord threw himself upon the upraised blade of his mighty weapon. 'With honor' were the last words he managed to gasp out . . . and then was cleaved in half the great heart."

It was damned near poetic. Even the vaunted Justus himself was becoming choked up.

There was dead silence. I realized that all eyes were turning toward the king. There might have been suspicion, confusion on the parts of the other knights, but ultimately, it all came down to the king. His thinking shaped the reality.

His gaze never waved from me. As withering an opinion as I'd earlier formed of him, I felt myself starting to get nervous. His reputation for incisiveness and canniness had to be based on *something.* If he'd seen through the nonsense, I was finished.

And finally, he said two words and only two:

"Good work." And then, with no further comment, he turned and left the room, the jester cavorting and drooling after him.

The relief that flowed through me caused me to sag and almost collapse, but I managed to catch myself before that happened. The other knights came forward, clapping me on the shoulder, clucking over the corpse of their fallen comrade, and offering succor to the lovely Rosalie. Rosalie in turn caught my eye and there seemed to be a slight glittering triumph in there, as if to say, *See? I could spout nonsense as well as you.* Clearly, she could. And she was in an excellent position as well. As widow, she would acquire all of Granite's lands and titles, and no doubt have a number of eligible men courting her. She wouldn't require the attentions of a lowly squire and stablehand, which was fine by me. As entertaining between the sheets as she was, I didn't need the aggravation. Besides, if anyone caught sight of us together or any whispering began about us, it could utterly shred the tissue of lies that was, at that point, my means of salvation.

Several knights had pushed Granite's corpse out of the way like so much refuse, and they were talking to me pridefully of honor and bravery. I said nothing in reply, because really, there was no point. They were speaking to hear their own voices, not to elicit comments from me. I bobbed my head, smiled, stated my appreciation for their well wishes, and counted myself damned lucky all in all.

I wasn't like the others, you see. I had no particular dreams of glory, no desire to do great things, go off on dangerous quests and the like. I simply wanted to survive, get some lands, acquire a title perhaps, avenge myself on my father, and find one particular man and kill him, all in the least hazardous means possible, and then retire in comfort. Until I managed to do that, I intended to keep my head down whenever and wherever I could.

One, however, attains power by being noticed. So I was walking a fine line, drawing attention to myself and casting myself to be as brave as any of the lords of the manor, while at the same time taking care to keep my head on my shoulders. That was my goal: the illusion of danger, as I liked to call it.

"Apropos . . ."

I turned and saw that the king had reentered. All became silent once more.

"I have a fairly hazardous mission to be assigned. I think you are just the man for it. Report in one hour." He nodded as a means of indicating that the meeting was over, and then exited once more.

"You lucky bastard," said Coreolis.

"Handpicked by the king for a dangerous job," Justus said. "I remember the first time I drew such an honor." He held up his right hand, which was missing three fingers. "Got off lightly for it. Damned lucky to have my opportunity. And now you'll get yours."

And as I felt a chill down my spine, I couldn't help but feel that the ghost of Granite was thinking that exact same thing, and laughing in anticipation of me getting mine.

Chapter 2

I am by trade neither writer nor historian; I am merely a master of fabrication, which I am told is all one requires to take up either of the aforementioned pursuits. I am also told that readers require something of an immediate nature—preferably something involving action—to draw them into a narrative. If nothing else, apparently, it gives the reader an idea of where the story is going to go. I can sympathize with that requirement. I have lived my life with not the faintest clue as to where it was going, walking an extremely angled and treacherous path in order to arrive at no place that I actually started out to get to. I've had no choice in doing so since, of course, it was my life and I had to live it. You, the reader, on the other hand, are entering my life voluntarily, and it would be the greatest cruelty to subject you to the same aimless sense of confusion that has permeated my existence. So the preceding chapter existed primarily to give you some footing, some certainty about my life, which is certainly more than I ever had.

Now that, ideally, you have been drawn into what I laughingly refer to as my career, I shall go back and recommence the narrative at the only truly proper place for it: the beginning. This, I assure you, will bring us back to the false beginning—which will actually be somewhere around the middle by the time we rendezvous with it. The ending will arrive in its own time, as it often does. So . . . let us begin.

I never actually knew my mother's name.

That's not to say she wasn't there. It's just that she never told me. Oh, she told me an assortment of monikers that she collected in the way that the underside of a bed collects dust. She would choose a different name from month to month, sometimes from week to week, depending upon her mood. I'm not entirely certain why she adopted this odd practice. Perhaps she was anxious to distance herself from whoever or whatever she once was. Perhaps she sought out a fanciful existence and thought that varied names would bring her a bit closer to that aspiration. Perhaps she was just crazy.

I will, for convenience's sake and the sanity of the reader, refer to her by the name she bore at the time that she also bore me, and that name was Madelyne.

Madelyne was a rather ordinary-looking woman. Once she was a pretty enough thing, but that had been many years before I made her acquaintance. She did not speak all that much of her early life. But based on things that she occasionally let slip, plus rather coarse comments that were made by others, I suspect that she got herself pregnant at a young age, possibly by some knight errant. Knights fascinated Madelyne, even at a tender age. She was prone to worshipping them, and indulged in that tendency by worshipping them while prone. An assignation with a knight was a dream come true for her. For him, I would assume, it was merely a lark, a tumble in the high grass with a willing young thing from the town. He went on his way, and about a month later, she went on her knees one morning and vomited rather convulsively, seized in the unloving arms of morning sickness.

She could have tried to abort the child, but no one valued life more devotedly, or more foolishly, than Madelyne. I say foolish because people who attribute any sort of miracle to life can only be considered fools. We humans pat ourselves on the back, strutting and preening when we manage to pop out a single child, and I've seen dragons lay nests of a half dozen eggs or more. Even the most common creature can generate the biological process that is reproduction. Life, miraculous? Nonsense. Putting infants on this planet, there's nothing miraculous about that. What's miraculous is when we let them live to grow out of infancy.

Upon informing her loving and understanding parents of her pregnancy, she was summarily shown the door by her father and informed that her presence would no longer be required, because they resided in a decent house, by God. A house of respect, a house of peace, where such things simply didn't happen.

In case you're thinking that my mother was sent out into the snow with poor, helpless little Apropos couched within her womb, you can set that aside right now. Would that my own conception had been that . . . tidy.

With nowhere to go and none to take care of her,

Madelyne resolved to care for herself. But a mere two weeks later, as she lay within the makeshift shelter she had created deep in the Elderwoods, Madelyne curled up in pain, her guts twisting and on fire. Thunder cracked overhead, adding a sense of morbid drama to the entire business. Melodrama aside, the outcome was that there was a puddle of bloody mess pooled around her by the following morning. Poor Madelyne. If she had only managed to keep her mouth shut, nature would have disposed of her indiscretion in its own good time.

But despite the loss of her child, she was still out of luck. Her father had made abundantly clear to her that she was no longer welcome in his home, having violated the strict rules of propriety set down. Pregnant she might no longer have been, but strumpet and tramp she quite permanently was. Since there was no going back, Madelyne opted to go forward.

She wandered, sticking primarily to the back roads and less-traveled areas, wanting to avoid the more common paths frequented by highwaymen. It was a brutal and grueling time for her, but when she recounted it for me, she tried to turn it into a grand adventure. She spoke to me of creatures that she had encountered . . . unicorns, dragons, and the occasional werecreature. If she was to be believed, the Elderwoods were simply crawling with such wondrous beasts.

Her most fanciful tale was her description of stumbling upon the birth of a phoenix. Such things happen with great rarity, particularly considering that there is only one phoenix at a time, reborn from the ashes of its predecessor.

Madelyne claimed that it was a particularly cold and bitter night when she witnessed "the event," as she was wont to call it. She was huddled within a makeshift shelter of well-placed branches, shivering against the elements because she had no money to stay at an inn, and she had been unable to secure any sort of gainful employment, times being what they were (as they so often are). She felt her toes and fingers going numb as she lay curled up, and flexed them as much as she could to try and restore circulation to them.

And then she felt something very curious. It was warm air, wafting in her direction. On such a cold night, it was hard for her to guess from whence such warmth might be originating. But if there was a heat source anywhere to be had, then she was quite determined that it should serve her as well as anyone else. The possibility did not escape her that it might be a fire lit by the exact type of criminal, robber, or highway bandit that caused her such concern, but at that moment she was not especially inclined to be concerned about anything other than avoiding freezing to death.

She made her way through the Elderwoods, following the heat source, blowing into her palms to try and get some bit of warmth into her hands, since her threadbare gloves were affording her almost no protection at all. There was a clearing just ahead of her, and what she saw astounded her.

A massive, birdlike creature was enveloped in flames.

She had never seen anything like it, although at first she fancied she was witnessing the pitiless slaying of a roc or some other creature. She looked around to try and spot whatever vicious hunters might have brought the poor animal to such straits. But slowly she came to realize that she was, in fact, the only human being in the area. She also realized that the creature was being immolated, not from without, but from within. The creature itself generated the flames consuming it, from deep within its own fiery heart. Nor was the creature crying out in any way, indicating that there was no pain involved. Indeed, it appeared to accept its fate with quiet, dignified resignation.

Within moments, the creature had been reduced to a huge pile of ashes. Even at that point, she didn't fully comprehend what it was that she was seeing. The fact was, she was concerned only about her own chill, and the growling of her belly reminded her that she had not eaten in some time. She took a step toward the pile of ashes in a vague sort of hope that there might be bits or parts of the bird—freshly cooked, of course—upon which she could dine.

Before she got anywhere near the ashes, however, they began to stir. It was a subtle movement, but enough to fully capture her attention and startle her out of her wits. She bolted back to relatively safe cover behind the trees and watched with goggle-eyed amazement as the ashes suddenly scattered to the wind, thus revealing a bird that was clearly in the image of the one which had just died. At first she thought that somehow the creature had survived, but quickly she realized that it was impossible. This new animal was utterly unscarred by any flame. Not a feather was so much as lightly scorched.

That was when she realized, finally, what she was seeing.

The phoenix stretched its wings to their full span, which my mother claimed was as wide as ten men. Its head pitched back and it let rip to the sky a screech so earsplitting, Madelyne maintained that forever after she had a slight ringing in her ears. Then the phoenix flapped its mighty wings, beating the ashes into a great cloud of soot, before leaping skyward with a final resounding caw and disappearing into the night sky.

My mother took this as a sign. An omen if you will. For a person does not witness one of the rarest occurrences in all of nature and un-nature and not be changed by such a moment. There are those who believe, for instance, that to view a shooting star is to be forewarned of some coming great birth or death. How much greater significance, then, was it to be spectator at an event of such rarity that it was mythic? By seeing the death and rebirth of the phoenix, by being guided there via destiny's mischievous hand, my mother became convinced that she was meant for a great destiny as well. Since death and birth were involved, she was quite certain that it had something to do with one, or both, of those processes.

I can't blame her, I suppose. She was alone, and scared, and really rather young. It was a foolish attitude for her to have, but it helped get her through the night.

The next morning, reinvigorated and convinced that she would have a great destiny if only she was willing to go out and find it, Madelyne set out to make something of herself. She took the main roads, no longer fearing highwaymen. Her reasoning was that whatever greatness she was intended for, it was certainly not to be accosted by robbers and then killed when she was unable to provide them with any money. Part of me shudders at the thought of such misplaced confidence. On the other hand, she traveled in that manner for a week without being molested or harassed in any way by anyone, so perhaps Madelyne did indeed know what she was about.

After a lengthy journey, she entered the outlying borders of the state of Isteria. King Rufus DeVane, who found himself beset by several neighboring chieftains who were would-be monarchs, governed Isteria at that time. DeVane was generally considered to be a weak ruler at best, although he tried as hard as he could to rule the land with an iron hand. Of those who challenged his rule, his major competitor was one Runcible the Crafty (a name that he himself had fostered and seemed rather pleased to maintain). Runcible was known as a man of few words, preferring to let his actions talk for him. When he did speak, it was of an idealized realm in which his followers—his knights, as he would make them—would fight on behalf of justice and tolerance, introducing a new golden age to the land.

All this talk was well and good, and of little interest to the peasants who watched the warfare go on year after year, and cared not a whit for politics. The odds were that whatever happened in the great castles of the land, and whoever it was who might be in charge, the average citizen would continue his life unchanged once all the shouting was done.

Finally, in her wanderings, Madelyne came upon a place of business known as Stroker's Inn, which was—unsurprisingly—owned and operated by a gentleman named Stroker.

Perhaps "gentleman" is not exactly the right word. "Brute" might be more on target, as would "thug," "bastard," and "bloody bastard." Stroker was massively built, with thighs the size of ham hocks and a mind as sharp as . . . well . . . ham hocks. Deucedly two-faced, Stroker was generally attentive and caring to his customers, and a total cretin when it came to his staff. However, much to Madelyne's "luck" (if such a word can be applied to the circumstance), Stroker was in need of help since another serving wench of his had been inconsiderate enough to die of food poisoning . . . generated, naturally, by Stroker's kitchen, although he denied it utterly.

So when Madelyne came to him, looking for a place to stay and for gainful employment, Stroker was happy to accommodate her. She knew from his loutish jaw, his unshaven face, his squinting left eye, his multiple chins, and the raspy cough which he had had for years (which I could only hope signaled the presence of some lethal illness)—she knew from all this that he was going to be a problem.

Which, of course, he was.

Before you get the wrong idea, no: Stroker didn't endeavor to have his way with her. You'd have thought he was exactly the type who would engage in such practices, but the opposite was true. He had no desire for or interest in assailing the questionable virtue of any of the women in his employ. He liked to claim that he was not interested in taking any risks of either contracting diseases or putting more brats into the world. A few suggested under their breaths, and far from his hearing, that perhaps he preferred his meat from the other side of the cow. In retrospect, knowing what I know of him and recalling his overall brutality and nastiness, my suspicion is that he simply wasn't capable. Couldn't quite get his sword out of the sheath, as they say. It would certainly explain his overall frustration with women in general. To have something so near and yet so far, the distance measured by . . . inches . . .

I think I've made my point.

But Stroker was hard on my mother in other ways. Harder than he was on the other girls, because they simply worked there, but had somewhere else to go when their workday was done. Husbands or parents, or even a simple hovel of their own. But not Madelyne, not my mother. She had none to care for her and nowhere to go. So Stroker gave her a small room that no one ever used because it was so far from the hearth that it was beyond freezing much of the time, even in the summer. My mother, though, was a veteran of nights in the forest, and so such extremes of temperature didn't daunt her. At least she could curl up upon a mattress, thin and pathetic as it might be, and she didn't have to worry about rain or snow upon her head. It was still a consideration since the roof leaked, but she was able to position herself so that none of it fell upon her.

Stroker endeavored to "push" my mother in other directions as well during her stay there. Particularly he urged her to provide . . . "company" . . . for the men who came by, for my mother was a comely wench and men asked after her. But she declined, politely but firmly. Stroker was the sort of brute who was perfectly capable of forcing her to bend to his will, but first and foremost he was concerned about his customers, and he was worried that an unwilling woman could claw up a patron's face, or worse, slip a knife between his ribs. So he did nothing to press the matter. She thought he'd forgotten about it. Actually, he was simply biding his time.

So Madelyne remained there, having found her niche, and becoming something of a fixture at the bar and inn. One day was pretty much like the next.

That is not to say that nothing changed in Isteria. King DeVane, as many suspected would happen, was forced out. Runcible came into power and, displaying mercy, exiled the fallen DeVane. Runcible's mercy was greeted with anger from DeVane, who—as he passed into banishment—swore a terrible oath that he would avenge himself upon Runcible one day. From what I heard, he swore even greater oaths a week later when someone, or perhaps a band of someones, went to his place of exile, and threw him bodily into a mile-deep canyon. Thus died DeVane, who might be alive today and perhaps even back in power somehow, if he'd only kept his big mouth shut at what could only be considered an inopportune time.

King Runcible sent royal proclamations far and wide, speaking of the new era that was to exist under his reign. The proclamations meant little to much of the populace, which was understandable considering most of them couldn't read the damned things. Those who could shrugged a bit and said that they would have to see it to believe it.

One has to credit Runcible's knights. They made a superb show of it. Jousts and open functions were held to which all inhabitants of the realm were invited, and they marveled at the knights' strength and power. But such warfare was for display only. Actual disputes had to be settled by ways other than trial by combat, which had been the method of choice. Instead, Runcible himself became a prime adjudicator, listening thoughtfully to disputes that were brought before him, saying little other than asking a few prodding questions, and then returning with a reasoned and fair decision. Runcible and his knights were quite well thought of in our little piece of the world.

And Madelyne was no less adoring of knights than she had ever been. She would speak of them constantly, in wide-eyed and impressed tones. Stroker kept saying that he found her incessant speculations tiresome, but she gave it no mind. Then, all unexpectedly, matters came to a head.

It was a dark and stormy night.

There had been a good deal of talk around the realm, far more than usual, about the activities of Runcible and his knights. There had been talk of a convocation of dragons which had been razing some of the eastern territories, although it had been unclear as to whether they were acting independently, or were in the employ of some individual—royalty or sorcerous, it was open to much dispute. But what everyone knew for certain was that Runcible's men had ridden out in force, and although some heavy casualties had been sustained, they had managed to beat back the threat.

Indeed, that evening at Stroker's, the storminess of the night was being attributed by some to the wrath of the Dragon God. Various customers, huddled in against the weather's ferocity, suggested that the hard rain falling was actually the Dragon God's tears, and the lightning cracking through the sky was the flashing of his eyes. Others ventured a related theory, that the battle between good and evil had been raised from the physical to the spiritual plane, and what was being seen on earth was nothing less than a full-scale war between order and chaos. There was also one poor bastard who attributed lightning and thunder to superheated particles too small for the eye to detect. He was driven out into the storm for his blasphemy and was promptly struck and killed by lightning, which caused a good laugh amongst the customers at Stroker's that evening.

Abruptly the door burst open, and in clanked about half a dozen knights in armor. It was, I am told, an impressive sight. They were huge, weathered men, but surprisingly seemed none the worse for wear. That was something of an accomplishment considering how foul the conditions were outside. There was a seventh man as well, although he was not armored but rather heavily cloaked . . . perhaps a druid, my mother would later speculate, or a retainer, or a priest or a squire, or even a magic user . . . a weaver, as they were called. Weavers didn't happen to wander into the area of Stroker's all that often. They tended to stick to the routes where the heavier thread lines were, and Stroker's was off the main thread paths. That was by design rather than happenstance. Stroker didn't particularly like weavers, and he'd carefully had the area sounded to make certain it was a weak junction for threads (or "ley lines," as some others called them). Weavers tended to show up, eat your food, drink your mead, then tap into the threads and convince you that they had paid you for everything. This was not grief that Stroker needed.

For a moment, no one said anything. Then everyone (except the knights) jumped slightly as the thunder rumbled so loudly that it seemed to have taken up residence within the inn itself. Stroker was clearly unsure whether the knights meant trouble or not. He came halfway around the bar and stood there, leaving the broadsword that he kept behind the bar for trouble within easy reach. Although he must have been a bit concerned, for he was outnumbered and not in a position to display a true show of force.

It did not, however, matter in the end. One of the knights—presumably the one of highest rank—took a step forward, his armor glistening in the candlelight. When he spoke, his voice was surprisingly soft. "We seek a private room so that we may take food and drink and entertain ourselves in relative quiet, away from prying eyes. And we wish to have our own serving girl, who will attend to all our needs."

The fact that the knights had not immediately torn the place apart apparently emboldened Stroker, who coughed a couple of times loudly and then said, "And I am to provide this for you out of the goodness of my heart?"

The knight reached into the folds of his cape and withdrew a small bag. He balanced it in his palm for a moment, as if weighing and considering the contents, and then he tossed it to Stroker in a casual underhand manner. Stroker caught it and glanced inside. Apparently there were enough gold coins within to satisfy even his avarice.

"That should suffice to obtain the services we requested," said the knight, and after a pause he added, "with funds left over to buy a round of drinks for everyone in this fine establishment."

This elicited a salutary cheer from the other patrons. There is no great trick to commanding the loyalty of a group of drunkards. Buy them drinks, and they're yours.

Now, it should be noted that during all of this Madelyne was watching from the corner, enraptured. She had seen but one knight in her life, and from what she told me, he could not begin to compare in magnificence to even the least of this group of soldiers who had wandered into her place of business. Unconsciously she began fiddling with her hair, straightening her potato sack of a skirt. Stroker must have noticed her fussing, because he turned to her and called her over. She came to him immediately.

"You belong to those gentlemen for the evening," growled Stroker, "and will attend to all their needs. Take them to . . ." He appeared to consider options, and then said, ". . . the Majestic Suite." He had raised his voice a bit when he said it so that the knights would hear. Most of them didn't seem to care. The one who had been doing the talking tossed off a small salute.

She stared at him blankly. "The what?"

With an irritated nod of his head, he said, "The room in the back. You know."

She did indeed know the room in the back. It was hard for there to be any confusion, considering that there was only one room there. But it had never been called Majestic or anything else other than the back room. Madelyne, in many ways, was still rather naïve—at least until that night's events were over—and she didn't grasp that Stroker might be posturing for the benefit of the knights. So she mentally shrugged and guided the knights to the back room. Their apparent leader glanced around with an air of vague indifference and simply said, "This will do."

There was a long table down the middle, with benches on either side. The knights took positions on the benches and Madelyne proceeded to serve them. The knights did not address her directly, but instead talked among themselves in low, cautious tones. Madelyne suspected that they were discussing affairs of state, secret matters that were meant for the ears of knights and kings and none other. She made sure to keep the drink flowing, biting back her natural inquisitiveness and instead being content to bask in their presence.

Minutes became hours. The storm had continued unabated, prompting a number of the customers to refrain from going outside. Consequently they had simply fallen asleep in their seats or at their tables, some of them with their drinks in hand. Madelyne moved among the snoring crowd, maneuvering effortlessly with more mugs of mead for the knights in the back room. The only other individual remaining awake at that point was Stroker. Nothing seemed to faze him.

When Madelyne walked into the back room with the drinks, she felt a little trill of warning down the back of her neck. The knights were looking at her in a way that they hadn't before. Indeed, earlier it had seemed as if they were barely noticing her presence, beyond the fact that she was the means by which they acquired more drink. But now they were studying her, appraising her, and apparently liking what they were seeing.

My mother, the poor thing, was flattered. She ignored the little buzz of alarm and instead chose to be pleased that she was garnering that sort of attention from such noble personages.

She placed the mugs down in front of each of them, *thunk, thunk, thunk,* just as she had repeatedly during the many hours prior to that. In those cases, their hands had immediately wrapped around the handles as if afraid that someone would burst in and steal their beverages. This time, no one did so. They didn't appear to notice the drinks were there. Their concentration remained upon her.

The fact that she was so much the center of attention actually emboldened her, when it should have warned her to get the hell out of the room . . . not that it likely would have made a difference. "Gentlemen . . . I know none of your names," she said, imagining that she sounded rather saucy. "Here I've been serving you all this time, and we haven't been properly introduced. I know you not . . . nor do you know me."

"We don't need to," said another one of the knights.

"Oh." She wasn't quite certain what else to say in such a circumstance, with a reply that seemed so harsh. "Well . . ." She curtsied slightly and then said, "If you will be needing anything else, my name is—"

She didn't get the chance to tell them.

One of them was on his feet, moving so quickly that

she never actually saw him rise. He clamped a hand over her mouth, cutting off her sentence, and then he pushed her roughly onto the table. She cried out in surprise and confusion, but since her mouth was covered her cries were muffled.

She heard a tearing of cloth, and was so disconnected from the moment that she didn't fully realize, until the chill air washed over her, that her dress was being torn from her. Pieces of metal were clanking to the floor as several of the knights were divesting themselves of their armor. "Hold her," growled one of them.

The thunder blasted, and the room seemed to light up with lightning, and then of course even the infinitely naïve Madelyne understood what was to happen. She managed to get her teeth around the fingers of the knight who was muting her, and she sank her incisors deep into his flesh. He let out a yelp, reflexively loosening his grip, and then Madelyne cried out at the top of her lungs. With perfect timing, thunder smashed once more, covering her cries so that none heard her.

That was, at least, what she believed. I think it perfectly likely that Stroker did indeed hear her cry out in fear and terror, but simply chose to do nothing. Why should he have? He had no particular love for Madelyne, and very great love for money. If she needed to be sacrificed upon the altar of his greed, then he would gladly twist the knife himself.

The ironic thing is, it's not as if my mother was a virgin, a delicate flower, or a prude. She worshipped the knights. They were like unto gods to her. They could easily, I suspect, have had their way with her if they had merely plied her with a drink or two and a few seductive words. I can't say she would willingly have taken on the lot of them . . . but I wouldn't have been surprised. But these were violent men, these knights. They were bloody bastards, is what they were. Warriors who had no grasp of niceties and sweetness. Oh, they likely had some notions of courtship and courtesy, but these things were reserved for noble ladies of standing . . . not ignoble ladies who were lying flat. Madelyne was not worth sweet words or seduction. These were men who were still riding the giddy euphoria that comes with war. They had displayed their armed might to one another, fighting battles that the simple peasant could only guess at. Now they were eager to show their abilities of conquest in other realms. Realms that should have been, as far as others were concerned, of a gentle nature. But these were rough men, and gentleness was not for them.

And so they took her repeatedly, right there on the table. Splinters lodged in her bare buttocks, and bruises were raised on her upper body where pieces of still-worn armor slammed into her when a knight moved atop her with less than caution. As for her lower body, well, at first she felt pain, but that was only for the first couple of "suitors." After that she was numb as they continued to spear her with all the compassion that a butcher displays for a hog. The numbness very likely originated in her mind as sort of a fail-safe, and all sensation below her waist simply shut down.

That was how the knights of King Runcible the Crafty entertained themselves that night. One after the other, and even the one who wasn't a knight, he took his turn with her, and when they were all done, they did it again. By that point she was not even trying to say anything. She simply lay there like a battered sack of wheat, her thoughts in a very faraway place filled with dancing unicorns which approached her shyly as she, virtuous and without stain, held out her hand to them and let them gently lick her palm. Nearby her in her fantasy realm, the phoenix bird birthed itself once more. High overhead, a great purple dragon flew by, wings outstretched and lazily beating the air.

She drifted off into that pleasant world, and there she resided until she felt some sort of warmth upon her face. Slowly her eyes fluttered open and she realized that it was streams of sunlight caressing her. The thunderous night had passed, and she had lain unconscious upon that hard wooden tabletop, her skirts hiked up around her waist, for who knew how long. The knights were gone, and the only thing to mark their passing was the soreness between her legs.

Stroker walked in, and whatever it was he was expecting to see it certainly wasn't that. For just a moment, surprise played across his face. Perhaps he felt a flickering of concern for the woman. He might have regretted his inaction of the previous night, for he must have known in his bones what the result was going to be; and maybe there was a spark of human compassion and guilt that clawed at him, which rattled his spine and chilled his blood.

If there was anything like that, it passed quickly, and his normal scowl darkened his face once more as he said gruffly, "Get cleaned up. You look like crap." He paused as if he was considering adding something, and then thought better of it, turned, and walked out, slamming the door behind him.

And thus was I conceived.

It occurs to me, as I read over the previous narrative, that I may come across as cold or hardhearted. I have described to you, after all, the brutal and pitiless gang rape of my mother. I have done so in a fairly straightforward manner. Where is the passion, you might wonder? Where is the sense of outrage? Did I not care about the awful circumstances that resulted in my being placed upon this earth?

Once, passion was all that sustained me. Anger burned brightly in my chest, and a sense of moral outrage consumed me. These were, after all, knights. King Runcible would boast at community fairs and such that they represented the best that mankind had to offer. They were to stand for fair play, for justice, for honor. My mother knew differently, of course. She knew what a pack of bastards they were. Either Runcible knew of their efforts and quietly endorsed them—in which case he was a screeching hypocrite—or else they acted without his knowledge, in which case his craftiness was a sham and he lived in quiet ignorance. But she said nothing. She kept her silence, as did the other girls who worked in the inn.

They did so out of fear, of course. Oh, they could have gone to the king, tried to accuse an assortment of the knights of their crime. But Madelyne would have had trouble identifying the men in question, for they had kept their hoods up the entire time they had been there, and the dim light had continued to cloak them in shadows as black as their own souls. Even if Madelyne had been able to single out specific knights, she would have had no proof to offer. Her bruised body, even the child growing in her belly, could easily have been the result of any other assignation with the types of brutes who usually consorted with tavern floozies. To accuse a knight without proof would have been slander, and slander against a knight of the realm was suicide.

So she said nothing. Indeed, as she rolled off the table and went to wash herself, she knew already that she was going to say nothing. She also claimed later, to me, that she knew even at that moment that I was already in process.

I have no rage now. I have no pity now. It has all been burned out of me, exorcised after decades of experiences and strife, of trauma, of triumphs and almost immediate setbacks. I look upon my life and I am simply left shaking my head, wondering how I managed to contain all the rage that surged in me without spontaneously combusting or in some other way experiencing an abrupt end.

My mother claimed it was because I had a destiny, and my anger was what I needed to survive.

Perhaps she wasn't all that naïve after all. Either that, or she simply learned from her harsh trials, just as I did, and dealt with it in her own way. At least she didn't lose her mind. Certainly other women in that position might have done so.

Or maybe she did, and I simply didn't know, since I was a little insane myself. Maybe I still am.

Chapter 3

My mother needed money, for she supposedly knew immediately that she would be preparing for my arrival. And she knew where her potential for earnings lay.

You see, what I neglected to mention in my earlier narrative is that when she awoke that next, sun-drenched morning, there was something of value upon her belly, in addition to something of value (albeit questionable) within it. It was a handful of coins, glittering in the sunlight. The oh-so-generous knights had left it there. Whether they intended it mockingly or sincerely, or whether they really gave it no thought at all, it's difficult to say. It was far more for a night's work, though, than she had ever received in all her time as a serving wench. The knights obviously considered it simply another form of service.

Her trembling hand wrapped around the coins, and only then did she truly believe they were there.

Money for sex.

It seemed a rather elegant solution to her. She had dreams of building up a sort of nest egg that she could use to buy me . . . well . . . I'm not quite certain, actually. An education, perhaps? A career? A means out of poverty? She might not have had her plans fully formed at that juncture. She only knew that a means of making money had been handed her.

Not that the idea of selling herself hadn't flittered through her head before, particularly on cold nights when she would have done damned near anything just to obtain a bit of shelter. But she still had enough ties to her old way of thinking that the notion of such activities was repugnant to her. Well, her evening with the knights had certainly realigned her thinking on that. The thing that struck her the most was how she had managed to take herself away to a happy place of fantasy and escape. Hidden away in the innermost recesses of her mind, she had very much liked it there. The prospect of returning to that place was not unattractive to her. And if it was possible to earn money while doing so, why then . . . it was almost like a paid vacation.

Besides, it wasn't as if she had to worry about getting pregnant.

And so my mother turned to prostitution.

She didn't quit her day job. She maintained her regular serving duties at Stroker's, if for no other reason than that it provided her with shelter. But she quickly developed a keen eye for seeing potential customers in the daily parade of ruffians and vagabonds who would pass through the inn. Just as quickly, she grew skilled at letting them know in subtle—and sometimes unsubtle—

ways that she could be easily had for a fairly reasonable price.

Stroker became aware of her activities in short order. Far from being morally outraged, he had no problem with it. As far as he was concerned, he supported anything that provided encouragement for return customers. He did, however, want to make certain that he benefited in the short term as well, and insisted on taking a portion of Madelyne's earnings as commission. She didn't argue the point. She was still bringing in more money, at a faster rate, than she would previously have thought possible, so she had no real reason to complain.

In the meantime, she was quite aware of my presence in her belly. Fortunately I developed slowly and was something of a runt, even at my eventual birth, so the fact of the pregnancy was something she was able to conceal for quite some time. If Stroker had had a brain beyond the brutish canniness that passed for thought, he might have figured it out. What woman is available for entertainment every day of the month? Nonetheless, it slipped past Stroker for a good long time. Eventually, though, even he—the oaf—noticed it.

In point of fact, someone brought it to his attention. A patron was lying flat on my mother's belly when I decided that that would be a good time to announce my presence to the world. Imagine, if you will, the surprise of the patron to feel a fluttering but firm kick coming through my mother's belly and bumping against his own stomach. He froze, as did she, for she knew what it was and he thought, but couldn't be sure. Just to make sure that there was no doubt, I kicked a second time, and he leaped off her as if her insides had suddenly become shards of glass.

"What the hell do you have in there!" he shouted.

"In where?"

"In your belly! Gods . . . you're pregnant!" he said without waiting for her to reply. "I'm not the father! Don't you dare say I'm the father!"

My mother was not given to bursts of wit, but her reply was about as close as she usually came. "This is our first time together, you idiot," she said. "What, you think you're so potent that you not only impregnate a woman, but you do it retroactively? Skip the first six months of the term? Why not just have sex with a woman and cause the child to spring out of her head fully formed before you even put on your hat to leave?"

He was not amused. Nor was Stroker when he found out when the irate customer told him moments later.

He dragged her into the back room. There was something of a sick irony to that considering that's where it had all started. "Who's the father, you damned trollop!" he shouted.

His wrath had worked on her before, nicely cowing her or prompting her to turn away in fear. But that didn't happen this time. It was as if, with the revelation of her secret, she felt strengthened rather than exposed. The angrier he became, the calmer she was. "I don't know who the father is," she said. "And it's odd that you would call me a 'damned' trollop. You made money off me and contributed nothing."

"I gave you a roof over your head!"

"Men who seek my services aren't concerned about architecture. I could ply my trade in a tent. If I'm damned, Stroker, you're twice damned."

He backhanded her then. He wore a large ring with a dragon on it for luck, and the thing tore at her lower lip. But she didn't flinch. As blood trickled down her chin, she didn't even reach to wipe it off. She just stood there, with a level and unwavering gaze. There was no contempt in that stare, or pity. There was, at most, vague disinterest.

He hit her twice more, trying to elicit some sort of response from her. Still there was nothing. He clearly considered doing it again, but it wasn't having the desired effect and he didn't have the will or the attention span to continue with the futility of browbeating someone who simply wasn't responding. So with an irritated grunt, which was what usually passed for pithy conversation from Stroker, he turned and headed for the door.

Just before he reached it, though, something seemed to click in his tiny little brain. Perhaps he was able to do something as simple as basic mathematics, but he suddenly appeared to figure out just precisely when it must have been that the conception occurred. He turned back to her, his hand still on the door handle, and he said, "The knights. The knights did this."

She said nothing, but there must have been something in her eyes—a fleeting look—that convinced him of the accuracy of his surmise.

"A child borne of rape." Amazingly, even the seemingly unflappable Stroker appeared daunted by that. "An ill-omened thing. You would have been wise to try and stop it from blossoming in your belly the moment you realized it." Such a thing would easily have been possible, and they both knew it. There were certain mixtures of herbs that, when consumed, could flush an unborn child from its resting place with alacrity, at least in the early stages.

"It's not an ill omen," she said sharply.

"It is. A child of violence only begets violence, and brings disaster to whatever it touches."

"I saw my own omen," she informed him, and for the first time, she spoke of the phoenix bird.

He stared at her skeptically, and when she finally told the tale, he said, "Even assuming it's true . . . of what interest is that? Of what moment?"

"It was a sign to me," she said firmly. "A sign of birth and rebirth. A sign of great things that were going to happen to me as a result of a birth. I asked a soothsayer about it," which was a flat-out lie, but she wanted to bolster her credibility.

"A soothsayer," he said with a snort. "A soothsayer will say whatever sooth you desire to hear if the money's right." But he didn't appear to want to press the point after that, settling for walking out with a final look of cold disdain, the loud banging of the door intended to signal his annoyance and opinion of the entire matter.

The thing was, even though she was lying about the soothsayer, my mother spoke the truth about her beliefs. She was of the firm conviction that her pregnancy was part of some grand plan. That her having witnessed the birth of the phoenix was indeed an omen, and that I was the centerpiece, the payoff, of that omen. In a sick sort of way, it's almost amusing.

My mother's carnal activities were curtailed after that. I was an active sort, you see, and since I had stumbled upon my motor skills, I became rather adept at letting my presence be known at inopportune times. Plus, several weeks after that, it became a moot point as my mother's belly began to swell in a distinctive manner, so much so that even a blind man would have seen the truth of things. So my mother restricted her activities to serving drinks and waiting for me to make my arrival upon the scene.

In a perverse sort of way, a family almost formed around her. There was another serving wench, named Astel, and she was a kindhearted young thing. Surprisingly bright for a mere server, Astel was younger than Madelyne, and yet seemed to take her under her wing. Astel had thick curly blond hair and a musical laugh, which I would have cause to hear later on in my life any number of times. She also had wide hips and an ample bosom, but when she ran she did it so lightly that it seemed she was made of mist. She heard of my mother's tale about the phoenix, and seemed entranced by it. She fancied herself a diviner of mythic matters, and told my mother that as far as she was concerned, Madelyne's reading of the situation was absolutely on target. This excited Astel somewhat, for she said she had never been in the presence of future greatness, and appreciated the opportunity that fate had afforded her.

She was the midwife the night that I was born.

When Madelyne went into labor, it was not a quiet affair. Oh, she described herself as being brave and silent, but that wasn't how Astel described it to me in later years. In point of fact, Madelyne howled like a tornado. Her caterwauling was so loud that it supremely disturbed the customers. So Stroker exiled her to the stable for the duration of the labor in order to spare the delicate sensibilities of his usual crowd of drunkards, layabouts, and petty criminals.

Considering the set of lungs Madelyne possessed, they likely would have heard her from the damned moon, if not for the fact that a hellacious storm showed its face that night. Astel told me that it was one of the most terrifying nights of her life, and I do not doubt it. Horses belonging to various patrons reared up in their stalls, whinnying fearfully, as Madelyne lay sprawled on a bed of straw and huffed and puffed away.

The calm that she had displayed all during the pregnancy, the quiet certainty that she was fulfilling some magnificent part of a greater plan, all evaporated during that stressful night. She bellowed profanities, she cried out for mercy, she cursed the knights who had done this to her, she cursed my name and she didn't even know what my name was. She just cursed it in spirit.

During all that, the dedicated Astel stayed by her side. Madelyne clutched Astel's hand so tightly that she nearly broke her fingers, but that didn't stop Astel from remaining right where she was, determined to help Madelyne see it through. She wiped the sweat from her brow, gave her small drops of liquid, spoke gentle words of support and endearment even though there were times that she was convinced Madelyne didn't hear a word.

Madelyne thrashed and screeched some more, and the horses were going mad with fear. It was a damned good thing they were tied to their place, otherwise they might have stampeded and my existence on this sphere would have been abruptly truncated as my newborn form was ground to pulp beneath panicky horses' hooves. Thunder smashed overhead, God apparently desiring to make a personal statement about the agonizing birth process that he had chosen to inflict upon humanity. Sort of like affixing one's signature to a particularly grisly masterpiece.

With one final, hair-raising howl that she seemed to be channeling from damned souls confined to the lowest recesses of hell, Madelyne's muscles convulsed and I was spat out of her nether regions into Astel's waiting arms.

It was not an auspicious debut.

Apparently not satisfied having exiled a woman in need to a stable filled with the pungent smell of sweaty animals and their droppings, Stroker felt the need—moments after my birth—to see for himself why something as simple as a woman trying to force something the size of a grapefruit through a bodily orifice the size of a grape should be causing such a hullabaloo. The door to the stable banged open, thunder cracking to accentuate the nominal drama of his arrival, and he stared at the scene in front of him.

My mother was gasping, covered with sweat, still not

having quite recovered her senses. Astel was cradling me in her arms and cooing softly. She looked up at Stroker and, apparently expecting him to share in the joy of the moment, said, "It's a boy."

"Good. He can pull his weight around here—" Stroker started to say, and then he caught sight of me. *"It's deformed!"* he snarled.

"He's a he, not an it," Astel said, but she didn't dispute his observation.

"Look at him!" said the angry Stroker, standing over me. "His right leg! It's withered and twisted! He'll never walk properly! And he's underweight! He's a runt, all shriveled and no meat on him! The first good cold snap will kill him!"

"He'll fill out . . . he'll be fine," said Astel.

"My baby . . ." It was Madelyne, speaking in a coherent and relatively calm manner. Her arms were weak but still half-raised, her fingers fluttering. "Let me hold him. . . ."

Astel started to hand me over to Madelyne . . . and then Stroker intercepted her and snatched me out of her arms.

"I'm exposing him," Stroker announced.

"No! You can't!" Astel said, horrified. She started to move toward Stroker to try and snatch me back, but he drew back a meaty hand and Astel, who wasn't always the most stalwart of things, retreated before the anticipated blow could land.

"I'm doing it a favor," Stroker informed her. "Better a quick death before Madelyne becomes too attached to something that won't survive anyway."

Madelyne was still confused, still not fully understanding what was happening around her, but she was able to grasp enough of it to realize what Stroker's intentions were. He was going to lay me out on a rock somewhere, or deposit me in the forest, leaving me to die from the elements or—just as likely—to be killed and devoured by the first passing predator looking for a light snack.

At that point, I started to mewl as infants generally do shortly upon birth, waxing nostalgic for the safety and warmth they have just left behind. This pitiful wailing was enough to spur Madelyne and, weak as she was, she still managed to lunge forward and grab at Stroker's leg. "No! He's mine! Mine! Give him to me! I'm his mother! Give him to me!"

"Stop your yowling, shrew!" he snapped, and he kicked at her with his free leg. He caught her squarely in her still weak stomach, and she lost her grip on him and rolled up in pain. But she didn't stop shouting, didn't stop demanding that he give me back to her at that very instant.

"I'm doing what's best for all concerned!" Stroker said, and he slung me over his shoulder like a sack of wheat.

My little mouth was right at the base of his throat.

And I sunk my teeth into him.

Teeth? I hear you say. Yes, that is correct: teeth. A right leg worth a damn, I did not have. Body weight, there was none. But God—in his infinite perverse wisdom—had chosen to endow me with a full set of teeth the moment I sprang from the womb. And they were, so I'm told, sharp little things, and powerful jaw muscles accompanied them.

My teeth crunched down into his neck as if I were a tiny vampire. I was probably just hungry. If so, the first liquid to cross my lips was not mother's milk, but blood, for that was what I drew when I bit him.

Stroker let out a startled yelp that was so high-pitched one might have mistaken him for a woman. *"Get it off!"* he shouted and, matching deed to words, he shoved me off him and sent me tumbling through the air. Had I landed on my head that might well have been the end of me, but Madelyne rolled across the floor and caught me.

"It bit me! *It bit me!*" Stroker cried out, waving an outraged finger at Madelyne.

To which Astel replied, trying her best to maintain a reasonable tone of voice, "Consider you were trying to kill him, Stroker. And consider who his mother is . . . and the violence of his conception. So he's born with teeth and bites you? That's certainly apropos."

And to the astonishment of both Astel and Madelyne . . . Stroker laughed. It didn't seem like something that was part of his character. He had appeared all bluff, bluster, and arrogance. He never seemed to have any sense of humor at all. But there was something about the insanity of being chomped upon by a newborn that appealed to his sense of the ironic . . . whatever that might have been.

"Yes," he growled. "That is most certainly apropos. That's the child's name."

"What?" Astel looked confused. "You . . . you can't name the child . . ."

"It's my stable, my inn. And I've never given a child a name before. Besides, you came up with the name, not me."

"But I . . . that's . . . but . . ." Astel, now completely befuddled, turned to Madelyne.

Madelyne, for her part, simply lay there and gently stroked my hair, which was already coming in as a fuzz of red. "It's all right, Astel," she said softly. "One name is as good as another, and 'Apropos' is as good as any."

"He's still going to be bad luck," Stroker said, and he rubbed the base of his neck and glowered at Madelyne, cradling her child in her arms. "At least now we'll have a name to curse when misfortune befalls us." Then he turned on his heel and walked out.

"I thought the child was finished for sure," Astel said. She looked wonderingly at Madelyne. "It's amazing how he changed his mind."

"Not amazing," Madelyne replied with a knowing smile. "It's . . . Apropos."

"It certainly is." Astel craned her neck slightly, trying to get a better look at me. My mother had used a wet cloth to remove the normal blood and slime that one accrues while being born. "He's certainly well on his way to having a head of flaming red hair."

"That's also apropos."

"What do you mean?"

Madelyne drew aside the blanket that she had wrapped around me, and exposed my hip. There, quite plainly, was a most unusual birthmark. It was in the shape of a small burst of flame. "You see? I was right. I witnessed the flaming death and rebirth of the phoenix . . . and here is a sign upon him. It's more than a birthmark, I'll wager. It's a linemark, a sign of lineage. Of greatness. Could there be any more clear a sign than that? Oh look . . ." she said as I began to whimper and squirm, "I think he's hungry." She held me up to her breast so that I could nurse.

"You know . . . that mark might still be a plain old birthmark . . . it could just be coincidence," Astel said doubtfully.

"No. No, Astel . . . there is no coincidence. There is simply . . ." she paused for dramatic effect, ". . . destiny."

I bit her.

It seemed apropos.

Chapter 4

The area around Stroker's Inn was hardly a hive of industry, but nonetheless, after a period of time, a village started to develop. I suppose it shouldn't have been much of a surprise. As near as I can tell, men were showing up in the evening, drinking well into the night, and then resenting the distance they had to stagger to get home (to say nothing of those who were drinking and riding, tumbling off their horses and being dragged behind when their feet snagged in the stirrups). Faced with the prospect of choosing between home and pub, a large number of men opted to combine the two, and relocated their homes to within easy staggering distance. Naturally their assorted businesses went with them, and that was more or less how the town was spawned.

There was some debate over what the town should be named. There was a sizable group of annoyed wives who advocated the name "Drunken Bastardville," and believe it or not, a number of the men embraced it as well before someone explained to them that the women were making fun of them. Finally they called it "the Town," so that even the most inebriated of men could remember it. As towns went, it wasn't much. Then again, it was probably what you would expect from a town that was created and centered on a tavern. Fortunately, as it turned out, the Town was well positioned along some of the more traveled paths, and so did a fairly brisk trade from transients. Furthermore, people procreated as is their habit, and a decent next generation of Townies sprang from the diseased loins of the founders.

My mother continued to ply her trade with willingness, if not great abandon. She didn't especially care one way or the other as some new passer-through huffed and puffed atop her. The only thing she was capable of feeling, really, was that she was helping to fulfill some sort of great destiny that awaited me, and she dedicated herself to that end. She told me about it repeatedly enough as I grew. She likely emphasized that for two reasons. First, she felt some sort of need to justify her activities to me, her son, since she probably felt that sooner or later I would judge her trade and find her wanting (a reasonable concern). And second, she wanted me to feel better about myself since I had to cope with my deformity.

A misshapen right leg is not something that one tends to grow out of. I was far slower to learn how to walk than the average child, and even when I finally did get the hang of it, it was only after a fashion. When other children would run, the most I was able to manage was a brisk limp. For the first years of my life, Mother fashioned for me some crude crutches, which enabled me to get around with some vague efficiency. I disliked them intensely, however, mostly because they underscored my vulnerability. This was driven home by the tendency that patrons of the bar had to kick the crutches out from under me whenever I would happen by. Since there was a steady flow of new patrons, each one thought that he was clever enough to have been the first one to think of it. So down I would go, time and again. Madelyne would always let out an aggrieved yelp, help me to my feet, and scold whichever patron it was who had decided to show what a tough man he was by abusing a helpless child. Her ire would invariably be greeted with guffaws, and a patronizing slap on the rump or a squeezed breast. This scenario played itself out so often that I came to think of it as a sort of ritual and took no personal offense. Nonetheless, the banged-up knees were certainly no fun, and I stopped using the easily targeted crutch by the time I was five. Instead I substituted a stout cane. I didn't get around as quickly as with the crutches, but it forced me to develop more strength in my left leg and a modicum of strength in my twisted right leg. Whenever possible, I would even disdain the cane and—in the tavern, most often—make my way by leaning on furniture or pulling myself around by clasping onto timbers in the wall. Consequently I gained some considerable upper-body power, although I didn't think much of it as I watched other boys, both older and younger, sprinting down the street with an ease that I could only envy and they could only take for granted.

Nor did I think much of my mother's frequent male

visitors. In retrospect, it is amazing what children will take in stride. I shared my mother's small room. She had her cot, and I had a bedroll shoved off in the corner. If it was night and I was in bed (or on the floor, as the case may be), and the back room was being used for some other private function, she would think nothing of bringing customers to our quarters. I would lie there in the darkness and occasionally be lulled to sleep by the rhythmic creaking of the cot. It meant nothing to me. It was simply what my mother did. I just assumed that everyone's mother behaved in a like manner.

I was disabused of this belief when I was about six or seven. I had been working in Stroker's since I was old enough to walk, or at least what passed for walking. I did whatever needed to be done, be it cleaning tables or mucking out horse stables. I didn't have all that much contact with the rest of the kids in the town, though. I was either too busy with my chores, or simply watching from a window and seeing the speed and alacrity with which they moved, knowing I couldn't possibly keep up. This particular day, though, Stroker had sent me on an errand, to fetch a new mug from the silversmith to replace one that had corroded. I limped past a group of young boys who were gallivanting fecklessly in the middle of the street—if a wide swath of dirt can reasonably be called a street—and they took notice of me. They stopped their ball game, and one of the larger ones stepped forward in what could only be called a challenging manner. His name was Skrit, and he was easily a head taller than I was. Still a child, of course, but to me at that time, he appeared a behemoth. Skrit had a broken nose and scarred lip from an earlier fight, and it was possible that he was looking for easier pickings.

I, in the meantime, was paying no attention to them, for I had found a coin lying on the ground. It wasn't much, but it was sitting there dirty and forgotten. I wrapped my small fingers around it and grinned. I had money of my own.

"Hello, Whore's Son," he called.

I glanced over my shoulder to see who was being addressed. It took me a moment to realize I was the addressee. What threw me was the deceptively pleasant tone in his voice. To him, it was sarcasm. But I was relatively friendless, knowing only the love of my mother the cot-creaker, the sympathetic looks of Astel, and the gibes and cuffs of the patrons of Stroker's. I had no experience with peer attitudes.

My hearing was also not the greatest.

"My name isn't Orson," I corrected him politely, or thought I had. I slid the coin into the pocket of my tunic without its being noticed. "It's Apropos."

"'Whore's Son' is apropos," replied Skrit.

"But that's not my . . ." I decided I was being unclear and started again. "Are you sure you're talking to me?"

"Are you the one whose mother is a whore?" he said with a sneer.

I leaned on my cane and scratched my head. "I don't know. What's a whore?"

Skrit stared at me, clearly trying to figure out if I was being coy or just stupid. But the expression of polite confusion on my face was probably too difficult to fake. "She's a woman what sleeps with men and gets paid for it, that's what! And the men what sleeps with them, they're whore-lovers!"

I thought of money clinking on the table next to the bed when the men would depart, and instantly knew that that indeed described my mother perfectly. Still, to me, that was the norm. Plus, I remembered times when my mother and Astel would be talking, and they would say things such as money was the only reason men were worth being with, and that what Madelyne did was no different than what the most respectable of women did. There were just different measures of what they were willing to sell themselves for. For other women, it was respectability, titles, land, gowns, and dresses. Astel would opine that Madelyne was more honest about what she did than those others. "It all comes down to money," Astel said. "The only thing that's different is where and how it gets spent."

With those thoughts ringing in my ears, I said to Skrit, "Does your mom get a place to live and food and clothes from your dad?"

Skrit blinked in slow surprise. He glanced at the others and they shrugged, uncertain of what direction this conversation seemed to be going. I wasn't responding to their taunts, as they would have wished, apparently: with rage or tears or some other thing they could reasonably lampoon. Instead I was simply earnestly confused and inquiring. "Yeah," Skrit said guardedly.

"Well, then . . . she's a whore, too, so I guess we're both whore's sons," was my cheerful response.

In retrospect, it was probably not the brightest answer I could have given.

For this comment was something that Skrit could easily understand. He saw it as an insult, and acted accordingly: He charged.

Alarmed that the conversation had taken a violent turn, I backed up, bumping up against a house. The much larger Skrit loomed over me, and he hit me hard in the stomach. I gasped, feeling my stomach tighten into a knot of pain, and then he hit me again on the side of the head. I went down, dropping my cane. Skrit took the opportunity to kick me full in the face. I felt my nose crack from the impact and knew immediately that it was broken. I rolled onto my back, blood fountaining from my lip and nose. One side of my face was covered with blood.

I had no idea what was going on, for it had all happened so fast. I heard the hooting and hollering of the other boys, and shouts of "Get him again!" and "Show him what-for, Skrit!"

I felt abandoned and alone, as if I didn't have a friend in the world, as if the entire universe had arrayed itself against me. I was unable to focus on a simple street fight: to me, it was a cosmic condemnation. My face stung, partly from physical pain, partly from humiliation and embarrassment.

I grabbed up my cane, gripping it firmly, gritting my teeth against the agony of my face that seemed on fire. Skrit was making no further move at that moment. Instead he stood over me, laughing, his hands on his hips. I had never desired much as a child, but at that moment, there was nothing I wanted more than to wipe that insufferable smirk off Skirt's face.

I swung the cane around. Cane? "Bludgeon" would be the more appropriate word, for it was large and thick and could serve as a weapon as easily as a means of aiding locomotion. The former was the capacity in which I used it at that point. I swung it as hard and as fast as I could, and it caught Skrit squarely in the side of the head. He staggered, not going down, but clearly surprised. A look of pure, glorious stupidity danced across his face.

I jammed the cane between his legs to trip him up, and succeeded. He went down onto the dirt and I was immediately upon him. I got in a couple of good whacks with the cane before the other boys converged upon me, dragging me off him.

They bashed me with whatever they could get their hands upon. Sticks, stones, rods, feet, made no difference. All I could do was curl into a ball and try and shield myself from as much damage as I could. Unfortunately that wasn't particularly easy. As poor a walker as I was, I began to wonder somewhere in the midst of all that punishment if I would ever be able to walk again.

Then a voice started shouting, "Stop!"

They didn't hear it at first, or chose not to. Above the raucous shouting of the boys, I could barely hear it myself.

Suddenly someone started yanking the boys off me, one by one. Before I knew it, I was suddenly clear of them. I had been crying in pain and humiliation, but considering my face was bruised and dirty, tears probably weren't especially noticeable. Still, I shielded my face until I heard a voice say, "It's okay."

I looked up.

It was an older boy. Rakishly handsome, a large hank of brown hair hanging down and in his face. He was grinning lopsidedly. "You okay?" He was dressed in a green tunic and brown leggings. He had several armbands, all of them multicolored in green, brown, and flares of orange. He looked like a giant leaf. "You okay?" he asked again.

It was a staggeringly stupid question, but I wasn't feeling up for sarcasm at that moment. "Yeah," I managed to get out. I paused a moment to spit, because my mouth felt full, and I was annoyed—although not surprised—to see a tooth land on the ground.

Skrit, however, didn't seem particularly inclined to let me off that easily—if a severe beating can be termed "easy." He pointed a quavering finger at the newcomer and shouted, "Get outta here, Tacit! This ain't none o' your business."

"It is now," Tacit said with quiet confidence that seemed far beyond his years. "This how you amuse yourself these days, Skrit? Beating up on crippled kids?" Tacit couldn't have been more than ten, but he used the word "kids" as if he were an adult.

The side of Skrit's face was already swelling up where I'd struck him. He rubbed it indignantly and said, "But . . . but he . . ."

"Come on, Skrit," Tacit said slowly. Skrit's protests didn't seem to have registered on him. "If you're that hungry for a fight . . . take a swing at me."

"Now . . . look, Tacit . . ."

But Tacit wasn't looking. Instead he struck a defensive pose, brought his fists up, and said nothing. No more words were required. It was time for Skrit to rise to the challenge or not.

Skrit appeared to consider it for a time, although it's difficult to know whether he really considered it, or just paused a good long time to make it look as if he was giving it serious deliberation.

I realized that Skrit was afraid of him. But not being willing to admit that, Skrit suddenly squared his shoulders and, for just a moment, I thought he was going to go after the newly arrived Tacit. Instead, however, he snorted derisively and said, "If you want to be pals with some crippled whore's son, ain't no never mind to me. You ain't worth wasting the skinned knuckles on."

It was an elegant means of saving face. If Tacit had pressed the issue, of course, Skrit would have had to run for it. But Tacit did no such thing, instead simply standing there, fists remaining cocked until Skrit and his cronies had swaggered off. Then Tacit turned to me and looked down. "Can you walk?"

"Kind of," I said.

He hauled me to my feet. I was amazed at the strength in the slim arm; it was as if I had no weight, he pulled me up so easily. "I'm Tacit," he said.

"I know," I said, partly leaning against him as I steadied myself. "I'm Apropos."

"What did you do to get on Skrit's bad side there, Po?" Tacit was the first person to call me by anything resembling a nickname. There was an implied instant friendliness there that I found appealing.

"I'm not entirely sure," I admitted. "He called my mother a whore."

"Oh," Tacit said sympathetically. "That got you angry?"

"Not especially. She is a whore. But when I called his mother a whore, that got him angry. I guess it's not good to be a whore, huh?"

"Well . . . that depends who you talk to," Tacit said thoughtfully, scratching his chin. "If you ask a man who needs a whore, then it's probably a pretty good thing to be. Anyone else . . ." And he shrugged as if the sentiment wasn't worth pursuing. "Where do y'live?"

"Stroker's."

"Come on, then." He looked at my leg in fascination. "What's wrong with your leg?"

"I dunno. Born that way."

"Oh."

He guided me back to the tavern, and when we arrived there, Madelyne let out a shriek and—for a moment—thought that Tacit was the one who had been responsible for the beating I'd taken. I quickly set her straight on that, but when she asked me what sort of words had passed between the bullies and me, I found that I couldn't tell her. I sensed—correctly, I think—that she would have been hurt by it. So I said, "They made fun of my limp." I caught Tacit's eye, but it wasn't really necessary. He was fast enough off the mark to know that utter candor with my mother wasn't a necessity.

Stroker, who was behind the counter pouring out mead, called out, "Well, you better get used to it! And where's my mug! The one you were supposed to bring from the silversmith, damn your eyes!"

Before I could explain that I'd never quite made it

there, Tacit stepped in. "I'll fetch it for you, sir," he said, and he was out the door before Stroker could utter another word.

Madelyne, bandaging my bruises and clucking over my ruined nose, looked out the open door through which Tacit had just passed and said in admiration, "What a nice lad. You were very fortunate, Apropos, that he stepped in to help you."

"I know, Ma," I said.

She wiped away the blood with a cool, wet cloth. "Making sport of a child's imperfections. Children can be so cruel."

"I know, Ma."

"Well . . . don't you make mind of none of them," she told me firmly. "Because you . . . you're a child of destiny. You're going to accomplish great things, Apropos. Great things."

"I know, Ma."

But I was looking at her with different eyes that day. From the things that the others had said . . . even from the tone that Tacit had adopted . . . I knew that somehow my mother was lower in the eyes of people than other women were. Lower because of what she did. It was as if my eyes had been opened, even as they'd swelled shut. I watched over the next few days the way that others treated her and truly saw it for the first time as degrading. I felt anger beginning to swell within me . . . but oddly enough, not for those that were doing the treatment, but rather her for letting it be done to her.

A week later, matters came to a head one night when my mother was entertaining a customer. I'd taken to sleeping in the stables, claiming that the room was a bit too cold for me, and I found greater warmth covered with straw and drawing warmth from the bodies of the animals that were clustered about. Madelyne thought it odd, but didn't press the point. Consequently, I wasn't there when her bed collapsed in, I presume, mid-coitus. But I heard about it not too long afterward when I heard her angry voice calling, "Apropos!" I wasn't used to hearing that tone from her. There was generally very little I could do that got her truly angry. "Where are you?"

"Over here, Ma," I called from the pile of hay I'd staked out.

She approached me, waving one of the legs that I recognized as having been from her bed. For a moment I thought she was going to use it to club me. Then she pointed to one end of it. "What is this?" she asked, her voice steady.

"I dunno."

"It's the leg of my bed, Apropos."

"If you knew, then why did you ask?"

"It's about three-quarters sawed through. And now it broke. Why do you think it broke, Apropos?"

I stared at her as if she'd lost her mind. "It broke because it was three-quarters sawed through. You just said so, Ma."

"The point is, who sawed it?"

"I don't know."

"I think you do." She tapped it gently into her open palm. "I think you sawed it, Apropos."

I shook my head so vigorously that the room seemed to spin around me.

As if I hadn't even offered protest, she continued calmly, "Why did you do it, honey?"

I started to tell her that I hadn't, but I found that I wasn't able to look her in the eyes as I did so. It is a rather disconcerting and annoying thing to discover that one cannot lie to one's parent. "I felt like it," I said, which was certainly true enough.

"All right, you felt like it. Why did you feel like it?"

"Because when you're with those men in bed, you're a whore, and you shouldn't be a whore because that's a bad thing."

Slowly she put the wooden leg down. I wasn't sure, as the words had all come spilling out of me, how she was going to react. I anticipated anger, or hurt. But she just seemed a bit sad. "Why do you think it's a bad thing?"

"Because . . ." I hadn't actually been able to wrap myself around the concept fully, and so I fell back on having my world defined by peer groups. "Because the other boys say so."

"I see. And do you always believe what the other boys say?"

"If they believe it enough to beat me up over it, I kind of do."

She shook her head sadly and sat down on the straw next to me. "And that's why you're sleeping out here now." It wasn't a question, and I nodded my head. "Apropos, you're going to have to learn sooner or later that you can't just let other people decide what the world around you should and shouldn't be."

"Why?"

"Because you have to make of the world what you want to make of it."

"Why?"

"Because," she said for what seemed the umpteenth time, "you have a destiny."

I sighed and flopped back down on the hay. It was quite clear to me that we weren't going to get any further that night. The destiny business was what my mother always trotted out when she had no answers. She tended to trot it out a lot.

To her credit, Madelyne didn't endeavor to press the point. Instead she simply sat next to me, running her fingers through my hair as if she wanted to reaffirm for herself that I was still there. When morning came, I awoke to find that she had fallen asleep next to me. And I realized that, as the sun shone down on her face, I still loved her, even though I vaguely understood that I should by rights be ashamed of her.

She'd slept with me, and I loved her. I pulled the coin out of my tunic, the one that I'd found on the street a week previous. I'd been trying to decide what to do with it, and at that point I knew precisely what it should be used for. My mother's hand was lying open, and I pressed the coin into her palm. Her fingers automatically wrapped around the coin, even in her sleep.

I was officially a whore-lover. It didn't feel too bad.

Chapter 5

Tacit was the one who taught me how to steal.

I enjoyed going about with him. I quickly learned that he was an orphan, and there was something attractive about that status. He answered to no one save himself, and whenever he came into town, it was always with a confident swagger, and coins jingling in a small leather bag that dangled from his belt. That self-confidence clearly translated into someone whom no one wished to cross, and it always amused me to watch the other kids give him a wide berth. I endeavored to imitate that swagger of his, but naturally with my lame and twisted leg, I was not overly successful.

Tacit walked a remarkably fine line with me. Since the day we met, he never made any mention of my handicap. One would have thought that he didn't notice it at all. However, when we walked about in the woods, he would always manage somehow to slow down, allowing me to keep pace with him, without ever giving me the impression that he was holding back himself. He never wanted me to feel as if I was a burden.

He maintained his home in the Elderwoods. This alone was enough to give him a certain cache, for the Elderwoods was considered a sorcerous place, where creatures of myth were known to gallivant about. It was said once that an entire army of weavers was set upon in the Elderwoods and was, to the very last one, slaughtered by a mad king who had vowed to rid the land of weavers once and for all. Although he had supposedly annihilated them, they unleashed a curse upon him so comprehensive, so frightening and so terrible, that the mad king's name of so long ago had been forever erased from the annals of mankind. His name disappeared from all histories, his image from all tapestries. He might just as well have never been born. A rather sad fate, really, for someone who set such store by trying to achieve fame for great deeds.

The slaying of wizards is a foolish endeavor, and should only be undertaken by those who are of a mind to commit suicide on a cosmic scale.

So supposedly the ghosts of the wizards strode the Elderwoods since that time. Tacit said that he had resided in the woods most of his life and had never seen any such evidence to support the rumor. He was not above, however, making use of this belief where he saw fit. For a number of shorter paths lay straight through the Elderwoods, and any number of travelers were inclined to brave the haunted forest for the purpose of saving some time. As a result of this tourist trade, Tacit would set traps and snares. But he was most adept at making his traps practically invisible, so that they could be ascribed to mystic forces.

Once, for instance, there was a rather portly merchant who was making his way through the Elderwoods with a most confident stride, until he stepped into a snare that hauled him upside down. Tacit had camouflaged the snare in such a way that it simply wasn't visible against the backdrop of the trees overhead—particularly difficult to spot when one was upside down and thrashing about. Convinced that he was in the hands of implacable spirits, the merchant did the only honorable thing under the circumstances and passed out. Relieving him of his purse of coins was but the work of a moment. Tacit cut him down before we dashed off into the woods, leaving the terrified merchant unconscious on the ground.

"Why'd you let him go?" I asked.

"Because we're more effectively served if he returns and speaks of his horrifying encounter with invisible creatures, rather than to speak of the cleverly camouflaged cable which snared him. Indeed, by the time he's finished telling and retelling the story, I guarantee you he will have been accosted by twenty decapitated ghouls all pelting him with their severed heads." He let out a low whistle as he emptied the contents of the pouch into his hand. Forty gold sovereigns poured out, the face of King Runcible looking at us in profile on each one of them. The coins glinted in the noon sun. "This," he said, "was a wealthy individual." He poured a little under half into his hand and offered them to me. "Want your share?"

"My share?" I looked at him askance. "Why should I get a share? You did all the work."

"Maybe. But you shared the risk. We're partners now, you and me. Partners and friends." He chucked me on the shoulder. "Or haven't you noticed."

Truthfully, I hadn't. I had simply taken to hanging about with Tacit, and as months had rolled over into years, I had always assumed that he kept me around more to kill boredom than out of any sense of loyalty or interest or any enjoyment of my company. "We're friends?" I said, which was probably not the most brilliant comment to make.

"Well, sure we are! What'd you think?!" Seeing that I wasn't reaching out for the coins, he took my wrist, opened my hand, and poured the coins into my palm. My fist closed reflexively on them and he smiled approvingly.

"Why are we friends?" I asked. "I mean . . . why are you my friend?"

"You don't know?"

I shook my head. "You do most of the talking," I said. "I just sort of follow you about. I limp. I'm not much use."

"How can you say that!" He perched on the edge of a rock and regarded me with open incredulity. A small insect nattered about in his face. He brushed it away without giving it any thought. "Why, you and me, we're . . . we're . . ."

"We're what?"

He appeared to give the matter a good deal of thought. He scratched the side of his head and pondered the situation for a time more . . . and then he looked up and pointed. "Do you see that?" he asked.

I looked where he indicated. All I could see was a hawk flapping gracefully through the sky. "You mean the bird?" I asked.

He nodded, brushing a hank of his hair from his face. "Do you know how it flies?"

"It . . . flaps its wings."

"And beyond that?"

There were certainly scientific answers to the question, but I had no clue as to what they might be. "It just . . . I don't know . . . it just does. It flies."

"It's the same thing with us, then, isn't it," said Tacit. "There's no reason to wonder why we're friends. We just . . . are. And you know what I see in you, Po? That hawk."

I flushed slightly at the thought. "That's silly."

"It's not silly. That's you, Po. That hawk." The creature swooped and dove over us. "I can see it in you. You're going to fly, Po. What matters a lame leg when you're going to wind up soaring over all of them."

"That's what my mother's always saying. That I have a destiny."

"Well, perhaps your mother knows what she's about, then."

At that moment, a large splotch landed smack on my head. As I felt its warmth dribbling down the side of my face, I didn't even have to wonder for a moment what it was. The hawk had shat on me.

To his credit, Tacit didn't say anything. If he wanted to laugh, he did a superb job of suppressing it. Instead he pulled out a cloth and handed it to me, and I wiped the bird crap from me as best I could.

I looked up at Tacit and noticed that he had stiffened. Tacit's instincts were second to none, and something had attracted his interest. His nostrils flared. Clearly he scented something. I tried to sniff the air but I detected nothing.

"Not great, heaping snootsful," he chided when he saw me trying to detect whatever it was that he had noticed. "You have to be more attuned than that. Just relax, Po. Don't think about smelling it. Don't think about anything. Just relax. Relax and let the forest talk to you. When there's danger, it will tell you right enough."

We had had talks like this in the past. Tacit seemed determined to transform the limping whore's son into a woodsman like himself, and the more I protested the uselessness of the endeavor, the more he seemed bound to proceed.

Once more, I tried to do as he said. I sat with my left leg crossed against my right thigh and tried to relax. There was a soft breeze blowing about me, and as I noticed the breeze, I also heard a gentle rustling in the trees and bushes. My imagination began to wander, and I forgot the immediacy of the situation. Instead I could almost begin to fancy that I heard the Elders of the woods whispering to me, speaking secret things of destiny and fate, of craft and wisdom, of smoke . . .

. . . smoke . . .

"A fire," I said slowly. "A big one." And then I started to hear voices as well. "And a crowd."

He nodded when I mentioned the fire, and then

nodded again when I further opined that there were people about. "These are my woods," he said, sounding rather possessive. "If people are loitering around, I want to know why. Besides, the last thing I'm interested in seeing are drunken fools letting a fire get out of control and level the Elderwoods. Haunted or not, trees hereabouts still burn."

I couldn't disagree with that. I shoved the coins into the pocket of my jerkin and followed Tacit as best I could. As always, he moved effortlessly. When he would push brush aside to pass through, it made no noise. Wherever he crossed, be it grass or dirt, he left no footprint.

There was still a great deal about Tacit that I couldn't begin to understand. His woodcraft was like nothing I'd ever experienced. It was almost magical, but he claimed no knowledge of weaving and indeed I'd never actually seen him perform any actions that could be ascribed to magic. I knew little about his early days, and one time I'd decided to press him on the matter. "Well," he had said, "you've read tales of infants being abandoned in forests and raised by wolves?"

I nodded, and then had looked at him skeptically. "You're saying you were raised by wolves?"

"No." And then he had smiled impishly and said, "Unicorns."

The disbelief on my face must have deepened. "Unicorns. You were raised from infancy by unicorns. That's ridiculous."

"Yes. It is." That was all he ever said of his youth, and I never knew for sure just how serious he had been. But it was moments like this one, as he made his way through the forest with almost supernatural ease, that I hearkened to that conversation and wondered whether or not it was possible that one of those rare and wondrous beasts had indeed suckled him in infancy. It would explain a lot.

As for me, of course, I felt—as always—like a great, galloping clod. As I approached early adolescence, my lame leg had strengthened a bit, but not much. Whenever I endeavored to obtain any sort of speed, it was always as if I were lugging along a great sack of meat attached to my right hip. I had substituted a staff for my cane, however, and with Tacit's guidance, had become rather deft in its use. It was longer and heavier than my cane, but my arms were strong from pulling myself along all these years, so the additional weight was of no consequence. Furthermore, it helped me to semi-vault distances rather than just limp along. Plus in those rare instances where other kids in the village decided that they wanted to have a go at me, it proved a rather nasty weapon. I was hardly a knight, or an entity to be feared, but one crack from my staff could make someone look like they'd been in a fight.

The smell of smoke grew stronger as I drew closer to it. Tacit had virtually disappeared into the forest ahead of me, but I kept gamely at it. Suddenly someone lunged at me from the side, clapping a hand over my mouth. Reflexively I started to struggle and then I realized that it was Tacit. "Shhhh!" he hissed in my ear.

Just over a rise, we saw the source of the fire.

There was a girl tied to a stake, thick ropes crisscrossing her breast. A massive amount of kindling had been clustered around the bottom, and the edges were already burning and crackling. The girl herself appeared nonchalant about the entire thing. She was dressed rather boyishly, mostly in gray leathers that looked fairly worn, including visible holes in the knees. She sported a black cloak. Her ebony hair was cut short and curled around her ears. Her face was round, except for her chin, which was rather prominent and, at that moment, outthrust in a wonderfully defiant manner. She appeared to be about Tacit's age, maybe a little older.

Surrounding her was about a score of what could only be termed angry villagers. They were waving torches, which would have been rather dramatic and underscored the mood had it not been high noon. Another one or two of them threw torches onto the kindling, and more areas started to go up.

A rather ratty-looking woman, toward the front of the crowd, appeared to be the ringleader. "You'll never ensorcell anyone again, weaver . . . especially helpless young men!"

The fire was already starting to lick at the toes of her boots, but the girl who'd been identified as a weaver—a magic user, or wizard, if you will—didn't seem the least bit disturbed by it. When she spoke, it was with clear contempt rather than any sort of alarm. Considering the straits that she was in, a touch less arrogance might have been advisable. "I told you, I ensorcelled no one! We had a dalliance, and that was all!"

"You're lying! You're a seducer and a thief!"

"He gave me the money of his own volition! He wanted me to have it; it was a gift!"

That was when I noticed that the ratty-looking woman had what appeared to be a ratty-looking son standing next to her. His gaze kept shifting between the weaver and his mother, and he didn't seem able to abide the sight of either of them for long. His shoulders were hunched and if his manner were any more timid, he would have made the most skittish of deer look positively intrepid in comparison.

"He wouldn't have given you any gift!" howled the mother. "He knows better! Don't you, Edmond!" And she slapped her son upside the head for emphasis. Edmond nodded mutely but took a moment to cast a longing glance at the weaver. She, for her part, didn't seem remotely interested in him. Instead the fire was drawing nearer and it had actually managed to snag, ever so slightly, her attention. The other onlookers, no doubt friends, relatives, or simply idiots with nothing better to do, shouted encouragement to the flames as if they were sentient and interested in anything the onlookers might have to say. "You bewitched my son and robbed him, and used the money for your own evil ends!"

"I used half of it to buy booze and get stinking drunk, and the rest of it I lost in a card game while I was three sheets to the wind! If I were as clever as you claim, don't you think I'd've put it to better use than that?!"

From where I sat, it seemed a rather credible defense. But somehow the crowd howling for her blood—and looking for an afternoon's entertainment—didn't seem interested in the particulars of her hastily cobbled explanation.

Tacit was crouched next to me, and he turned and

said intently, "I'm going to make a move here. Are you with me?"

"With you? Are you insane?" I looked at him disbelievingly. "That's an angry mob. The girl's a weaver that they've got a grudge against. Weavers can take care of themselves, and mobs take care of anyone they want to. She's not our concern."

He didn't appear to have heard me. Instead he was studying the area of the conflagration, which was about thirty feet away from us. "There must be no threads in that area. That's why she can't weave a spell to help herself. Po, we can't just stand by and watch them take the law into their own hands!" he continued with growing urgency. "If the girl has done something wrong, she should face true justice."

"If she did something wrong, being incinerated for it is about as true as justice gets."

"And if she didn't?" he demanded.

"Then it's her rotten luck! Tacit, listen to me! Number one, weavers aren't to be trusted as a rule. And number two, I guarantee you that if the situation were reversed, and it was our necks on the line and she happened by, she'd continue on her way without giving it a second thought."

"Well, then I guess that's how we're going to stay different from her, isn't it," he said.

The only weapon that Tacit ever carried was a short sword that was strapped to his thigh. I'd only seen him wield it for matters of a practical nature—skinning a recent kill, or hacking through some particularly impenetrable section of the forest. But when he drew it this time, the rasping of the metal as it slid from its sheath sounded particularly ominous. "Are you with me?" he said again.

I looked at the girl, the fire getting steadily closer. And I looked at the demented expressions of the townspeople. And I looked into the face of possibly the one person on the planet whom I considered a friend.

"Absolutely not," I said.

A look of disappointment crossed his face, and then it hardened into anger. "Don't you know the meaning of the word 'bravery'?" he demanded.

"Yes, I do. Do you know the meaning of the word 'foolhardy'?"

He was about to reply, and then a gust of wind fanned the flames higher. There was suddenly no more time, and nothing to be gained by trying to talk me into joining him in an adventure that was likely to get him killed.

He leaped out of hiding, crossing the distance between us and the girl with great bounds. She spotted him first, since she had the better vantage and was the only person in the immediate area who wasn't fully focused on watching her burn. An expression of complete bewilderment crossed her face. The reason for her confusion was immediately evident to me; she was doubtlessly wondering if Tacit was insane as I thought him to be.

Some members of the mob caught sight of Tacit as he drew close and sounded an alarm. They must have realized instantly he meant them no good, a logical conclusion since he was charging them and wielding a blade. Several of them instantly formed a wall of bodies, blocking his path. Tacit swung his short sword, and they fell back but still obstructed his way. Suddenly he turned and dashed up the trunk of a large tree just to his right. The move completely befuddled his attackers, and then they understood as Tacit scrambled along a high and strong branch that stretched directly over the girl. Smoke was rising and it was getting harder to see her. She was starting to cough, but if she was at all afraid, she wasn't showing it. I envied her. If I'd been in her situation, I'd have been screaming my head off.

It wasn't until that moment that I truly understood that I was lacking something that others, such as Tacit, possessed. There are some for whom the good of mankind is their primary concern, and others who basically put their own considerations before everyone else. I was among the latter. Truth to tell, if Tacit hadn't been my friend, it wouldn't have bothered me in the least. But watching Tacit's heroics frustrated me, because I saw what he was doing and realized that it was something I wasn't capable of.

I should have admired him for it.

Instead I felt a cold envy growing within me for this person, for my friend. I resented that which came so easily to him, or at least appeared to.

Momma was screaming in fury, and her son Edmond didn't seem to be doing much of anything except cower. Tacit dropped from overhead, and one quick slash of his short sword severed the cords that held the weaver in place. He grabbed one of the flaming sticks from the bundles beneath their feet, holding it at the nonflaming end, and waved the torch with one hand into the faces of the crowd while swinging his sword with his other hand. "This way!" he shouted to the girl, spotting one small area where the flame wasn't especially high. Without waiting for her to acknowledge it, he threw an arm around her waist and vaulted. The wood shifted under his feet and threw off his trajectory. As a result, he cleared the pyre, but he came down, falling on top of the weaver and landing in a heap.

Immediately the mob was upon them. They pulled Tacit free from the girl. She struggled mightily in their grasp, and it was the most emotion I'd seen from her since this whole misbegotten adventure started.

Tacit was even more determined to give a good accounting of himself, but he had inhaled too much smoke while rescuing the girl. He was hacking away, but it wasn't with his sword; his coughing was so violent that I half-expected one of his lungs to be ejected from his mouth. No matter how noble the heart or pure the determination of any warrior, it does him no good if he can't draw a breath. Tacit was borne to the ground and held immobile, his arms and legs pinned like a butterfly's.

"Let him go!" shouted the weaver.

"Friend of yours?" asked Momma contemptuously.

"I never saw him before!"

"So a complete stranger decided to risk his neck for you. How idiotic."

It was disconcerting to realize that I was in agreement with someone whom I considered to be only slightly smarter than a mushroom I'd just mashed beneath my foot. It *had* been idiotic. And Tacit hadn't listened to me, and now the weaver was still going to die and she was likely going to have company. They'd probably just tie up the both of them and toss them on the pyre, which was burning rather rapidly and with great enthusiasm.

"He's some do-gooder. This isn't his problem. Let him go."

"He made it his problem," Momma said firmly, "and that was his decision. So now he'll share your fate, you cheat and harlot."

Well, that appeared to be that. Tacit was going to die . . . horribly, it seemed. His grandstanding heroics had come to nothing. I was going to be without the one friend I had. Nothing had been accomplished.

I wondered if a sudden wave of bravery would overtake me. But no . . . nothing surfaced. I was no more inclined to risk my neck now than I was before, even if Tacit's life was on the line. He'd been the one who decided to risk it. Let him bear the burden of that decision.

Gods, he infuriated me, Tacit did, for being so concerned about this girl that he'd run off and leave me behind. That he'd throw away his life, in fact, for this utter stranger. What sort of friends could we truly be if that friendship meant so little to him, that he was willing to risk ending it—and himself—all to save someone he didn't even know?

And suddenly I wanted to save him. And I wanted to make it look easy. I rose from behind the brush and slowly made my way toward the crowd.

They didn't see me at first. They were busy hauling out large quantities of rope and tying up Tacit and the weaver. But then one of them spotted me, and pointed me out, and then another did and another, and within moments all attention was focused on me. The shouting of the crowd had died off, and the only sound to be heard was the crackling of the fire.

If I moved too quickly, my limp would be evident and make me look weak. So instead I moved very slowly, very ponderously. I said nothing. When one says nothing, it heightens both the interest and importance of the words when they eventually come. I must have looked a rather bizarre sight . . . a rather young man, wielding a staff, coming toward them with no hurry, as if the imminent disaster which awaited Tacit and the weaver were of no consequence to me.

I drew within a few feet of them and then stopped. I surveyed the lot of them, adopting a gaze and attitude so imperious that one would have thought I could have caused them to discorporate with a single harsh word.

Still nothing was said. Finally, Momma couldn't take it any longer, and she said angrily, "What do you want, boy?" But she sounded no more comfortable with my curious presence than did anyone else.

I appeared to ponder the situation a moment longer, and then I said slowly, "How much."

They looked at one another, these judges, jury members, and executioners. "How much what?" one of them asked.

As if the question was so self-evident that I couldn't believe the fool had needed to pose it, I said, "How much did she take?"

They looked at one another, and then at Momma, who seemed confused by the question. It was Edmond who spoke up, which was rather unexpected considering he hadn't said anything until that point. "Fifteen sovs," he said.

I sighed inwardly. Somehow I'd had a feeling it would be about that much. But in order to pull it off, I had to be as casual as possible.

I shook my head and gave a small, derisive laugh. "All this over fifteen sovereigns." I reached into my jerkin and pulled out the twenty that Tacit had handed me earlier. "Twenty sovs to put an end to this sorry affair. Take it or leave it." As if I didn't give a damn about their opinion . . . indeed, as if the entire matter were already decided . . . I tossed the coins. Like a cloud of gold they hovered in the air and then fell to the ground.

Had I simply tried to hand the money over, there might have been temptation on their part for dickering. But when people see money on the ground, they have no choice but to obey the impulse to grab it as quickly as possible. Which was precisely what they did. Immediately they were on their knees, scrambling after the fallen sovereigns.

"Wait!" shouted Momma, but her cries received no attention whatsoever and quickly she realized that if she didn't try to lay claim to the coins, she'd wind up with nothing. So she joined in the scrabbling about. Edmond, for his part, simply stood there, looking confused.

No one was paying any attention to Tacit and the weaver. Indeed, they appeared almost as puzzled as Edmond.

With a tilt of my head, I indicated that they should follow me, and promptly they did. Within moments we had obtained the safety of the brush while the erstwhile mob was still rummaging around on the ground, trying to find all the coins I'd thrown there. The fire, meantime, was burning fiercely. Indeed, burning so fiercely that Tacit couldn't help but let a look of concern cross his face.

Sensing his concern, the weaver said, "Allow me." She reached out, appearing to caress the air, and then her fingers moved together as if she were playing "cat's cradle" with invisible string. Perhaps the point where they'd chosen to try and toast her had no threads, but the area where we were now hiding, a safe distance from the madding crowd, apparently possessed what the weaver needed.

Immediately there was a crack of thunder from overhead, and then the skies ripped open. At first there were only a few splatterings of rain, but within moments we were faced with a genuine downpour. It descended upon the fire and, in no time at all, reduced the whole pyre to a huge pile of smoldering ashes. By that point, the three of us had withdrawn from the area entirely, the weaver pulling a hood up from the back of her cloak to afford her some protection from the rain. Lucky her.

We hightailed it through the woods, wanting to put as much mileage between ourselves and the mob as possible. After all, there was really nothing to prevent the crowd from keeping the money and throwing Tacit and the girl (and me, for that matter) on the fire anyway once things dried out. There was a network of caves that Tacit used for shelter on those nights when the Elderwoods proved inclement, and that was where we headed. We said nothing during that part of the trip. There seemed little to say.

Once we made it to shelter, Tacit pulled some wood from his stockpile and gathered it at the front of the cave. "Now let me just get it lit up . . ." he began.

The weaver extended a finger and made a small circling motion with it. Lightning cracked from overhead and slammed downward into the cave. The blast sent both Tacit and me tumbling backward in alarm and confusion. The weaver never even budged. She just sat there with a smug smile as the lightning struck the tinder. Within moments a warm fire was crackling.

"Very flamboyant," said Tacit, pulling himself together as best he could. Me, I was still waiting for my heart to climb down out of my throat.

"No less flamboyant than a harebrained rescue stunt," retorted the weaver.

Clearly Tacit took offense at her tone. "I was doing it to save you," he said.

"You were doing it to show off."

There was so much contempt in her voice that I almost felt as if I'd discovered a kindred spirit.

Tacit threw up his hands in disgust. "That's it. It is now official. Chivalry is dead."

"Stupidity is alive and well, however," said the weaver. "I assure you that if the situation had been reversed, I'd have left you to your fate."

I didn't say anything. I didn't have to. Tacit couldn't even bring himself to look in my direction.

"You know," I said slowly, "I don't know who's the bigger fool . . . you or him. Him because he thought you mattered . . . or you because you don't know enough to be grateful."

She stared at me long and hard, and something in her face seemed to shift. She lowered her gaze. "I don't like being in someone's debt," she said, almost to herself, wringing the rain from her cloak.

"Well . . . you are. You're in his," and I indicated Tacit.

"What, not yours?"

"No," I said.

"You," Tacit said, pointing at me. He smiled and shook his head. "You . . . I knew you'd come through. Damn, but you're an inventive little cuss. I should have known that when things really got difficult, you'd step in. You were right: I was foolhardy. You were the real hero. You used your brains and you got the job done, rose to the occasion to save her and me. You're the noblest, bravest one of all."

Noblest. Bravest. What rot. There was no bravery in buying oneself out of difficulty. I hadn't risen to any occasion. I should have felt ashamed, I suppose. Instead, all I felt was annoyed that he didn't realize how stupid I'd made him look. Naturally, I said the only thing I could say, given the circumstance.

"Thanks."

The rain was beginning to lighten, and the weaver was clearly preparing to depart. "Wait," Tacit said. "What's your name?"

"None of your business. Names have power. I'm not about to give you power over me."

At this, Tacit began to bristle. I thought he'd shown

remarkable restraint to that point. "Power over you? I . . . we . . . saved your damned life. You'd be a broiled corpse if it weren't for us. If owing someone your life doesn't give them power over you, I don't know what does. Deny it if you want, be arrogant to us if it pleases you, but you're not fooling either of us. In addition to having a weakness for liquor and gambling, it seems you also have a weakness for common decency."

She pulled the hood up over her head, and seemed to glower from deep within it. She rose and headed for the cave exit, and then stopped momentarily and said, "Sharee."

"Is that your real name?"

But she didn't reply. Instead she drew her cloak tightly around her and walked out.

Neither of us spoke for a moment, and then Tacit reached over and patted me on the shoulder. "The hell with her," he said. "The important thing, Po, is . . . you proved what you're made of today."

Oh yes. I'd proven it, all right. I was made of spite and craven fear that could only be overcome when I thought that I might be able to make my one friend in the world feel inadequate. I was a definite prince among men.

He pressed half of the sovereigns that remained to him into my hand. "It's the least I could do," he said.

"I can appreciate that," I said. "I always do the least I can do."

He laughed. He thought I was kidding.

I wasn't sure if I felt more sorry for Tacit or for myself.

That night . . . I dreamt of her. At least, I thought I did.

I was sleeping in the stables, which was where I had

taken to spending a good deal of my time in the evening. I wasn't expecting to dream of Sharee. I thought I had put her out of my mind. But she was hovering over me in my dream, looking down, and there was something in her eyes that I couldn't quite fathom. Then her face drew near and her lips pressed against mine. They were both warm and cold at the same time, which was most puzzling. When our mouths came in contact, I felt something like a spark, as if lightning had struck me, and suddenly—for just a moment—the world seemed to be not itself, but a shimmering array of multicolored ribbons, glistening in glorious blue, green, every color imaginable. For that instant, I saw the world the way that weavers must see it. It was astounding, amazing . . .

I opened my eyes, sat up suddenly . . . but there was no one there. And as I settled back into the straw, a recollection of the shimmering threads racing through my mind, I suddenly remembered that I always dreamt in shades of gray, not color.

Chapter 6

Resentment can be a powerful motivation if properly utilized.

It was from that point on that my resentment for Tacit grew with each passing day. I hid it effortlessly, however. As far as he was concerned, we remained bosom friends. Indeed, he perceived a marked change in my attitude and actions from that day forward. I was far more aggressive than I had been, more eager to participate in various ventures. Whereas before Tacit had to offer me a share of whatever money we took in, in short order I was more than happy to take whatever he felt was due me. I was always quick to bring it home and stash it away in the corner of the stables that I had staked out for my own. I had gotten my hands on a small strongbox, and managed to loosen a few boards in the floor so that I could secret it away. No one knew of its existence, not even my mother. Every so often I would take it out simply to let the coins run through my fingers and clink into the box. I felt as if I was building toward something.

I just wasn't entirely yet sure what that might be (although every so often Madelyne would mutter something about "destiny" again).

Sometimes I found myself thinking about Sharee. I wasn't quite sure why I did, but Tacit could somehow always tell when she was in my thoughts. He would kiddingly, but firmly, whack me upside the head and say, "You're thinking about her again. Stop it."

"She was rather attractive," I'd say, or something to that effect.

"She's a weaver. To rescue one is not a bad thing. Weavers are favored by karmic forces and such endeavors as the saving of a weaver's life can rebound to one's benefit at the most unexpected times. But they are not like you and I, Po. They have their own concerns and priorities, their own world, and we merely stand on the outside of that world looking in. You do not want to go too close, I assure you, and you certainly do not want to open yourself up emotionally. That way lies disaster."

"I know, I know," I'd say, and I'd manage to put her out of my mind for a good long time, but every so often she would creep back in with the stealth of an invisible cat, and we'd have the same conversation again.

As for Madelyne, she continued to ply her trade. But such a life takes a fast toll on a woman. It is easy to be a remote, untouchable beauty and stay that way for many, many years. And if a stunning tapestry is hung upon a wall, it remains unsullied and a work of art. However, if one drapes it across the floor of a pub and all manner of men tread upon it with their heavy boots, it's going to be worn rather thin, and rather quickly. Such was the case with my mother. The wrinkles in her face deepened, her body sagged from the constant wear. The spark in her eyes became dimmer and dimmer through the passing years as she became resigned to her rather pathetic status in life. Men were not quite as quick to seek her out, as she became less pleasing to the eye.

My feelings toward her remained mixed. She was, first and foremost, my mother, the one who had borne me, protected me in infancy when others would have just as soon left me to die. I suspect that many other mothers would willingly have left me to my fate. Not her, because she believed that my fate was one of great importance. On the other hand, it is difficult to maintain respect for one who may be utterly deluded. She was, in the final analysis, a harmless enough creature. I suppose I should even have been flattered that her dreams for my future were the way that she defended herself against encroachment of unfortunate reality into her own life.

As for me, I worked on my own means of defense.

Tacit was a formidable fighter. I personally had little patience for fights. If I could walk away, run away, or in some other manner simply keep clear of them, then that would have suited me just fine. However, I was quite aware that sometimes combat was unavoidable. Indeed, my first encounter with Tacit had been a consequence of one of those instances. On that occasion, Tacit had been there to prevent me from being smashed into a meat sack of shattered bones. But I couldn't count on him always being there; my natural and burgeoning cynicism prompted me not to count on anyone for anything.

So it seemed incumbent upon me to find ways of defending myself, which was no easy task considering my lameness of leg. Tacit, however, was happy to aid me in my endeavors. The key lay in my staff, which served as a walking aid, but also could be utilized as both an offensive and defensive weapon. Tacit worked with me every day, running me through exercises that were designed to accommodate my natural handicaps. When there was any surface available for me to lean against, be it building, tree, or whatever, I would brace myself against it and wield the staff in a manner similar to that of a windmill. As I became defter and more dexterous, even Tacit had trouble breaking through the whirling defensive screen I was able to create. Any weapon thrust into the "circle of death" (as Tacit liked to flamboyantly call it) could be broken or, at the very least, knocked out of the grasp of whoever was wielding it. A fist or outthrust leg would meet with an even worse fate. During our practice sessions, I nearly broke Tacit's arm on more than one occasion.

I was also capable of shifting from defensive to offensive stance rather quickly. If I had nothing to lean against, I would angle forward on my good leg, allowing it to absorb most of the weight of my body, balancing lightly on the ball of my lame right foot so that I could hop/pivot with facility. I was far from being a formidable fighter, but that wasn't the purpose of the exercise. Tacit felt—and I agreed—that any that looked upon me would consider me easy pickings. If they suddenly found themselves faced with a genuine fight, they might be less inclined to press an attack. That was the theory, in any event.

Plus, Tacit added a few tricks. He retooled the staff so that it could be separated in the middle by a quick twist. This would provide me with a lengthy baton in either hand, giving me more defensive options. And he added a secret compartment in one end in which I could store small objects, which was nicely convenient if I should happen to smash someone on the back of the head and steal their purse.

But the nastiest addition was at the other end of the staff on which he had mounted a headpiece depicting a dragon wrestling a lion. Tacit rigged a devilishly clever spring-loaded blade as the dragon's "tongue," about four inches long, which was triggered by my tapping a hidden button in the middle grip. It wasn't meant to serve as a substitute for a sword, but rather to provide a nasty surprise where the circumstances warranted it.

Madelyne was unaware of the full extent of activities that Tacit and I embarked upon, and naturally I had no interest in filling her in. However, she approved of him nonetheless, considering him a good influence, for she saw that my confidence built as I spent more time with him.

Poor Tacit. How limited he was, I felt. How circumscribed his idealized world of bravery and daring. Obviously Tacit was not someone who preferred only the purest of morality; he was a cutpurse and a thief, after all. Then again, he had an annoying habit of keeping only the smallest measure of his spoils for himself, preferring to give whatever money he obtained to me, or to the needy . . . in short, to anyone except himself. It was as if he engaged in his activities purely to keep busy.

This I also found most annoying. Someone with his talents, I felt, should be endeavoring to get rich or build a base of power for himself. It was a subject I gently broached to him one day.

"Power," Tacit said, shaking his head, "is not something that any truly wise person wants."

"Why is that?" I asked him. It was a warm day and we had both just bathed in a nearby river. We were lying bare-chested on the grass, letting the sun dry us. I've always had a sketchy concept of my own age, for my mother—in her fairy-tale mentality—felt that I was "ageless" and never wanted to saddle me with anything as mundane as birthdays. If I had to guess, though, I was in my middle-to-late teens by that time.

"Power is a finite resource, Apropos," Tacit said. "Once one person has it, others want to get it. And usually they want to take it away from the one who has it. It's not a game I choose to play. Let the others above me struggle with one another, engage in their contests and wars as they see fit. I would prefer to exist beneath their notice."

"But you could bring yourself up to their level."

He shook his head and smiled. "I am perfectly content to wait for them to come down to mine."

That was when we heard them.

By that point my own woodcraft had improved to the point where I didn't need Tacit to bring my attention to things. Any sort of major disturbance to the relative peace and quiet of the Elderwoods, I could detect almost as quickly as Tacit. "Horses," I said. "Men on horseback." I listened a moment more. "About five, six . . ."

"Ten," Tacit said with confidence, waving for me to follow. "Come on."

The hoofbeats were far in the distance, but approaching quite rapidly. We made our way through the forest with alacrity, or at least as much alacrity as I could muster. There was an area of the Elderwoods where the hills angled upward to form a natural lookout point, and that was where Tacit and I headed. It gave us a valuable vantage point to see what was going on, and what was coming from which direction. However, the area was nicely covered with vegetation, so that anyone looking in our direction would have his vision obscured.

We lay down flat, looking at the oncoming horsemen. Ten, just as Tacit had said. Their horses were magnificent beasts to look at. Their coloration was somewhat amazing: Every single one of them was purest gray, their hides seeming to shimmer into black with every great thrust of their powerful legs. When they moved, they seemed like a mass of storm clouds coming toward us. That impression was underscored by the fact that the sky truly was darkening up; I suspected that we were in for a storm before too long.

The riders themselves wore garments of different styles, but which featured a color scheme that was uniformly black and white.

It was a most impressive array. All of them had swords dangling from their hips, and a number of them had shields. The shields bore a crest that consisted of a globe, with renderings of what appeared to be marching feet encircling them.

At first it seemed that the riders were approaching the

Elderwoods, but soon it became readily apparent that they were simply circumnavigating it. Apparently they had no intention of actually trying to enter the legendary forest. Wherever they were heading, it wasn't here.

Their emblems, their colors, all meant nothing to me. But when I glanced at Tacit, his expression and body language immediately alerted me to the fact that he did, indeed, have some familiarity with these individuals. He didn't appear scared, actually. It took a lot to scare Tacit. But he was obviously concerned.

"Journeymen," he said. When he saw my blank expression, he added, "Meander's people."

"Meander!" The name filled me with that unique combination of interest, awe, and dread that his name usually summoned. "Are you sure? I mean, are you absolutely sure?"

Tacit nodded. In the distance, thunder rumbled as if to underscore a sense of drama.

Meander, the Keepless King. Meander the Vagabond. Meander the Mad. All of these appellations, and more, had been applied to him, and probably none of them truly began to capture the full picture.

Meander had once been a king in a frozen region far to the north, and had come into his title with the passing of his father, a man named Sentor who was reputed to be relatively wise and fair. Sentor had constructed what was said to be a glorious, sparkling castle that was known far and wide as the Ice Palace. It was his crowning glory, so much so that Sentor abruptly died within days of completing its construction, and thus did Meander find himself king of the Keep of the Frozen North. It was rumored that Meander had done away with his father, but no one had ever been able to verify it.

Once in charge, Meander took himself a princess from a nearby realm . . . the only other one within distance, in fact. She was a lovely young thing named Tia, and despite the arctic aspects of the Keep, it was said that her very presence brought warmth where before there had been none. With the two major frigid realms united through the marriage, matters were quite peaceful, albeit cold, in the frozen north.

One day Meander and Tia embarked on a journey to Tia's home, accompanied by the normal escort of guards. But along the way, a fearsome storm came up that was unlike any that even the longest residents of the Frozen North had ever experienced. The king and queen became separated from their escort, and the escort found itself snowblind. For a solid day the storm continued, and when it was over, Meander and Tia were nowhere to be found. A search was called off after many days, and for a time there was great mourning within the Keep.

Then, to the astonishment of all, Meander staggered out of the wilderness one day, making it all the way to the Ice Palace before collapsing in a heap. There was no sign of his beloved queen, and the only utterances out of Meander's mouth indicated that Tia was, in fact, dead. It was almost too cruel, the kingdom having to mourn a popular ruler for a second time. As for Meander, frostbite had claimed several of his toes.He fell ill immediately upon returning home, as if the last of his strength had been used up in making it back. For two weeks he shivered, tossed, and turned as the doctors tended to him, and it was unknown for quite some time whether he would live or die. When he finally returned to his court, his outward demeanor was calm, almost supernaturally so. And his next pronouncements utterly floored the court.

"We have come to understand the world better," said Meander, or so the story goes. "We have restricted ourselves to the Frozen North, but that is foolishness. There are no borders, no boundaries upon this world save those which we construct for ourselves. But they are artificial, and mean no more to the world's surface than the illustrations we call constellations mean to the actual stars. From this place atop the world, we hereby abolish all borders. We will recognize no territories. We will go where we wish, when we wish, as we wish. We will be king of all we survey . . . and we are tired of surveying this frozen wasteland. So we shall survey other climes, other areas, and wherever we are, that is where we will be king until it pleases us to go elsewhere."

"But Your Highness," said one courtier, "what of this magnificent castle?"

"Castles are foolishness," replied Meander. "They provide enemies with somewhere that they can find you and strike at you. They give you something to hold on to that can be taken away from you by others. Ours will be a roving kingdom, a vagabond kingdom. To be satisfied with one place is nonsense. Let the other kings of the world dwell within their fortified walls and believe themselves safe. Castles can be attacked, sacked, siege laid to them. We will be," and he smiled, "we will be like the ocean. Strike at an ocean, and your blow means nothing, for there is nothing there to meet your fist. You cannot imprison or border the ocean. It is endlessly useful, and endlessly powerful."

There was some spirited discussion of the king's new philosophy in the court, but ultimately he was their king. Besides, I expect that he might have hit a bit more resistance if his realm had been in sunnier climes and he was proposing relocation to somewhere in the Frozen North. As it was, no one was tremendously averse to the concept of heading someplace warmer. However, just to make certain that no one had any second thoughts, Meander waited until the entire castle was cleared out of everything easily transportable, and then he destroyed it. The Frozen North is, so I hear, a remarkably quiet land, snow falling there with an eerie hush. It is said that the crash made by the Ice Palace when it collapsed reverberated for days across the perpetual silence of the land, and by the time it finally ceased its echoes, Meander and his people were long gone.

Thus did King Meander consciously choose a life of perpetual wandering. He cared nothing for borders or treaties, and would move across lands with no regard to the sovereigns who were already there. He recognized no rule save his own. At first, various monarchs reacted with fury over Meander's utter lack of respect for their respective authority. One of the first notable skirmishes involved King Verona, who had long ago decreed that no foreign king could set foot in his realm of Upper Montclair without heavy tax or copious offerings. When Meander crossed into his territory and set up his portable realm, Verona sent messengers demanding that Meander pay homage. The messengers never returned. Assuming that Meander had slain them, King Verona sent the famed Fifth Regiment against Meander. When the Fifth arrived, they found that not only were the messengers in perfect health, but they had, in fact, switched loyalty to Meander. It was difficult not to. The Fifth discovered that Meander was in the midst of what he referred to as his "movable feast." Paying no attention to the posted signs or warnings, Meander's people had slaughtered some of the succulent game (deer and such) that were maintained purely for the highly refined taste buds of the king and his higher tier of nobles.

Now, the Fifth had two or three nobles in command position, but the majority of the Fifth—as was the case with most regiments—was composed of grunts and ground pounders. Well trained, but grunts just the same, and they were accustomed to being treated as such. It was just the standard pecking order. But Meander, with no regard for such things, treated them as if they were lords themselves. "Sit down at our movable feast, good sirs," Meander welcomed them rather than taking up arms against them. "Enjoy, for once, the best that your land has to offer, instead of those handouts which your lord deigns to give you."

This was met by howls of protest by the nobles, who demanded that the men immediately slaughter everyone in Meander's court and take the king himself prisoner. But they underestimated their own control over their people. It is a simple matter to order men into battle against an opponent who is shouting war cries. But to meet generosity with violence is another matter entirely. Plus it is said that the ladies of Meander's court, now that they were out of the frozen clime,, had "thawed" considerably and were most anxious to indulge their newfound warmth with all comers. Between such enticements as food and sex, the hardy men of the Fifth Regiment were happily helpless. The nobles faithful to King Verona blustered and threatened and swore and stamped their feet until the grunts, their bellies full and their palates tingling, got tired of them and put them to the sword. Thus did Meander take the Fifth.

It proved a significant lesson to other monarchs, who realized that they had a serious problem on their hands. From Upper Montclair, he moved through Upper Echelon, and the entire Upper Lumbar region, and none of the kings, liege lords, and others in charge knew what to make of him. He took what he wanted, acquired followers with ease, but showed no interest in the traditional challenging of power or capturing of land that other roaming monarchs so frequently displayed. And heaven help anyone who made a foray against him, because long practice made Meander's court the most mobile and terrain-adaptive of any in the land.

Consequently, when Tacit and I saw a number of his soldiers—known as the Journeymen—passing through, we had absolutely no clue how to react. One never knew what one was going to get with Meander or his people, because his followers were a hodgepodge and agglomeration of whomever happened to have joined him at that time. It was said that Meander was sort of a free-floating pocket of chaos. It was said he cared nothing about anyone, as if all his actions subsequent to his wife's death were a means of isolating himself from anyone or anything truly being able to touch him.

It was said that, in truth, he was a madman.

All I knew was that seeing ten of his Journeymen pounding through the area was something that filled me with a vague sense of dread, and I had no real idea why.

"What are we going to do?" I asked.

Tacit looked at me with confusion. "'Do'? We're not going to do anything. They're not heading into the Elderwoods, which is fine by me. If they did, we'd have a problem on our hands. As it is . . ." He shrugged.

Thunder rumbled overhead, and it began to rain, big fat drops pouring down. We made for the nearest cave and holed up there, trading stories that we'd heard about Meander. Tacit seemed disturbed by him, but the more we spoke of it, the more the entire concept began to intrigue me. "Perhaps I should take up with him," I mused out loud. "Join his ranks."

"What would you want to do a bloody stupid thing like that for?" Tacit demanded.

"Maybe it's not so stupid. Maybe Meander is the only one out there who sees things for what they really are."

"Meander is a madman," Tacit said dismissively.

"Perhaps. Or perhaps it's simply a mad world, and Meander is the only one with clarity of vision."

Tacit leaned forward, drawing his knees up under his chin. "Meander has no sense of justice, or order. He's the incarnation of pure impulse. There's something to be said for spontaneity, granted. But there's also something to be said about knowing where one stands at all times, and you'll never get that with Meander. Not ever."

The rain came down all the harder. We stayed in the cave and spoke of this and that, liberally mixing matters of importance with matters of no consequence at all. The rain formed such a steady beat above our heads that, as day rolled toward evening, slowly I found myself being lulled to sleep.

And I dreamt with a clarity such as I had never known before.

I saw my mother, saw Madelyne, and she was speaking to me as if from very far away. To this day I cannot remember exactly what she said. Certainly her incessant carping about my destiny figured into it. But there was something more, something fearful in her manner. Even in the dream, there was an attitude that came through above all else: She was acting as if this was the last time she was going to be able to speak with me.

She cried out in pain, and when I awoke it was as much to her scream inside my head as it was being startled from my slumber by the roar of thunder.

The abruptness with which I woke startled Tacit awake. "I have to go home," I said, without knowing or understanding why.

"What's wrong?" Tacit asked.

But I didn't wait around to tell him. Instead I bolted from the cave. It was still raining. I didn't care. I was being compelled by something greater than anything that I was able to understand. My lame leg was almost forgotten as I ran through the forest. I knew the path so well that, even in the darkness, even in the rain, I was able to maneuver through the Elderwoods as if it were broad daylight and I were fleet of feet.

He had no idea what was going on, but Tacit nonetheless followed me. I wasn't aware of it at first, because even when he was making no effort to conceal himself, Tacit still moved like a ghost. But a carelessly snapped twig under his foot tipped me that Tacit was behind me. I didn't care. All I knew was that I had to get back to the tavern.

I burst through the door and saw Stroker standing by the fireplace. There were only a handful of regular customers there, and they were clustered together and muttering in low tones. Everyone turned and looked at me, and there was darkness in their eyes that held something ominous within. Even Stroker, who had never given two damns about me, looked as if he was actually, albeit momentarily, concerned.

As if we were already halfway through a conversation, I said, "Where is she?" I must have been quite a sight at that moment, with my hair flattened around me from the rain, my clothes disheveled, tracking in mud from the Elderwoods. But I didn't care about any of that. More alarmingly, neither did Stroker seem to care.

Stroker indicated the back room with a quick tilt of his chin. I headed toward it and threw open the door, to discover Astel sobbing over my mother's corpse.

I stood there for a long moment, the reality now having caught up with my most fevered imaginings. Madelyne's eyes were open, but she was staring at nothing, her soul having departed the body and left the lids up in the way that someone might hurriedly flee a house and leave the door ajar.

I felt a hand on my shoulder, realized it was Tacit's, and pushed it aside. I entered the room and stood over Astel. To my distant surprise, I felt exceptionally calm. "What happened?"

"A . . . a Journeyman," Astel managed to get out. "I . . . there were raised voices. I heard, everyone heard. He wanted her to do things . . . disgusting things . . . she wouldn't have any part of. She was a good and decent whore, and wouldn't have any truck with what that . . . that pig wanted." She accentuated the "p" in "pig" so that she spat upon saying the word. "His friends caroused outside, and he tried to take her here, to do his filthy . . ." Her voice shuddered and she took a moment to compose herself. I didn't rush her. What would have been the point? "We heard furniture being thrown about. And the snap when he broke her neck, the bastard . . . I heard that, too. We all did."

"His name," I said tonelessly. "Did any of you get his name, so he can be found."

"No. But before she died, she left her mark on him a'right. If you see him, that will help you identify him, sure as I'm breathing."

"Her mark?" Tacit spoke up.

Astel flexed her hand in a clawlike motion and made a sweeping gesture. I understood immediately. Madelyne had always kept her fingernails long and sharp. If she chose to employ them as weapons, I certainly wouldn't have wanted to have the damn things raking across my face. And sure enough, I could see traces of blood on the fingernails of her right hand. She'd bloodied her murderer something fierce, that much was certain.

Her murderer . . .

A cold fury was beginning to build in me, as I walked slowly across the dirty room and, passing my hand over her face, shut her eyes. Something had to be done about this.

I would like to tell you that I was motivated by a sense of justice, of honor. But these matters were of little relevance to me. I knew that this was an unjust world, and to expect any sort of equity within it was a complete waste of time.

But . . . she was mine. She was my mother. I had, by turns, loved her, pitied her, loathed her. In the final analysis, however, she was the only mother I had, and some brute had come along and taken her from me, had stolen from me. He had taken that which was mine, that which he had no right to take.

I had so little. So little. How dare some thug try and rob me of what little I had.

"Can you describe him beyond the mark?" I asked.

"Tall. A big man . . . at least two heads higher than you. Massive built he was, with a scowl dark as thunderclouds and the strength of five men, at least. Maybe ten."

I didn't like the sound of that.

"Tell me you'll find him . . . find him and kill him for what he did," Astel continued with bubbling ire. "Tell me you will."

"I'll do better," I said. "I'll find *his* mother . . . and kill *her*."

"Wait a minute," Tacit said immediately and even Astel seemed taken aback. "You can't do that," continued Tacit.

"The hell I can't. Watch me."

"Kill some woman you don't even know!"

"He did!" I pointed out, indicating my mother's body.

"But that's not the point! If you were going to try and kill him, that'd be one thing—"

"It certainly would. It would be suicide. You heard her description of him. He'd annihilate me."

"Po," Tacit said slowly, "you can't do it. You can't just kill an innocent woman because of something her son did."

"Well, I have to do something!"

"Not you. We. We have to do it. We will find him . . . we will find the man who did this . . . and we will exact vengeance on your mother's behalf."

"Why?" I stared at him incredulously. "Why 'we'? Why are you mixing into this? This isn't your concern."

"Of course it's my concern. You're my friend!"

I looked at the dead body of my mother, which Astel was just in the process of covering with a sheet. "Why do you have to do that?" I muttered.

"Do what? What do you mean?"

Thunder cracked overhead, and something about the sound of the heavens, combined with something in Tacit's voice—such a matter-of-fact, "how-could-you-even-ask" attitude—pushed me over an edge that I didn't even realize I was standing near.

"Why do you have to try and be heroic all the time!"

I said in frustration. "Why do you have to see everything so 'clearly'? What do you think you're trying to prove?"

"Prove?" He shook his head. "I'm not trying to prove anyth—"

"Oh, the hell you aren't!" I was shouting by that point, uncaring if anyone outside heard me. "That's all you ever do! Try to prove how much better you are than I am! How much nobler, how much more heroic! Tacit, who can move with the grace of a unicorn! Tacit, with the heart of a gryphon! The heroic cutpurse and rogue, trying to make everybody's life a little bit better! I'm sick of it! I'm sick of you! Haven't you gotten that yet? Don't you understand that?"

"Po," he said slowly, moving his hands in a "calm down" gesture, "I know that you're upset. Your mother's body is not even cold, her murderer protected by a vast army . . ."

"An army that you'd take on single-handedly, no doubt, in order to accommodate a friend! And you'd probably win, too!" It all came spilling out, everything I'd bottled up. "Damn you! God damn you! Damn you for your perfection and innate wonderfulness! Damn you for being so much better than I am, and leaving me to look at you and be sick with envy!"

"Apropos, my friend—"

"I'm not your friend! How many ways do I have to spell this out for you! I cannot stand you, all right? I can't stand the sight of you! Whenever I look at you, all I see is all that I am not! I can never measure up to everything that you are!"

"But we're not in competition, Apropos!"

"That's the worst thing of all. You see, *you're* not in competition. You're so skilled, so wonderful, so perfect, that you don't even realize it!" I was sweating profusely, my forehead positively dripping, and the salt from it sopped down and stung my eyes. I wiped them furiously, hoping that it didn't seem as if I were weeping. That would have been simply intolerable. "You're just someone who served a purpose, that's all! Nothing more than that!" His face was resolutely stoic. I stepped closer in, suddenly consumed with an overwhelming desire to hurt him. "Must I spell it out? I used you! Used you for protection, for knowledge. You were a means to an end, that's all. All your heroics and your taking on this quest or that cause. And now you're going to do it again, with my mother, and drag me along with it as if throwing my life away against some behemoth is going to bring her back. And the worst is, you'll probably expect great deeds out of me! Probably fix it so that it's my hand that lays the villain low or something equally noble. The hell with your nobility! The hell with you! Do you finally comprehend? Do we finally have an understanding, Tacit? Do we?"

I wasn't sure what I expected him to do. Rant, perhaps, or strike me, or hurl invective.

But all he did was just look at me with what seemed infinite sadness, and then he shook his head and said quietly, "Perhaps . . . you are right. Perhaps this is something you'd best do alone. Handle the matter as you wish. May you find whatever justice you deem your mother worthy of, Apropos. May you find everything you seek."

I was fairly trembling with rage. "Stop being so damned polite! Didn't you hear anything I said?"

"I heard everything you said. And I forgive you."

He bowed slightly to Astel, placed a respectful hand upon my mother's cold one for a moment as if wishing her good journey, and then turned and left.

"I don't need your forgiveness any more than I need your friendship!" I shouted after him. I doubt that he heard me, and truthfully, it wouldn't have made much difference if he had.

It was done. I was rid of him. It was about time, really. I'd learned from him every reasonable skill he had to offer. I didn't need him anymore. Particularly if he was going to lead me on some quest that would get me killed, as if my mother would ever know or care. "Exact vengeance on your mother's behalf," Tacit had said. What a colossal crock that was. My mother had no more behalf. She was beyond such human concerns as justice.

"Justice. There has to be justice for her," Astel said, as if she could read my thoughts. She pointed a quavering finger at me. "And you have to get it for her. You're her son. She believed in you."

I looked at her body, now covered by the sheet, and thought about her natterings about destiny and such. Then I caught a glimpse of myself in a mirror mounted on the wall nearby. Moderate height was I by that point, with a fairly well muscled upper torso. But my right leg was still a fairly useless object, and overall I looked very unimpressive, leaning on my staff and assessing my abilities and worth.

"More fool she," I said.

Astel's movement was quick. I never even saw her

hand swing in its arc. But I certainly felt the impact as it cracked against my face.

There was cold, hard fury in Astel's face. "You little creep," she fairly snarled. "I caught you when your mother's womb expelled you. I was there when you sank your teeth into Stroker's throat. Your mother sold her body to buy you a roof over your head, and what have you done in return? Never offered her so much as a soft word, much less made any effort to support yourself or make her life better!"

"I . . . did . . . from time to time," I protested, but it sounded rather lame the way I said it. My face was smarting but I didn't want to give her the satisfaction of seeing me reach up and rub it.

"You did nothing, except hang about with Tacit or glower at your mother ever since you found out what she did in order to provide for you."

"That's not true." I thought about the time that I'd pressed the coin into her sleeping hand, but I wasn't about to share that memory with Astel. It would seem as if I was defensive, providing excuses. So I simply repeated, a bit more sullenly, "That's not true. And. . . and I've made money. I have. Lots of money, hidden away. Money I was going to give her!" And at that point it was a complete lie, because I'd never had any intention of giving her a single sovereign. But just as before I'd wanted to upset Tacit, now I was seized with the desire to do something about those contemptuous looks that Astel was giving me.

She shook her head in haughty disbelief. "I don't think you know what true and false are anymore."

"You don't know anything, Astel," I said angrily. If she could be accusatory, I could be, too. "You've known me my whole life, and you don't know anything about me!"

"I know that Tacit at least had some measure of the right idea, and you treated him like garbage!" she said, pointing at the door in indication of the direction he'd gone. "I know that at least he had his heart in the right place! Where's your heart, Apropos?!"

"Hidden away where the likes of you can never find it!"

We were very close, taking step upon step toward each other, our bodies both trembling with our respective fury. "I wouldn't bother looking for your heart!" she shot back. "Why should I seek out such a shriveled and pathetic thing as that! Your mother lies dead, and your only plan is to track down some helpless woman and murder her!"

"What would you have me do, Astel? Throw my life away combating some brute that'll slay me, like as not? And what good will that do her?!"

"You're a coward!"

"I'm a realist! If living in the real world makes me a coward in your eyes, then fine! Who gives a damn what you think?"

"You do!" She shoved me. With my lame leg, I almost stumbled, but I recovered and shoved her back. When she came at me again, I caught both her wrists and held them easily. Thunder blasted even louder, so loud that it seemed as if it were in the room with us.

"You have no compassion!" she shouted over the

thunder as she struggled in my grasp. "No care for anything save yourself . . . no love . . . no . . ."

Her body was right up against mine, and that was when I kissed her fiercely. It was a clumsy movement, my skull cracking against hers so hard that we were both momentarily dazed. She was nearly twice as old as I, but still damned attractive. She tried to pull away from me. I kissed her again, feeling something building deep within me, something that was demanding it be unleashed. Rain was pouring down, slamming against the walls, and the wind was howling. She sunk her teeth into my lower lip, drawing blood, and I pulled away momentarily. Triumph flashed in her eyes, but there was something else in there as well, something that prompted me to bring my mouth savagely down upon hers once more, and this time there was only the mildest resistance. When I bore her down to the floor, all resistance was gone.

With my mother's corpse lying covered on a table five feet away, I had my first woman. It was hardly the ambience that one could have wished for, but I suppose in retrospect that there was something symbolic about it.

Chapter 7

We lay close to each other for some time, holding each other tight, skin against skin so that it took our bodies as long as possible to cool. "That was . . . unexpected," I said, my voice sounding a bit huskier than it had a little while earlier.

"Life is full of surprises," said Astel. She was idly fingering the wispy curls of chest hair. "Do you know what I think you lacked, Apropos?"

"Is this going to be an alphabetical list, or are you going to go from largest to smallest?"

She smiled at that. I guessed I had amused her. "I think you lacked confidence. The sort of confidence that can only be gotten by . . . by becoming a man. A true man," she added.

"Is that what it takes, then? What of monks who swear themselves to lives of celibacy?"

She made a dismissive noise. "They're busy making love to God, or whatever permutation thereof is interesting to them." She drew herself even closer to me. If she'd held me any tighter, she would have been in back of me. "Confidence," she said again, as if she'd just settled a dispute for herself.

"And is that why you and I had it off just now? So that you could help build my confidence?"

She sighed contentedly. "A little, perhaps. But also . . . I hate to admit it . . . I've wondered about it for a long time. Fantasized about it. I know, I know how strange it is. After all, I held you in my arms when you were newborn. But perhaps that was part of the excitement as well. Watching you grow into young manhood, coming into your own."

"And before, when you spoke of my heartlessness?"

Propping her head up on one hand, Astel said, "We say things when we're angry, Apropos. Things we don't really mean. I think it's what we do when we're not angry that has greater weight, don't you." She leaned over and kissed me once more, and I felt my body begin to respond on its own. The second time we had sex was far less rushed. I was hardly what one would call experienced, but I did have the benefit of being a fast learner.

It was a short time later when we finally dressed and emerged from the room where my mother's body lay. Only a handful of people remained in the tavern at that point, most of them so drunk into oblivion that they could have been on the sun and wouldn't have known their whereabouts. Stroker, however, cleaning glasses behind the bar, was stone-cold sober. Since he usually relegated those chores to wenches and such, clearly he had things on his mind. He glowered at us from beneath his beetled brow.

"I've sent for the funerian," he growled. "He'll take the body and dispose of it." Not for Stroker were the niceties of asking after the state of mind of the newly orphaned.

"Dispose of it how?" I asked. "Where will she be buried?"

"Buried!" He snorted. "'Less you've got money for a grave site, she'll just be made ashes in the funerian's kiln."

It was clear that his mentioning my having money was such a preposterous notion that my temper started to flare. "Money!" I retorted. "I'll have you know that—"

Then I felt Astel's hand gripping my arm warningly. I wasn't quite sure what the problem was, but it was clear that she didn't want me to continue. Cutting myself short in what I hoped was a vaguely smooth manner, I ended the sentence lamely, "—that if I could get it, I would. Wait a minute . . . what about her money?"

Stroker looked at me blankly. "Her money?"

"My mother's earnings! All these years . . . where are they? She must have banked them with you. Where is it!"

"Your mother gave me squat, boy, 'side from what I was entitled to. I think she kept it with her, in her mattress."

Immediately I headed back into the room. I would have pitched my mother's corpse off the bed to inspect the mattress . . . except that I quickly found one section had been torn away 'round the other side. I shoved my hand in, probing . . . and came away with a single sov that the thief must have missed. That was probably the real reason that he'd killed her. Sitting on the mattress, he must have felt the wealth contained therein, disposed of her, and taken it for himself.

I muttered a string of profanity and stomped back into the main room. "It's gone! It's all gone! But if you have a shred of decency . . ." Then I stopped, remembering who I was talking to.

Stroker snorted once more, like a horse with an allergy, and turned away. Astel led me over into a far corner of the tavern and sat me down. "Don't you be mentioning that money of yours to anyone," she whispered. "Not a word of it." She took my hand in hers and squeezed it tightly. "Your mother was right, Apropos. You do have a destiny; I could always sense that about you. But we both know that if it's to be found, it's not going to be in this place. Let's face it, there's nothing to hold us here. We can get out, you and me."

"We?" Things seemed to be moving much faster than I'd anticipated. It was only within the last hour that I'd come to think of Astel as a real, flesh and blood woman rather than simply some individual who had always been there. A woman of passion and fire, and desires all her own, that was Astel. To go from that state of mind to thinking of us as a "we . . ."

Still, it didn't seem particularly out of the question. She had awoken my carnal side, had brought me over the threshold into manhood. Already I felt an attachment starting to develop. I couldn't look upon her without imagining what it would be like to be horizontal with her once more, sampling the amazing heat that the woman seemed to radiate from every pore. "We" didn't seem such a terrible idea at that, truth to tell.

"Yes, we. Does the notion . . . repulse you?" she asked. Her voice contained potential for a world of hurt.

"No," and I smiled, genuinely smiled, which is something I rarely did. "No, it doesn't repulse me at all."

"I could use some help here!" Stroker called angrily from behind the bar, and Astel immediately got to her feet and moved behind the bar to start cleaning up and settling down matters for the night. Stroker walked around the bar, carrying a large stein of what was probably mead. He swaggered toward me, and I wondered what he was going to say and do. What charming *bon mot* was going to tumble from his lips, what new insult or snide remark?

He stood at the edge of the table where I was seated, regarding me for a long moment. And then, to my surprise, he placed the stein in front of me. The froth of the mead swirled around the top. It was the good stuff, not the stuff he watered down, I could tell. And when he spoke, it was without any of the bluff, bluster, and arrogance that I had spent my entire life hearing.

"I'm sorry about your mother," said Stroker in a low voice. "She deserved better. And she deserves justice." That was all, and then he turned away. For a moment, just a moment, I thought I caught the smallest amount of moisture starting to form in the corner of his eye.

"Justice from whom?" I asked.

He looked back at me, as if surprised that the question needed to be asked. "The king, y'fool. Who else?" He walked away shaking his head, as if he couldn't quite believe that such a stupid question needed to be asked.

I had to admit, it made sense. It was known far and

wide that King Runcible was quite the adjudicator. People from around the land came to him with disputes to be settled, which seemed a far more reasonable means of handling arguments than resorting to combat. There was a place in his palace known as the Hall of Justice, where he sat once a week and welcomed all comers, the great and the ingrate, attending to their grievances.

I myself had always held such practices in general, and the court of Runcible in particular, in great disdain. Who better had the right? Runcible made a great show of his knights standing for something good and moral, but my very existence on this planet put the lie to that. Runcible's men were just as violent, just as self-centered, just as capable of great evil, as were any other individuals who made no pretense of moral posturing. I was a bastard, spawned from a group rape of my mother. It was hardly the sort of origin that was likely to give one a warm, generous feeling toward those who were responsible.

Still . . . there was something to be said for the notion. Hell, it had been a long time ago. For all I knew, those knights who had participated in the barbaric assault against my mother had been weeded out of Runcible's court. There was no real way for me to tell. Besides—and here was the aspect that I found most attractive—if Runcible sicced his knights on the Journeyman who had slain my mother, my neck was not on the line. Let his trained brutes deal with the situation. That way I could have my revenge against the cad who had stolen from me, and at the same time do so without having to worry about running into difficulties myself.

No, it was not a half-bad plan at all.

The funerian showed up promptly at dawn, which was fortunate since with the passing of a bit more time, my mother's poor corpse might have started to get ripe. He was a tall, pale individual, the type who seemed born to the profession. Stroker, who was becoming a fountain of surprises, slipped the funerian a few coins. Not enough to pay for a burial site, but at least sufficient to obtain a right and proper funeral and a solo cremation. There was somehow more dignity to that than watching a body tossed on a pyre with a half a dozen strangers.

The attendance at my mother's funeral was small. It was in the open air, of course, the funerian's kiln heated up ahead of time for maximum efficiency. Her body, wrapped in funeral cloths, was eased into the kiln, and the heavy metal door banged shut behind her with such finality that I jumped slightly. Astel was next to me, clutching my arm. Ever since our "bonding," she had become a bit clingy. That might have caused problems in the long term, but for the moment it was acceptable. Stroker was there as well, plus a handful of regular customers who had come to appreciate Madelyne for her "talents" and her perpetually upbeat manner. The kiln belched out black smoke, which tailed away high into the sky. The funerian performed a fill-in-the-blanks sermon, and when he asked if any individuals wished to speak on her behalf at that time, no one volunteered. I felt I should say something, but I couldn't for the life of me imagine what. There were things I wished I'd said to her while she was around, but it was a bit late for that.

So I maintained my silence rather than risk saying anything foolish.

Astel nudged me in the ribs. I looked at her in annoyance and she inclined her head toward the front of the assemblage. Clearly she wasn't going to let me off that easily. I sighed heavily and trudged toward the front, accentuating my limp even further as, perhaps, a slight bid for sympathy. I turned to face the people there and, after a moment's reflection, I said, "Madelyne was my mother, and she had . . . a vision of what the world should be. And it never really matched up with her dreams. So what I'm going to do is dedicate the rest of my life to fulfilling her vision. Because that's what she'd want me to do." I hesitated, then mentally shrugged and said, "Thank you."

There were actually tears in Astel's eyes. I couldn't believe that she had gotten misty-eyed over such a pathetic speech. Someone patted me on the back; to my horror, I had a feeling it was Stroker. This wasn't the way I needed the world to be. The last thing I required was a brute like Stroker revealing a soft underbelly, or Astel—whom I'd always viewed as being one of the more pragmatic of women—to be a sucker for a few sentimental words.

Not too far off, there was a grove of trees that was part of the outermost ridge of the Elderwoods. I glanced in that direction, and of course . . . of course . . . I caught a glimpse of a figure clad in green and brown. Then it vanished into the concealing woods.

We stood there and watched the black smoke belch from the top of the kiln, stray ashes and such fluttering upward. My mother had aspired to so much. Perhaps, wherever she wound up next, she might be closer to whatever it was she was seeking. Some minutes later, the funerian handed me a large urn with her remaining ashes.

"What am I supposed to do with this?" I asked.

"Whatever you want," said the funerian.

I lugged the thing back with me. No one made an offer to help. Maybe they felt it would be something of an insult or some such nonsense. Damned foolish of them. If anyone had asked if they could help, I could gladly have shoved the urn over to them. Astel kept pace with me, and I said, "Any ideas as to what I should do with this?"

"When the time comes, you'll know," she said cryptically.

The mood in Stroker's was somber that night. I sat at a table alone, staring at my mother's urn, and Stroker walked over to me and sat down. "Look," he growled, "I never had much use for you. But if you want to stay here, you can. Course, you'll have to pull your own weight from now on. You've always been a lazy little shit . . ."

"Have I," I said tonelessly.

"You know it, I know it. So you'll have to bust your ass from now on to keep room and board. But if you're willing to do that, then fine." He paused, and then tapped the base of his neck. "I've still got your mark, y'know. Right here. You can barely see it, but it's there just the same. You were a nasty little creep from the day you were born."

"A lazy little shit, a nasty little creep. So why keep me

around at all?" I looked at him levelly. "Because you want to see me squirm? Because you want to treat me like the shit and creep you think I am? How much do you want to make me grovel just so I have a roof over my head?"

His gaze hardened. "I was trying to be nice. Should've realized that was pointless with someone like you."

"Yes, I guess you should've."

He shoved the chair back with such force that it hit the floor. I'm not sure what else he intended to do, but finally he just shook his head and walked away, leaving me alone. I felt a gentle hand on my shoulder then, and knew that it was Astel.

"We're getting out of here," I said.

It took us no time at all to gather the few belongings we had, and then I led her to the stables, still hauling my mother's ashes in the urn. I went to the corner, pulled up the floorboards where I had been secreting my stash for the past years. I actually felt some degree of pride. For so long, I had wanted to pull out the fruits of my "ill-gotten gains" and show them to my mother, or shove them in Stroker's face whenever he made some disparaging comment about how I would never amount to anything. At least I would be able to show it off to Astel. There was, after all this time, a small fortune in there. Probably far more than my mother had stashed away, since I didn't have such considerations as food and rent to be deducted from it.

"Astel . . ." I started to say, ". . . come take a look at this . . ."

I half-turned and barely had time to see the urn in

Astel's hands. She had planted her feet firmly and was twisting at the hip, gripping the urn and swinging it straight at my head. Before it could fully register on me, the urn cracked against my skull. I tumbled backward, hitting the ground heavily. I tasted blood swelling from my mouth, and even though I couldn't string a coherent thought together, I still managed to pull myself halfway upright just as she whipped the urn around again. This time it hit me with such force that the urn shattered, spewing ash everywhere. Most of it, however, was on me, choking me, stinging my eyes. I coughed violently, trying to clear my lungs.

Through my limited sphere of vision, I saw Astel's hands grab up the strongbox in which I had taken to keeping my stash. I lunged for it, trying to get out the words "Give it back!" She gave it back to me all right. She slammed me on the back of the head with it, and that was the end of that. Blackness spiraled around me and my head hit the straw. Just before I lost consciousness, I heard Astel say, "I'm sorry, Apropos. This will probably make it even harder for you to trust anyone in the future. Unfortunately, well . . . I just don't care."

And then there was nothing.

That would have been a fortuitous time in my life to have all manner of portentous dreams. To have my departed mother's shade show up in my imaginings and put forward some useful advice. Or perhaps see visions of things to come. Unfortunately, such was not the case. I saw nothing but darkness, and then eventually there was dampness on my face. That was enough to bring me out of my enforced slumber, although I had no idea how long I'd been out. The dampness was coming from a leak in the ceiling of the stables. I heard rain outside, although it was not remotely as fearsome as it had been the other night.

I hauled myself to my feet. Standing up was always problematic, even on my best days, thanks to my lame leg. But this was even worse, because my head was throbbing and I could feel the world tilting wildly around me. My jaw ached, and when I rubbed my lower face, dried blood came away on my hand.

That bitch.

"That bitch," I said out loud, as if simply thinking it wasn't enough. "That damnable bitch."

Had any of it been real? Our lying together, the emotions that had been stirred . . . had she done it in order to put me off guard, so that I would lead her straight to my nest egg? For that matter, had she been the one who had stolen the money from my mother, seeing the corpse and figuring she'd have no need of it . . . and then lay with me to augment her riches? Was she capable of doing such a thing? Well, hell, maybe. The truth is that, even though I had known her my entire life, I didn't really know her. In fact, I was becoming increasingly certain that I didn't know anyone, or anything about anyone.

I let out a ragged cough, and then another. My lungs spasmed as the last of the ashes which had gotten in there were propelled out. Other lads my age had complained about having their mothers getting in their hair, but I seriously doubt that any of them had ever meant it quite so literally.

She had left me my staff. Now, wasn't that a sweet

thing of her to have done. The way things were going I was surprised she hadn't picked the damned thing up and used it to stave in my head once and for all. I bent over, nearly stumbling again, before getting a grip on the staff and using it to steady myself. Then I limped toward the door of the stables, and out. The fact that it was raining was of no consequence to me at all.

I stood out there in the rain, the heavy drops pouring down, and I stretched my arms out and raised my face to the sky. My mother's ashes were washed off me, although some remained in my clothes, discoloring them permanently. And there, in my fallen state, I laughed. Because it had been all so ridiculous. The cynic had lowered his guard. I had listened to the siren call of lust and love, and for just the briefest of moments, I had surrendered the eternal vigilance that was my credo. Naturally, I had paid for that, paid for it with the loss of all the money I had saved up. Astel could have gone anywhere by that point, in any direction. She had a head start of hours. She'd probably even arranged for a mount, for she had most certainly planned this ahead of time; on horseback, she could be miles away.

She had a head start, she had my money, and I had absolutely nothing except the clothes on my back and a few pathetic possessions in a small bag inside the barn. All that . . . and the taste of ashes in my mouth. How classically Apropos.

I had no idea what the hell I was going to do. I could seek out the shelter of the Elderwoods, go crawling back to Tacit. But that wasn't going to happen. I could seek out Stroker's help, but I doubted he was going to think much beyond the notion that, whatever had happened to me, I deserved it. Who knew, perhaps he was right.

"You have a destiny," she'd said to me. Perhaps I did, but at that moment, I had no purpose at all. No plans, no direction, and nothing in particular to do. Nothing except a burning need for vengeance against those who had done me wrong.

I wiped the soggy ashes from my face, very likely making a bigger mess than before, and decided at that point that I might as well seek vengeance on he who had murdered my mother. That need burned more brightly than wanting redress for the ills that had been done me by Astel. In a way, I was almost grateful to her, for she had driven home to me the remarkably useful lesson that one must never relax, never trust, not for a moment. It had cost me money now, but with any luck, it would save me money in the future. I would trust no one, ever again, and put my needs, wants, and desires ahead of everyone else's. That was, after all, the way of the world. My aching head was more than sufficient reminder of that.

The wrong that had been done to Madelyne, however, needed avenging. Not only had she been deprived of her life, but also I had been deprived of her company. Much to my surprise, I found that I missed it, and her. Someone had to pay for that. It was not a matter of honor in particular, for I had none to defend. It was simply a matter of the natural order of things. Personal grievances require response.

But I knew that I, alone, could not possibly seek satisfaction from Meander's Journeyman. Even if I managed to find him, from what I'd heard he would make short work of me, and where would be the point in that? I had been toying with the notion of employing a sword-for-hire, and there were certainly enough of them about. Some bruiser with a huge blade who could act on my behalf while I watched from a safe distance. Such men did not come cheaply, though. Had I the money I'd been stockpiling, it would have been an easy matter. But I was now a pauper, devoid of any funds, and I would never be able to afford such an individual.

No, the idea bandied about earlier seemed to be the way to go. I would go to the court of King Runcible and seek redress of grievances there. I would demand the head of the marked man who had slain my mother, and Runcible would certainly listen to reason and acknowledge the fact that his subjects could not, should not, be treated in such a cavalier fashion. An attack on a free-woman would not be tolerated. Yes, definitely the king would see to that.

I would go to King Runcible to seek justice, to avenge my mother's death . . .

. . . and, truth be told, to kill time, because I had nothing better to do.

As for Astel, wherever she was, I hoped that she would have a long and lingering death, and that said death would involve multiple open sores and scabs, preferably in the vicinity of her private regions.

It was not a gentle notion, but it brought me some small measure of comfort.

Chapter 8

The long journey to Runcible's palace went without incident. That was certainly a refreshing change of pace.

I couldn't help but notice the change in the realm of Isteria as I drew closer to the king's palace. The quality of homes and places of business enjoyed a definite upswing. I was not simply approaching the power of Isteria, I was also approaching the center of money. If one is looking for the true places of puissance, one need look no further than to see where wealth is concentrated. I suppose that is the fundamental difference between places where the rich dwell and places where the poor dwell. The wealthy are grouped together because it gives them a warm feeling to look upon others of their own kind. The poor are lumped together because they have no choice.

I drew within sight of the castle, and truly it was a most impressive affair . . . at least, from what little I could see of it. There was no moat around it, as I had heard some other such structures had. Instead there was a high and extremely sturdy-looking wall that ringed its perimeter, and I could see—if I looked very carefully—bowmen casually strolling along the upper recesses. For guardsmen they seemed rather relaxed. I could only assume that if danger presented itself they would be a bit more on their guard. As for the castle proper, I could see very little except for hints of the tops of towers, with flags bearing the Isterian crest fluttering in the vagrant breeze. It was a lovely day, for what that was worth, the blue sky bereft of clouds.

At what I perceived to be the main gate, there were a goodly number of people hanging about. There were also several rather self-important-looking guards who were not letting them through. I strode up to them with as much swagger as I could muster considering I had a limp and said, "I wish to see the king in the Hall of Justice."

The guard looked me up and down. He did not seem impressed. "You'll have to wait."

"Until when?"

"Until the day that he sees commoners in the Hall of Justice. That would be noon tomorrow. And he only sees ten people on judgment days, so you'll have to wait your turn and hope you get in." He indicated the others who were milling about. "Why don't you go stand with the others . . . presuming with that crippled leg, you can make it that far." Then he chortled at his impressive lack of wit.

At first I was going to raise my voice in protest, but then I realized that there was no point. This was simply a brainless guard, following orders, given a smidgen of power and savoring it like a fine wine. He wasn't worth my time, and it would only amuse him, even empower him, to see me objecting to cruel or callous treatment. Without a word I turned and walked over to the others who were waiting. I hoped they wouldn't notice that my belly was already growling. The only food I'd had to eat was some provisions that I had managed to swipe from Stroker's before setting out. Two skins full of water, some assorted table scraps. I'd rationed them carefully, but they were starting to run low, and my stomach was definitely drawing that to my attention. Furthermore, because of my exhaustion, my lame leg was sorely tired from the long walk it had taken me to get there, and it felt as if I were dragging along a slab of iron rather than something approximating a human limb. I endeavored to conceal it as best I could, but the limp was still even more pronounced than it usually was. I heard the snickering of the guards and did my best to ignore it.

The others glanced at me briefly before returning to either talking among themselves in low voices or, more prevalently, simply standing in silence. Every so often some new noble or important person would ride up to the gates, and they were naturally ushered in immediately. Rank had its privileges, although I had to admit that a few of our number truly did smell rather rank. As for our group, I did a quick head count and found that there were approximately twenty people ahead of me. This did not bode well. Perhaps some of them were together, and the number of cases the king had to face was fewer than it appeared, but I still didn't like the look of it. If I didn't get in this go-around, I might have to wait around until the following week. By then my supplies would have long run out, and I frankly wasn't entirely sure how I was going to go about replenishing my stock. Certainly I'd learned sufficient woodcraft during my time with Tacit that I could take to a forest and hunt game, but I wasn't overwhelmed with the notion. More likely I'd probably just resort to stealing money or food from others. That, of course, carried its own risks. I wasn't seeing a large number of choices being presented to me, though.

As the sun drifted lazily toward the horizon, dark clouds began to roll in. More foul weather was clearly on its way. I couldn't quite understand it. Isteria had a rainy season, but this wasn't it. Generally, around this time of year, the weather in Isteria was quite mild, bordering on warm. In recent weeks the weather had been unseasonably foul. It bothered me, and it also bothered me that it bothered me.

Before long the skies opened up. This time, however, there was no thunder. Instead cold rain, quickly transforming itself into frozen rain, began to fall.

There were loud profanities from the others in the group, whose number had swelled to about thirty. Several of them had brought lean-tos or other means of convenient shelter. As for the guards at the wall, they had small guard booths into which they could step, keeping them safe from inclement weather.

I had nothing. I simply leaned on my staff and endured it. I wasn't about to go running around, trying to find someplace where I could hide from the frozen rain.

From their shelters, I could see the guards pointing and snickering at me. Let them. As if I cared what they had to say.

The frozen rain came down harder and harder. I felt my hair stiffening, icicles forming on my eyebrows. I didn't move. I remained utterly stoic, as if I was challenging the gods to throw their worst at me. As for the others in our waiting group, the weight of the collecting ice soon became so overwhelming that the lean-tos collapsed. There were moans of frustration, more cursing, as the crowd shook their fists at the sky and howled over their bad luck. As for me, I said nothing. What was the point? Since the loss of my mother, my virginity, and my life's savings, all in rapid succession, I felt emotionally numb. I had run the gamut and was simply exhausted from it. I couldn't even muster enough emotion to get upset over slowly becoming coated with ice.

The icy rain showed no sign of letting up and one by one the crowd began to scatter. Whatever issues they felt they wanted to take up with the king, apparently they decided that it could wait for a time when the weather was going to be more cooperative. Although the first few departed with reluctance, within minutes the rest of them were in full flight. Soon I was the only one remaining.

For the first time in a while, I moved. My clothes felt stiff and partly frozen to me. I made my way to the closest point to the gate, where the ones who had previously been first in line had been standing. Then I planted my staff resolutely and took up my vigil once more.

The guards had stopped laughing by that point. They simply watched me, as if I was some sort of oddity. Later that night, with the rain still coming down, there was a changing of the guards. The newcomers looked at me with open curiosity as the others whispered in their ears, pointing at me. There was no laughing, no snickering.

My tattered cloak, the only protection I had against the weather, hung heavily around my neck. It was frozen solid. There were icicles decorating my lips, and I sucked on them, appreciative of the moisture and glad that it meant I didn't have to dip into my water skins for a bit longer. Sometime around midnight, I think it was, I fell asleep. Yes, I slept standing up, leaning on my staff for support. At one point I partially woke up and was convinced that I was dead, for I couldn't open my eyes. It took me a few long moments to realize that they had frozen shut. I also became aware, however, that the rain had stopped. It was quiet as the grave. I forced my eyes open, and could hear the ice cracking as I did so. I maintained my posture, continued to stand there as immobile as a statue. It was still dark, but I sensed that the sun would be rising soon.

And rise it did. It was nice to know there were a few things one could count on. The chill that had brought the frozen rain the night before was now gone, replaced by a glowing warmth. The ice was melting off me, collecting in puddles at my feet. I gave it no more heed than I had given it when it was forming upon me in the first place. I just stood and endured.

As the sun climbed higher on what promised to be a glorious day, my wet clothes slowly dried on me. But I began to feel a chill to my bone. The extremes of cold and hot were wearing on me, and it was becoming that much more of an effort to cling to the staff and not tumble over. I was stubborn, though. There was another changing of the guards, and the ones who had been on post when I first arrived returned. They made no pretense at that point of doing anything other than just staring at me, and then they looked at each other and shook their heads.

Slowly people started approaching the gate. I recognized many of them from the night before. They were the ones who had fled when the weather became too much for them. It was approaching noon, and one of them . . . a burly individual . . . strode up to me and jerked a thumb behind himself. "Back of the line, cripple," he said.

It was everything I could do to repress my shivering. I was loath to let him think somehow that I was trembling out of fear. If I had in fact been feeling anything other than exhaustion, I would indeed have been afraid. More than likely, I would immediately have acquiesced to his demand. He was a head taller than I was, and infinitely better rested.

At that moment, however, I was too exhausted to give a damn about anyone or anything. Furthermore I was concerned that if I tried to walk, I might fall. That's how tired I was. "You left," I said. They were the first words I'd spoken in nearly twenty hours. My lips were cracked and a bit blistered, and what I'd said came out as something of a croak. "You left," I said again. "I stayed. I'm front of the line now."

"The hell you are," said the burly individual. "Move, cripple. Now." And he grabbed me by the arm.

There is no sound in the world quite like the sound of a sword being drawn from a scabbard, particularly when it's a big sword. It was that very distinct noise that froze everybody in their place, as a guard—the one who had spoken tauntingly to me the day before—pulled his weapon and held it in a casual fashion. He appeared physically capable of separating one's head from one's shoulders with minimal effort, and from an emotional point of view would do so with impunity.

"Let him go," the guard said evenly.

"But . . . but he—"

"He," the guard continued, in a voice surprisingly soft for one of his size, "is now the front of the line. Remove your hand from his shoulder, or I will remove your arm from your shoulder." He was tapping the flat of his blade gently into his palm. He looked like someone who hadn't used his blade in a while, and was eager for an excuse.

Just like that, the restraining hand was gone from my arm, and the rest of the crowd took up its position—in most desultory fashion—behind me. I wasn't quite sure how to react to what the guard had just done, and I looked at him with clear confusion on my face. He simply tapped his blade to his forehead in a sort of salute to me, and then sheathed it and went back to his station.

I didn't know what to make of it. As far as I was concerned, I had displayed the questionable attribute of not knowing when to come in out of the rain. And because of this, the guard was suddenly treating me as if I was worthy of respect. Only in this world of topsy-turvy attitudes could outright stupidity, such as I had displayed, be something that got me high marks. I had an amused glimmering of a notion at that point: If I ever turned out to be a complete and utter fool, I could wind up running the whole kingdom. It was something to consider.

I heard a bell chiming the noon hour from somewhere behind the walls, and the guards stood back as the great doors opened of their own accord. Another guard was now standing just within, but unlike the others his tunic was deep purple. I guessed from that, along with the self-important way that he was carrying himself, that he was from the king's personal guard.

The guard at the door whispered something to him, and the purple guard's gaze flickered in my direction for a moment. Obviously I was the topic of discussion, but both of them were trying to be subtle about it. They weren't terribly successful.

The purple guard then paced out the people waiting on line, selecting the first ten who had issues and disputes they wished to bring before the king. As I had suspected, it wasn't a one-for-one. Some had come in couples, and one was a group of three. All in all there were about eighteen of us, but there were still a number of frustrated individuals who had to turn and walk away. I couldn't help but notice that the burly fellow who had tried to send me to the back of the line had fallen just below the cutoff . . . all thanks to me. He growled in my general direction. I ignored him. It was easy.

The inner city, the city within the walls, was also called Isteria, the same as the kingdom. We entered through the gate and I could immediately see the palace much more clearly. There was a main street that cut through the center of Isteria, which lay within the walls. There were shopkeepers, vendors. Two blacksmiths, and three weapons makers. Four pubs, which frankly astounded me. What could people possibly need more than one pub for?

I also noticed something else. There was no poverty in Isteria. No hint of want, no sign of crime prompted by desperation to put food on the table or bread into one's stomach. No matter where one wandered in the rest of the outer realm, want and need were represented in some way, shape, or form. Beggars here and there, or stores that were shuttered for lack of business. A former pickpocket, wandering about forlornly because two fingers of his right hand had been chopped off in punishment. And of course, there were always the smells. The aroma of a charnel house wafting from one direction, perhaps. Or the odor of excrement, sometimes human, sometimes animal. One always had to watch where one walked. And mud. Mud everywhere, particularly after some nasty weather such as we'd been having lately.

But in the capital of Isteria, there was none such. It seemed pure and perfect. The main street was layered with a sort of hardened clay, smoothed off for easy transport. There was no crap anywhere about, and not a whiff of any offal odors. All the people seemed happy and healthy and just pleased to be alive. It was as if I were looking upon a world that never existed, and yet here it was all laid out for me.

Some of it could be ascribed to money, of course. Isteria City had the highest concentration of wealthy individuals, from the king and queen on down. It was likely that even the guard who was escorting us, as far down as he was in the grand scheme of things, probably earned as much in a year as the average citizen of Isteria proper earned in five or ten years. I had mixed feelings about it, which I found disconcerting, because usually I had such a steady and endless wellspring of cynicism that my feelings—except for flashes of genuine affection for my late-if-benighted mother—were uniformly consistent. On the one hand, I looked with contempt upon a capital city that so poorly reflected the land that it ostensibly represented. On the other hand, I was envious and wondered what it would be like to be a part of it.

The palace only seemed to get larger as we drew closer, spires reaching so high from this angle that they seemed to be scratching the sky. Flags fluttered in the breeze. I felt my legs start to buckle, and the guard noticed and steadied me. "Quite a few people get weak-kneed from being impressed," he told me in a low voice. The sentiment was much appreciated, although in my case I was simply hungry and exhausted.

Without preamble, we were escorted directly into the palace itself. I was immediately struck by how cool the air was. Perhaps the reason it was so striking was because it caused me to shiver even more. I didn't like the feel of the raspiness building in my lungs. More than anything, I would have simply liked to lie down on a bench for an hour or so. Obviously, however, that was not an option.

"In here," said the guard, and we were ushered into a room that was fairly stark. A table had been set up at one end with small refreshments. I was the first one at the table, gobbling down whatever I could, even shoving aside an old woman to get at a small morsel of food which others would have considered an appetizer, but for me was an entire meal. I gorged myself on what amounted, comparatively, to little more than table scraps.

Unfortunately, because I gulped whatever I could

down, my stomach was caught off guard. I felt it starting to heave, but with sheer force of will I kept everything down. I engaged myself by looking more closely at the others in the room with me. I was struck by the variety of expressions they bore. Some seemed hopeful, as if this was the culmination of a lifelong dream. Others appeared apprehensive, fearful of what they would experience. Still others appeared resigned, as if they were convinced that this entire endeavor was simply a waste of time. I wondered where my own expression fit into the array.

The door opened and this time another purple-clad guard was there. He pointed at me. "You. Come."

I did as instructed, limping after him as best I could while trying to keep my shoulders squared and what I laughingly referred to as my dignity intact.

I was struck once more by the coolness of the castle. Cold air kept things preserved. That made sense, of course. It was entirely to the advantage of the nobility to preserve the status quo, to keep things entirely as they were. After all, since they were at the top of the heap, what advantage was there to risk knocking out any of the supports?

Knights passed me by. I wouldn't have recognized them as knights at first, since they weren't wearing their armor. Nor was there reason for them to be. They were "off duty," as it were, the castle not under attack. Nor were they planning to ride out at the moment and enforce the king's justice, or perhaps rape some poor helpless trollop in the city.

Elaborate tapestries hung along the walls, with depictions of adventure and feats of derring-do portrayed upon them. On most of them, words were interwoven along the borders, and the words were always some sort of uplifting comment. JUSTICE ABOVE ALL, proclaimed one. PURE OF MIND, PURE OF BODY, PURE OF SPIRIT, said another. All charming phrases designed to educate and impress anyone foolish enough to buy into them.

Two knights were approaching, engaged in conversation. I wondered if either of them was my father, and tried to see something of myself in their faces. One of them had eyes that reminded me of my own, while the other had reddish hair that was evocative of mine.

It was hopeless. A hopeless game that existed only in my mind. As the knights passed me by without giving me a second glance, I knew all too well that the notion of determining who was my true father was purest folly. First of all, I had no way of knowing whether he was even still alive. There had been skirmishes, quests, and such during the intervening years, certainly. My father might have fallen to an opponent's arrow or a blast of dragonflame. Anything was possible. Being a knight was not the safest of occupations, after all. And if he was alive . . . if he did lurk somewhere within these walls . . . did he even remember that night? The night that I had been so violently conceived? Was it all a drunken blur to him, indistinguishable from who knew how many other nights of revelry and debauchery? Did he remember Madelyne's face at all? Had she meant anything to him?

As my erratic footsteps echoed in the great corridors of the palace, I became convinced—with greater clarity than I'd ever known in my life—that the answer to all of those questions was no. None of it meant anything to these protectors of justice and morality. Perhaps I had an abundance of siblings wandering about from similar evenings of entertainment by these great and just individuals; all of those siblings equally meaning nothing. The slight fluttering in my stomach from before was replaced by a slow, burning anger. In a way, I almost welcomed it. It made me feel truly alive.

I heard voices up ahead, laughter echoing. Powerful laughter, the laughter of strength and confidence. For a moment—just a moment—I envisioned going in there and pointing an accusing finger at the assemblage. "One of you," I saw myself stridently declaring, "is my father!" And the reaction to that would be . . . what? Shocked looks? Embarrassment? Shuffled feet, scuffed toes, an inability to meet my gaze or the critical stare of their fellows?

Nonsense. Very likely they would laugh at me derisively before throwing me out. Very likely, they wouldn't believe me. They probably bought into the nonsense of their little homilies about truth, justice, and morality.

Or even worse, they would believe me . . . and simply not care. The notion of being laughed at by these . . . these holier-than-thou mighty knights was more than I could bear. So I resolved to say nothing of my parentage, preferring instead to focus on the matter at hand, the slaying of a freewoman of Isteria by one of the minions of the mad king, Meander. Perhaps it would lead to a full-blown war, which would result in the death of whichever one of the bastards present—if any—happened to be my father. It wouldn't be much in terms of evening the scales of true justice, but it would be something.

I was ushered into the main hall and looked expectantly to the throne. There were twin thrones, although one was a bit smaller than the other . . . presumably that one being for the queen. Both, however, were vacant. Instead, there were several knights grouped around, and they were dressed a bit more formally than the others I'd seen roaming the halls. They sported nicely adorned tunics, one of them with gold epaulets. They were also armed with short swords hanging from their hips, although considering the number of guards standing about at the ready, I could only assume that this was more for show and ceremony than anything else.

What truly caught my eye, however, was the huge tapestry that hung behind the thrones. I couldn't quite believe it, and just for a moment, I felt a winter chill finger my spine. It was unmistakably a representation of a phoenix, rising from the ashes of its predecessor. Moreover, someone was astride it. It was impossible to make out the details, for the bird was so large that it dwarfed its rider by comparison. Perhaps "rider" was too generous a word, for to call it such would be to call a flea a jockey.

"She would have loved to see this," I said.

I sensed an immediate change in the atmosphere of the room. Until that moment, there had been relaxed chatting, albeit in muted tones. When I spoke, however, there was immediate silence. I looked around, making no attempt to hide my confusion.

One of the knights, the one with the epaulets, had a foot propped on one of the steps leading to the thrones. He had an air of confidence about him, and he looked at me as if I provided him with amusement. "You speak out of turn, young sir. Youth may excuse much . . . but not everything."

I supposed that, had I a brain in my head, I would have taken my cue to be properly quavering. Instead I said, "I thought that, since the king isn't here yet . . . well, there was no harm . . ."

"The king?" The knight sounded properly entertained, and there was now a ripple of laughter through the court. There were several ladies in waiting, and their high-pitched giggling was added to the mix. For some reason I found that even more irritating than the sneering of the men. "The king is not in attendance at the present time, young sir."

"But I . . ." The confusion must have been all over my face. "I . . . thought this was the time when he heard petitions, complaints . . ."

The knight sauntered to a podium that stood somewhat left of the throne. He moved with a fluid and easy grace. He was not especially tall, and his black hair—tied back in a tail—was streaked with gray. His eyes glittered with a cold intelligence. "The king is the court of last resort. Most matters are not of sufficient moment to warrant his attention. I am his chief magistrate, Sir Justus. Whatever issues you have, you will tell them to me and I will settle them."

"But I was told the king—"

He cut me off, politely but firmly . . . a bit more the latter than the former. "I am telling you differently. Since I am here, and whoever told you otherwise is not, I suggest you attend to me, not him. If you wish, think of me as the king, in that I speak with his authority . . . and therefore, in that sense, you are dealing with him. Now . . . what weighs on you, young sir."

I realized that I wasn't going to get anywhere demanding to see the king. Furthermore, I started to feel slightly light-headed, as my exhaustion began to catch up with me. If it hadn't been for the small amount of food and drink I had managed to grab, I likely would have passed out right then.

"My mother," I said slowly, "is dead. Her name was Madelyne, and she worked at a pub called Stroker's."

I was hoping that some reaction would accompany that announcement. I wasn't quite sure what, but . . . something. But there was nothing. Simply blank stares.

Sir Justus affected some vague interest. "What was her position there?" he asked.

"She . . ." I could have come up with a lie, but Sir Justus had pale green eyes that seemed to penetrate into portions of my mind that I would have far preferred to keep private. So instead I said, "I . . . do not think that is especially relevant."

"She was probably a whore then," said another knight, and there was rough laughter from all around. All of a sudden I would have liked nothing better than to crush their skulls if there was a way to take all of them at once.

"Yes," I said, making no attempt to hide my annoyance. "She was." I wanted to shout out, *And a group of you raped her years ago, and I was the result, you sanctimonious pack of bastards!* Instead I restrained myself sufficiently, and simply inquired, "Do any of you have a problem with that?"

If there had been a surprised silence before, the quiet that greeted my newest outburst was positively deathly. "Have a care, child," said the knight who had just spoken. He was a burly fellow with a bristling mustache.

I wasn't backing down. I was too tired and not thinking clearly enough to worry about normally overwhelming concerns such as my continued health. Considering what was truly tumbling through my mind—the accusations, the vituperation—what I was allowing myself to say was incredibly restrained. "It is a simple enough question, milord." There was nothing in the way I said the honorific that could have implied any true respect on my part.

It was Sir Justus who replied. "All creatures serve their purpose in their own way, and in that respect are equal. She was what she was, and I see no point in dwelling on it. Am I correct in assuming that the manner of her death is why you are here?"

"Yes." Clearly he was endeavoring to move on, and probably I should follow his lead. "She was slain by a Journeyman."

"One of King Meander's men." He didn't sound surprised.

"You know? You know of Meander's presence?"

"Of course." There were nods from the other knights now. There were no longer any expressions of contempt or annoyance. Apparently Meander's presence was something that they took rather seriously.

"Well then . . . I demand justice for her. Her life was ended, brutally, tragically, and prematurely. She was a freewoman of Isteria. There must be a . . . a balancing of the scales."

"True enough," said Justus. He appeared to consider the matter a moment. "Was she a young woman, your mother?"

"Reasonably young, from a chronological point of view."

"What other point of view is there?"

"Well, sir . . . a woman in her profession tends to age a bit faster. Wear and tear and all that."

"Ah." He nodded. "A good point, and an honest one. And because you are honest, you will not be penalized for it in the settlement."

"Penalized? Settlement?" I made no effort to hide my befuddlement. "I . . . do not understand, milord."

He wasn't replying. Instead he was digging deep into a pouch hanging from his belt, and from it he produced a handful of gold dukes. A single duke was worth fifty sovereigns each. He was handling the huge amount casually, as if he did this sort of thing all the time. I felt my breath catch in my throat.

He counted out ten dukes, walked toward me, and pressed them into my hand. "This," he said, "will certainly make up for the years of lost revenue."

I stared at my still open hand, the coins glittering in my palm. It was a considerable amount of money. But I wasn't entirely clear on why it was being handed to me. Furthermore, I was having trouble focusing on anything. My hand seemed very far away, as if it were attached to the wrist of someone else entirely. I felt clammy, but did my best to push through it. "I . . . don't understand."

As if addressing a simpleton, Justus said, very slowly,

"This will make up for the money that she will not earn, since she is dead."

"But . . . what of the man who killed her? What of him?"

"What of him?" Justus replied. But the accent was different. I had emphasized the word "him" while he had hit the word "of." My priority was her killer, but Justus seemed nonchalant. Everyone else appeared to share the blasé attitude.

"Well . . ." I gestured helplessly, unable to believe that I had to spell out something that should have been so painfully obvious. "He killed her!"

Now it was the burly knight, the one who had been remonstrating me before, who spoke up. "And you've been offered compensation. What more do you want?"

"Justice!" I couldn't help but find it ludicrously ironic that I was echoing the words of Astel, a woman so bereft of morality that she had knocked me unconscious with my mother's ashes and robbed me of my life's savings. But the situation was rapidly spinning out of control, and I found I was willing to say just about anything, including spouting moral indignation that I only marginally bought into, simply so I wouldn't look the fool.

"You have your justice in your hand," said Sir Justus, indicating the coins.

"But . . . but aren't you going to track down her killer? I can describe him! At least, I can describe the marks she likely left on him!"

"That won't be necessary," said Justus.

"But it should be! It . . . I . . ." My mind was at war

with itself. Part of me was urging me to pocket the money, which would be more than enough to stake me to a decent lifestyle, at least to start. But I couldn't get past the image of her corpse lying beneath a blanket, the image of a life cut short. The life that had given me my life. *Take the money, fool! Take the money and simply get out!* My mind made a tremendous amount of sense, and I can only blame temporary insanity, aggravated by my weakened condition, for what happened next.

"Why aren't you going to go after him! She was a freewoman. Whore or not, she was still a freewoman of Isteria. She was murdered. Why aren't you going to do anything about that?"

"What would you have us do? Go to war with Meander?" There was a ripple of derisive laughter throughout the so-called Hall of Justice.

I wasn't laughing. I wasn't even cracking a smile, although the gold dukes remained in my hand. "If that is what it takes . . . yes. Yes, that it exactly what I would be expecting."

"Listen, young sir," said Sir Justus. "We know his habits, his patterns of movement. The vagabond king never resides in one place for very long. However, if you want to make sure that Meander's stay in your territory is a lengthy one, then the best thing you can do is attack him. Once attacked, he will extend his stay just out of sheer perversity. His madness, however, is a predictable one. Try to make him leave, he will remain. Take no action, and he will depart. That is the official position of His Majesty, King Runcible, and frankly it is one with which I agree."

"But that's insane! You're supposed to defend the people!"

"We are supposed to defend the land and kingdom, and I do not appreciate being lectured, young sir," Justus told me. He was much closer to me, and there was clear anger beginning to build beneath the placid exterior. "Many factors come into consideration besides simple application of brute force. There are other, far more aggressive rulers to worry about. Berserk tribes, warlike monarchs. Plus we have knights out on quests. Manpower is not endless, and we must pick and choose our fights. Meander is simply not worth it."

"You mean my mother isn't worth it," I said flatly, the stench of their hypocrisy suffocating me. "If one of Meander's men had slain a noblewoman, that would be a different story. But my mother, she was a prostitute. She isn't worth your time."

"Her line of work certainly leaves her open to violent advances. Her end was unfortunate, granted, but not completely surprising, given the givens." His impatience was becoming more and more evident. "Engaging Meander in war is a pointless pursuit. Good King Runcible chooses those fights that are in the national interest, and this one simply is not. But your ire is quite evident. Tell you what," and he took another two coins from the pouch and placed them in my hand, then wrapped my fingers around them to indicate that as far as he was concerned, the matter was finalized. "If it is particularly upsetting to you, you can use the extra money I've just given you to hire a freelance mercenary to attend to the situation. An attack by an independent operator wouldn't be construed as reflecting the opinions or attitudes of King Runcible, and so he could act with impunity. That, of course, is up to you."

"But . . . but . . ." I had apparently developed a stammer. My brain was locking up, and I was beginning to feel an uncomfortable tightness in my chest. "But . . . it should be your job!"

"I have done my job," Sir Justus said, and there was no disguising the fact that his good humor and patience was on the verge of totally dissolving. "Take the money and be done with it. There are others waiting for justice. You have permission to take your leave of us. Good day, young sir."

Well, that's that, take the money and go, just go. My brain seemed rather pleased with the way everything had worked out.

But there was another part of me . . . a part that was picturing my mother. Deluded, true, but never anything other than a good-intentioned soul who had believed in me and sold her body to try and provide a home for mine. A woman who took her brutalization and transformed the result of that trauma into her reason for living. I thought about the gentle words she had spoken to me, about the endless patience, and the sweetness of her face.

And that other part of me said angrily, *In the final analysis, then, is that all she's worth? She believed in you, and you would sell her memory for twelve dukes? A handful of gold coins? Is that the going price for the life of one's mother? Because you know you won't use any of the money to hire someone to track down her murderer. You'll use it for yourself. And these men, at least some of these men treated her like trash when she was alive, and would buy you off now that she's dead. Do you accept this, then? Will you simply take the money . . . and run?*

And the answer, all in my head, came quickly and cleanly and clearly:

Yes.

The battered and pathetic thing that represented any claim to conscience I might have had turned away from me in disgust. Oddly, I couldn't blame it. I was disgusted myself. Disgusted at my weakness and my lack of resolution, at my refusal to see justice through in the name of the woman who had borne me. And the most disgusting thing of all was . . . I knew it wouldn't last. Oh, at the moment I was filled with self-revulsion. But I was walking out of there with twelve dukes in my pocket. That would buy me plenty of mead in which to drown my sorrows, plenty of women in whose soft loins I could hide, plenty of nights in comfortable, warm beds. Properly managed, I could parlay it into a homestead, or perhaps purchase an already existing business. Hell, perhaps I could even buy out Stroker and take the place over myself. Wouldn't that bring everything pleasingly full circle.

There would be guilt, yes, but the guilt would fade, erased by comfort and pleasure. And the simple truth was that there was nothing I could do that would truly be of interest to Madelyne. She was dead and gone, and all the justice in the world wouldn't be of any use to her.

For no reason that I could quite discern, that remarkable tapestry with the phoenix on it momentarily caught my attention. I wanted to try and emblazon it in my memory, carry the image with me although I didn't know why.

All of this went through my mind in what must have been only a moment, and then the great heaviness in my chest suddenly started to buck, as if trying to force its way out. There was an awful congestion within my lungs. I tried to fight it, for I did not want to appear weak in front of the assemblage—at least, any weaker than nature had already made me—and in doing so, I tried to bring my right hand up to cover a cough. As I did so, the coins flew from my hand, scattering across the floor with a musical tinkling sound.

There was a gasp from the assemblage, and the face of Sir Justus could have been carved from stone. The burly knight nearby gave even more visible evidence of what appeared to be outrage, his face positively purpling as if he were a swelling pustule about to explode. There was also a giddy peal of nervous laughter, originating from one who had apparently just entered. His garb marked him unmistakably as the court jester. Aside from that one high-pitched giggle, however, he didn't contribute anything else to the moment, which had suddenly become etched with tension.

I had no idea what had just happened, or why they appeared so angry, and then I realized: From their point of view, I had just thrown the money on the floor in what could only be regarded as a gesture of utter contempt.

I was about to explain, to drop to one knee and try to gather the coins up and beat a hasty retreat, and then Sir Justus said, "How dare you, you little whore's son. This . . . this is how you respond to my generosity? I have been patient with you, from pity for your lame state if nothing else, but my patience is done. Out! Now!"

It occurred to me at that moment that I might make a good recruit for King Meander, for my nature was apparently no less perverse than his. I had been ready to leave . . . until Justus ordered me to go. I looked at the clear fury in his face, betrayed by the veins on his temple, which were throbbing.

For once in my life, I felt truly empowered. My head was swimming with the giddiness of the sensation. Here was a knight, a highly ranked knight, surrounded by his fellows, getting himself into an uproar owing to a perceived insult by me, an individual who was so comparatively low on the social scale of Isteria that I might as well not have existed at all. It was as if I, a lowborn lame son of a whore, had been elevated to peer of a knight just by dint of appearing to be an ingrate.

It was a heady, intoxicating experience, the joyous sensation accentuated, no doubt, by the fact that I could barely think straight as I felt illness crawling through me, invading me. Yet in a way, that illness was suddenly my closest friend, for I was doing everything I could to ignore it and, thus, became more focused.

I didn't want to let go of this power. I liked making the knights mad. I wanted to do it because it gave me twisted pleasure to be able to affect them in that way. Here I had been, subject to their sneers and clear attitude of superiority, as if I was shit on their shoes. They weren't sneering now, no they weren't. They were disconcerted, bewildered that such as I would openly hold such as them in contempt. They didn't know, of course, that I—bastard offspring of one of their number—knew them for the hypocritical cretins that they were. Yes, I was definitely keeping that piece of knowledge to myself, for knowledge was even more power, and I was becoming drunk on that power.

"How dare I? How dare you!" Putting all my strength into holding on to my staff with my right hand, I made a sweeping gesture that encompassed the rest of the room. "How dare you call yourselves knights and lovers of justice! I spit on your offerings! I spit on you!"

The burly knight was trembling with rage, but he was remaining where he was. I was presupposing that these mighty soldiers wouldn't want to sully themselves attacking a mere lame peasant. He said, "Have you forgotten where you are? Who you are? Who we are? This . . ." and he pointed a shaking finger in the direction of Justus, "is Sir Justus of the High Born! I am Sir Coreolis of the Middle Lands! Who do you think you are, to speak so to us!"

"I?" And my voice seemed to soar, louder and stronger than ever, despite the congestion in my chest that threatened to choke me. *"I am Apropos, of nothing, and as far as I am concerned, you can kiss my lame, whore's-son ass!"*

I figured this was the point when they would have the guards evict me. It was only when Justus and Coreolis yanked their swords free of their scabbards that I realized I had figured wrong.

"Now," said Justus, very quietly, very dangerously, "you're going to be Apropos, less of nothing. Less an ear, less an arm . . . or maybe I'll just relieve you of that useless leg of yours."

The softness in his voice was enough to make me

believe, just for a moment, that he was still giving me a chance to leave. That was another miscalculation on my part, however, for without another word, Sir Justus charged. Although he wielded only a short sword, it made him no less dangerous, and I could see even from where I stood the razor sharpness of the blade. I also noticed, much to my surprise, that Justus was missing two fingers on his right hand.

Coreolis was coming in as well, but from a different angle and a bit slower, clearly more than happy to let Justus have the initial pleasure of carving me to bits. From all through the court, there was a collective roar of approval from the other knights, who were looking forward to seeing their insulted brethren slice and dice the lame peasant upstart.

Naturally, I did the only thing I could under the circumstances. I ran like hell.

At least, that was what I tried to do. But at that moment, everything that was wrong, and had ever been wrong with me, caught up in one shot. My lame right leg gave out, and I wasn't able to recover because a staggering spell of dizziness went through me. I tried to reverse myself, to clutch onto my staff and balance myself that way, but it didn't work. Instead I tumbled to the floor, my staff still in my hands, but otherwise helpless. One would have thought that, considering the fact that I was fallen, Justus would have backed off. But there was bloodlust in his eyes, his honor too much at stake, and he didn't slow his charge in the least. He came within a couple of feet of me and, setting himself in a stance, brought his blade up and back like a butcher about to cleave the skull of a hog.

And as my vision blurred, I realized that I was still clutching my staff angled up across my body . . . and that the dragon end of the staff was in proximity to Justus's crotch.

I squeezed the handle . . . and the four-inch blade, rigged up by Tacit, obediently snapped out of the dragon's mouth, positioned no more than a cat's whisker from Justus's most vulnerable area.

The snap sound of the blade was most distinctive, and the area from which it originated caught Justus's attention so that he was wise enough to look down and see his peril. He froze in position. Coreolis, on the other hand, didn't notice his associate's jeopardy, and was standing nearby my waist on the other side, apparently ready to hack me in two.

"I wouldn't if I were you," I said with a calm that surprised me more than anyone.

Their view of what was occurring was partly blocked by the positions of the knights' own bodies, but others were starting to draw nearer to the little standoff we were having, and their eyes bulged when they saw the predicament.

"You wouldn't dare," blustered Coreolis, his sword still poised to bisect me, but he didn't sound terribly sure of that.

"Your swords," and from my position on the floor, I calculated the arcs involved, "each have to travel approximately six feet down in order to strike. My blade, on the other hand, has only half an inch to its target, and requires not much of a thrust to strike home. Even a dying jab will suffice. The question presented is . . . can you kill me . . . before the lowborn unmans the highborn."

It was, in retrospect, an impressive speech considering that every word was an effort for me to form. My tongue felt as if it had swollen to twice normal size, and my voice sounded thick to my ears. But obviously I had gotten my point across . . . so to speak.

No one moved. For a moment, I thought we might be there forever.

And then an unfamiliar voice, speaking with an odd mixture of amusement and confidence, said, "What's all this, then?"

There were gasps, and murmurs of, "Your Majesty!," and everyone in the court went down to one knee, with the exception of Justus, Coreolis, and myself, who remained human statues.

The owner of the voice stepped around, and from there on the floor, I got my first look at King Runcible of Isteria.

"Well, well . . . what have we here?" he asked.

At that moment, the jester leaped forward, spinning about, doing a little jig, and . . . plucking a lyre . . . he sang out . . .

"A rude but daring whore's son has braved the Justice Halls,
Offended good Sir Justus, whom he's now got by the—"

I didn't hear the end of the rhyme, because that was when I lost consciousness. But I suspected I could figure it out.

Chapter 9

It was raining on my face.

At least, that's what it felt like to me. Cold water, moisture sopping into me, and I tried to reach up and brush away whatever was causing it. I was surprised, in a distant sort of way, to discover that I couldn't move my arm. It wasn't restrained; there simply wasn't enough strength in it. It was as if my muscles had shut down from disuse.

I tried to speak, but all I could manage was a slight croak. Everything seemed dark and damp, and then a wet cloth was lifted off my face. I blinked against the sunlight that was streaming in through the window next to my bed. "Wha—?" I said, which was a brilliant thing to say. I'm not even sure the word was recognizable coming from my constricted throat.

There was a woman leaning over me, smiling. I took her to be a maidservant of some sort. She was in her late forties, I thought, wearing a simple blue gown. She looked rather maternal; in a way, she vaguely reminded me of my mother. Her eyes were dark brown, and her silvery hair was tied back in a bun. Her first words weren't addressed to me, but rather to someone I couldn't see, probably standing outside my field of vision. "Send word. Our young rebel is awake." Then her smile widened as she continued to dab at my face with the cloth, as if she were mopping up a stain. "Hello," she said. "You gave us quite a scare for a while."

"Scare?" At least the word sounded a bit more intelligible. "Why . . . scare . . . ?"

She dipped the cloth back into a small basin of water, wrung out the excess water, and bathed my face again. I was bare-chested, lying under sheets that were cool and pleasant. "You've been unconscious for three full days. Just keeping water flowing into you has been challenge enough. Fortunately, we have a most excellent medi-weaver in our employ. Far more reliable than doctors."

I shuddered slightly. The thought of someone using magic to cure my ills was rather disconcerting for some reason. I actually preferred the methods that Tacit used. In our time in the forest together, Tacit had given me a basic grounding in the sorts of roots and herbs that were helpful at times of illness.

"Three . . . days . . ." I asked, and became aware of just how parched my throat was. She held up a mug of water to my cracked lips. Certainly they'd been trying to keep water going down my throat, but that hadn't stopped me from becoming dried out just the same. I drank deeply and fast, and immediately started to gag, coughing up the water quite violently. The woman didn't seem the least bit put out, even though I hacked a bit of the water up onto her. She simply dabbed at the moisture with a cloth.

"Three days?" I said again.

She nodded. "You had a fever and chills something fierce. The guards said you froze at night and warmed during the day. That would be enough to do damage to even the hardiest of men."

"So I've . . . proven." It was a very weak attempt at humor, but she rewarded it with a game and encouraging smile. I found myself taking an immediate liking to this older wench.

"Am I . . . in a hospital somewhere . . . ?"

She shook her head, the smile never wavering. Either she was a woman of infinite patience or she found me amusing. Or possibly both. "No, you're still in the palace."

"And I'm still alive?" I made no effort to hide my surprise. "I would have thought the knights would have butchered me the moment I was helpless."

For just a moment, there was a flicker of annoyance in her face, but then it passed. "Knights," she said crisply, "do not do such things."

"Pardon me for saying so, madam," I said, with a touch of bitterness in my voice, "but I think I'm just a bit more versed in the realm of just what knights will and won't do."

"Indeed." Her eyebrows arched slightly, but she made no comment. Instead she dipped the towel back into the water and reapplied it to my face. "Well . . . I wouldn't dream of contradicting someone so worldly."

"Worldly." I laughed softly. "That, madam, I am not.

I've seen very little of the world, really. And what I have seen, I've been on the bottom looking up."

"It must hurt your neck, craning it so."

I drew myself up a bit, propping my torso up with my elbows. "So . . . what is your name?"

"Beatrice. Bea, to my close friends and intimates. And you, I understand, are Apropos of Nothing."

"My name is known. I'm not entirely sure whether that's a good thing or not."

"As with all things, Apropos, it has both its positives and negatives. Life is a double-edged sword."

"That's why I try to live it to the hilt."

She laughed at that, rather heartily. It was not exactly a ladylike laugh. Then again, that wasn't all that surprising, since a serving wench didn't require the attitudes of a lady.

Her next words, however, completely startled me. "The king wishes to make you an offer."

I looked at her askance. "Does he now."

She nodded. "He has heard your tale."

"And he's going to attack Meander?"

"No. He is doubling the number of patrols, to keep an eye on Meander and prevent matters from getting too out of hand. But he is not going to strike against the Vagabond King."

"Because he doesn't give a damn about the life of one lousy whore."

"That is one way to view it," she admitted. "However, I am curious as to whether you've ever seen the result of a war with Meander." When I shook my head, she continued, "Devastation. Entire towns laid waste. Meander's consistent plan of attack is one predicated on total chaos, and much of that chaos spills over onto the helpless citizens of the land. I sympathize with you for your loss, Apropos. But is going to war over your mother worth the loss of lives that many other parents—and their children—will suffer?"

Her gentle voice, when putting the matter in that way, seemed to make eminent sense for some reason. There was none of the arrogance and preaching that was characteristic of the way that Justus had put it. Or maybe I was just viewing her with a lack of negative attitude.

"Well?" she urged.

Her statement hadn't seemed to need a response, but since she pressed me for one, I found myself nodding regretfully. "I . . . suppose there's nothing to be gained from further loss of life. But—"

"But you still burn with a desire for justice or vengeance."

" 'Or'? They're the same thing, aren't they?"

"That," she said, "is a debate for another day." She was sitting on a small chair and she placed the cloth back in the basin. Then she leaned forward, her fingers interlaced. "Am I correct in assuming that you have no plan for the rest of your life?"

"Well . . . nothing definite . . ." I admitted.

"The king is prepared to offer you a position as a squire."

"A squire." I looked at her askance. "That's absurd. You're mad, woman."

"Am I?"

"Yes!" Shaking my head, I informed her, "Squires are

sons of noblemen. Landed, titled individuals. I am Apropos of Nothing, as you so kindly reminded me. I stand to inherit nothing except whatever dirt I'm buried in when I die. No one is going to allow me to be a squire."

"The king was impressed by what he heard and saw," Bea said, appearing quite certain of herself. "You were brave and resourceful, standing up to Sir Justus and Sir Coreolis in a way that even the healthiest and stoutest of individuals would have hesitated to emulate. And you did so while you were ill."

"The illness clouded my judgment. That is all."

"Perhaps. Or perhaps you have potential that you do not suspect."

My head thudded back onto the pillow. "Oh, gods, you sound like my mother. And what would be the purpose of my becoming a squire, even if such an impossible thing were, in fact, possible."

"The purpose would be that you would be trained. You would learn the ways of true soldiers. You would—if you were clever, brave, and smart enough—rise through the ranks. You would acquire friends and influence all your own. You would, in time, become more than a match for the evil individual who deprived your mother of her life. And at that point, you would be able to seek him out yourself and take your vengeance upon him."

"But you speak of a time years hence. Meander and his men could be anywhere by then."

"That is true," she allowed. "And that is indeed part of it. After all, if you track him down over land and water as a freelance, take him down and kill him . . . that would be so far removed from Isteria that it could not rebound against us. I admit, it would be a challenge for you. But only you can know: Are you the type who shrinks from a challenge, Apropos?"

I started to think about it. In point of fact, I had very little to lose. Considering the huge and boisterous point I had so foolishly made of "refusing" the money that had been offered me, the notion of now taking the funds was anathema to me. The sneering looks of contempt I would get from the knights, the validation they would receive for their own arrogant view of the lowborn . . . it grated on me fiercely.

"No," I said, sounding far more confident than I felt. "I am not the type who shrinks from challenges."

"Then it is settled," and she slapped her open hands on her thighs as if indeed there wasn't a single other thing that could possibly be discussed. "You will be given lodgings with the other squires. They will be instructed to treat you in all matters as their equal. You will be assigned a knight who will be your mentor. You will learn and grow. You will become skilled and knowledgeable in matters of honor, and in time, you will discover your destiny."

I moaned softly. There was that damned word again.

But even as I heard it, I recalled the tapestry that hung on the wall, the one of a rider astride a phoenix. I asked her about it.

"That?" she said. "That tapestry was woven by a far-weaver, years ago."

That indeed caught my full attention. True far-weavers—magic users who depicted scenes of the future with the combined skills of their hands and their sight—

were among the rarest of all weavers. "And . . . what is it supposed to signify?" I asked.

"The coming of the greatest hero. The one who shall rule over all Isteria . . . indeed, some believe over all the known world, and unite the kingdoms into a golden age." She cocked her head and looked at me with amused interest. "Why? Think you that you are that great hero?"

"Me?" I laughed. "Madam, if I am a great hero, you are the queen of Isteria."

There was a knock at the chamber door. I saw that there was a woman-in-waiting standing near the door, but she made no move to open it. Instead she looked at Beatrice, clearly waiting for some sort of instruction. Obviously Beatrice was the head of the housekeeping staff. "Come," called Beatrice.

The door swung open and the king entered, his great purple cape sweeping about him lightly on the floor.

The chamber woman immediately went down to one knee, bowing her head in the appropriate response. Since I was already reclining, and in a sickbed at that, protocol did not require that I immediately genuflect.

Beatrice, to my astonishment, rose to her feet and simply stood there, her hands placed daintily one atop the other, as she smiled at the king and nodded once in acknowledgment. The king crossed the room, took her hands in his, and gently kissed them on the knuckles. "How fares the young sir whose mouth outstrips his prudence?"

Confused, I said, "I . . . I . . . fine, Highness . . ."

Beatrice told him, "I had given him your offer, milord. He seems a bit . . . skeptical. Perhaps," and she showed her pure white teeth, "perhaps he believes that a mere woman would not be privy to the king's offers or business."

He looked taken aback, although he reacted in such a mannered way that it was clear he was feigning outrage. "Say you what? He doubts the word of the queen herself? A saucy lad, this one."

"The . . ." I looked from one to the other as if they were tossing a ball back and forth between themselves. "The . . . the queen?"

"Queen Bea, at your service, squire," she said, and curtsied slightly.

"At *my* service?!" I was totally flummoxed, and now felt the need to leap to my feet and try and show proper respect. Unfortunately, leaping wasn't exactly my forte. Furthermore, since I'd been lying unmoving for so long, most of my muscles were rather flaccid. So in my rush to try and display respect, all I wound up doing was tumbling weakly to the floor.

"Very dignified," said Runcible, shaking his head.

Queen Bea automatically reached down to help me up, but I waved her off and Runcible, gently, but firmly, took her elbow to indicate to her that she should let me be. Slowly, summoning all the willpower I had at my disposal, I forced myself to stand. I was wavering slightly as I did so, but at least I wasn't on my back. I was barechested, but I endeavored not to be deterred by my partial state of undress, even in the presence of the monarchs of the state of Isteria. I lowered my gaze so I was not staring either of them straight in the face. I had the uncanny feeling, however, that the queen was smiling.

"May I be so bold as to ask," I queried, still without looking up, "why the queen herself would be tending to my bedside?"

"Because it amused me to do so," she replied. "And believe it or not, Apropos, one of the main endeavors for a queen is to find ways of distracting herself from the boredom that is so frequently a part of her station."

Not caring particularly about matters that were concerning me, Runcible asked brusquely, "Is he accepting my offer, yea or nay?"

I snuck a glance in their direction, and saw that Queen Bea was looking at me expectantly.

"I would be ten times of an ingrate, Your Highness, were I to turn away from such a tremendous opportunity to learn and grow."

"Indeed," said Runcible. "She did mention the counteroffer . . . ?"

"Counteroffer?" I looked at her in puzzlement. She shrugged.

"Yes," continued Runcible. "Twenty dukes if you simply leave. That is nearly twice the amount you were offered."

I felt my throat closing up. Nearly twice as much. I would have no problems, ever again. It was . . .

It was . . .

It was too perfect. Too pat.

As much as I wanted to lay claim to the coins—as happy as I would have been to take them and get the hell out of there—something stopped me. And that something was suspicion. It was too easy, too damned easy.

I bowed slightly at the waist and said, "Thank

you . . . no. I will not sell my mother's memory. It would not be . . . honorable," I said, faking sincerity with great élan.

Beatrice nodded approvingly. "Well said, squire. I have no doubt that, had you tossed aside the opportunity to become a squire to the great knights of good king Runcible—taking instead the empty comfort of money—my majestic husband would have—"

"Thrown you out with nothing in your pocket save your hands," Runcible was gracious enough to conclude for her. "Welcome, squire." That was all he said, and then he turned and walked out of the room. He paused, however, just before he left, and said six words that struck cold to my spine:

"Report to Sir Justus for assignment."

It was at that point that I was prepared to pull my clothes on and sneak out of the castle through the nearest exit, wherever that might be.

But then I envisioned the conversation that must have gone on between the king, or the queen, and Justus. *You know that young fellow who nearly sliced off your privates, Justus? The one who made you look like a fool? Well, we've decided to put him on the training track toward knighthood.*

Oh, how Justus must have paled. How disconcerted by that news he must have been. *But . . . but Your Majesty,* he probably stammered, *you cannot be serious! He is lowborn! He is a threat to our sanctimonious little club! Why, for all I know, he's the bastard son of somebody right here at the castle! Perhaps even my own little bastard!*

What care I for your indiscretions, the king would have

replied. *I have given you an order, Sir Justus, and you will disobey it only at your extreme peril!*

My, what a lovely little chat that must have been.

I could always depart the palace at some other time. Granted, there were guards, but I could likely slip out without much difficulty. This, on the other hand . . . this had the promise of providing amusement. No matter how much Sir Justus would bluster and complain, the bottom line was that he had to assign me to a knight, who would serve as mentor to me. For a moment my blood ran cold as the notion occurred to me that he might hold on to me himself, or perhaps—even worse—toss me over to Sir Coreolis. But somehow, I didn't think he would. If he were out for vengeance, I doubted he would do something quite that overt. In fact, he'd probably assign me to one of the better knights of the realm, someone for whom there'd be no excuse if I failed to succeed in my efforts.

I was certain that was to be the case.

More fool I.

I had never seen a knight quite like Sir Umbrage of the Flaming Nether Regions.

To say that he was not what I was expecting would be to understate it. In truth, I hadn't been entirely certain what to expect when—sufficiently recovered from my illness—I had been conducted to the magistrate chambers of Sir Justus.

Justus was seated behind a very wide and impressive desk. This was clearly where he conducted private business, and when I was ushered into his presence, at first he gave me not so much as a glance. Instead he appeared to be totally involved in reading some piece of parchment. Truthfully, I had no idea whether the paper was really that damned interesting, or whether he was simply keeping me standing in order to try and annoy me. In either event, I gave no sign that I was remotely inconvenienced. Instead I simply leaned on my staff and waited for him to acknowledge my presence. If he was out to ignore me, he could probably keep it up all day. Then again, so could I, and besides, I was used to being ignored.

But the silence only lasted a minute or so, and then Sir Justus put the paper down and looked up at me. "Well, well . . . Squire Apropos. I am told you will be staying with us for some time."

"So I was told as well, milord."

"I think 'sir' will do at this point, rather than 'milord.'" He seemed to consider the situation a moment, and then rested his hands flat on the table. "Obviously, squire, we got ourselves off on the wrong foot . . . no offense," he amended, casting a glance at my infirmity.

"None taken, sir," I replied. No reason not to be magnanimous.

"We are all on the same side, after all. Nothing is to be served by carrying a grudge, eh?"

"I would like to think not, sir."

"It's settled, then," said Justus, and he certainly made it sound as if it were indeed settled. He even smiled in what appeared to be a most sincere manner. "So . . . if you are to be a squire here, then naturally you will need to be assigned to a knight who is, in turn, in need of a squire. Correct?"

"That is my understanding, sir."

"Well, as it so happens," and he leaned forward, gloved fingers interlaced, looking quite pleased to be passing the information on to me, "I have just the knight in mind for you. One of the most experienced in the king's service. Been with him for years, in fact. Years and years."

"And he does not presently have a squire?"

He sighed heavily, seeming a bit downcast that the subject had been broached. "Regretfully, no. Not at present. He is rather hard on them, I'm afraid."

I should have expected as much. Justus was going to assign me to a taskmaster. Someone who he was sure would be able to break me. Well, I might just have a surprise or two for them up my sleeve. It was just like Justus and his ilk to believe that I would be disposed of that easily. I would not leave until such time that I chose to. "You mean he's demanding of them?"

"Oh. No, not at all. They just, well . . ." and he shrugged apologetically, "have a habit of getting killed . . . usually in his defense."

"What?" I didn't quite understand . . . but then, a few moments later, I did.

For there was a clanking behind me that sounded more like tumbling chunks of armor spilling from a closet than the approach of a genuine knight who was fit to wear them. I turned and gawked at one of the most extraordinary knights I had ever seen.

He had thick white hair that grew from his head in all directions, as if it had exploded from his scalp. He sported a long white beard as well. His armor might once have fitted him properly, but apparently he had shrunk over time, and now seemed a bit lost in his own suit. He had tired eyes and a general air of fatigue about him. He was taller than I, but probably weighed about half of what I did. His sword hung low off his belt, his scabbard dragging on the floor, and consequently he was able to use his sword as a sort of walking stick, for he angled the hilt and leaned upon the scabbard every few feet to pull himself along.

"I give to you Sir Umbrage of the Flaming Nether Regions," Justus said proudly. "Sir Umbrage . . . your new squire."

Umbrage licked his chapped lips and stared at me with tilted head. When he spoke, it was with a voice that was reedy and quavering. For a moment the sound of it startled him slightly. He seemed surprised that he was still capable of speech.

"New squire?" he said, blinked at his own voice, and then continued, "What happened to my old squire?"

"You remember." Sir Justus came around the desk and touched Umbrage gently on the arm. "That rather ugly business with the Blue Knight of the Marsh." He looked at me and half-whispered, as if Umbrage were not in the room, "Poor devil. Never seen a human being cut into quite that many pieces before. But at least," and he raised his voice for the latter part of the sentence, "at least Sir Umbrage got away."

"At least I did," said Umbrage agreeably, and then looked at Justus. "Away from what?"

"We have to talk, sir," I said from between gritted teeth.

"We are talking," Justus pointed out reasonably.

"Don't you have someone who's a bit . . ." I tried to find the most delicate word I could, and finally settled on ". . . younger?"

"Certainly you're not thinking of turning down this assignment," Justus said in mock horror, overplaying it just enough that there was no longer the slightest chance of misunderstanding between us. This assignment was not remotely coincidence. I had underestimated him, however: He had not chosen to associate me with a brutal or difficult knight. Instead he'd tied me to an incompetent one.

"It had crossed my mind," I said in a flat tone.

Justus squared his shoulders and turned to face me. "Sir Umbrage is one of the king's oldest and proudest allies. I will grant you that he is not what he once was, but in his prime, no one could touch him. I have considered the options very carefully before deciding to assign you to the fine care of Sir Umbrage. I assure you, squire, that if you should turn down this offer, it will be nothing short of an insult to the king. And the king has very little patience where insults to his honor are concerned."

"But . . . but I . . ." For once my normally glib tongue was at a loss.

"There will be no 'buts,' squire. If you do not desire the king to take offense, then you will have to take Umbrage. Do I make myself clear?"

Slowly I nodded. I was completely boxed in. "Yes, sir."

"Very well, then. You may go." He went back around

his desk, picked up a new parchment, and began to read it as if I were no longer in the room. But I could see enough of the self-satisfied smirk on his face to know that he was enjoying every moment of my discomfiture.

I walked up to Sir Umbrage. The view regretfully did not get any better as I drew closer. "All right, Sir Umbrage," I said. "Where do we start?"

He appeared to consider the question for a time, and then said in what actually sounded like a vaguely sage tone of voice, "The beginning is usually the best place."

"Yes, sir."

He waddled a bit as he headed for the door. I followed him slightly behind and to the right, as was proper for a squire. But just as we were leaving the room, he stopped, turned, and stared at me as if seeing me for the first time.

"And you are again . . . ?" he asked.

"Your squire, sir knight," I said formally, doing everything I could to ignore what I thought to be snickering coming from the general direction of Justus's table.

"I thought you were killed by the Blue Knight. Chopped to pieces."

"I heard that too, sir knight."

He nodded, apparently satisfied with the response, and moved on.

I had no option except to try and deal with the situation the best I could . . . and hope that Sir Umbrage of the Flaming Nether Regions dropped dead before I did.

Chapter 10

Considering what my existence had been until that point, it is impressive to state that what followed was easily the worst period of my life.

Riches, potential camaraderie, and an existence of ease and wealth surrounded me but at the same time was denied me. As I had suspected from the start, Sir Umbrage provided me no help or guidance at all in terms of even the most minimal skills required to be a knight. Herewith, a typical day in my service to Umbrage.

As per his strict instructions, I would awaken him in the morning. Then I would awaken him again. And again. Each time he would assure me that he was awake, and then I would return an hour later to suggest yet again that this time it might be an excellent idea if he actually managed to haul himself out of bed. By the time he truly joined the land of the living, it was usually noon or slightly thereafter. In the meantime, I spent the morning polishing and honing his weapons, which he never used, and tending to his horse, which he never rode.

What a magnificent beast he had for a horse. The horse's name was Titan, and an apt name it bore, for it was massive. Apparently the horse had been a gift to Umbrage from no less than the king himself.

After the noon hour, Umbrage would partake of his midafternoon meal. It was the only time he truly seemed alive, for the man could certainly put away food. Considering his frame, I could not quite figure out where he stashed it. But eat well he did, and with impressive alacrity. Barely was beef or fowl or mead put in front of him, and the next thing I knew, it was gone from the plate while Umbrage would sit there with a contented look upon his face. Whereupon, happily fed, Umbrage would then doze in his chair for another hour or two, digesting the meal like a languid snake.

In the late afternoon, Umbrage would be at his most active. During that time he would wander about in the great square, chat pleasantly with merchants, smile at passersby. It turned out that Umbrage was quite popular with the non-knight crowd, for he actually took the time to converse with them. Most knights, you see, had neither the time nor patience to converse with commoners. Umbrage did. The thing was, his conversations tended to go off on tangents, or perhaps even start over again since he forgot that he had begun them in the first place. The lower classes chose to find the disconcerting behavior charming.

The other knights, however, held a contrary view.

I quickly learned that Umbrage was widely considered a joke among the nobles. Oh, they never said as much to his face, although they probably could have since he would have forgotten it a short time later. Instead they were content to speak of him behind his back. Once several knights were grouped together, making cutting remarks about Umbrage that I could not help but overhear as my "lord" and I approached. Umbrage, on the other hand, appeared oblivious. In fact, when he heard the laughter, he joined in merrily without even knowing what they were laughing about. This, of course, made them laugh all the more.

Umbrage was maintained at the castle out of the king's sense of gratitude. In the king's youth, you see, he once found himself at the hands of a rather merciless group of marauders. Umbrage was a freelance at that time, and stumbled upon the sight of a beardless youth defending himself as best he could against a pack of brutes and thieves. Umbrage stepped in and smote them, rather handily to hear the king's description of the encounter. Young Runcible learned his savior's name and swore that, should he ever become a mighty king, Umbrage would always have a place in his service. Umbrage thought nothing of the vow at the time, but years later Runcible did indeed fight his way to the throne of Isteria, and he made good on his promise. By that time, many years had passed, and they had not been especially kind to Umbrage. That did not matter to the king, however. Whenever he looked at the elderly knight, he saw him only through the eyes of his own youth, viewing him as a still-vital warrior and canny gladiator who was deserving of all honors and respect that could possibly be laid at his feet.

All of that was well and good in the abstract. But the

knights did not see Umbrage as anything other than a walking, talking joke.

I should not have cared, and would not have, save that it had direct impact upon me. Since I was the squire of such a knight, naturally I held the exalted rank of Idiot-By-Association. Therefore I was viewed with the according contempt. In retrospect, I suppose I cannot really blame them. Had I been in their position, I likely would have regarded me in the exact same way. My own infirmities did not help my status, of course, and my ties with the most ludicrous knight in the realm didn't improve matters.

As for the other squires, naturally they followed the lead of their lords and masters. They saw that whenever Umbrage was spoken of, it was with disdain, so of course they imitated that attitude when it came to dealing with me. The ringleader of them all, and not coincidentally the squire for the ever-belligerent Sir Coreolis, was a squire who called himself Mace Morningstar. I doubt very much that that was his real name, but rather a nom de guerre that he had adopted for reasons passing understanding. Perhaps he felt that it gave him something to live up to.

Mace was everything I would have wanted to be, had I actually wanted to be anything. Mace walked with a permanent swagger, and when he spoke, it never seemed as if he was speaking just to one person. Instead he had a tendency to declaim to whomever happened to be in earshot. Furthermore, his voice ascended and descended to peaks and valleys in such a way that it seemed as if the fellow were constantly singing. What he was singing, more often than not, was his own praises.

Mace was tall, sandy-haired, and powerfully built, and insufferably convinced that he could do just about anything. The most annoying thing was that he was apparently correct. The squires, as a whole, were a fairly tough bunch, but Mace was the toughest of them all, their acknowledged leader. He set the tone to which the others responded.

Unlike the toughs of my youth, however, Mace and the others felt no need to beat the crap out of me. They made great pretensions over the proper way that "gentlemen" were supposed to act. Whereas as a child I had received bruises and cuts, as a squire I sustained only cutting remarks. I have to admit, I almost preferred the former type, for the latter took much longer to heal. Indeed, sometimes they never did.

"How fares the brave squire of Sir Umbrage?" Mace would ask with derision. "Get much fighting in? Much training? Slay any dragons today, Apropos? Off on any quests, are you? Look, Apropos! A damsel needs saving! Get to, quickly!" This would, of course, be quickly followed by laughter and looks of disdain.

I hate to admit it, but it got to me.

It should not have. Really, I did not care overmuch for the ways of knights. For the most part, I held them in contempt, remember. I knew their dark underbelly, I knew the evil of which they were truly capable. My own presence in the world was a constant reminder.

But I would watch them during their training periods. Observe their combat skills growing under the careful tutelage of their mentors. They would practice with jousting machines, or with each other. I was never invited to participate in such activities, because we always had to have the knights to which we'd been assigned overseeing us, and since Sir Umbrage was never awake for more than a few minutes at a time, that made my participation somewhat problematic.

Day passed into month, slipping over into year, and with each day my resentment grew. I believe it surprised the other squires that I continued to remain in their presence. One would have thought that they would admire my dedication. Far from it. They simply assumed that I was too stupid to know when to leave, so they treated me with even greater scorn than ever.

There were two fairly hideous occurrences during that time. First: Meander the Vagabond King left the area. That was inevitable, of course. It was his nature. Truth to tell, King Runcible played it precisely right. Left to his own devices, facing no challenge or overt threat from the regional monarch, Meander's attention wandered much as he himself tended to. So off he went with his Journeymen to seek new climes, new challenges, new regions to engage his interest. And with him marched away the unknown murderer of my mother. A great, dangling loose end had just been affixed to my life, and there wasn't a damned thing I could do about it. After all, I was busy training to be a knight so that I could learn the skills necessary to engage such an enemy, except that the skills were not being given me.

The second hideous occurrence was when a regional warlord named Shank decided to flex his muscles and muster an army as a means of testing Runcible's defenses and resolve. Runcible gathered his knights, and announced to them that such a challenge could not go unmet and that he was immediately going to assemble a small army by means of the Draft. The Draft was Runcible's customary way of choosing who would fight in a war. All the names of the knights were written on small pieces of parchment, and placed in a large circle drawn on the floor in one of the draftiest sections of the castle. It never took very long for a good, stiff breeze to come through, at which point the names would swirl about in a small whirlpool of wind, and a number of them would invariably be blown outside of the circle. These names, selected by the Draft, would be the knights chosen for the army. Odclay the jester would gather the names up, gallivanting and japing as he did so, and then the king with great ceremony read each of the names accompanied by much cheering.

That particular day, for that particular mission, Sir Umbrage's name was called. There were the requisite huzzahs, yes, but also an undercurrent of snickering and amusement. It was clearly felt that Umbrage would be less than useless in the endeavor. I also noticed an assortment of sympathetic looks in my direction, accompanied by shaking of heads and sad clucking noises. All of which Mace neatly managed to summarize by sidling up to me, patting me on the back, and saying "Nice knowing you" in that damnable singsong voice.

Thank God I was drinking heavily by that time. I had Odclay to thank for that.

The jester had come upon me one evening, sitting in the stables, where I'd been shoveling Titan's manure, looking and smelling about as pleased over the situation as one might assume me to be. Having had enough of that joyful activity, I had plopped myself down in a far corner and was just staring off into space, probably looking rather forlorn. Odclay rang his little bells in my face. I glared up at him and said, "Get those things away from me or I will shove them so far up your ass that you'll jingle when you think."

He laughed. It was not, however, a condescending laugh. It sounded almost commiserating.

"You," he said after a moment, "need a drink." He had not spoken with his customary jester gibe. Instead he almost sounded as if he were talking man-to-man.

I looked at him askance. "Indeed. And what of it?"

"Can you keep a secret?" He hunkered closer to me and looked most conspiratorial.

I thought of my origins, of the things that I had wanted to blurt out to the knights but had kept securely tucked away within my breast. "More than you can possibly believe."

"Come, then."

He rose, shoving his bell stick into his belt to secure it so that it wouldn't continue to jingle and betray his whereabouts. He paused at the door to the stable, saw that I was just sitting and watching him, and waved with impatience. With a mental shrug, I stood and followed him out, pausing only long enough to shove my hands into the trough outside in order to cleanse them.

He led me across the courtyard to one of the far walls of the castle and stood there a moment, his hands resting against the structure. Then he pulled, and I realized that he was yanking on some sort of grip in the stony face that I had not seen before, even though I had passed that wall a thousand times during my stay. Without a sound, the section of the wall slid aside on oiled hinges, and he gestured for me to follow. Since he was a jester, he couldn't help but tiptoe in a mincing manner into the darkness. For my own amusement, I imitated his walk as I followed him.

We crept down, down a winding stairway that was so dry and dusty that I could barely breathe. Moments later, however, we emerged into an area that I had never ventured into before. We were deep in the castle's wine cellars. I couldn't believe it. Barrels, kegs stretching as far as I could see, and no one was guarding it because, really, who would dare drink from the king's private stock? Well, the jester would dare, of course. Jesters dare all. As for me, I was the titleless, landless squire of a joke-of-a-knight. I had naught to lose.

Odclay and I drank in silence. He didn't seem much for conversation, and really, he was a jester. What was there to discuss? Jokes? Mindless cavorting? We simply sat in quiet contemplation of our own progressive inebriation.

Still . . . as he drank, somehow Odclay seemed . . . sad somehow. One wouldn't expect such from a jester, but this misshapen little man nevertheless came across as something of an object of pity. I wasn't sure why I pitied him . . . but I did.

I would like to tell you that Odclay became my drinking buddy, but I would be lying. I didn't see him again in the cellars after that. Indeed, he didn't even appear to acknowledge that we'd spent any time together at all. The next time I spotted him, doing his usual gallivanting for the king, he barely glanced my way. And when he did, it was with no hint of recognition. There was no secret look between us, no wink, no indication that we shared some mysterious and confidential bond. It might as well have not happened at all.

But it had happened, and I did not forget that secret entrance. I snuck down to the wine cellars every so often, drowning my ennui and boredom in the king's impressive wine stock. No one noticed. Keep in mind, I had worked and lived in a tavern for my formative years. I knew what was what in terms of the best wines and such, even if I had never seen most of them firsthand before. I knew that if certain bottles disappeared, it would cause a hue and cry that would run the length and breadth of Isteria, and none would rest until the culprit had been found. But no one was keeping track of the contents of ale and mead casks, and it was with those that I concentrated the majority of my imbibing. Once or twice I was almost caught out as unexpected footsteps warned me that the wine steward or some other servant was approaching through the more normal means of entrance. But the wine cellar was vast and I never had any trouble secreting myself away until the danger of detection had gone.

The day of the departure to fight the dreaded Warlord Shank came upon us apace. I should have been panicked or terrified. I should have been considering packing up everything I owned and vanishing into the nothingness from which I had come. But I was surprisingly calm as the morning sun shone down upon me when our departure date dawned. I can only attribute that composure to the extreme boredom that had enshrouded me during the year or two (time had blurred) that I had spent in useless residence at the castle. One day had become so much like another, with my lack of knightly education and the daily sneers of the other squires, that anything—even personal risk—seemed preferable.

Besides, I knew that I had a secret fall-back plan. In the event of true, mind-boggling danger . . . I would simply fall back. Retreat. Run like hell should the need arise. What did I have to lose? No one was going to pay attention to the actions of a mere squire. Besides, if matters looked that disastrous, anyone who saw me flee would likely wind up spitted and gutted by an enemy blade anyway, and would only be able to speak against me if he happened to find a means back from the great beyond. In the absolute worst-case scenario, any survivors who claimed that I had run . . . why, I would simply say that Sir Umbrage had ordered me to try and maneuver around behind enemy lines, an action that I—as obedient squire—had to oblige. Heaven knew that Umbrage wouldn't be around to gainsay me. After all, if pitched battle broke out, one did not need to be an oracle to know that Umbrage would be among the first to fall.

Little did I suspect that he would be, in fact, the very first to fall.

We were to assemble in the main courtyard at ten in the morning to prepare for the great move-out. Naturally this meant rousting Sir Umbrage earlier than his customary noon. I went to his chambers and woke him, and then woke him again, then again and again, repeatedly, every ten minutes from dawn until about nine. Finally he sat up, blinking away the last vestiges of sleep, and he looked up at me with slightly glazed eyes and said, "And you are . . . ?"

"Apropos," I said.

"Indeed," grunted Umbrage. "I'd consider you damned irrelevant, actually, insofar as a good night's sleep is concerned. Why wake you me at this ungodly hour?"

It was the most coherent I'd ever heard the old soldier. It almost gave me cause for hope. "War calls, sir. Duty. Battle in the king's name against a foul enemy."

"Oh." He considered that a moment. "Well . . . nothing for it then," he sighed. He swung his veined legs from under the covers and hobbled off to immerse his wrinkled body in a morning bath. When one is engaging an enemy with the intent of slaughtering him, one does not need to offend with bodily odors as well.

I watched out a high window as the knights assembled. Everyone's armor was polished to an impressive sheen. I even spotted Mace Morningstar secretly admiring his reflection in Sir Coreolis's back. There was laughter and raucous merriment, and they exuded such confidence that I almost wanted to be one of their number. Almost. Then sense and reality reasserted their grip upon me. I never wanted to lose sight of the fact that they were, at heart, the enemy. To destroy my enemy, I had no intention whatsoever of becoming him as well.

"Squire," came Sir Umbrage's voice. I turned and saw

that the old man had bathed and was now wearing the appropriate undergarments. "My armor, if you please."

I went to the cabinets where the armor was stored. I had taken the precaution of polishing it the night before. It did not shine as much as the armor tended to by obsessive squires who lovingly treated it every day, but 'twas enough. 'Twould serve. Umbrage looked it over and then nodded with brisk approval. "You'll help me on with this, then?" he asked.

There was something about him . . . a sense of lost nobility, of inherent tragedy. Somehow I instinctively knew that he was not one of those number who had assaulted my mother that stormy night long ago. I knew that such an action would be beneath Umbrage. He, of all the knights in the castle, was so "old school" in his manner that he would probably have been repulsed by the deeds done that awful evening. For the first time in our association, I found myself not only warming up to the old man, but to the very concept of knighthood itself.

"It'd be an honor, sir," I said, and I meant it.

"Good. You're a much brighter lad than that fool who woke me this morning out of a sound sleep."

"Thank you, sir," I said, and meant it somewhat less.

I armored him. The suit was still loose on him, apparently held over from a time when he was more muscular and filled it out better. But there was nothing to be done for it at that point. We headed out to join the others in the main courtyard.

If the other knights held Umbrage in contempt, as I knew they did, they did not let that sentiment show.

Instead, as Umbrage slowly made his way through the assemblage, he received only nods of acknowledgment and kind words about how healthy he looked. He was silent throughout, nodding and accepting the comments without reply. I, in the meantime, brought Titan from the stable. The horse looked tall and proud, and I suspected that of the three of us—Umbrage, the horse, and myself—it was the beast who was the most likely to acquit himself honorably in combat. As the king prepared to address us from the upper balcony, from where he made all such speeches, I helped Sir Umbrage climb aboard Titan. I had my own equipment, meager as it was, with me as well. I gripped my trusty staff with my right hand. My sword was slung over my back. Since my right leg was still quite weak, I had no desire to impede my already questionable ambulatory skills by weighing down my stride. I saw little likeihood that I would have need of the blade anyway; I had no real formal training with it, and besides, I had no intention of dueling with some monstrous soldier. My main use for it would be cutting through underbrush. I noticed the sidelong glances from other squires, the barely contained snickering, but chose to ignore it.

"My brave knights!" the strident voice of King Runcible rang out. Queen Bea stood obediently and proudly next to him. We all turned to attend to the king's words. "Freedom from tyrants and from conquest is never simply granted us. Freedom must be fought for, constantly. And you have been chosen to fight on behalf of Isteria against the dictator of the Outer Lawless regions. The dreaded Warlord Shank himself has sought to expand his influence, but you . . . you, my fine and gallant knights, will—"

He was interrupted by the loudest snoring I had ever heard. Sir Umbrage's head was slumped forward, his torso rising and falling peacefully, his eyes closed, his lips fluttering with the buzzing of his snore.

I wanted to sink into the ground. I wanted to pull out my sword and I couldn't decide whether I would throw myself upon it, or use it to decapitate the old fool, or go on a murderous rampage and simply annihilate everyone who bore witness to this travesty, including every damned knight, the king, and his lady. Or perhaps some cheerful blend of the assorted options would do.

No one said anything, but laughter rippled through the assemblage. The king, to his credit, did not choose to acknowledge the interruption, but instead pressed on. "You, my gallant knights, will show the enemy what you are made of. You will—"

The snoring grew louder. I couldn't believe it. It sounded like a stampede. His head snapped around and for a moment I thought he was going to rouse himself, but then it slumped to one side and the noise escalated. The king couldn't be heard over it, that's how loud it was. Unable to stand it anymore, I walked quickly over to him, trying not to allow my cheeks to turn bright red as I felt every eye upon me. "Sir!" I hissed. "Sir Umbrage! Awaken! You're embarrassing us!" Nothing. He didn't stir. I did the only thing I could: I reached over, grabbed his leg, and shook it.

He reacted instantly. He snapped up, his eyes wide, shouted, "Back, villain, you shall not have me that easily!," and lunged to grab his sword, which was mounted just to the right of the saddle. The sudden movement completely overbalanced him and before I could do anything to prevent it, Sir Umbrage slipped out of the saddle. He tumbled to the ground with a hellacious clattering.

The roar of laughter from the other knights was promptly extinguished when they saw the scowl darkening Runcible's face. Umbrage, for his part, lay on the ground looking rather stunned. My impulse was to crawl into a hole somewhere and die. Resisting it, I ran around Titan and went to Umbrage's side. But when I tried to haul him to his feet, Umbrage let out a most alarming yell and clutched at his right arm. It projected at an odd angle and I could tell immediately that he had dislocated it.

There was dead silence as all waited for the king to speak.

"Bad luck, Sir Umbrage," he said after a time. "'Twas not meant for you to join your comrades on this excursion. Report to your chambers and a healer will attend to you anon. Fortunately, you are as revered for your mental prowess as well as your physical. Good knights . . . I say ye, Sir Umbrage!"

"Sir Umbrage!" shouted the knights in unison. And perhaps the king was unable or unwilling to discern the clear contempt that the knights clearly possessed for the pathetic individual to whom I had been attached, but it was more than clear to me.

As I helped Sir Umbrage to leave the courtyard, the puzzled knight looked at me with bewilderment and said, "And you are, again?"

"Apropos, sir."

"Yes. Yes, you certainly are," he agreed, and smiled in that vacant manner to which I had become all too accustomed. As we walked, the king continued his parting speech to the troops . . . a speech that no longer had any relevance to us. Our moment had passed, and no one was interested in giving us the slightest bit of attention anymore. Actually, that was not strictly true. There was one. As we passed Mace Morningstar, standing next to the great white horse that Sir Coreolis was perched upon, Mace never took his gaze from us. He said nothing. He didn't have to. His smirk said it all.

And so the forces of King Runcible set off to quell the uprising of the dreaded Warlord Shank. At one time, it would have been an endeavor that I would gladly have passed upon. Indeed, I would have sought whatever means I could find to get out of it. But if I had done so, it would have been on my terms. Instead, it was upon the terms of Sir Umbrage. Sir Umbrage, who was peacefully back in his bed and snoring, sleeping through the ministrations of the mediweaver who set the arm, guiding it back into place.

The battle against the dreaded Warlord Shank took weeks, and we received frequent updates as to its progress. Naturally the updates were filled with tales of derring-do and great exploits by the noble legions of King Runcible. Every so often we got word of a knight having fallen, and lo there would be a great uproar and crying and beating of breasts, but invariably when one of ours went down, he took ten, twenty, or thirty of Warlord Shank's men down with him. I suspected a good deal of inflating of the battle figures. As for me . . .

. . . well, until that time, I had been taking myself down to the wine cellar and getting drunk every so often. But I decided that it was time to cut back. And I did: I cut back on the "every so" part, preferring to get blind, stinking drunk as often as possible. Every evening, when I finished with my nonexistent duties in the service of Sir Umbrage—who was well on the mend and actually remembering my name two out of every five attempts—back down I would go to the wine cellar. I still displayed reasonable caution. No one ever spotted me. But truthfully, even if they had, what would the consequence have been? What was the worst they could do to me? Throw me out? I served no useful purpose. Disgrace me? I was already disgraced, associated with a useless knight and living out a useless existence.

By the time word came back that the battle was over, that the dreaded Warlord Shank had been beaten back into his stronghold deep within the Outer Lawless regions, there to lick his wounds and hopefully threaten us no more, I knew that I had had enough. The castle of King Runcible was no place for me. If I felt like having people laugh at me, I could simply limp down the street and there would always be wonderful examples of humanity, ranging from small children to drunken sots, who would be happy to make sport of me with no encouragement. My stay was serving no purpose. I was learning nothing in the ways of war except from what I had been able to observe. I was gaining no rank, title, or riches that might serve me down the line. My mother's murderer was who-knew-where. Certainly he was beyond my ability to reach him, and since I was garnering no skills or allies where I was, I had no hope of hunting him down or being able to accomplish anything against him once I had. Besides which, I kept coming around to the simple truth that nothing I did to the bastard, providing I did find him, was going to matter one bit to the ashen remains of my mother. The only thing being satisfied was my ego, and that poor tattered object had been so completely beaten down and defiled, so permanently in a state of starvation, that there was no point in even trying to feed it.

I knew it was time to go. But something kept me from doing so, and that something was a deep-seated desire to leave the damned place at least moderately better off than when I'd come in. I had turned down quite a fair bit of change for the questionable privilege of remaining among such great samples of humanity as the king and his knights. I needed *something* to show for it. For I remained, as always, a great believer in the theory of pass-along aggravation. And if I suffered and knew grief during my tenure at the castle, then by God, someone else was going to experience the same by my hand.

"They come! They come!" one of the lookouts in the great outer wall shouted, with lungs so powerful that his voice carried all the way to the castle. He was quite correct. Like a great, twisting serpent, the line of returning knights stretched back and across the hilltops. They were still several miles off, but people were already lining up, forming a welcoming throng whose cheers could be heard throughout the countryside.

I was among that throng, but unsurprisingly, I cheered not. But neither did I glower. I simply watched with as detached an expression as I could. More than an hour after they were sighted, the pro-cession finally arrived at the front gate. Truly, they were impressive-looking. There were fewer of them than had left, of course, but the strongest, bravest, and most truly obnoxious of the knights remained, and they were more than happy to drink in the crowd's adoration. At first my hopes swelled, because I didn't see Mace Morningstar, and could only hope that the square-jawed lout's head was serving as a table ornament somewhere in Warlord Shank's main foyer. But no, my hopes were too quick, and just as quickly dashed when I saw Morningstar marching alongside the annoyingly alive Sir Coreolis. More than that, Mace was generating a certain degree of advance wagging of tongues, as word spread of the mighty squire who had wielded a sword to defend his fallen master and had laid waste to half a platoon. I later found out that Morningstar had in fact laid waste to a mere three men, two of whom were reliably reported as being blind drunk, but these things tended to grow upon the retelling. In any event, there was much discussion of the likelihood that Morningstar was headed toward knighthood far sooner than anyone could have expected. I would have been boiling with jealousy had I (a) any interest in being a knight myself and (b) any expectation that I would be around to see such a thing come to pass.

I still had no idea what I was going to do to even the score, but as so often happens in such situations, I found myself thrust into a predicament—of my own making, admittedly—that resulted in my stumbling most unexpectedly into a satisfying means of retribution.

One evening, shortly after the much heralded and applauded return of those annoyingly brave knights, I was making my way across the courtyard toward the castle. I had finished up with my late-evening grooming of Titan. Tending to the horse had developed into the one pleasure that I enjoyed in the whole damned place. I got to the secret entrance to the wine cellar and was preparing to press against the stones that would trip the hidden door when I was halted in my tracks by the irritating baritone of Mace Morningstar, hailing me. I froze in place, fortunately enough. A few seconds later and he would have observed me disappearing through the passageway, and I would have been undone.

Morningstar was not alone, as several of his cronies were at his heel. I had observed that when they were walking singly or in smaller groups, their individual strides were normal. But when they kept company with Mace, they automatically and unconsciously adopted his swagger. So when a group of them would approach me, I often had to check to make certain that the ground was not quaking beneath me, or that there was not a good, stiff wind which was threatening to blow all of us over.

"You smell of horse manure, good squire," Mace said with his customary false cheerfulness as he drew near. "Why lean you against the castle wall? Are you holding it up for us?" This drew the requisite chuckle from his associates.

"Simply providing reinforcement," I replied. "I had heard that your ego had swelled to such proportions since your return, Morningstar, that it overtaxed the support structure while you were within. But since you're out here, I can relieve myself from my post." With that, I stepped away casually from the wall, giving no hint as to my true intention.

My rejoinder drew a brief titter of amusement from the others which was quickly silenced with a glance from Mace. Then he looked back to me and smiled that square-jawed smile of his. "I imagine you have been preparing good Umbrage's horse for the tourney two days hence."

"Tourney." I was blank on what he was referring to for a moment, but then I recalled. A tournament had been scheduled to welcome the return of the victorious troops. A joust which was to be a celebration of the mighty men-at-arms. All knights were to compete in a contest that was really little more than an organized exercise in mock head splitting. The average joust is fairly on par with the average bar brawl, without the purity of spirit. Nevertheless, Umbrage was expected to participate.

Umbrage had been involved with such contests before. His record on that score was not particularly impressive. To be specific, my lord and master had consistently been unhorsed in his first passes in all jousts going back for the last fifteen, twenty years or so. He was not what one would remotely consider a serious threat to triumph upon the lists.

"Yes, of course . . . the tourney," I continued. "Naturally, yes, we are preparing for that."

"I could see that, yes," said Mace. "When he fell off his horse just before we rode against the warlord, we knew that was his way of preparing himself for the joust." This remark drew rather louder guffaws from the squires accompanying him.

I didn't even bother to respond other than a forced smile, and I turned away.

"What is your hurry in leaving, Apropos?" inquired Mace.

"What is my point in staying, Mace?"

"We're simply chatting. Trying to be friendly. We are all of us, after all, squires. That is not to say that we shall all remain as such," he said with a smirk. "Some of us have greater destinies."

Gods, I hated that word.

I rubbed the bridge of my nose. The desire for alcohol was becoming almost a physical need; I could feel it burning in the base of my throat, and my brain was urging me to bring it to that pleasant place where it could float in numbness. "Mace, is this conversation going somewhere? Because if it is not, then I most definitely am . . ."

"I just wish to understand, Apropos."

"Understand what?"

"Understand what it is like . . . to be such a loser."

His words should not have stung me, but they did. I should not have cared what he said, but I did. And most of all, I should not have bothered to respond to him, but I did. "You're trying to bait me, Morningstar. And you're quite good at it. You are," and I doffed an imaginary cap, "a master baiter."

There was dead silence then. The full moon above seemed to shift its light directly upon us, as if having taken an intense interest in our conversation.

Morningstar didn't lose his temper, didn't come close. The most that happened was that his permanent smile of confidence thinned ever so slightly. "Perhaps I am," he said affably. "But better that . . . than a loser."

And I slipped into his game, which was regrettable. "I am no loser, Morningstar. Umbrage's fortunes are not mine."

"Nonsense, of course they are. When our lords triumph, we bask in their reflected glory. When they are . . . less triumphant . . . that likewise reflects upon us. We," and he gestured to the group with him, "have all known our triumphs, our successes, individually and in association with our lords. You have known nothing like that. I am more than simply a knight-in-training, Apropos. I am also interested in matters scientific. From a scientific point of view, your predicament fascinates me." His tone dropped, became even more mocking. "Does it rot your spirit slowly and steadily? Or does it plummet by great degrees, then even off, then tumble once more. How does it work, I wonder?"

"You underestimate me, Morningstar. And you underestimate Umbrage as well." In truth, that was complete nonsense. I had been demoralized to the point of wanting to flee, and Umbrage was useless in all ways.

"Do I? Perhaps you will surprise us, then. Perhaps Umbrage will win the tourney two days hence. I would dearly love to see that. Wouldn't you, lads?" This generated the loudest laughter of all. It echoed from the castle walls, it sailed to the sky, and in my imaginings, the moonlight itself trembled slightly as the moon shook in silent mirth at the very notion.

And the words sailed from my mouth before I could pull them back. "How much would you love to see that?"

The challenge in my voice was unmistakable. Mace took a step closer, as if not quite able to believe what he had just heard. I understood his incredulity. I could not quite believe I had said it. "Are you suggesting a wager?"

I said nothing, hoping that they would laugh it off and walk away. I should have known better. I had presented a chink in my armor, and naturally Mace shoved a sword in and twisted it with glee. "Ten sovs," he said immediately, and then amended, "No. Double that. Twenty sovs."

"I don't have that sort of money."

"Afraid you'll lose already?"

"It's not a matter of winning or losing," I lied. "If I cannot cover the bet in any way, then it would not be honorable to engage in it in the first place."

"I would be willing to take it out in trade," he said. "You acting as my servant for a time, taking some of the more onerous duties off my hands. Your time and energies," and he held out a pouch, "against hard cash. Does that not seem reasonable?"

I'd been outmaneuvered. All I could do was nod.

But that wasn't bad enough. "Gentlemen," and he turned to the others with him. "Would you be interested in getting involved in the wager?" Immediately there were choruses of agreement and laughter as they all tossed their own twenty sovs into the wagering.

Naturally they could afford to do so. They were all the sons and scions of wealthy men, knighthood being a privilege of the rich and entitled. I, on the other hand, had no resources other than my questionable and occasionally nonexistent wits.

"Well, Apropos?" said Mace challengingly. "Have we a wager?"

So smug. So full of themselves. In a few years, they would be so suffused with arrogance, so insufferable, that they would be the new generation of bastards who went about assaulting barmaids. *Teach them a lesson!* a voice within me screamed. *Find a way! You're clever, you're resourceful, you can do it.*

"Yes," I said.

I wasn't sure exactly how I expected them to respond. Perhaps, for the most fleeting of moments, I thought that they might actually have respect for me for standing up to them. Instead all they did was laugh all the more loudly and saunter away, chuckling among themselves and speaking loudly of all the tasks they would put me to. Then Mace, seemingly struck by an afterthought, turned and walked back toward me. He stopped a few feet away, his massive arms folded across his broad chest, and he said, "And Apropos . . . when you lose . . . I hope you won't be getting any ideas about fleeing. A bet is a bet, and we take such things most seriously. If you attempt to desert our fair grounds, I assure you I will track you down. I mean it." I could see by the glint of his steely eyes that he did indeed mean it, and I also did not doubt for a moment that he was capable of accomplishing it. "Should that come to pass," he continued, "I can personally guarantee that your servitude will be far longer than you ever expected and far more brutal . . . and with large manacles attached to you so that you do not attempt a repeat of such dishonorable behavior. Good evening to you, Apropos," and he doffed an imaginary cap before turning and strolling away.

Some time later, I sat in the wine cellar, staring at the walls while cradling a wineskin in my lap like a child, murmuring over and over as if lulling the child to sleep, "I am shat upon. I am shat upon." Indeed I was. From a moment of sheer reckless impulse, I had allowed myself to be thoroughly outmaneuvered by Morningstar and his lot. What the hell was I supposed to do? Umbrage had no chance of winning the tournament. But I had no means of obtaining the funds necessary to pay off the bet. Squires were not paid for their services; room, board, and training were supposed to be all the payment necessary. The richer squires—which described all but me—received additional funding from their families, but I had nothing and no one. I could go to Umbrage for the money, but I doubted he would give it to me. He was quite stingy, never becoming involved in any games of chance or gambling with the other knights, keeping his purse strings tightly closed. It did not seem likely he would endorse my gambling endeavors. If it meant losing his squire to become the virtual slave of others, well, what did it matter to Umbrage? The odds were that before long he would forget I was ever associated with him. I had to keep reminding him every day or so as it was.

I was thoroughly without hope.

And then, as I stared at the wineskins . . . an idea hit me. When one is that far down into the pit, such notions provide glorious shafts of light, and suchlike struck me at that moment. It was an idea that seemed simplicity itself. Suddenly not only was I no longer afraid of the upcoming joust, I was in fact eager for it to arrive.

—

It was a glorious day for the tournament.

Of all my memories of my time at King Runcible's castle in the state of Isteria, that may be my fondest. Not simply because of my knowledge of what happened, but because it was everything that a knightly convocation should have been. King Runcible and Queen Beatrice were seated in a royal box at the edge of the grounds, the box itself festooned with banners and ribbons, an honor guard proudly arrayed around them more for ceremony than from any serious concern that an attack might be imminent. The knights marched in crisp, surefooted display, their swords extended and saluting their liege. The horses, the mighty mounts who would serve as their vehicles of battle in the upcoming joust, munched contentedly on their feedbags, watching the pageantry with bored eyes.

As for me, my gaze never wandered from Sir Umbrage. I was relieved to see that he kept in step with the other knights. When they whipped their swords around in their ceremonial salute, at least his blade didn't fly from his hand. I had a vision of it sailing from his grasp, whipping through the air and decapitating the king in front of the entire horrified assemblage. Granted, such an action would likely have caused the festivities to be canceled, but it certainly seemed an extreme length to go just to get out of a bet . . . even just a potentially calamitous bet as this one.

The squires were divided into two groups and positioned at opposite ends of the field, the running order of the jousts having been already determined. By serendipity, Mace Morningstar was at the far end. Yet I could feel his annoyingly cold stare upon me, surrounded by a face that displayed nothing but charm and cheer. I could see that he was already imagining the various backbreaking chores that he was planning to submit me to. Were I him, I might very well be doing the same thing. Then again, if I were him, I might have bashed my head in with a brick rather than live with my own insufferable nature.

The lists having officially presented themselves to the king, the knights sauntered into their respective areas to await their challenges. Sir Umbrage was the first of the knights to have a go. This was considered an honor, and the fact that the king had selected him for it was not lost upon the others. The king still had a fondness for Umbrage; clearly the king remembered the knight from his glory days and maintained an almost unbalanced determination to see a flash of the old magic.

Unfortunately, Umbrage's opponent was no pushover. His name was Sir Rambert, although he was popularly known as the Ram. The nickname had been acquired specifically because of his jousting ability. Once the knight was in motion, he was something of an irresistible force.

I helped Sir Umbrage buckle on his armor. He seemed surprisingly lucid, even invigorated. "Superb day for it, isn't it, son," he said.

"Yes, sir," I replied, inwardly flinching at a knight calling me "son."

He lowered his arms as I finished buckling on his breast- and backplates. I then went to work on his arms, affixing the pauldron, the rerebrace and couter. Then he extended his arms forward as I slid the gauntlets on. "Good of you to help me," he said.

"Not a problem, milord."

"And you are again . . . ?"

I sighed. "Your squire, Sir Umbrage."

As he had so often, Umbrage squinted at me as if first encountering me. "When did I get a squire?"

I had long since tired of telling him how long I had been with him. So I simply said, "As of this morning, sir."

"Ah! Welcome aboard, then."

"Glad to be here, sir."

Fully armored, Umbrage walked toward Titan as I guided him with a firm hand on his elbow cup. The knight walked straight and proud, perhaps caught up in the majesty of the moment. I prayed that his mounting of the mighty horse would go smoothly, and for once whatever supreme beings there might be chose to grant my wish. Umbrage, his armor gleaming in the sun, walked up the short flight of steps which led to Titan's powerful back and he swung his leg over with no problem. After a moment's consideration, he took his buckler and held the shield comfortably on his right arm. He took the lance in his left, a green and white pennon fluttering from toward the end.

I looked to the far end to see how fared Sir Ram. He was astride his horse, but I could see through his still-raised visor that there was concern on his face. He didn't seem comfortable on his horse, but couldn't quite discern what precisely might be the matter.

The queen, as was her place in these matters, then rose in her seat and took a step forward, holding a ceremonial purple cloth which fluttered gently in the soft breeze. As she did so, all grew quiet in anticipation. She savored the moment, and then released the cloth, which caused a massive roar from the crowd. It seemed as if everyone in the entire town had crowded in to watch the spectacle.

Sir Umbrage slammed down his visor, Sir Ram doing likewise, and both of them urged their horses forward. I could see Mace at the far end, laughing in anticipation, already envisioning Sir Umbrage being knocked clear of his saddle on the first go about. The knights charged toward each other, and Titan picked up speed at Umbrage's urging . . .

. . . and Ram began to slow. Even though his visor was down, the knight's confusion was visible as he looked down at his mount, jamming his feet against the beast's sides and trying to get more speed out of him. His endeavors had the opposite effect. The horse slowed even more, and even staggered slightly.

The pike of Umbrage's lance struck just below Ram's gorget, at the base of his throat. The blow, propelled by Titan's stalwart legs, drove the pike forward and Ram backward. The knight was overbalanced, yanked completely from his saddle, and with a clatter of metal he tumbled to the ground in a glorious crash that wiped that insufferable smirk right off Mace Morningstar's face.

There was a stunned silence for a moment, for Sir Ram had been heavily favored. Umbrage wheeled his horse around at the far end of the field, raised his visor, and stared with no less incredulity than was on the faces of anyone else watching. Ram's horse still seemed dazed by the entire encounter, wobbling somewhat. Sir Ram staggered to his feet, looking around in obvious confusion, and then he raised his visor and his disfocused eyes snapped together on Umbrage. Then—and I have to admit, it was the mark of a gentleman—Ram bowed slightly to the victor, and this gesture resulted in a thunderous burst of applause from the assemblage. It started small, but grew quickly like crashing waves, washing over both Umbrage and myself.

Mace Morningstar was not looking at Umbrage. He was looking right at me, the first cloud of dark suspicion hanging over him. I didn't look away, of course. That would have appeared guilty. Instead I simply tossed off a salute, and the cheery gesture was enough to get Mace to turn to his cronies and huddle in what seemed a most intense discussion.

There were other bouts then between other knights, but Sir Umbrage, as the winner, was required to take on all comers.

He beat them.

One after the next, he beat them.

The crowd became aware, as triumph piled upon triumph, that they were witnessing something truly remarkable. Umbrage should have been little more than an opening act for the great show; instead his prowess brought him higher and higher in the ranks of knights. He graduated rapidly from woeful joke to valiant underdog and then, ultimately, to unexpected hero. It was as if God had reached down from on high, tapped him on the shoulder, and granted him new strength, vigor, and luck for this amazing day.

In a sense, I suppose that was accurate enough. It was God's grape, to be specific. The grape which had grown upon the vine, which had found its way to the king's wine cellar . . . and from there, into the feed of the horses of all the other knights. Basically, I had absconded with some of the most potent liquor from the king's stores, my time at Stroker's having served me well in determining just what the most powerful drink might be. I had then snuck into the feed stores and, after taking sufficient quantity to feed Titan separately, I had spiked the horses' food supply. The moment the mounts had strapped on the feedbags that morning, it was the equivalent of bellying up to the bar. Ultimately, every single knight of the lists rode horses who were, to put it delicately, functioning at less than their full potential. To put it less delicately, they were drunk off their horses' asses.

It didn't occur to anyone that any such thing was amiss, for such a stunt would have been wildly dishonorable, and the entire purpose of the joust was to see honor in its most pure display.

He had just dispatched Sir Justus, a triumph that had

given me particular pleasure. As the confused Justus pulled himself to his feet and staggered off, followed by his equally staggering horse, I was pouring water down the throat of the somewhat confused Sir Umbrage. He was looking at me with near befuddlement. "Am I winning?" he asked.

"Yes, sir, it would seem so."

"How is that happening?" There was something in his eyes that I had never quite seen before, but I couldn't place my finger on what that might be.

"It would seem the gods of the joust have smiled upon you, milord," I told him. I thought I sounded rather smooth about it.

But once again, his gaze shifted, as if layers were being peeled from his eyes. And there was something deep and cold there that I had not expected. To my surprise, I found myself looking down, suddenly taking great interest in shining up his armored leg. "Just . . . one more opponent, sir. Sir Coreolis."

"Coreolis."

"Of the Middle Lands, yes, sir."

"And I am Sir Umbrage of the Flaming Nether Regions."

"That would be you, yes, sir." I finished polishing up the leg and suddenly a hand of surprising strength was on my shoulder, hauling me to my feet.

He looked at me in a way that seemed capable of seeing into my very soul, and he murmured, "And you . . . you are Apropos of Nothing . . . are you not. My squire."

"That's right, sir." The change in him was almost frightening.

He was silent for a long moment. He seemed on the verge of asking me something . . . but before he could, the fanfare of trumpets indicated that the combatants were to get to their horses. I helped him to the stairs that led up to Titan, but he paused with his foot on the first step, turned to me, and said, "I will lose this match."

"I hope not, sir" was all I said.

He harrumphed then rather loudly, coughed in a decidedly disgusting manner, and climbed atop Titan. I could have sworn that Titan looked at me with disdain, as if he knew what I had done. Perhaps he had. Perhaps horses had a means of communicating with each other, or could at the very least discern weakness in one another. Perhaps he knew that his compatriots were three sheets to the wind, and had a pretty good idea who had reduced them to that state. Or perhaps I was simply becoming obsessed with second-guessing everything. Certainly my nervousness was understandable. The bet was still very much in force, and if Sir Umbrage's prediction was correct, everything that had been accomplished up to that point would be for naught.

Sir Umbrage was poised and ready at one end of the field, Sir Coreolis at another. Of all the knights, Coreolis had the largest horse of them all, a pure white monster of a mount with the rather intimidating name of Bonecrusher. He had his own special feed that Coreolis kept separate from the others, but since most of my incredibly important duties revolved around the stables, I'd had no trouble at all gaining access to it. The problem was that, because of Bonecrusher's sheer size, I felt it necessary to mix a higher percentage of wine into his feed than I had with the other steeds. Wanting to err on the side of caution, I had more than doubled the amount that Bonecrusher was ingesting compared to the others. Nevertheless, I still didn't know for sure that it was enough. I was operating on pure guesswork.

As I watched Bonecrusher and Coreolis, my heart withered, because it appeared to me that Bonecrusher was in fine fettle. He had already taken on several other opponents and seemed none the worse for wear. He stood there proud, confident, looking not the least bit wavery. I muttered a low curse and envisioned myself spending the next year or two as Mace Morningstar's personal slave. It was not a pleasant contemplation.

There was Mace, sure enough, patting Bonecrusher's rump and nodding approvingly. Coreolis had his lance prepped, as did Sir Umbrage. They merely awaited the dropping of the cloth that would be their signal to gallop toward each other with the single and soul intent of knocking the living snot out of one another.

Queen Bea stretched out her hand for the final time of the afternoon. The crowd had been roaring, louder and louder, up until that point, but when she extended her arm they became utterly silent. She sustained the suspense with a teasing smile—and then released the cloth.

"Yah!" shouted Sir Coreolis, slamming down his visor and urging Bonecrusher forward. Umbrage followed suit, albeit without an overdramatic shout. Their lances were leveled at one another, the distance between them quickly closing. I was certain that my heart had ceased beating, my breath frozen in my paralyzed lungs.

The two knights pounded toward each other, weapons at the ready.

And Bonecrusher fell over while Sir Umbrage and Titan were still a good ten feet away.

He did so completely without warning. One moment he was in full gallop, the next his feet went out from under him. The majestic horse simply went down, his legs collapsing beneath him. That Bonecrusher did not break a leg was nothing short of miraculous, considering the abruptness of the fall. That Bonecrusher did not fall atop Sir Coreolis while toppling was also a remarkable bit of luck. Not for me, you understand. I wouldn't have cared if the horse had landed on him and crushed him into sheet metal. It was, however, Coreolis's good fortune to be thrown clear of the beast and crash to the ground with an earsplitting clatter of armor.

There was dead silence for a moment. No one knew what to make of what they had just seen. The horse was lying there, staring off into space, and I was quite certain that purple unicorns were probably dancing around him at that moment, laughing at his stupor. Sir Umbrage drew Titan up short and looked in amazement at the fallen knight, who was staggering to his feet and yanking off his helmet.

"The winner of the day—Sir Umbrage!" called the king then, and because the king had said so, naturally this engendered a huge ovation from the crowd. Umbrage reined in Titan and nodded in acknowledgment of the accolades, but there was still polite confusion on his face.

Because of the collective volume of the shouting people, it took a few moments for Coreolis to shout over them. But everyone could tell that he was bellowing at Umbrage, because he was pointing and waving at the old knight in a most belligerent fashion. And when he yanked out his sword and pointed it straight at the still-mounted Umbrage, his meaning could not have been more clear. That was when the crowd quieted enough for Coreolis's voice to rise above them as he shouted, "Trickery! Base trickery! I was not defeated! My horse collapsed!"

"Horsemanship," Queen Bea said coolly, sounding quite majestic as she spoke, "is part of the test of the jousts, good sir knight. If you could not control your steed . . ."

"He did something!" snarled Coreolis, his face purpling with rage. "He, or his damnable squire, or—" He was so furious that he couldn't get the words out, and then he waved his sword once more and said, "Fight me, Sir Umbrage! Down here! Man to man, sword to sword!"

"I have had a long day of fighting, sir knight," Umbrage said mildly. "I am not as young as you and your ilk. Let the day end without vitupera—"

"I do not yield! Fight me now or be known as a coward!"

There was deathly silence then. The significance of the charge was not lost on any. The situation had spun entirely out of my control, and when Coreolis cut Umbrage to ribbons, the fault would entirely be on my head.

I knew what I had to do. I had to step forward and take responsibility for my actions. It meant disgrace, punishment, who-knew-what, but I couldn't just stand there and let Umbrage take on the infuriated Coreolis.

I tried to make my mouth move, to own up to what I had done. But nothing came out. My fundamental weakness had consumed me completely. I had tried a subterfuge, and it had come damned close to working. Now that it had fallen apart, I couldn't bring myself to try and make it right. I cursed myself for my paucity of spirit, but that still didn't prompt me to put myself forward as the perpetrator of the stunt that had rigged the afternoon's festivities. I feared the consequences. I feared the punishment. I feared what awaited me at the hands of the angered knights, of the squires.

And so I said nothing and stood there, knowing that I was about to see Sir Umbrage have his head handed to him, perhaps literally.

Sir Umbrage, without so much as a glance in my direction, eased himself off Titan and withdrew his sword from its scabbard. There was no cheer from the crowd this time; they knew what they were witnessing. Indeed, everyone understood what was at stake. Technically, this was still simply a joust. No lethal, killing blows were to be struck. That rule usually sufficed when one was dealing with two knights who were simply out to prove who was the more skilled combatant. But Sir Coreolis was furious beyond endurance, and in combat, things could happen very quickly. To say nothing of the fact that Umbrage was not exactly a young man. A blow dealt to him that would simply knock cold a younger man could very well prove lethal to the old knight.

They strode toward each other, taking up positions

within range of one another. Umbrage seemed barely able to lift his sword. He did not, however, seem especially concerned. I couldn't help but wonder if he even knew where he was or what was about to happen.

Sir Coreolis let out an infuriated roar and, with no more warning than that, charged. His sword whipped around toward Umbrage. Coreolis was not mincing around. He was coming straight for the attack, counting on his aggression and brute force to carry the day. It certainly seemed like a safe bet.

I never even saw Umbrage's sword move. Nor, I think, did anyone else, including Sir Coreolis. All anyone knew was that one moment, Umbrage had the sword at his side, and the next it was a blur. There was a loud *clang* and Coreolis staggered slightly, and the sword was out of his hands. It was pinwheeling through the air, making a "whupp whupp" sound as it spun, and then it thudded to the ground at the far end of the field, right where Mace Morningstar was standing. The blade speared the ground directly between his legs, missing circumcising him by inches. Morningstar stared down at it, ashen, as the sword wavered slightly from the impact.

Before Coreolis could make the slightest move, Umbrage had the point of his own sword right at Coreolis's throat.

"Do you yield?" asked Umbrage. His voice was strong, his posture firm, and there was absolutely no question in any witnesses' minds that if the answer was anything other than an affirmative, Umbrage could and would kill him where he stood.

Of course, Coreolis said the only possible thing, given the circumstances. "Aye."

And oh, the roar that went up then, and oh the cheers, and oh the huzzahs, and never, but never, had there been any hero of the lists like Sir Umbrage. As for me, I still couldn't believe it. At a time like that, I should have been looking at Mace. I should have been smiling, seeming quite smug, perhaps rubbing my fingers together to indicate coins between them, drinking in his fury. But instead I couldn't take my eyes off Umbrage in his triumph.

And Umbrage looked at me.

And he did not seem the least bit happy.

Chapter 11

I took a great deal of time with Titan that evening, cleaning him and washing him down. The big fellow had seen more action in that one afternoon than he likely had in the past several years combined. In the distance I could hear the sound of revels, for there was great partying going on in the main banquet hall of the castle. I chose to absent myself from it. Somehow I was not in the mood.

After I settled Titan down, I started across the main courtyard. It had been such a hive of industry that afternoon that it was almost frightening, the silence which lay upon it now. The only noise, aside from the celebrations in the castle, was the steady tap-tap of my staff. It was then that I heard more footsteps behind me. I suspected the identity of those behind me before I even turned to verify it.

Sure enough, Mace Morningstar and a handful of his cronies were there. The moon was only just beginning to wane in its cycle, so there was plenty of light for me to see them. None of them looked happy. No, I amend that: They looked happy in the way that someone does when they are looking forward to making someone else unhappy. They carried no weapons except the customary daggers tucked in their belts. Chances were they didn't need any.

Remember, I was not completely without physical resources. I could handle myself quite well . . . under certain circumstances. Against a half-dozen knights-in-training, however, any one of whom could likely give me great difficulty . . . well, those were other circumstances again.

Nevertheless, there was nothing to be lost in trying to bluff the matter through. "Ah. Mace. Here to give me my winnings?"

His mouth was upturned in a grim smile, but the smile did not extend to his eyes. "We know what you did, Apropos."

"Oh? What would that be?"

I waited. No response was immediately forthcoming, verifying for me that they in fact had no clue what I had done. They were on a fishing expedition, hoping I might panic into blurting out some sort of admission. They did not know me very well.

"Morningstar . . . are you planning to renege on our wager?" I asked coolly.

"Not at all, Apropos, not at all. Here." He removed a purse from his belt and held it up. He jingled it lightly. "Would you care to count it?"

I bowed slightly. "Since we are all gentlemen, I am more than happy to take your word, along with your purse."

"Indeed." He lofted it through the air with a casual underhand toss, and I caught it easily. "There. I have given you the agreed-upon funds."

"Yes. You have. No one could deny it." I bowed once more and turned to walk away.

"And now," continued Morningstar, sounding quite cheery about it, "we're going to take it back."

I turned back to them. "You're going to what?"

"Take it back. We made no promise that we would not, did we, gentlemen?" There were nods and grunts of confirmation.

"But that's . . . that's . . ."

"Dishonorable?"

"Yes!"

He took what was, for him, a short step, but it brought him much closer than I would have liked. "And what care does one such as you have for honor, except where it serves your ends?"

It was a valid question. The answer, of course, you already know. But I hardly saw the need to share my philosophies with Morningstar. Nor did I see it worth getting the snot kicked out of me just to hold on to some winnings. I could always get more winnings. Teeth, on the other hand, would be somewhat more difficult to replace.

"I've better things to do, Morningstar, than bandy words with you. If it means so much to you . . ." I tossed the money back. I admit it annoyed the hell out of me. It seemed that all I ever did around the damned castle was give back money that was rightfully mine. I knew by that point that within the next day or so, I was going to take my leave of the place. My goal had been at least to depart in financially a superior position to what I'd been in before. Faced with the clear vexation of the other squires, however, my goals had reconfigured. Now I was aspiring simply to get out of there in one piece.

Even that drastically downscaled aspiration, however, seemed doomed to failure. Because Morningstar tossed the purse to the ground, making less and less effort to confine his anger. "This isn't about money, you peasant bastard. It's about respect."

"Oh. I thought it was about money. Thank you for clarifying that, Mace. Good evening to you, then."

I started to walk away then, but Morningstar was right behind me. He grabbed me by the scruff of the neck. I squeezed tight on the handle of my staff and the blade snapped out of the end, but as I whirled to bring it around, he knocked it effortlessly from my grasp. I had underestimated not only his anger, but his strength. The staff clattered to the ground.

"That trick played well against Sir Justus, but I've had the warning of it," said Mace. "You've had this coming for a long time, whore's son."

"I'd rather be the son of a whore than a spoiled arrogant cretin like you," I shot back. If I was going to be speaking with fewer teeth in the future, at least I wanted to make my last words with the full set memorable.

The others shouted encouragement, closing on us, and then there was a very very loud clearing of a throat from behind us. We looked around.

Sir Umbrage was standing there. Just standing there. His arms were folded. His sword hung from his hip.

He said nothing. I hadn't even heard him approach, although naturally with all the shouting he would have been able to move with relative stealth. He was in formal attire, dressed mostly in gray with black trim.

"This is not your affair, good sir knight," said Morningstar. "I believe that you were as duped as the rest of us, and not a party to this bastard's trickery, whatever form it took."

He said nothing still. Just stood there.

"So good evening to you then, as we conclude our . . . discussions," Morningstar continued.

No reply. No movement. Still more silence.

"Sir Umbrage, with all respect, it would be best . . ."

Mace's newest statement got no more response than the previous ones had. Just more stony silence.

For a long time, no one said anything. There was something indefinable in the air. Even the crickets that had been chirping earlier ceased so as to hear better.

Finally, Morningstar—who had been holding me backward by the tunic—slowly righted me. He dusted his hands off, looked as if he was about to say something more to the knight, and then apparently thought better of it. He backed away, as did the others, pausing only to pick up the purse that he had thrown down. Then he extended a finger to me angrily and said, "This is not over, Apropos."

For the first time, Umbrage spoke. "Yes," he said in a tone that did not invite disagreement. "It is."

There was nothing for them to say in reply. Moments later they had retired toward the castle, there to join in the mirth and merriment that was in full bloom within the castle's walls.

I picked up my fallen staff, turned to Umbrage, and started to say, "Sir, I thank you for—" But I didn't even get that far before Umbrage's right fist landed squarely in my face. I felt a crack that I knew all too well; my nose was once again broken. I staggered, but managed to keep myself righted by clinging to my staff, even as the world spun around me. I closed my eyes and that was even worse, so I opened them again and fought to keep myself steady, staring rigidly at the ground and trying to keep myself upright. As soon as my vision began to straighten, I looked at Sir Umbrage once more. His arm came toward me once more and I flinched automatically, certain he was going to strike me a second time. But instead he was holding a cloth. "Here," he said. "Stop the blood flow."

I did so. The blood was indeed coming fairly profusely from my nose. I moaned softly as I pressed against it, for the break was fresh and the pain in applying pressure to it was fearsome. But I did so nonetheless until I got it under control.

"Why did you do that?" I asked tentatively.

"Because you deserved it." He sighed. "You've doomed and damned us both, boy. Well . . . there's no help for it now. Come with me, and I'll explain it to you." Without another word he turned and walked away, and naturally I had no choice but to follow.

Once inside his chambers, Umbrage secured the door so that we would not be disturbed. From far away, I could still hear the noises of merrymaking. I almost felt as if they existed in another world altogether, which I could only observe from a distance while forever wondering what it would be like to be a part of it.

He pulled a large decanter from a cabinet and unstoppered it. "Drink?" he asked.

"What is it?"

"It's of the grape. That's all you need to know."

In fact, it was. For a moment my natural caution flared, and I wondered if he was out to poison me. But then I realized the absurdity of the concern; if he'd wished me harm, he needed do nothing else aside from leaving me to the tender mercies of Mace and his ilk. For that matter, there were many other subtle ways I could be disposed of besides something that would bring so much direct questioning to he himself.

Pouring myself a flagon of the brew, I drank deeply of it, and it burned in a most satisfying manner as it went down my throat. I wiped the liquid away from the edges of my mouth, noting distantly that there was still some crimson from my blood on the back of my hands.

Umbrage likewise drank and sat down opposite me, staring at me in an odd manner that I couldn't quite decipher. "When I was a young knight . . . even a middle-aged knight . . . I was most formidable," he said abruptly. His voice had none of the quavering and uncertainty to it that I was accustomed to hearing. "King Runcible's . . . respect . . . for me is not without its basis in fact. And then, one day I decided to take an oracle. Never take an oracle, young Apropos. It will bring you nothing but misfortune. That was indeed advice given me by elder knights, but naturally I knew better since youth always does. My reason was that my beloved wife had died, you see, and I had no idea what a future without her could possibly be like. It was all a great, black wall to me. So I had to know. And the oracle said to me, 'You shall die in a great battle.' Well, as you might suspect, I was rather pleased to hear that. For a knight to die in battle is the most glorious end that any warrior can desire. At least, that is what they tell you when you are training to be a warrior. Besides which, if I died in battle, that would reunite me with my beloved. So . . . so much the better. Knowing that to be my fate, I launched myself into campaign after campaign. This was the period during which I gained my greatest fame. I was unstoppable, feared by all, truly awesome to behold in the heat of battle . . . at least, so I'm told," he added with a slight flash of modesty. "But as year passed into year, several things happened. First, and most obviously . . . I did not die. 'Twas a combination of skill, bravado, and luck, basically. And second, the loss of my spouse lost its sting as the seasons turned, for time has a tendency to heal hurts, even the deepest ones. Here's an odd thing, Apropos: The older one gets, the more enamored one becomes of life. As I got older, I found myself with a growing desire to continue walking this mortal coil. Furthermore—and I know this is irrational to some degree—since I knew I was to die in combat, why . . . all I had to do was avoid combat, and I would be effectively immortal.

"I would happily have retired to the backwoods and lived quietly for who knew how long, but good King Runcible, well . . . he knew me of old. And he had his own attachments to me, as you well know. He thought he did me honor by bringing me here, making me one of his knights. I tried to refuse, but once our liege gets an idea in his head, he is loath to release it. Particularly when it's an idea that he is convinced is going to benefit the individual being helped. He didn't want to 'waste' me, you see. And I could not bring myself to admit that my taste for battle had turned to ashes on my tongue. 'Coward,' they would have called me. I could not tolerate that."

"But you could tolerate being called a senile old fool?"

"Of course," he said mildly. "Age comes to us all, Apropos. Besides . . . if I were to be thought senile and bereft of senses, I could smile inwardly, knowing that not to be the case. But to be called 'coward' . . . that would have stung far more deeply, for I would have known it to be partly true."

It was all so clear. "You faked your infirmities, then."

"Those of the mind, yes. My body, I admit, is not what it once was . . . although, by God," and he shook a fist defiantly, "I may be less than I was, but that still leaves me more than many of them."

"You fell off the horse on purpose."

He nodded.

"But you dislocated your shoulder as a consequence."

"No. That is an old injury, which I am capable of repeating when the need arises." He shrugged. "We all have our talents." Then his face darkened. "Now you . . . your talent seems to be primarily that of botching up the lives of others. I had no desire to reveal that I was still puissant. But suddenly I found myself at the top of the jousting lists. By the time I was riding against Sir Coreolis, I knew that something was amiss and had divined that you had to be behind it, you young fool. I was fully prepared by that point to fall against Coreolis. I would have, too, if his damned horse hadn't collapsed."

"You dissemble, milord," I said, leaning forward, taking another swig of the brew. "You could have fallen against any of your previous opponents. Admit it: You liked going up against your 'peers' and defeating them. Deep within you, some part cries out in fury against the way they regard you with such utter contempt. You enjoyed making up for some of the injustices they've done you."

"You are wrong," he said, but he wasn't entirely convincing, and I knew that at least on some level I was correct. He seemed distracted by a thought for a moment, but then he shook it off. "In any event, it did not matter once Coreolis was coming at me with sword in hand. At that point, I had no choice. I had to defeat the fool, and quickly. So I did . . . and in doing so, made clear to our dear king just how capable I truly am. My name was securely among the bottom ranks of knights to receive assignments, and that more than suited me."

"I was told that your previous squires met with accidents. Did you . . . ?"

"Do them in?" He guffawed at that. "Of course not, and I think you already know that. The problem was that, even on routine missions, they would see my caution and try to pick up the slack. Youth believes itself immortal. There is a cure for such an attitude, but unfortunately it is a cure from which one never recovers. Nonetheless, it served my purposes, for nobles complained to the king about the high mortality rate of my squires. No noble wanted his son attached to me. And one can't send a knight places without a squire. A knight with no retainers? Unthinkable."

"And then I showed up," I muttered.

"Yes, you did. My assorted 'disasters,' even on the most routine of missions, had dropped me to the lowest point on the list of knights who were likely to be sent out on missions, aside from random selections such as the Draft. But thanks to you, good squire, we have now jumped to the top of the king's list, I daresay. We're very likely for it now, and you've none but yourself to blame."

"You should have told me. Told me earlier, I mean. If I'd known what you'd been about, I'd have . . ."

"You'd have what? Assisted me in my subterfuge? Yes . . . yes, perhaps you would have, at that. Anyone capable of rigging an entire joust for his own ends certainly has a dim enough grasp of honor. I should have told you then, I suppose."

"But you've told me now. Why?"

"Why?" He laughed bitterly. "Because we're in the same boat now, me lad. I will do what I can to repair the damage you've done to my pleasant state of semi-retirement. Failing that, well . . . I shall have to attend to you."

I did not like the sound of that. "Attend to me, sir? What do you mean?"

He did not answer. "You may leave now."

"But—"

"I said . . . you may leave." And with that, he turned his back to me. Realizing that the interview was over, I headed for the door, but his voice pulled me up short. "Apropos," he said, "one who has no honor, and no use for it, might feel tempted to flee at a time like this. I am not saying you are without honor . . . but if you are . . . then I would not let that thought cross your mind. If I am in a difficult situation, then you who put me there are going to be right along with me. If you try to depart prematurely . . . I will find you. And things will not go pleasantly, I assure you."

I couldn't help but feel that, considering I was someone whom no one seemed to like, people were going to great lengths to make sure that I remained where I was.

The next day I understood what Sir Umbrage meant about repairing the damage. When Umbrage rose late, as he customarily did, he sauntered into the great hall where knights (many of them with hangovers) were eating a light lunch, and he called out, "A glorious day for a joust, isn't it, my lords! When do we start?" He appeared to have no recollection of what had transpired the day before. Not only was this, in and of itself, enough to utterly confuse his fellow knights, but furthermore it was in fact a terrible day for a joust considering that it was pouring rain, the field having been reduced to a massive mudhole. When informed that he had in fact won the previous day's bouts, Umbrage expressed laughing incredulity and refused to take anyone seriously who pressed the point. Thus did he endeavor to reestablish the status quo, and I believe in some measure he was successful, although there may have been a few who were slightly suspicious.

As for me . . .

That evening, after I finished my chores, there was a large man-at-arms waiting for me. I'd never seen him before; he might very well have been a freelance. He had a barrel chest and sloped brow, but he seemed quite intelligent. "You are Apropos?" he demanded.

"No," I said quickly.

"That's what I was told you'd say. Come along, then." He turned and walked toward the training area where squires worked out every day. I followed him, curious as to what was happening.

He produced two practice swords, tossed one to me, then took a stance and said, "Now do what I do."

And there, in the still of the night, we practiced and I was trained in the ways of knightly combat. This happened every night for several months. My mysterious, unnamed tutor only showed up at night, was never around during the day, and never engaged in any conversation other than to tell me what I was doing wrong (never what I was doing right). I could only assume that he had been hired by Sir Umbrage, who felt that I was going to need all the training I could get.

I hoped he wasn't correct.

As it turned out, he was.

Chapter 12

All of which, reader, brings us back—as promised—to the beginning. For those of you whose memories do not stretch back quite that far, I had just been responsible for the death of Sir Granitz and covered up that culpability rather adroitly, when the king had dropped a rather charming comment upon me before departure:

"I have a fairly hazardous mission to be assigned. I think you are just the man for it. Report in one hour."

The words hung over me as I hastily packed my belongings and prepared to get the hell out of Runcible's castle.

The body of Sir Granitz was already being readied for its funeral, and I was preparing to put as much distance between it, and my then-current surroundings, as I possibly could.

The king's pronouncement after Granitz's death was not anything I needed to hear. A hazardous mission? I thought not. Report in one hour? I could be half a league away, farther if I managed to get my hands on a fast horse. Just the man for it? If anything underscored for me that the king had absolutely no idea with whom he was dealing, it was that.

I didn't have all that much in the way of belongings, so I had my pack filled just before Sir Umbrage entered the room. When we were alone, he no longer maintained the blank and vacant stare that he reserved for the other knights. I got the full impact of a glare that was loaded with quiet anger. "I just spoke to the king," he said. "I informed him that I did not think you were ready for any sort of hazardous mission, in my humble opinion."

"You . . . you did?" I couldn't believe it, and felt a wave of relief seizing me. "Thank you, milord. I mean that, from the bottom of—"

"So he said I should accompany you."

I considered those words a moment, then slung my pack over my shoulder. "Good day to you, then."

"Where do you think you're going?"

I laughed bitterly. "Anywhere but here." I headed for the door.

Umbrage grabbed my wrist in a grip that was nigh unto iron and swung me around. Instinctively I shielded my nose, but he made no effort to strike me. I was relieved, but only slightly.

"You," he said tersely, "whether you like it or not, are my squire. As such, your actions reflect on me. To be perceived as a doddering, less-than-effectual knight is one thing. To be dishonored by mentoring a squire who would flee rather than face a quest given him by the king himself . . . that I will not tolerate."

"And am I supposed to tolerate risking my life just because of a misplaced sense of duty?"

"Yes, Apropos. That is exactly what you are supposed to do." He smiled wanly. "You are the one who set these wheels into motion, squire. You've no one to blame but yourself, and I will be damned if I allow you to slip away and leave me behind to face the dishonor that you leave in your wake. I could have allowed Morningstar and his cronies to smash you to stew. I still might, if the mood suits me. For that matter, I may yet. Now . . . our king is expecting us in his chambers in ten minutes. We will both be there, or by God, it will go the worse for you. Do you understand me, squire?"

Once again it struck me that, for someone as unpopular as I, it seemed an amazing number of people were intent on keeping me around. It would have been nice if any of them had been motivated by goodwill rather than wanting me to suffer.

I dropped my pack to the floor, and Sir Umbrage nodded approvingly. All I could do was shake my head and say, "This is a fool's errand and it will probably be the death of me."

"Well, my lad," said Umbrage with disgusting cheerfulness, and he patted me on the shoulder. "Better you than me, that's what I always say."

Unsurprisingly, it brought me little comfort.

We proceeded to the king's private audience chamber, as we were expected to do. The king, after all, did not conduct all of his business while seated upon a throne; that was for more stately affairs than the relatively simple task of sending a reluctant squire on some damned-fool mission that would likely get him killed. For something as trivial as sending me off to my death, nothing more was required but something relatively small and intimate. Of course, that is all relative; even the king's smallest chamber was still three times as big as any other quarters in the place.

There was a guard standing outside, but he was largely for show. We were, after all, in the heart of the castle proper. He nodded slightly to Umbrage and me, and we returned the gesture. We carried no sword or daggers, even the ceremonial type. It was against palace policy for weapons to be kept in private audience with the king and queen. No one expected trouble, of course . . . but anticipating trouble and expecting it were two different things.

The guard, maintaining the proper form at all times, rapped on the door without turning his back to us. Anticipation, as I said, although I have to say there were few people in the castle who were less of a threat than us. In point of fact, I couldn't readily think of any. From within, a voice called crisply, "Enter, please."

We did so, Umbrage prodding me lightly in the back to make certain that I stood up straight. Inside we saw a chamber elaborately furnished with gorgeously carved furniture and thick, purple curtains hanging draped over the windows. There was a work area, and also what was clearly a sitting area for entertaining company, with several comfortable-looking chairs, an equally plush bench, and a table in the middle. Seated in one of the chairs was Queen Beatrice, and she was pouring out tea. Three cups had been set out, and obviously two were intended for

Umbrage and myself. "Please, gentlemen . . . sit." She gestured toward the couch adjacent to her.

I couldn't help but glance around as we obeyed, and she caught the look. "No. The king isn't here, if that's what you're wondering." She smiled. She was as exceedingly pleasant and unaffected as she had been that day when I had awakened to my "new life." There was something about her that commanded respect, not out of any sense of fear as was often the case with royalty, but instead just a pure decency that she seemed to exude.

"Your presence is more than enough to honor us, Your Highness," I said.

She laughed lightly. "Sir Umbrage . . . your mentor takes after you in the art of flattery, at the very least."

"Thank you, Highness," Umbrage said. "Teaching him that technique was the least that I could do. And I always endeavor to do the least that I can do."

Her brow knit slightly as she considered that sentiment as she poured out tea for us. "I made it myself."

"Really? We're honored."

"So much honor, squire. You must set great store by it."

I shrugged noncommittally.

"Well . . . to business, then. You have been polite enough not to inquire why I am attending to this rather than the king. The reason is that this is a matter of a somewhat personal nature. 'Woman's work,' one might say."

"You require us to do . . . woman's work?" asked Umbrage. I couldn't tell what he was thinking at the moment. It might very well have been relief. How much trouble could one get into doing woman's work? "I was under the impression that the king had some great quest in mind."

"There are all sorts of quests," said Queen Beatrice. "This is more of an . . . emotional quest, I suppose. Which is why the matter has fallen to me."

"I will serve Her Highness however I can," I said. "What would you have of me?"

She looked into her tea glass for a moment as if endeavoring to read her fortune in the leaves. I took a sip of it. It wasn't bad at all, actually. Then she said, "Entipy has come of age."

The phrase meant absolutely nothing to me. I looked questioningly at Umbrage, who said, "Entipy? The princess?"

"That's her name? Princess Entipy? What sort of name is Entipy?" I asked.

Umbrage fired me a rather dire look, but the queen only smiled, taking no offense. "A fabricated one, good squire. There was a family dispute over the name. Family disputes at our level can lead to somewhat lethal consequences unless all are mollified. Her true name, to satisfy several different highly placed individuals, is Natalia Thomasina Penelope."

"N . . . T . . . P," I said, and my smile mirrored the queen's. "An excellent compromise, Highness. Not that it's for me to judge."

"I will take it as a compliment rather than a judgment, squire."

"If I may ask . . . where is the princess? In all the time that I've been here, I don't recall seeing her."

"She has not resided here for several years," the queen

said with a heavy sigh. "I've missed her terribly. But she was quite . . ." Her hands fidgeted. She looked quite uncomfortable. ". . . wild . . . is the only term I can use that adequately describes her. Her behavior was rather unseemly, particularly during state functions. Her father and I love her dearly, but I freely admit that we were somewhat at our wit's end. For the past years, she has been in the care of the Faith Women at the Holy Retreat. Someday . . . Entipy will be queen. She is our only child, the heir, but before one can be the best ruler possible, one must be the best person possible. Her father and I felt that removing her from an environment where she was pampered and pandered to would be the best thing for her. The Faith Women are a severe, strict, but loving order, and very knowledgeable in the ways of the world. We felt they would give her the grounding she needed. But now Entipy is of age, and she will have duties here in which she will be schooled."

"Have you seen her in all that time?"

That seemed to be the toughest question of all for the queen to field. "The . . . Faith Women felt it would be best if we did not. They are good, knowledgeable women, the Faith Women are, and their wisdom in such matters is second to none. I wanted the best for my daughter. No woman wants any less."

There was silence for a time, and then Umbrage said tentatively, "Highness . . . I am still unclear as to the nature of our mission."

"Ah. Of course. How foolish of me." She took another sip of tea and put the cup down. "Now that my daughter has reached maturity under the care of the Faith Women, she will be coming home. We are sending a group of knights to serve as her escort from there to here. You, squire, along with your mentor, will be among that group. But you will serve a different purpose than the others."

"I will?"

"Yes. I want you . . . to be the princess's friend."

I stared at her, then looked to Umbrage, whose face was a complete blank. I was certainly accustomed to such a look from him, since he had spent many years cultivating a stare of perpetual vacancy. But this time, I sensed, it was not manufactured. He seemed as much at a loss as I.

"Her . . . friend?"

"Yes. Technically, you will be assigned as her personal bodyguard. But more than that . . . I want you to be her friend. The princess had no one her own age with whom she could associate while she was here. I want you to make an effort to ingratiate yourself with her. Be friendly to her. Be pleasant. That may not be easy; she can be quite . . . a handful. She has fire within her, and I doubt that the Faith Women were entirely able to extinguish it. Nor should they, for she will need that inner fire if she is to rule. But I want you to let her know that it is not necessary to burn everyone who comes near. Be attentive. Listen to her. Accommodate her whenever possible, but don't be afraid to stand up to her. No harm will come to you as a consequence of your saying no to the princess, you have my personal assurance of that."

"Highness, I . . ." I looked to Umbrage and back to her. "I'm not certain . . . if I'm the right person for this job. I do not pretend to be a student of the human psyche. Perhaps she'd do better with another woman . . ."

"Another woman," the queen said, "will become more a co-conspirator than a friend. Or a servant, bowing to her whim. That is not what she needs, squire."

"I bow to your wisdom in that regard, Highness . . . but surely you must see that I may not be what she needs either."

"Are you refusing my request, squire?"

My lips suddenly felt rather dry. I wasn't sure what to say.

"Because if you are . . . no offense will be taken, I assure you."

I let out a sigh of relief. "That is . . . very generous of you, Your Highness." I saw from the corner of my eye that Umbrage likewise looked relieved.

"Oh, no, no offense at all. It's . . . a pity, I admit. I had a feeling that you and Entipy would get on famously. A fiery young wench, quick-witted and the equal of any man. I thought you and she would take to each other . . . but, if nothing else, I wouldn't want to force something upon you that you feel isn't worthy of you."

"It's not so much a matter of worthiness, Highness . . ."

She continued as if I hadn't spoken. "I mean, granted, this was a royal assignment, but that's of no matter. There are other royal assignments, squire, to which I would be more than happy to attach you."

I felt my hair starting to prickle on the nape of my neck. "There . . . are?"

"Yes." She rose, gently setting her teacup down and then walking over to the work area. She whistled softly as she rummaged through some papers. "Ah. Here we are. The Screaming Gorge of Eternal Madness." She said it with an air of anticipation.

"The what?"

"There is said to be," the queen told us with clearly growing excitement, "a creature which lurks within the Screaming Gorge of Eternal Madness . . . a creature whose gizzard contains a fortune in diamonds. The royal treasury has taken something of a dip since the entire taxation fiasco in Pell. You could go to the Screaming Gorge of Eternal Madness, brave the creature, slay it, cut it open, and remove the diamonds. Granted, one hundred and seventeen . . . I'm sorry, eighteen," she made an adjustment, scratching with a pen, "have made the attempt over the past several centuries. Only a handful have returned, and they were in varying states of insanity. One poor devil tore his own eyes out, another swallowed his tongue . . ." She shuddered. "In any event, the rest have not been heard from again, although it is said their screams can still be heard emanating from the gorge to this day. But perhaps you will be the fortunate pair. It could be the creature has mellowed with age."

She smiled sweetly.

I rose then and said, "It would be my honor to make the princess's acquaintance."

"I thought you would say that," Queen Bea said. "Finish your tea before it gets cold. It's good for you."

I finished it . . . because if there was one thing I knew, it was what was good for me.

No one knew anything about her.

I couldn't understand it. Not only did Umbrage

know nothing of the princess, aside from her name, but everyone I asked about her greeted me with shakes of the head, shrugs of the shoulder, and unvarnished ignorance of the subject at hand. It seemed most puzzling to me. How could it possibly be that the princess of the realm, the heir to the throne, was an enigma to all concerned?

As near as my inquiries were able to determine, the princess had been kept apart from everyone else at the castle, starting at quite a young age. A special suite of rooms had been set aside for her, and there she had resided. There was speculation about her. Some opined that she was so ghastly to look upon that no one could stand to do so. That she had some sort of considerable deformity, or that she was an imbecile and in all ways an embarrassment. But no one knew for sure. They couldn't even lay claim to having seen her even once.

I had been endeavoring to acquire information so that I would have some inkling of what to expect, but I found the dearth of knowledge about her to be almost alluring in its way. Apparently we had a genuine mystery girl on our hands. There were few enough things in my life that could fall under the heading of "intriguing," but this was definitely one of them. The only thing I could ascertain for sure was that she had tended to pass tutors in the same way that others pass water or gas. During the time that she resided in her private quarters, teachers would come and go. No one lasted terribly long, and there was a widening gap of time in finding a new teacher every time that an old one resigned . . . usually looking several years older and considerably more wan and wasted than when they had first arrived. Then one day the parade of teachers ceased, and a casual query to the king had revealed the fact that Princess Entipy had been shunted off to join the Faith Women at the Holy Retreat. "It will do her good" was all the king said. He was not forthcoming with any further information, and that more or less ended the matter, since, really, one cannot exactly start grilling a monarch for information, particularly about such a sensitive subject.

The night before we were to depart, however, I was busy brushing down Titan and preparing him for the journey, when I heard a soft laugh from behind me. I turned to see Mace Morningstar there, leaning against the doorframe, his arms folded. Instinctively I reached for my staff, which was leaning against a post, but Mace made a dismissive gesture to indicate that such defensive tactics were not necessary. "I'm just here to wish you goodspeed on your journey, Apropos," he said. "Will you have a mount of your own?"

"A small steed is being brought in, so I'm told," I said cautiously. I still didn't trust him.

"Well, that's good. That's good." Morningstar's insufferable grin didn't diminish one bit, and he said with a snicker, "Well, good evening to you then, squire."

"Wait." It occurred to me that I had not asked Morningstar if he knew anything of the princess. Obviously I endeavored to avoid Mace whenever possible, but he was the one who had approached me this evening. What had I to lose? "Do you know anything of the princess?"

"I? What would I know of her?" But he said it in such

a way as to practically shout at me that he was indeed cognizant of some information.

Naturally, given the situation and my knowledge of the way such buffoons as Morningstar thought, I said the only reasonable and logical thing: "Nothing. You'd know nothing of her. It was foolishness of me to inquire. My pardon, Mace." I bowed slightly and returned to grooming the horse.

It worked like a charm, of course. Oh, Mace didn't come out with it immediately, of course. He picked up a strand of straw and began to chew on it idly, clutching it between his teeth. Then he sauntered over to me, leaning against the wall, his arms folded across his chest. I barely afforded him a glance as I asked, "Oh, are you still here?"

"She's beautiful," Mace said.

"Really. When did you see her?"

"On a dare, some years back, on my first visit to the court. It was before I became a squire. Some other boys challenged me to climb up the side of the castle after I'd boasted that I could scale any surface."

"And you did it, of course."

"Of course," Mace said matter-of-factly. "I climbed halfway up the side of the castle. Heights didn't bother me; nothing did, or does, really."

"I'm happy for you."

"Anyway," continued Mace as if I hadn't spoken, "I found myself at eye level with a window. Naturally I peered through it."

"Hoping to catch a female undressing?"

"That's right," Mace said, unabashed. I think he was

incapable of feeling any sort of shame. Granted, so was I, but at least that was a conscious decision on my part. I think he was just too stupid. "What I saw instead was this young woman—hair the color of an early autum, eyes like a raging sea, and when she spoke, a voice like a southbound breeze . . ."

"Is she a person or a weather report?" I asked.

"She was speaking with a tutor, a fairly heavyset woman with a brutish accent and a mole on her chin that had hair growing from it. She asked a question of the woman, and when the tutor turned to a particular reference volume to check the answer . . ."

"Yes?"

"She stabbed her."

My eyes widened. "What? Who stabbed who?"

"The princess stabbed the tutor. Oh, nothing lethal, mind you. She used a quill pen that was to her right. She just took the thing and drove it into the top of the woman's hand which had been resting on the table."

"Good lord," I murmured. Then I said suspiciously, "Wait a minute . . . if you're making this up . . ."

"On the life of my father, I swear it so," said Morningstar with enough sincerity that I couldn't help but believe him. "Jammed the thing straight down. I have to admit, I wasn't aware that one could drive a quill that far down into someone. A good inch or so it penetrated. Tutor started screaming like a stuck hog, and a string of invective in her native tongue poured from her throat, and in ran the queen all in a dither, asking what's happened, and the tutor who, by this point is in agony, pointed helplessly at Entipy. And there was our royal princess, as cool and calm as you please, and she looked up from her text and said, 'She's clumsy, Mother. What can I say?'"

"And you saw it all happen. With your own eyes."

"With these very two hawk-eyed orbs you see before you. Her mother and the tutor left in a lather, and then I began to climb down. Just as I started to go, I thought I saw Entipy glance in my direction. But I was already starting down, and so figured that I was in the clear. So what happens? I'm halfway down the wall, and suddenly an inkwell dropped—nay, hurled—from overhead caromed off my skull. It knocked me clean off the wall and I fell the rest of the way. Broke my leg from the fall. Took six months to heal properly, and even now I still have a barely noticeable limp. That minor impediment is why I feel some slight sympathy for you, Apropos, believe it or not."

"I don't believe it, thank you, considering you tried to beat me to a pulp after the jousts."

"That was simply a matter of pride. It was nothing personal. If I did not feel for you, Apropos . . . why would I be telling you what I know of Entipy?"

"I don't know."

"Yes, you do, for I've explained it to you. Look." He pushed back a hank of his sandy hair. I could see the trace of a scar, shaped in a small semicircle. "That's what's left of the place where the ink bottle struck me. It was my very first combat scar. One would have hoped for something more impressive, I should think."

"Indeed." I paused and then said, "If I am to believe you . . . I shall need more of a reason that you have shared this with me besides the notion that you are doing so out of the goodness of your heart."

"It is of no consequence to me whether you believe or not," he said with a shrug.

We stared at each other for a short time, and then he genuinely smiled at me. It was the smile that I found most disconcerting of the entire encounter.

He never did give me any further explanation as to the reason for his "warning." Perhaps he had no other that he could truly articulate. In retrospect, I can only assume that his desire was to make me nervous. I think he wanted to see me sweat, or at the very least plant in my head some degree of apprehension about the task that lay ahead. In short: He didn't want to take the slightest chance that I might actually take some pleasure in what was to come, no anticipatory glee in the prospect of being trusted by the queen herself to be the personal escort to the future ruler of the throne. Morningstar might very well have confused my motives with his own. I knew his type all too well from having seen it not only around the palace, but all my life. He had his own serious ambitions for social climbing. He probably thought that I was of a similar persuasion, and that I would have regarded some sort of mandated close relationship with the princess as a potential tie to the king or the throne. In that spirit, he probably didn't want to take a chance that I might, even for a short time, be pleased about the assignment. So he thought he'd spoil my mood.

He didn't comprehend that my mood had been spoiled the day that I was born, and it had only been downhill from there.

Chapter 13

It was comforting to know that I still retained enough of my skills in woodsmanship to smell smoke when it was out there.

The journey to the Holy Retreat had gone without incident until that point. Indeed, it had been so utterly trouble-free that I found myself getting a bit nervous about it for no reason that I could determine. Our escort party numbered about twenty, which seemed more than enough. We were under the command of Sir Nestor, one of the king's personal guards. He was affable enough, although all business when it came to matters of security. He kept an advance party lurking about, making sure that the way was clear. He exuded a quiet confidence that I found somewhat heartening. Sir Umbrage, for his part, didn't seem especially heartened by it at all. Instead he had a tendency to keep looking around the woods, squinting against the sun, trying to see something that did not readily appear to be perceptible. Perhaps he was trying to find random threads of fate and sort them out.

I had asked him before we set off why, if he was so apprehensive about our little mission, he didn't simply pull some sort of stunt similar to that which had gotten him out of our war effort. "There is a fine line between unfortunate happenstance and perceived deliberate ineptitude," he had replied.

"You're saying you think they might have caught on."

He nodded. He was probably right although, considering how things turned out, he might have been well advised to take that risk.

For my part, I had found myself doing the same thing during the trip as Sir Umbrage. I scoured the forests, the beaten pathways ahead of us, for some sign of pursuit or some danger that might be approaching us. None had been readily apparent.

And yet . . .

And yet I couldn't help but feel that something was out there. I couldn't determine precisely what that might be, nor was I able to figure out what might prompt me to think that. Yet I thought it just the same. I would glance deep into the woods, sometimes quickly snapping my gaze in that direction at random intervals as if trying to catch someone watching us. I never saw anything. Yet I kept having the feeling that there was something out there, just beyond my perceptions, dancing just outside of my field of vision and—worst of all—laughing at my inability to spot him or her or it. The woods and forest areas through which we traveled had none of the sheer oppressive mood of the Elderwoods, which had been my primary former haunt. My new surroundings were innocuous enough. But I still felt there was something there, and I misliked that I couldn't begin to guess what it might be. In all likelihood, it was simply my imagination. The problem was: I wasn't that imaginative a person. So when such things presented themselves, it tended to make me . . . apprehensive.

I had restrained my worries, though, because we had a journey of several days ahead of us, and nothing was going to be served by my fretting and voicing concerns the entire way. All I would do was annoy Sir Umbrage, who was already in an apprehensive enough mood, and the other knights and squires in the company who seemed to regard my presence as something of an aberration at best, an annoyance at worst.

At least I had been given a horse for the purposes of the journey. That was a bloody great relief. I managed to get about well enough on my lame leg, but even with the aid of my staff, lengthy walks were not my favorite pastime. Not unless I had the opportunity to rest repeatedly along the way. The horse was nothing special. She was a relatively small, dabbled beast named Alexandra, and I doubted she was very fleet of foot. Then again, neither was I, so I could hardly condemn the poor creature for not possessing that which I also lacked.

The weather had been quite temperate, the conversation pleasant if a bit strained from time to time, and the entire trip had been fairly free of stress, aside from my free-floating anxiety that we were being pursued, watched, or in some other way being monitored. So it was somewhat jolting when I first scented the smoke. I could tell from Alexandra's reaction that she sensed it too. There was some slight hesitation on the part of a couple of other mounts, but the puzzled looks on the faces of the other knights indicated that they weren't quite certain what was putting the horses out of sorts.

"There's a fire ahead," I said.

This drew looks from Nestor, Umbrage, and several others. "I smell nothing," said Nestor. "Are you sure? I don't smell anything."

"Yes, I'm sure. The horses smell it, too. Look at them."

Nestor raised a hand, palm up, indicating that the rest of the group should come to a halt. They did so and he tilted his head back, sniffed the air. Finally he nodded slowly. "Yes. Yes, you're right. Redondo, Messina." He summoned two of the more reliable members of the advance scouts. "Check on ahead. Report back. See if it's a camp of some sort. If so, see if it's hostiles."

"It's not an encampment," I said with conviction. "It's bigger than that, I'd warrant."

"Perhaps. We'll see."

We waited then for what seemed an interminable time, although I doubt it was really all that long. Then Redondo and Messina returned, and they appeared quite agitated. They went straight to Nestor and the three of them spoke in low whispers. I didn't have to see Nestor's face to tell that he was clearly upset, and then he turned to us and said, "Full speed, lads. It's the Holy Retreat. Someone's torched the place!"

The announcement galvanized everyone in the group. Even Umbrage seemed inclined to drop his usual air of quiet befuddlement and called out, "The princess? Is she there? Is she unharmed?"

"We don't know," returned Nestor. "The squad spotted some people milling about, but it was hard to discern. No talking now! Full speed, I said, damn your eyes!"

I can tell you, there's nothing like having someone say "Damn your eyes" to let you know that they're genuinely concerned.

So with our eyes in serious danger of damnation, we spurred our steeds onward until we were practically thundering through the woods. Soon the smoke was strong enough that one could have smelled it through a raging head cold. We emerged from the woods then and we were able to see, in the near distance, the Holy Retreat of the Faith Women . . . or at least, what was left of it.

I had never been to the Holy Retreat, although I had heard that it was a simple but elegant structure which had served the unadorned needs of the Faith Women. I would never have been able to tell firsthand, however, because the place was in ruins. We arrived just in time to see one small, still-remaining part of the structure collapse in on itself. It simply gave up and fell with a groan of splintering wood.

Clustered around the front of the Holy Retreat were a number of forms which I would have assumed to be women. It was an assumption because the Faith Women tended to dress in rather dreary, asexual garb. Indeed, the only reason we knew for sure that they were female was because they called themselves the Faith Women. I'd spotted Faith Women from time to time, embarking on missions of mercy and such. A couple of them had more of a mustache than I, so in a way we were all more or less taking their word that they were as advertised.

We thundered across the open ground, we knights, and I fancy that we made a rather impressive sight. After all, there's nothing like seeing twenty armed men arriving too late to do anything about a disaster that truly stirs the heart to bursting with emotion. We reined up a respectful distance from the Faith Women, who were simply standing there and staring at us. Their faces were inscrutable. We had no idea whether they were happy to see us, or distressed, or even cared one way or the other.

"Who is in charge here?" he called to the group.

The Faith Women looked at one another, and then one of their number stepped forward. We should have been able to tell that she was in charge. She was the only woman I'd ever seen who had so much facial hair, she could have braided her eyebrows. Her hands were hidden within the folds of her garment, her hair obscured by a hood. Her eyes were hard and cold. She said nothing, simply waited. That she said nothing didn't surprise me. Faith Women tended to be a fairly conservative lot, cherishing words as if they were coins, and loath to toss them around in a wasteful fashion.

"I am Sir Nestor, dispatched by King Runcible to retrieve his daughter, the Princess Entipy." His horse moved around slightly, apparently still a bit spooked by the smoke wafting into the air. He steadied his mount and continued, "Obviously, you have had a great disaster here."

The Faith Woman nodded. Her face remained impassive.

"Do not think me insensitive to your plight, or uncaring of the fate of all of your order, but my mandate requires me to be a bit single-minded," Nestor continued. "My first, my only, priority is the princess. So let me get to the heart of the matter: Is the princess all right? Was she injured? Is she—" He obviously didn't want to say the word "alive." None of us were looking forward to the prospect of returning to the king carrying a large vase and informing His Highness that his only child was in residence within.

The Faith Woman did not answer immediately. She seemed to be searching for words. Then, apparently opting for a mute reply, she stepped aside and gestured toward her associates.

A hooded figure stepped forward. She was smaller than the rest, the face fully obscured by the hood. She took a few steps, stopped, then squared her shoulders, arched her back, and withdrew the hood.

She looked rather small, almost swimming in the outfit she wore. Her face was carefully neutral. Her long hair was unkempt, although that was probably understandable given the circumstances. I saw nothing of autumn and raging seas in her, as Morningstar had described her. She seemed rather sullen, actually, fairly unremarkable in appearance, although there was a sort of vague prettiness about her. She did have a regal bearing, I'd certainly credit her that. She was no longer a child, but instead clearly a young woman.

"Princess . . . are you all right?" asked Nestor with concern that was mixed with obvious relief.

She nodded. That was all. Just nodded. So far none of the females had spoken a word.

"We're here to bring you home. Your father and mother very much look forward to seeing you once more."

Another nod.

Nestor turned his attention back to the women. "Now . . . my dear Faith Women . . . this is clearly a great tragedy. Would you care to tell me how this came about? Was it by accident, or did some swine attack you? If the latter, we can make sure that justice is done. If the former, we have means of offering compensation, for the king and queen are most grateful for the fine tutelage you have given their daughter . . . and their gratitude will be vastly increased upon learning that you have clearly managed to save her from any jeopardy this unfortunate conflagration might have presented. In short, I am asking: How may we be of service to you?"

The Faith Woman looked at her compatriots in stony silence. Their expressions were as granite-etched as her own. She looked back to us, and then one of her hands emerged from within the folds of her sleeves. It was long and a bit bony, and she pointed it, trembling somewhat, at the princess.

And the Faith Woman, speaking each word in a careful, measured tone, said, "Get . . . her . . . the *fuck* . . . out of here."

There was no reaction of horror or shame at the profanity spoken by their leader. Instead all the heads of the Faith Women bobbed up and down in silent agreement.

That was when Entipy smiled. Really smiled.

I had never seen a smile quite like it. She looked at us—looked at me—with that smile, and the smile seemed to say, *Hello. You're going to your grave, and it's going to be my doing.*

And Umbrage leaned over in his saddle and murmured to me, "Well, *this* certainly doesn't bode well."

Master of understatement, Sir Umbrage was.

Nestor angled his horse toward me as we prepared for our ride back to Isteria and he said in a low tone, "Good luck." He didn't seem sarcastic in that respect; I think he genuinely felt bad for me. I couldn't blame him. I felt bad for me, too.

Demon spawn.

That's what I saw when I looked into those eyes. Demon spawn. A quiet look of cold contempt, as if we were bugs to her. Not for a moment did I doubt why this . . . this individual . . . had been sent to the Faith Women for tutelage. Her parents simply did not want to have to deal with her. It was a no-lose proposition for them. The longer she was away, the calmer their own lives were. And if the Faith Women managed to bring her under control, well, so much the better.

Apparently, considering the smoldering ruins of their home, the Faith Women had had a less-than-stellar success rate with her.

Sir Nestor offered to leave a couple of knights behind to aid with the organizing of a rebuilding, but the Faith Women seemed to want nothing more than for the lot of us to be on our way. Naturally we obliged them. I think, however, given the circumstances, we would have felt a little more sanguine about the entire affair if we hadn't caught sight of the Faith Women dancing a gambol of celebration upon Entipy's departure. Entipy, for her part, sat perfectly erect in the saddle, straight and tall. She looked as if she had been born in a saddle, that much I had to admit. She looked neither right nor left. Truth to tell, I wasn't certain if she knew or even cared that any of us were there.

This did not stop Sir Nestor from taking the time to guide me to her personally and say, "Highness . . . Apropos is squire to Sir Umbrage. He will be your personal escort and retainer for the duration of our trip home. If you have any needs or desires, request them of Apropos and he will shatter every bone in his body rather than disappoint you."

I glanced worriedly at Nestor, less than ecstatic about the characterization of my willingness to carry out my duties. He winked at me. That hardly mollified me. But rather than dwell on it, I simply bobbed my head in acknowledgment of her and said, "Highness."

She glanced at me, one flicker of her eyes seeming to take in not only my presence, but my very soul. The young woman chilled me. Then again, she was royalty, and what point is there to being royalty if you can't discomfort those below you.

The princess and I were situated in the middle of our escort, in order to provide maximum security. My initial thought was to say absolutely nothing to her as we began our ride. In retrospect, perhaps I should have maintained that strategy. I couldn't help but feel, though, that I should say *something* to the silly girl. It was several days' journey, after all, and riding the entire way in silence seemed unnatural somehow.

"We have good weather for the ride, Princess," I ventured after a time.

To my surprise, she laughed. It was neither a guffaw nor a titter, but simply a small chuckle. "Have I amused you somehow, Highness?" I asked.

She looked at me in an almost pitying manner. "Nearly an hour we ride, and you've had all that time to come up with a conversational gambit . . . and that was the best you could do?" She shook her head in pitying contempt.

"No," I replied sharply. "But I thought starting off with 'So, burned down many Holy Retreats, have you?' might be considered a bit off-putting."

There was a loud clearing of throat from Sir Umbrage, who apparently was riding just within earshot.

Entipy simply smiled at that. "Is that what you think I did?"

"I wouldn't presume to judge, Highness."

She looked me up and down appraisingly. "Don't lie to me," she said. "I've no stomach for it."

"Lie, Highness?"

She said nothing in reply to that, but merely focused her attention on the road ahead of us. I moved my mount a bit closer to hers and said in a pleasant tone, "I don't appreciate being called a liar, Highness . . . even by royalty."

"Then try not lying and you'll find it will happen less." She afforded me a glance. "I know people, squire. Know them at a glance. I know you. You judge. You look around at the world and judge it constantly. And that judgment is the same no matter what you are perceiving: Disdain. Me, these knights, everyone . . . you hold all in disdain."

"Why would that be the case, Highness?" I asked, fascinated.

"Because," she replied easily, "you reserve your greatest disdain for yourself, and everything else simply radiates from that."

Her words stung. That came as a surprise to me, because I had thought that there was nothing that could be said, and no one who could say it, that could possibly lance through the shell I had built around myself. Yet she had struck through with relative facility. I was not about to let that be evident in my response, of course. "My, my. How comforting it must be to be a princess and know everything."

"Not as comforting as it must be to be a squire and know nothing," replied the Princess Entipy.

My conversational endeavors having been summarily brushed aside, I lapsed into silence for a time, allowing the ride to pass in relative peace. Then Sir Umbrage caught my eye and he made a prompting gesture, clearly indicating that he wanted me to take another whack at social discourse. At that point the only whack I was interested in taking was at her head with a stout branch, but I did not think that would please the king and queen overmuch, nor aid in my standing or in that of Sir Umbrage.

"You ride quite well," I said finally.

She looked at me askance, with cool detachment. "You mean, 'for a girl.'"

"I tend to say what I mean. You ride well, male or female. None of this sidesaddle nonsense. Good posture, good frame . . . gods, girl, it was a compliment. Ascribe nothing more than its intent."

"I need no compliments from you."

"Fine."

At which point I resolved that I wasn't going to say a damned thing for the rest of the four-day ride, even if someone tried to pry my mouth open with a dagger.

The sun continued to crawl across the sky, and it was late in the afternoon when she abruptly said, "Thank you."

By that point we were not riding. Sir Nestor had brought us over to a nearby lake where the horses were being allowed to drink, and we were all stretching our legs. I was leaning against a tree, skipping stones across the lake and picturing Entipy's head squarely in the middle of the lake as my target, when I heard her "thank you" almost at my shoulder.

I turned to regard her. She was staring at me with that same impassive face, that same chilling look that reminded you there were probably demons gleefully playing tag somewhere in this creature's brain. "You're welcome." Then, almost as an afterthought, I added, "What for?"

"For the riding." She paused and then added, "I had a good teacher."

"Really. Set him on fire too, did you?" I tossed another rock.

"No. He's going to come and take me away. We're never going to reach the castle."

That was certainly sufficient pronouncement to prompt me to hold up throwing the next stone. "Is that a fact?"

She nodded. "Yes. That's correct. He's likely trailing us through the forest right now. And once the moment presents itself, he's going to take me away and we're going to reside in the forest and make love like wild beasts, freshly fallen leaves serving as our bed as our naked bodies writhe in—"

I held up a hand and said, "I get the picture. Well, well, Princess . . . I had no idea you had such plans. And you are telling me this . . . why?"

"Because I find you annoying."

"I see."

When she spoke, it was in a curious little up-and-down voice, almost singsong like a small child. "And I want you to know what's going to happen ahead of time. So you can know it's going to happen, and still be unable to stop it, and know that my father will be ever so angry with you for letting it happen and you're still helpless to prevent it. He'll probably lop off your head."

"If it means not having to listen to your drivel any longer, I'd lop it off myself."

"Drivel? Is that how you speak to a princess?"

I had completely had it. I do not suffer fools gladly, even to this day, and back then my patience was not remotely approaching levels of maturity. "No, that's how I speak to a deluded, fire-starting loon. Where did you meet this savior, this hero of yours?"

"He came upon me while I was doing chores outside for the Faith Women. *Chores.*" She repeated the word as if it were the name of a vile disease that had claimed all her loved ones and a bevy of cuddly animals besides. "I . . . a princess . . . chores. Can you imagine?"

"Happily," I said.

She ignored my response. Instead she draped her hands behind her back, clearly taken with the doubtlessly false memory. "He had no idea who I was. He fell in love with what he thought was a peasant girl. It was only recently that he learned who I truly was . . . and vowed to me that he would take me away with him and we would live happily ever after."

"Four words that have no business in each other's company," I snorted. "One doesn't live ever after. One dies. And there's very little happily about it."

She shook her head. "You could not be more unlike him. He's been through such hardships, but still believes in love triumphant and heroism being rewarded."

"Then he's as deluded as you, which would be consistent since my suspicion is you're imagining him from whole cloth." I tossed another rock, watched it skip and sink. "Tell me then, Princess . . . why did he not simply take you away from the Faith Women? Why wait until you were surrounded by a squadron of armed men? Wouldn't that make it more difficult for him?"

"He doesn't care," and she snapped her fingers, "for however many armed men may surround me. But he did care that the Faith Women had promised my parents that they would teach and protect me. He did not wish to undercut their vows, despite my wishes to the contrary. That is his way."

"How very convenient for him. Princess . . . even if he

exists . . . which I doubt . . . you've seen the last of him. He had his fun with you while you were around, and now you're gone, and he'll move on to some other crazy young girl."

"You think I'm crazy?" When she spoke, her eyes flashed ever so slightly.

"What could have given you that impression?" I asked with ill-concealed impatience. "Perhaps the fact that I keep referring to you as such. Could that be it?" I cocked my arm to throw another stone.

And then she ricocheted a rock off my head.

"Hey!" I fairly shouted, an overloud exclamation which naturally attracted the attention of the other knights, who looked in our direction. She was sitting there with that same damnable smile, the one that spoke volumes of her quiet arrogance and contempt for life in general and me in specific. I could see it, all there in her face.

This was not what a princess was supposed to be. A princess was supposed to have an elegance about her, a sense of the regal. She was supposed to be a marvelous creature, an incarnation of hope and purity. She was supposed to be an abundance of things, in short, which were lacking in the Princess Entipy.

And then, with only a few words, she transformed herself from a mere loon to an exceptionally dangerous loon.

"You will see," she said. "You will all see . . . when Tacit One-Eye comes for me."

She turned and walked away, which was fortunate because that way she didn't see me with my arm frozen in place and the blood draining from my features.

Tacit.

She had been cooped up in the Holy Retreat for years. The Faith Women were notorious for keeping news of the outside world away from the retreat, and word of Tacit and the revolt in Pell—which was the first time his name truly began to be spoken—could not possibly have reached her.

Which meant that Tacit had.

Which meant that everything she had told me was true.

Which meant that we had a serious problem.

If the princess's intention had been as she had said—to place a fear within me and a feeling of dread over the impending calamity of a simple mission gone completely wrong—then she had succeeded beyond her wildest dreams.

I thought of how I had been regarding the woods around us with suspicion during our ride, but had not had any clear idea as to what was causing that suspicion. Now I knew. Tacit had been there, following us like the forest-spawned ghost he was. Yes, it *would* be just like Tacit to honor the vow of the Faith Women to watch over the princess. Furthermore, if we were in his element, the deep forest, Tacit would be utterly confident in his ability to make off with the princess at any time . . . particularly since this was not a kidnapping. She was going to go willingly.

I already felt as if I had enough concerns with keeping an eye on Entipy as it was, since I considered her eminently capable of slipping a dagger between my ribs any time the fancy took her to do so. For that matter, she was just deranged enough—once we had set up camp for the night somewhere—to set fire to the entire encampment. The prospect of waking up with a dagger protruding from my chest and flames closing in from all sides was not a pleasant one.

I knew I wasn't going to be sleeping well on the trip back as it was. But all that was as nothing compared to my concern that Tacit, phantom-like, would abscond with her at any time and we would return to the palace empty-handed.

My hand reflexively went for my throat as I pictured the king nodding to a royal executioner to get on with it.

I immediately went to Sir Umbrage, who was chatting amiably with Sir Nestor, and drew them both aside. I told them of my rather disconcerting conversation with the princess, and they both cast apprehensive glances in her direction. At that point, she seemed perfectly content to stare out at the lake in a somewhat dreamy fashion. I could only imagine that she was trying to figure out if there was some way to set the lake on fire.

"I am not concerned," Nestor said at last, words that directly belied the initial reaction I had seen. "I have heard of this Tacit One-Eye, the same as you gentlemen. But he is, after all, just one man. We are many. Even if the princess desires to go with him, that does not mean she will automatically be heading off. Thank you, Apropos, for apprising us of the situation."

"So what will we do?" I asked.

"We will do as we have been doing. The fact that we

have a name for our enemy does not change in the least our procedures, for we have been allowing for the possibility of an enemy all along. We will sleep in shifts, we will keep an eye on the princess. There will be knights on watch at all times. In short, do not worry yourself, young squire," he said, patting me on the shoulder. "The princess will not be going anywhere; not while we attend her."

I nodded, taking some comfort in the words, but I still could not shake the feeling that we were underestimating the incendiary nature of the situation.

We mounted up shortly thereafter, I once again taking my place by the princess. She did not even so much as afford me a glance. Obviously I no longer mattered to her, if I ever did. She had told me what she thought the way of things was going to be. So of what possible future relevance was I to her?

As we continued our ride through the forest, I found myself consumed with watching the woods around us. Knowing that Tacit was out there now made every shadow seem to come to life. I strained to hear the slightest crack of a twig or displacement of a stone. Even as I did so, I felt a sense of hopelessness. If Tacit was indeed out there—and I had no reason to think not at that point—then he was not one to tip his presence through such a happenstance. Part of me wondered if his claims to having been raised by unicorns had some basis in fact. Even if they did not, his woodsmanship and forestry were second to none, and he was about as likely to reveal his presence through a mishap as I was to sprout wings and fly the rest of the way to Isteria.

I heard something far in the distance then. A faint cawing that sounded like a bird's call, but there was something about it that seemed peculiar somehow. I looked around but saw no reactions from any of the other knights. They seemed too busy scouring the woods around us, looking for some sign of pursuit or danger.

That's when the rustling from overhead drew my attention.

I looked up, but the branches were thick with leaves and it was impossible to discern anything. They seemed quite still, though. Perhaps I had imagined it . . .

. . . or perhaps not.

I drew back from Entipy a bit so that I was alongside Nestor. His eyebrows knit into a questioning look.

"I heard something. A rustling from overhead."

"Overhead?" He looked up as I had and then shook his head. "Nothing to worry about. Probably just some sort of animals."

"Possibly the two-legged kind."

"No. No, the branches are too thin. Anything of any weight climbs up there, it would come snapping right off. Actually," and he licked a finger and held it up, "it's fairly gusty hereabouts. I would imagine it's even more so up there. So you probably heard nothing more than the wind."

"All right. If you're sure."

Nestor smiled. "Your concerns are natural enough, squire. This is your first major mission. Of course you feel that there are enemies lurking about, hiding everywhere, waiting to spring out at you if you give them the slightest opportunity. That's good. That's a good attitude to have. Care and attention to the world around you is what any knight needs to survive. But if you worry too much about too many things, you can drive yourself to such a state as to be virtually useless to others. You're surrounded by good knights here, strong and true. The princess, although a little . . . odd . . . offers no true threat to us, nor does her supposed paramour. Do not work yourself into a frenzy of distress, young Apropos. Such actions will be the death of you."

That was the last thing he said to me before the arrow thudded into his chest from overhead.

Nestor didn't even realize at first. He heard the sound and felt the impact against him without fully comprehending the significance. It was only upon his looking at the protruding shaft, still quivering, that he understood precisely what was going on. He opened his mouth, probably to bark some sort of order, but he never even managed to get it out. All he did was slide off the horse, tumbling to the ground with a crash that brought everyone to a dead halt.

"We're under attack!" I cried out, and even as I shouted the alarm, another arrow descended, slicing straight through the head of my unfortunate horse. The creature was killed instantly and fell over. I had no time to dismount or clear the creature's corpse before it hit, and as a consequence the animal fell squarely on top of me.

Shouts started coming from everywhere. "Shields!" cried some and "Protect the princess!" called others, and then the air was alive with arrows. Some knights did indeed manage to get their shields up in time, blocking the initial salvos. Others were far less fortunate, and both knights and squires were falling right and left, crying out in anger and confusion, unable to see the face of the enemy that was dispatching them in a manner both cowardly and yet quite efficient.

At first I tried to push Alexandra's corpse off me, but as several more arrows slammed down into the horse's unmoving body, I realized I had stumbled upon a rather serendipitous buffer. My sword was strapped to my back and, pinned flat on my back as I was, I was unable to get to it. But my walking staff was lashed to the side of the horse and, reaching over tentatively, I managed to work it loose. I figured I was going to need it if I was to have any hope of levering the beast off me.

I tried to catch sight of what was happening. Sir Umbrage was still standing, holding his buckler high, his sword gripped and ready in his right hand. He had dropped all pretense of the vacuous, easily befuddled knight. There was determination in his face, and he was scanning the branches overhead, trying to catch some sight of the opponent.

Entipy was also there. She looked a bit confused, though, and I wasn't surprised. She was probably thinking that this sort of mass slaughter wasn't Tacit's style. The same thing had occurred to me. I had no idea why Tacit would resort to such a tremendous force of arms when subtlety would do just as easily. Why not wait for nightfall and simply slip away with her into the darkness, particularly when she was so willing and eager to go? Why a frontal assault?

The arrows stopped. The knights, whose number had been cut by close to half, looked around at each other in dread and confusion. Surprisingly—to them, if not to me—it was Umbrage who called out sharply and in a firm voice, "Keep those shields up!"

"Shall we close ranks, sir?" called one of the squires. I could tell from his voice, he was terrified but trying not to show it.

"And serve them up a better target? I think not! Apropos! Take the princess and run for it! We'll cover your retreat!"

He had not seen my slightly inconvenient position, lodged as I was beneath a dead horse. "That might prove difficult, sir!"

He turned and saw me there, and then the princess decided to switch into royal mode. "I run from no one!" she declared. "I'm in no danger! I'm—"

And that was when the enemy descended *en masse.*

Chapter 14

You have heard of Harpies, I am quite sure. Those screeching bird-women with claws that can rip you to shreds, and high-pitched, piercing voices that can finish off whatever's left of you after the talons have done their work.

However, as widely known as the Harpies are, far less known is the fact that Harpies go into heat once every twenty years or so. I can assure you that it is not a pleasant time, for the only thing less attractive than a Harpy trying to kill you is a Harpy trying to make love to you. At least, I can only imagine it, since I have been fortunate enough not to have witnessed such a sight firsthand.

Unsurprisingly, their attempts at cross-breeding often do not work, because what man in his right mind would willingly couple with a Harpy? It may very well be that their frustrated "love lives," as it were, is the explanation as to why Harpies are perpetually in such a foul mood. For one thing, it is impossible to distinguish the charge of a killer Harpy from the charge of an amorous one, so even brave men would flee at the sight of them. Certainly it was difficult to find men who were remotely in the mood or capable of performing under the rather demanding circumstances.

There was one occasion, though, when a flock of in-heat Harpies descended upon a leper colony. By that time the Harpies' urge for mating was so overwhelming that they were not exactly choosy. As for the lepers, a number of them were already blind, and certainly—what with being lepers and all—any hopes of sexual congress had long been adjourned. So when they heard women coming in droves, even though they were women crying out in extremely annoying voices, the lepers perceived it only as good fortune and perhaps even a divinely inspired errand of mercy.

Naturally mating with the Harpies resulted in the deaths of the chosen lepers, but at least it provided them with an opportunity that they never thought they would have: They went out with a bang.

The Harpies, in turn, returned to their nesting grounds and finally reproduced after many decades of fruitless attempts. The result, however, was not remotely what they expected. Every single one of the offspring which resulted from the assignation was male. This, of course, was revolting to the uniformly female Harpies. They could not, however, kill the little monstrosities, for the Harpies had very strict rules against slaying one of their own. So they simply abandoned the creatures, leaving them to fend for themselves.

Which they did.

The creatures had only existed as rumors for quite

some time. There were fleeting reports of having seen one here or there, but it had been impossible to ascertain whether they genuinely existed or not. What everyone seemed to agree upon, though, was that the little grotesques were as fierce as their mothers, but—unlike the creatures that had spawned them—they had superb voices, almost melodious. Indeed, it was believed their victims were lured in by the sounds of their singing. They even fashioned crude musical instruments which they used for accompaniment.

Because of their outlandish nature, and their masculine bent, they had acquired the name of the Harpers Bizarre. And bizarre they most definitely were.

I knew, because it was these creatures who descended upon us now.

They were a fright to look at as they spiraled from the trees overhead. None of them was much over three feet high, but their diminutive stature was not to be confused with helplessness. From the waist down, they were covered with feathers, and their legs ended not in feet but in talons that I suspected were razor-sharp. They had human chests, arms, and heads, but their hair was wild, their blazing red eyes looked more birdlike than manlike, and they had small wings on their backs. The wings did not seem large enough or powerful enough to enable them to beat the air and go aloft, but they were sufficient to allow gliding. That was how they were coming at us now.

They didn't appear to notice me at first since I was not exactly easily spotted beneath the horse. Instead they went straight for the knights and squires.

"Close ranks!" Umbrage now shouted, seeing that the arrow barrage had ceased and been replaced by a frontal assault. If he was at all intimidated by the sight we were facing, he didn't show it. Their blades out, the knights were trying to keep their nervous mounts from bolting as they swung their swords, hacking and slashing at the Harpers.

But the Harpers were too agile, moving like a cross between birds and monkeys. They would flip back, out of harm's way, ricochet off a tree and come back in at a different angle. Seeing the knights' vulnerability, the Harpers Bizarre would come to ground and then bounce up, getting at the underbellies of the now-terrified horses.

Knights, even knights on horseback, are accustomed to battling foes of a normal height. Because they were under assault by lethal beings who were so short, it made it impossible for the knights to get at them before the Harpers got at the horses. Frantically trying to get away, the horses bucked, stumbled, fell over one another, with the result that all of the gallant armored men were sent tumbling over one another, thrown from horseback and forced to carry on the battle on foot.

But on foot, they had no chance. While they staggered about in their armor, stiff and clumsy in comparison, the Harpers Bizarre moved with speed and alacrity that was frightful to behold.

I heard a melodious screech and looked up. One of the Harpers Bizarre was descending right toward me, his face twisted in a delirious look of joy, his talons fairly quivering with anticipation. He saw I had no sword in my hand, and my staff certainly didn't appear to present any threat. He plunged straight at me. It was all I could do to steady my nerves, because I was trembling with terror. I had no choice but to wait until he was closer, closer, almost on top of me, and I smelled the ghastly odor of him as he let out a shout of glee in anticipation of the bloodletting.

That was when I popped the blade in the end of my staff.

He struck it dead center, the blade skewering right through his chest. He had a look of utter astonishment on his face. Immortal their mothers might be, but the Harpers Bizarre had human blood in them, and that blood was flowing from its wound and down my staff.

I had never killed anyone in my entire life. I suppose I should have been relieved or depressed or something, anything. But I was too frightened to feel anything except numb.

Then the creature writhed about, spasming wildly. I swung my staff and pitched the Harper away, and it tumbled through the air, still seized by its death throes, before landing some distance away where I could no longer see it.

I heard more cries, and screams, and the sounds of flesh being rended. There had been no female shriek, which made me wonder what Entipy's status was. But naturally I was far more concerned about my own.

Still clutching my staff, I started to ease my lower body out from under the fallen horse. As I did so, something large and apparently wet thumped to the ground nearby me. I craned my neck around to see what it was and my breath caught in my throat. It was Sir Umbrage. To be more specific, it was his head, covered with blood, one eye gone, apparently having been torn out or even consumed. The other dead eye seemed to be staring right at me in a most accusatory fashion.

My stomach heaved in protest, and it was all I could do not to become sick on the spot. I tore my gaze away, hauled my lame leg out from beneath the horse, and started to do the only reasonable thing given the circumstances: crawl away.

I actually managed to get three whole feet before my escape route was cut off.

A Harper was directly in front of me. He was not in attack mode, however, nor did he seem to be looking at me. Instead he was staring at the bladed end of my staff with the blood on it. I noticed that, unlike the others, he seemed to be wearing some sort of ornamentation on his head, a glittering half-circle that looked vaguely like a crown.

It was then that I heard the princess's voice. She was shouting, "Let me go, you feathered idiots!" Her protests were being met with raucous and sneering laughter. Hearing her made me realize that I was no longer hearing the voices of the other knights. While trying to keep an eye on the Harper in front of me, I still managed to cast a glance behind me. A quick look was all I needed; the piles of bodies certainly told the story eloquently enough.

The Harper in front of me called out "Briiiing her! Here! Heeeere!" in a tone that indicated he was accustomed to being obeyed. He didn't simply speak . . . he seemed instead to "caw" his sentences, as if shouting from a great distance with a voice that was both deep and yet had a certain brittleness to it. Clearly he was the leader of the flock. Then he looked back to me. "My peeeeople. Yooooou kiiiiilled one of my peeeeeople," he said.

"I did?" I asked, trying to buy time. With a nod of his head, he indicated the bloodied staff. "Oh . . . this. I have no idea how it got this way."

"Noooo lie youuuu! Seeeefla the Annoyyyying . . . yoouuu killl!"

"No, really, I didn't—"

His eyes widened in surprise. "Cowwaaaard you are, eh? Kiiiiiller . . . successful kiiiiiller . . . but coowaaard toooo! Amaaaaaazing!"

Entipy was surrounded by the Harpers, and she was pushed to the ground next to me. There was no fear in her, I had to give her that. She simply looked irritated. I couldn't help but wonder if she was really that brave, or whether she was just so stupid that it hadn't occurred to her that we were in mortal danger. "You," she told the lead Harper, "are in serious trouble."

This caused raucous laughter to filter through the assembled Harpers Bizarre. Now that I saw them all together, I realized there had to be about fifteen of them. Considering the way they fought, however, and the viciousness with which they could attack, they were capable of bringing down opponents numbering far greater than they themselves.

"Aiiiiileron am I. Aiiiileron of the Harpers Bizaaaaarre! Yoooouuu, Priiiincess, in more trouble than meeeeee, I think."

I couldn't help but feel that Aileron had a point.

Entipy clearly felt otherwise. "That may be what you think now. But things are going to change. You'll see. You have no clue what's coming."

"Aaaaahhhh . . . yoooouuu think Taaaacit will come, eh? Taaaacit, eh?" The mention of the name caused much chuckling and snickering among the Harpers Bizarre.

Their reaction and apparent knowledge of Tacit's involvement clearly had an effect on the princess, but to her credit she covered it well. "I don't know what you're talking about. And turn your face the other way when you speak; you tend to spit."

This resulted in only more raucous laughter. With the ground and surrounding foliage red with blood, at least it was nice to see that somebody was in a good mood.

"IIIIII thiiiink you know. Taaaacit One-Eye. Heeeee thiiiiink he stop us. Thiiiink heeee match for Harpers Bizaaaaaarre," sneered Aileron. "I throoowww him off cliiiiiiff into riiiiiver. Waaashed away. Noooo mooorre Taaaacit."

"You're lying!" Entipy said defiantly, and then in a fury, she lunged at Aileron. She didn't get very far, though, because the Harpers bore her to the ground and essentially sat on her. Struggling beneath their weight, she cried out, "Apropos! You're supposed to be my body-guard! Do something! Get them off me!"

This declaration of hers seemed to seize Aileron's imagination. "Bodyguard? Yoooouuu?" he inquired.

I cleared my throat uncomfortably.

"Wellllllll?"

I looked at the princess. Her head was flat against the

ground, one of the Harpers keeping her head immobilized by the simple expedient of having one of his taloned feet atop it. And for a moment—just a moment—I saw fear in her eyes. She had been so filled with arrogance, so confident that Tacit was going to be taking her away, so sure that she would be associated with me for the briefest of times and then whisked off by her hero. And now, in just a few short moments, it had all fallen apart. Despite her bluster and bravado, she was a ship with no anchor, and she was looking to me—her last hope—for some sort of succor.

I did not hesitate.

"She's lying," I said.

"Apropos!" she bellowed, or at least came as close as she could to bellowing considering she was near to being smothered.

"I'm not even one of them, okay?" I was speaking very quickly, nearly babbling. "I'm not a knight or anything . . . I'm just a guide . . . look at me! Look at my leg! See? It's crippled! I'm a cripple! Who's going to want a cripple for a knight?"

"Apropos!" I now knew why purple was considered the royal color, because that was certainly the hue her face was becoming.

"Hoooowww aboooouuuut," Aileron crowed, "if we killllll her . . . and let yoooouuu go. Yeeesss or noooo?"

"You . . . you'd do that?" I couldn't believe it.

Aileron waved in the direction of the dead Harper. "Yooooouuu kiiiiill Seeeeefla the Annoyyyyying. No mooore annnoooyyyance, thanks to you. Yooouuu beg for liiiife . . . weeeee let you gooooo."

So I begged.

Naturally.

Five minutes of imploring and pleading, with outright sobbing visible toward the end. I thought Entipy's head was going to explode, she was clearly so furious. I didn't care. She'd been a right pain in the ass and whatever she had coming to her, I didn't give two figs about.

My display was greeted with great amusement by the Harpers Bizarre, however, who hung on every word and chortled and laughed and in general had a great old time. Finally Aileron put up a hand, his chest so convulsed with laughter that he clearly could barely get a word out. "Yooooouu go! Goooo, cooowwardd! Gooo and liiiiive full, coooowwardly life. As for giiiirl . . . we haaaave plaaaaans. We sennnnnd home to faaaather . . . one piiiiiece at a tiiiime. You oooookay with thaaaat, Aproooopos?"

I bobbed my head. The princess was beyond fury. If she could have killed me with a glance, I would have been dead on the spot.

"Faaaaareweeelllll!" cried the Harper Bizarre, and the rest of his kind joined in. With their contemptuous laughter and wishes for a safe journey ringing in my ears, I hobbled off into the forest as fast as my good leg would carry me.

Once upon a time, I had been able to move through the woods with something vaguely resembling alacrity. The woodcraft that Tacit had taught me had served me well. Certainly I had not been at Tacit's level, but I could nevertheless handle myself quite well in virtually any forest environment. At least, I could do so when my mind was clear, my thoughts not tumbling helter-skelter over one another.

Such was unfortunately not the case here.

I tripped, I fell, I sprawled, I pulled myself to my feet and kept on going, and all that was going through my head as I did so was that I had to put as much distance between myself and the Harpers Bizarre as I possibly could. I was giving no thought to the princess whatsoever, nor considering my failed mission. She had been a royal pain in the ass to me, and I held little sympathy for her.

Still . . . "little" sympathy I did have. I envisioned her in the clutches of those creatures, and felt that she was probably more than a little frightened. Then again, I could not be sure. Considering the princess's temperament, it was entirely possible that at that moment, the Harpers were the ones finding themselves in a disadvantageous position. I tended to doubt that they were going to kill her. She was far too valuable a prize. But I certainly didn't think they were going to make life easy on her. Not that she had tried to make life easy on me, or anyone else. She was a bully, an arsonist (I suspected), and not particularly lovable.

Still . . . did anyone, *anyone,* deserve to fall into the clutches of the Harpers Bizarre with no means, no hope of escape? With no one to act as her hero or rescue her?

I slowed in my flight. This was as much an acknowledgment of the reality of my personal situation as it was any thought being given to the princess's predicament. My breath was ragged in my chest, sweat cascading down my face. My good leg was throbbing since I had been favoring it so heavily. I balanced myself on my staff, taking in great lungsful of air, licking my dry lips and wiping the stinging perspiration from my eyes.

I pondered. I thought, Should I do it? Should I risk myself, in the hope of doing the genuine, heroic thing? Even though it meant likely throwing my life away—

The thought got no further as I resumed my voyage away from the princess. I felt a sizable degree of self-disgust and self-loathing, but these paled in comparison to self-preservation, so my survival instinct told my new-born (stillborn would be more correct) conscience to shut up and let me get on with the important business of saving my own hide. Truthfully, I have no idea how far or how long I ran. Every time I slowed down, I was certain I could feel the wings of the Harpers beating somewhere nearby, as if they were tracking me and waiting to descend upon me when I slowed down or displayed weakness. It was always more than enough to spur me on, and I kept going.

I felt a chill beginning to settle into my lungs. The air was cooling again. I had to admit, this was beginning to disturb me. We had developed some very odd weather patterns, and I had no idea what that could possibly portend. Although there were cold seasons moving into other regions, Isteria should have been fairly temperate. The paranoid aspect of me began to wonder if this weren't happening for the simple and sole reason of inconveniencing me. Certainly the colder it got, the more raw my lungs began to feel. With my luck, some sort of virus would settle into them. How ironic—and yet just—a way that would be for me to expire. Not at the point of a sword, as I feared, and not of old age, a peaceful death that I never truly figured would be mine. No, I would probably meet my end thanks to a really nasty cough that developed into something worse.

It was then that I felt a gust of warmth. The contrast between that and the air around me was so significant that it felt like a hammer blow of heat. I almost ran past it when the current snagged my attention, and I took a few steps back to appreciate truly the warmth of it. I stood there a moment, allowing the warmth to wash over me. It seemed to be coming from somewhere to the south. I didn't know what was causing it, but I did know that warmth was preferable for my purposes than cold, and so I set off in that direction.

I continued to cast furtive glances over my shoulder every so often, still alert for any possible pursuit by the Harpers Bizarre. But as time passed (how much, as I noted, I could not discern nor do I really know now), I slowly became more confident that they would not be after me. I posed no threat to them. They thought me an object of contempt. Indeed, they probably would not have wanted to waste a claw on tearing me to pieces. Such efforts would likely have been considered a needless squandering of effort.

I should have been insulted, I suppose. But the fact was that I was able to see me from their point of view, and to be honest, if I had been in their position, I wouldn't have bothered with me, either.

The warmth was growing, indicating that I was getting closer to the source. I didn't know what that source might be, but I tried to be alert to all possibilities. It might very well have been some sort of enemy camp, with a great fire burning in the middle being stoked by individuals who would take one look at me and see me as potential kindling, just another fagot to be tossed onto the fire. Well, I had no intention of being considered a fagot.

I strained my ears, tried to listen for the sound of talking, or boasting, or snoring . . . anything that might indicate that a large number of men had gathered and therefore posed a potential threat. And after a time, I did hear something. I heard it only once, and even as I heard it, I didn't know what it was. Not at first.

What I heard was a high-pitched screech. At first I thought it to be a cry torn from a female throat, and I wondered whether I hadn't accidentally gone in a giant circle. Perhaps what I'd perceived was the dying screams of Princess Entipy herself. For the briefest of moments, I felt a twinge of guilt, but quickly pushed it away. Better her than me, I kept telling myself.

But even as the screech died away, I ran the echoes of it through my mind and came to the conclusion that I had been mistaken. That was no human sound. It was the sound of a creature . . . a bird, most likely. From the depth and volume of it, though, I was certain that it was a large one.

A very large one.

I had stopped walking and didn't even realize it at first, because my mind was racing so frantically that it had left my body far behind. All my mother's blatherings about destiny and such came roaring back to me, for I was remembering things that she had told me about when she had witnessed the death and birth of a phoenix. Of how that rare event seemed somehow inextricably intertwined with my own fate, right down to the flame-shaped birthmark I bore. Could it be . . . ? Was it possible . . . ? A phoenix, dying and being reborn somewhere nearby?

Suddenly, everything seemed to make a hopeful sort of sense. Even as it clicked into place, I was moving. Believe it or not, it was as if my lameness of leg was forgotten, a minor thing, a triviality. I moved through the forest with the speed of a deer. Well . . . a lame deer, admittedly, for I did trip a few times, but I did not let such mishaps even begin to slow me down. I was absolutely positive that the warmth was definitely wafting from the south, and the gusts of wind that bore it into my face only confirmed it. Moreover, the faster I moved, the more intense the warmth became. I felt it searing the hairs of my eyebrows and inside my nostrils, and my mouth and throat were becoming completely dried out. I didn't care. At that point, it would have been irrelevant to me if my entire body became overheated and blistered. I was dedicated . . . no. No, not dedicated. Consumed. Consumed with a need to witness the miracle that my mother had spoken of so often.

I had spent so much of my life drifting, and hadn't even realized it. I had told myself that the fact that my existence seemed to have no purpose was not a problem for me. It was only at that moment, on the trail of the possible phoenix, that I really and truly began to think for the first time that there might be something more.

Not only that, but that if there was something more, then I might indeed be entitled to some of it.

I gave up any effort to move with stealth. Branches cracked under me, brush was rudely shoved aside, and at least twice I sent small animals running away while making annoyed chittering noises. Anyone who was listening for an intruder would have no trouble detecting my approach, but it didn't matter. I felt as if events directly pertinent to my life were moving forward with unstoppable force, and I was happy—no, delighted—to be a part of them. I suppose the timing factored into it, in part. After all, the men all around me had been wiped out, and I dared not return to the palace at that point. Not without the princess. I was going to wind up with less than I'd started out with.

But if there was a phoenix up ahead . . . truly a phoenix . . .

The tapestry, as I'm sure you can surmise, was uppermost in my mind. The tapestry that hung on the wall back in the palace, depicting the great hero of Isteria, the savior who was to come. There was coincidence there that could not be ignored. It could be me. Why not me? Granted, it didn't seem terribly likely. I had never had aspirations to be anyone's savior aside from my own, but . . . anything was possible. The timing was just too perfect. To be snatched from my lowest ebb and brought up to a point of triumph . . . why not indeed?

I heard a second screech, and this one was of a different timbre than what I'd heard before, I was sure of it. Instantly, even as I clambered over a fallen tree, I realized what the difference was. The first cry had tapered off with what could easily have been a sort of fading energy. It was a death cry, the last gasp of something aged. What I had just detected now was the birth cry of the new. It was young and vital. The first cry had been like a last answer being provided; the second cry was that of a first question being asked.

The heat was now almost overwhelming. The energy being unleashed in the process must have been unimaginable. It was coming from just over a rise, and I climbed it with no problem, as if my lame leg were a thing of the past.

It was then that I heard another voice. This, however, was not a bird or some other creature. This was a voice emerging from an all too human throat. Worse: Not only was it all too human, but it was all too familiar.

I peered over the rise, my heart pounding, knowing what I was going to see before I even saw it.

It was Tacit.

He looked a bit banged up, and his clothes were still a bit sodden, obviously from having been tossed into the river by Aileron of the Harpers Bizarre. However, he was clearly not dead, but simply a bit the worse for wear. Furthermore, his clothes were rapidly drying off from the heat of the emerging phoenix.

And that was definitely what it was: A phoenix. The ashes of its predecessor were scattered everywhere, and the newborn was sniffing the air in curiosity. It did not appear to have focused its vision upon Tacit yet, but it was definitely aware of his presence. It let out another ear-piercing screech, then leaned forward and nuzzled Tacit's chest. For a joyous moment, I thought the creature was going to bite him in half, but it did no such thing. Instead it seemed quite content to bring its entire massive head up against him. Even though the creature was newborn, it was still as big as five full-grown men, and when it experimentally beat the air with its wings, all the brush and undergrowth within a thirty-foot radius bent.

Not Tacit, though. He kept a firm grip on the phoenix's feathers and held his place. He was singing to the damned thing. Naturally he had a great singing voice.

It was a ballad that he sang. From the refrain, I could discern that it was about the Coming of the Great Hero. It was further evident, from the way that he sang it, that he was quite certain that he was singing it about himself. The verses all centered on mighty deeds that the Great Hero was to accomplish, of the enemies and dangers that he was to overcome. It smacked of prophecy, of verses crafted by farweavers who enjoyed producing "future histories," as they liked to call them. I had heard them from time to time in my life, but since they usually involved matters that were of little consequence to me, I'd rarely paid them any mind. They were of a unique style, though, and I could recognize their cadences and rhythms.

What Tacit was singing now, though, had tremendous relevance to me. Because every word out of his mouth sounded like aspects of his life; at least, some of them were aspects that I was familiar with. And as he sang each successive verse, the phoenix bobbing its mighty head up and down as if keeping time, it became clear from the touch of pride in his voice that all the accomplishments of the "Great Hero" in the ditty were things that he himself had done.

And then I heard the one that brought the greatest chill over me, even though the warmth of the newly born phoenix bird still filled the air.

"The Hero grew to help the poor, and they all cheered his name
"Except for one, a foolish lad, who had a leg so lame
"Who cursed the hero's name because his nature was so frail
"And wandered to obscurity, to vanish from our tale,
"And then our hero—"

So the song went on as Tacit bonded with the phoenix and sang of the Great Hero's future, rescuing the princess, ruling the land.

And I stared into the small ring of fire that surrounded the phoenix . . . and I understood.

For the first time in my life . . . I truly understood.

Most people do not have an epiphany, a sudden revelation and comprehension that realigns their thinking. Usually something occurs to them, but even if it is a major revelation, they cannot encompass it or embrace it all at once. It filters through their sensibilities a bit at a time, and does not have an immediate impact upon their lives. Instead it changes things for them in a hundred different ways, and it is only upon looking back, with clear hindsight, that one is able to localize one moment in a life and say, "Yes. Yes, that is when it all changed for me. That began it."

Such was not the case here. I got it all, right then and there.

In retrospect, I would have to recommend against epiphanies. They are very difficult on an emotional level, and they also sometimes move you to foolish and inopportune acts, which was what happened in my case.

My epiphany, in case you are wondering, was this:

All people are, at heart, egocentric. We all exist in the center of our own little universes. We believe that we are living out our lives as best we can, and that we have our own sphere of influence which exists of both friends and enemies. They in turn have their own friends and enemies with whom they interact. That is a given. But we, each of us, tend to put ourselves ahead of others because we believe that we are significant. We must attend to our own needs, desires, wants, and aspirations, because each of us is our own greatest priority. No one else cares for us as much as we do, no one else can exist in our skin. We think we're important. It is where our sense of self-worth comes up, where our egos reside, where "we" are. And we believe that each of our lives means something.

In staring into the great truth of the fire of the phoenix, in seeing Tacit bond with the creature and prepare for his next great deed, I came to an understanding that I would have reached even if I hadn't heard Tacit performing his charming ditty to point the way.

My life meant nothing.

I meant nothing.

In all these years of attending to my mother's talk about my great and glorious, but unknown, fate, and even nursing the hope that she was right, I had overlooked one of the inescapable realities of destiny. If it truly existed—and I was beginning to believe that it did—it meant that nothing I did mattered. Everything was preordained. Destiny, and predictions thereof—ranging from my mother's convictions to the Great Hero tapestry in the palace—hinged entirely on the concept that the future was immutable. It was all laid out, all planned, and all foreseeable if one had the foresight to see it.

Basically, all of life was nothing more than a story. A tale, a fable, with all the beats and twists and turns meticulously mapped out, all the parts assigned, all the characters positioned in their proper places and carrying out their ordained tasks.

Which was all well and good if one was the hero. It meant that your destiny would be a magnificent one, with many hardships that you would overcome before getting your just rewards.

But now I saw clearly, the shrouds dropping from my eyes. I saw myself for who and what I was. Saw all my weaknesses, both in body and spirit, heard my position in the scheme of things, looked back upon my life and where I was in relation to Tacit, and was forced to an inescapable and inevitable conclusion.

Tacit the brave, Tacit the determined, Tacit the unstoppable, was clearly the protagonist of some sort of epic tale. He was the Great Hero, whose coming was foreseen. Gods help me, Entipy—that raging brat of a princess—had been right. He would indeed save her, most likely with the aid of his newly found phoenix bird, which he'd probably been led to through some riddle or sorcerous turn or clue in a quest or some other damned twist of fate that was so prevalent in those annoying fantasy yarns. Tacit was the hero, THE hero.

Me . . .

I was a supporting player.

I had a bit part. I was a walk on, a one-off, whose presence was worth a chapter or two at most, a few lines in a ballad. I was there not to serve any purpose or goal of my own, but instead to highlight and underscore Tacit's greatness. I was comedy relief at best, a throwaway character at worst. I was never intended to amount to anything. I had been placed at the outskirts of the epic to be someone who fleshed out Tacit's world. I existed to showcase the fundamental humanity and gallantry of Tacit, who was the leading player.

My entire life didn't matter. Everything that had happened, from the circumstances of my birth to the nature of my mother's death, from my betrayal by Astel to my experiences in the castle . . . and anything I was to do in the future . . . none of it was remotely relevant to anything or of any real consequence.

I didn't have a life, not a real one. I simply had a backstory which existed to flesh me out as a mildly interesting subsidiary character.

On some level, I must have sensed it all along. Perhaps it had derived from the constant sense that I needed Tacit far more than he needed me. Or perhaps it came from the realization that Tacit probably had given me not a moment's thought since that day I had told him what I really thought. He had walked away secure in the knowledge that what I believed didn't matter one iota in the grand scheme of things. Because he didn't disappear from my life; I disappeared from his. I became an offstage, forgotten character, relegated to the early chapters of Tacit's great adventure and then forgotten. At most, I would be mentioned in passing, with appropriate contempt, by Entipy, as she clutched onto his middle while they rode astride the phoenix, being carried away to their new home and his new position as ruler of Isteria. All his previous "crimes" would be forgiven, for his greatness would be recognized immediately and his incontrovertible place would be assured.

He had moved beyond me. He was on to the climax of his adventure. All he had to do was gain the phoenix's trust, use the creature to free Entipy from the Harpers Bizarre, and head back to his new home in triumph. Oh, Entipy wouldn't want to go back to the palace, but he would probably insist. "Your parents must know that you're safe," he would say nobly, and when they returned to the castle, then would come the hero's welcome and the happily ever after . . .

And I would be stuck living out the rest of a life that had no purpose, no point, no worth . . .

. . . other than to make Tacit look good.

And that song he was singing . . . the one to the phoenix, about precisely where I stood in the order of things. Only two possibilities existed: Either it was some sort of tribute to his own wonderfulness that he was in the process of composing, in which case my so-called friend was putting together ballads which aggrandized him and made me the fool . . .

. . . or else, as I had first surmised, it was some weaver ballad that he had learned, in which case it was entirely possible that he had known it when we were younger, and had befriended me not out of generosity but because he knew it was supposed to happen, and was fulfilling that which had been predicted so that he could have his great, happy, wonderful ending.

To hell with me, and my concerns, and my own aspirations. Only Tacit the Mighty, Tacit the Daring, Tacit the Hero, mattered. The one ostensible friend I'd ever had in this world . . . and even to him, I was nothing but something to be stepped over . . . or stepped on.

That was when I snapped.

In all fairness, I think if you had realized that you were fairly irrelevant, you would have, too.

For the briefest of moments, my rage went inward, and I came that close to throwing myself upon my sword as a final testament to my frustration and sense of bleak hopelessness. But just as quickly, I aimed my hostility in the proper direction: Outward. Outward toward the one who had made my life inconsequential: Tacit.

There was a rock in my hand. I had no idea how it came to be there. I didn't even remember picking it up. It was perfect and smooth and cool in my overheated palm. It was as if my hand was moving before my head had processed the information, and then I drew back my arm and I threw.

Under any other circumstance, Tacit would have sensed it. A movement of a rock hurtling toward him would have been as loud as a gong to him, just from the violent way in which it sliced through the air. But Tacit was completely lost in the bonding between himself and the phoenix, oblivious to the world around him. And that obliviousness cost him.

The rock struck him squarely in the side of the head.

Because he was completely unprepared for it, Tacit went down. He looked stunned and confused, as if ejected from a place of peace, even ecstasy. Clearly he hadn't even fully registered what had happened; all he knew was that he had been severely jolted and he wasn't entirely sure why or how. As for the phoenix, it seemed just as confused. The way its head whipped about, I could tell that its eyes were still not completely focused on the world around it. Doubtless within the next minute or two it would know what it was about, but at the moment it was as perplexed and uncertain as any newborn.

In all my wretched existence, I never moved as quickly as I did then. I covered the distance between us in just a few strides, using my staff to vault the final few yards. Tacit was still dazed, and only in the last second did he see me coming. Even as he did, though, his mind was trying to make sense out of what was happening. Consequently, he did nothing to stop me because he still hadn't quite figured out what the hell I was doing there. In his perplexed state, determining the why of why I was there was more important than anticipating and blocking my next move.

I braced myself and swung my staff as hard and fast as I ever had in my life. I slammed it into his skull, and if the rock had dazed him, the damage my heavy staff did was far worse. I heard something break, and it wasn't the staff. Instead it was the satisfying snap of bone. Tacit went down, his jaw at an odd angle, little "unhhh" sounds floating from his throat. He tried to sit up. I saw a small puddle of blood where his head had been a moment, and spotted a couple of his teeth in the middle of it. I wondered if he was in pain. I wondered if he was feeling anything. I wondered why I wondered even as I swung the staff once more. This time he tried ever so slightly to put up a defense, but it was utterly inadequate. The staff came in on his blind side, on the side covered by the patch, and it struck home, opening a huge gash in his forehead. Blood poured down his face. There was always a lot of blood in such wounds, far out of proportion to the severity of the cut itself, but in this case the collateral damage was devastating, for the blood blinded his good eye.

The phoenix now knew that something was desperately wrong. It screeched in fear, and flapped its wings. This time it managed to do more than move air around, and I saw the wings developing the strength required to move the creature. This was a being of a magical origin, not bound by normal rules of natural development. Its strength and abilities were growing not by days, but by seconds. The phoenix started to rise into the air.

Tacit began to stand, his legs bending wildly, and I swept his legs out from under him with the staff. He went down and I heard him call out my name, heard him say "Apropos!" in a tone that had confusion, betrayal, anger, and a thirst for revenge all intertwined. At least I think he said "Apropos." With the combination of the newly missing teeth and apparently broken jaw, it wasn't the most articulate couple of syllables I'd ever heard.

Then I drove the staff home. I didn't swing it in an arc this time, but instead rammed it forward like a spear, taking Tacit squarely in the forehead. Mercifully for Tacit I didn't have the blade extended, or I would have driven it straight into his brain. I figured I owed him something for all the help he had given me, and here I had repaid the debt: I was letting him live.

Tacit tumbled backward with a huge bruise on his forehead. He lay on his back, staring sightlessly toward the sky, and for just a moment I wondered if he wasn't actually dead, my "mercy" a bit too late. Then I had no time to give it any thought, for the phoenix was airborne. Confused, frightened, and determined to put as much distance between itself and this place of violence as it possibly could, the phoenix was getting out of there.

I wasn't about to let that happen. As I had moments before, I took several quick steps forward, jammed the pole into the ground, and drove my body upward powered by the only part of my body worth a damn, my arms. For a split second I thought I wasn't going to make it, and then my desperate hand snagged onto the feathers on the phoenix's back.

The bird let out an alarmed yelp, pivoted, tried to shake me off. We were already twenty feet in the air and rising fast. A fall from that height was not going to do me a lot of good. Several feathers came loose from the creature, and I almost lost my grip. Somehow, displaying strength I would not have thought I had, I propelled myself upward and snared one arm around the phoenix's neck, securing my hold.

Thirty, forty feet in the air, higher still, moving at a

dizzying pace, and then the phoenix flipped over, trying to toss me, and I was dangling. My right leg was useless, my left leg seeking purchase and finding none, and the only thing that was preventing me from falling was my left arm wrapped around the bird's neck. In my right hand was my staff. The blade was still contained in the staff, which meant I could probably have killed the stupid thing, but one quick glance down convinced me of the folly of that notion. If the bird died at that moment, it would predecease me by only a very short time.

I thrust upward with my right hand, bringing the staff across the phoenix's neck, then shifted my grip from the bird's neck to the other side of the staff. *"Stop it, you overgrown parakeet! You're mine now!"* I shouted, even as I performed the equivalent of a midair chin-up. In accomplishing that I was able to bring my left leg up and around, under the creature's belly, so that even though I was upside down I was now flat against the creature's back and clearly not being shaken off anytime soon.

"You're mine!" I said again, not knowing if the creature understood me and not caring, hoping that my tone of voice alone would underscore the fact that I was serious. The creature screeched in protest, but I ignored it. "You're mine, and you will go where I tell you, now! *Now!"*

And with that I secured my grip on the back of the bird's head and angled the beast forward and down. It continued to try and fight me, but I could sense its resolve was weakening.

The creature was confused. I couldn't blame it. On some level, it sensed that it was supposed to figure into the grand scheme of things. It knew—as Tacit obviously had—that it had a role to fulfill in destiny's master plan, and that role was to be fulfilled now. But it obviously sensed that something wasn't right. It wasn't sophisticated or intelligent enough to determine just what precisely was wrong.

As for me, I no longer cared about right and wrong. All I knew was this: I had "wanted" my entire life. Wanted something, anything, to call my own. Wanted to break out of the little box that I had been placed in, first by society, then by the knights, and now by destiny itself. I didn't want to go through my life and end up Apropos of nothing.

And there had been Tacit, ready to step into his designated spot.

It had all been so hideously unfair. I was not ready to accept or concede the possibility that Tacit might be better, worthier than me. Instead I saw in him, with his self-aggrandizing ballads, a smug symbol of everything that had been lacking in my life, and if I usurped that symbol, then maybe my life would no longer seem so empty, so filled only with bile and frustration and cynicism.

If I could take Tacit's place in the story . . . I could be the hero.

It was really that simple. I would hijack destiny's plot, laugh in the face of the author, and write my own ending. I would turn it around. No longer would I be Apropos the disposable character. Instead I would take over the narrative and drive it in a direction more to my liking.

That was my plan, at least, provided I could get the damned bird to cooperate.

The phoenix tried to shake me off once more, but I was holding on too tightly. It struggled beneath my grip, fought to throw me off, failed. It flapped around in midair, not going in any particular direction, but instead simply hanging there like a swimmer treading water.

I knew that this was it. This was the moment to firmly grasp the reins of destiny and send it galloping in a direction that suited my fancy. Unfortunately, I had a slight drawback: not being a hero, I had no clue as to what I should do next. I had thrust myself into the role, rather than been destined for it through fate and nature, as Tacit had been.

For a few seconds, I felt panic welling up inside me. Perhaps this had not been such a great idea after all.

The phoenix, possibly sensing my hesitation, let out another ear-piercing scream and then threw itself through the air. I let out a shriek of my own—rather girlish, I hate to admit—but held on nonetheless. Fortunately the noise I had made was drowned out by the phoenix's own.

Tacit probably would have enjoyed the ride. He would have considered the experience and adventure somewhat exhilarating. Me, I was just doing everything I could not to heave up what I'd eaten that morning as the bird banked sharply and wheeled through the air.

It was then that I spotted, from on high, the Harpers Bizarre.

The phoenix did as well, and it angled its head in curiosity as it stared down at the strange creatures. The Harpers were gliding across the tops of the trees, clutching onto high branches and thrusting themselves forward, their wings moving their distorted bodies through the air with considerable alacrity. I strained my eyes and was able to make out the struggling form of the Princess Entipy. No one Harper seemed able to control her. Instead she was being carried by four Harpers, one each gripping one of her limbs. Even in such an uncomfortable and unfortunate position, she continued to struggle. I had to credit her this: She didn't take defeat easily.

It was at that moment that I realized what the heroic thing would be to do: rescue Entipy. Clearly that was what Tacit had intended. And if he had intended it, why . . . that meant that it was supposed to happen. Destiny's plan, as fate would have it, and all those other niceties. But since I had impulsively commandeered the role of hero, it was incumbent upon me to assume all the responsibilities therein.

Except I had no stomach for going up against the Harpers again. I had gotten away from them once, and counted myself lucky.

The phoenix, however, had other ideas. For it should be remembered that the phoenix was still a newborn, and newborns tend to be rather hungry. Now, there was no record of any phoenix ever having attacked, devoured, or tried to devour a human being. Smaller winged creatures, on the other hand, seemed to be well within the confines of the phoenix's preferred menu.

Consequently, the phoenix took one look at the Harpers Bizarre and sensed its first meal. I have no idea whether the phoenix even remembered I was on board at the time. If it did remember, it certainly didn't attach much importance to my presence. Instead it folded its wings back and dove toward the Harpers, who were still unaware that they had been targeted as an entree.

Aileron was in the lead, as was appropriate for a leader, and it was he who spotted the phoenix first. The phoenix had not made any noise at that point; some instinct simply warned Aileron to look up. He saw the phoenix dropping like a boulder, its claws outstretched, descending at horrifying speed. Aileron shouted an alarm to the rest of his warriors, and the phoenix—knowing that it had been spotted—let out a *screeeeeee* of such deafening proportions that I could only assume it had done so for the purpose of freezing its intended prey in their tracks.

To some degree, it worked. A number of the Harpers Bizarre looked up at the oncoming bird and stopped right where they were. They stared upward with eyes so wide and so terrified that I thought their orbs were going to leap out of their faces and try to make a break for it on their own.

"Arrooooooowwws!" shouted Aileron, and his order got through to some of them, but not all. Even as some of the Harpers nocked their arrows, the phoenix tore into them, its claws out and slicing through them with such ease that one would have thought the bird was sliding a knife through cheese.

Entipy continued to struggle, and her captors had no idea which way to look. They saw several of their fellows gutted in seconds, saw others firing arrows, saw the bird bearing down on them, and did the only thing they could—scattered and ran. This left Entipy with no support at all, and she fell, but not far. Where she was at that point, the branches were particularly dense. She didn't plunge more than a couple of feet before coming to a halt on upswept branches. She thrashed about, the branches tearing at her clothes, shouting imprecations and letting anyone within hearing distance know that they were going to rue the day.

Aileron wasn't concerned about ruing any days. Instead he had spotted me, holding on for dear life to the back of the bird. Our gazes locked, his eyes widened, and he shouted "Aaaaapropohhhh!" even as the Harpers unleashed a volley of arrows at us.

The phoenix was fast, but not that fast. It could not angle out of the way as arrows thudded into its underbelly. The phoenix let out a cry, but it was not a death scream so much as it was a *That hurt and now I'll kill you even more* scream. And if that was indeed the bird's sentiment, it certainly did not hesitate to put deed to thought.

The great creature took in a deep breath and then puffed out its chest. The arrows exploded from where they had struck, tumbling end over end with vicious speed. The Harpers scattered as they tried to get out of the way of the returning shafts. Many of them managed to get clear. Several of them did not, and crashed into the treetops, writhing with arrows lodged in their torsos or throats or legs.

Aileron's fury was beyond any that was measurable on a human scale. From I-know-not-where, he pulled a dagger and waved it at us defiantly. "Yoooouuuu will diiiieeeeee!" he cawed, and then he saw Entipy still thrashing about in the top of the tree some yards away. "But sheeeeee will dieeee fiiiirst!"

The phoenix didn't seem particularly interested in cooperating with me. It was much more interested in feasting upon the struggling bodies of the Harpers. The creature had just snagged one of them with its powerful talons, shredding the Harper's wings effortlessly. It flipped the thrashing Harper into the air and then snagged it in its beak in the same way that you might toss a grape in the air and catch it on your tongue. Like a great cat worrying a mouse, the phoenix shook its head violently, keeping the upper half of the Harper securely within its beak while allowing the lower half to be torn free and fall away. Apparently the phoenix preferred white meat.

As fascinating as this insight into phoenix culinary tastes was, it did nothing to attend to the fact that Entipy was in mortal danger. When she saw Aileron advancing on her, though, she displayed not a jot of fear. Instead she unleashed a string of invective so overpowering that it stopped the surprised Harpers leader dead. Apparently he was accustomed to intended victims begging, pleading, or railing against the unfairness of their situation. He was not used to being cursed out.

His brief hesitation was what I needed to close the gap between myself and the princess. I still had the staff positioned across the phoenix's throat. I hadn't been pressing it particularly hard, giving the bird the opportunity to attack and feast as it saw fit. Now, though, I had to take charge, as problematic as that might seem. I drew the staff tight against the phoenix's throat, which certainly got the bird's squawking attention. "Down!" I shouted, and pointed with emphasis toward Entipy. "Down! Hurry!"

The phoenix had obviously fully acquired its vision by then. It looked down, saw Entipy, and then saw the Harper advancing on her. Whether the phoenix acted out of a sense of wanting to rescue the girl, or out of interest in grabbing another snack, I could not really say. Either way, the result was the same. The phoenix flapped its powerful wings once and then headed straight down toward Aileron.

Aileron, I could see, was assessing the distance between himself and the phoenix, which was in the midst of a spectacular dive. Then he calculated how far it was to get to the still thrashing Entipy. The choice before him was clear: Could he get to Entipy and gut her before the phoenix got within range and gutted him?

Apparently he decided that the answer was yes, for with a mighty howl he leaped the remaining distance toward Entipy, his blade outstretched, ready to be rammed into her heaving (if modest) bosom and redecorate the treetops with her lifeblood.

At that moment, Entipy snapped off a large branch and brought it up right into Aileron's path. He became entangled in it, cutting free of it with his dagger. The action only delayed him seconds . . . but it was all the seconds I required. Wrapping an arm around the phoenix's neck, I extended the staff with the other hand and shouted, "Princess! Grab it!"

For once in her arrogant little life, Entipy did not argue. She lunged for the staff and gripped it firmly, and then the phoenix pumped its wings and we angled upward once more. Entipy curled up her legs as Aileron lunged for her, but he missed her clean and crashed through the upper level of the branches. He vanished into the lower level of the terrace of branches, and as he did so he howled, "I will geeetttt youuuuu, Aproooooopooooosssss!"

The rest of the Harpers had scattered, realizing that they were hopelessly overmatched by the powerfully flapping phoenix. Filled with determination, Entipy hauled herself up the staff, hand over hand, grunting slightly but otherwise giving no indication of the effort involved. I had to admit, I was a bit impressed; I had simply figured that she would dangle and that I'd have to pull her up myself. But she obviously wasn't waiting for me.

She drew herself up to the back of the phoenix and clambered aboard. There wasn't a lot of grace or artistry to her doing so; she just sort of flopped aboard. "Are you all right?" I asked, or at least I started to ask. She didn't give me the time to get the entire sentence out. Instead she slugged me forcefully in the shoulder, hard enough to get a rather loud yelp out of me. *"What did you do that for?!?"*

"You *abandoned* me, you asshole! You begged for your miserable life and left me in the hands of the Harpers Bizarre!"

Trying to recover my self-possession, I said serenely, "All part of my master plan."

"Master plan? You're telling me you went to find this . . . this . . ." She looked the bird over. "What is this, anyway?"

"The phoenix."

I informed her of that with a certain degree of smug satisfaction, and clearly that smugness carried over, because Entipy finally looked ever-so-slightly impressed. "This is a phoenix that we're on? A . . . real phoenix?"

"That's right," I said. At which point I made a rather horrendous mistake.

I became overconfident.

I reached down and patted the phoenix on the side of the head, as if we were astride a sort of overgrown horse or some other docile creature, rather than a monster of myth which was newly hatched, cranky, and confused. In short, the phoenix's reaction to my paternal pat was not a positive one.

The creature went berserk.

Bucking wildly, the phoenix suddenly vaulted heavenward as if it intended to rip free of gravity and hurtle into deep space. Entipy was almost tossed right off, but she barely managed to maintain her position by throwing her arms around my stomach. To be accurate, she was holding on to where my stomach previously had been. Thanks to the sudden jolt of the phoenix's upward thrust, my stomach had relocated to somewhere in my boots. The wind hammered so hard against me that that alone was almost enough to blow me right off the creature.

The phoenix wasn't doing any more flips. It was as if, angered over being used and abused, it felt that simply tossing us off wasn't sufficient punishment. The phoenix continued to climb, higher and higher, then suddenly pivoted and angled back down again. This time Entipy slammed forward, and I yelped as her jaw dug into my shoulder. Considering that it was her teeth smacking up against me, it probably didn't feel any better on her end either.

"Do something!" she howled.

"I am! I'm holding on!" I was grasping the creature's throat with one arm, and was desperately clutching my staff with the other. I tried to bring it up and around the bird's neck, but this time he was entirely too active for me to accomplish that seemingly simple feat. Every time I thought I could get an angle around, the bird changed course.

Suddenly the phoenix traded in pitches and curves for pure speed. It was hard to believe that it had only been born minutes before, because its command of its wings was complete. Screeching, the bird thrust forward, moving at high velocity. The ground became a blur beneath us.

"Where is it going?! Control it!" shouted Entipy over the roaring of the wind around us. I certainly tried my best, but the phoenix was becoming stronger with every passing moment, and my thrusts and shoving on the great beast's head didn't even warrant its attention. At one point it snapped its beak warningly at my fingers, and I withdrew. Of course, I had my trump card; I could try to slay the beast, using either my sword or the blade in my staff. But that wasn't exactly the wisest of courses to pursue, because we were far too high. If we skewered the beast, its demise would shortly be followed by our own. So I didn't exactly see the advantage.

Besides . . . I had the sinking feeling that I knew precisely where the beast was going. Or, to be more precise, where it was going away from.

My mother had known what she was about when she spoke of destinies, that much was clear to me now. Unfortunately for me, the destiny that she had foreseen belonged to Tacit. I had hijacked it. The phoenix was a creature of myth and legend, the sort that is both born into, and dies from, destiny. If any being knew what was supposed to be what, it was the phoenix. And somehow it knew that the man riding astride it was not the right person at the right time. The destiny of the phoenix, the role that it was supposed to play, was to bring the triumphant Tacit back to the palace where he and Entipy would live happily and majestically ever after, I was quite certain of that. But because that destiny had been diverted, the phoenix was resolutely and instinctively heading away from the place that it was supposed to go. As much as we desperately wanted to get to the castle of King Runcible . . . that was how much the great flapping beast that we were riding wanted to head in the completely opposite direction.

Entipy had demanded to know where the phoenix was going. The answer to that was that the phoenix was not heading toward any place in particular, but rather away from somewhere else. We were racing not to the phoenix's destiny . . . but to mine. And I had no clue as to what that was.

Then again, I had always been fairly good at improvising.

Chapter 15

Entipy lapsed into silence, which was enough of a blessing in and of itself. I paid no attention to her, since I was devoting my concentration to tracking just where in the world we were. The one thing I knew for certain was that we were heading west, because the sun was hanging directly in front of us on the horizon, dropping lower in the sky as sunset and evening approached. That was not a situation that I was looking forward to, because once night fell, I was going to have no way of knowing which way we were heading. At least with the sun still up, I could try to catch sight of a few landmarks—castles, distinctive mountain peaks, something.

We were no longer in Isteria, of that I was quite certain. We had passed far beyond the boundaries of the city/state, and I couldn't even begin to guess just where the phoenix was going to have us wind up. Fancifully, I almost felt as if the phoenix, born of fire, wasn't going to stop flying until it had sailed directly into the sun itself, erupting in one glorious conflagration that I would have been in a far better position to admire had I not been stuck on the damned bird's back.

The phoenix started to angle off, and for a moment I thought it was descending. But a stronger, more furious pumping of its wings drove us to the northwest. The farther we went, the colder it was getting. I began to worry that the creature might take us to the Frozen North, and that we would possibly wind up in the clutches of King Meander (should he have decided to return to his former place of power). I saw my breath starting to mist up in front of me. It was not a comforting feeling. I didn't say anything to Entipy about it. I had the feeling that if I indicated any hint of concern or uncertainty, she would see it as weakness and use it as an excuse to verbally shred me. Considering my state of mind at that moment, the last thing I needed was her haranguing me. The temptation to shove her off might prove to be too great.

Unfortunately, Entipy finally decided to grace me with her verbal presence. "Where are we?" she said, and then—as if reading my mind—she added, "And if you say that we're on the back of a phoenix, so help me, I will knock you off."

"Being abruptly deprived of your company, Highness, is hardly what I would call a threat," I replied.

"Why are you so nasty?"

That actually prompted me to laugh. "You would ask that of me? You?"

"Yes, I would. I'm a princess. A princess is entitled to ask anything she wants, of anyone she wants. Why are you so nasty?" She paused, apparently considering the matter since she probably figured out that she wasn't going to get much response from me. She decided to answer for herself. "Don't you like women? You don't, do you," she added suspiciously—even contemptuously—after a moment's thought.

I sighed. "I have no more hostility for women than I do for anyone else."

"Meaning?"

"Your Worshipfulness," I said, "I would give anything, seize any excuse, not to have to continue this conversation."

Naturally, the phoenix decided to take me up on it.

With long fingers of night caressing the ground, the creature chose that moment to angle steeply downward. This abrupt movement was accompanied by two ear-piercing screams. The first was the phoenix itself, a howl of defiance torn from its throat. The second was the princess, who let out a most unhighnesslike screech of alarm. I managed to avoid emitting any unmanly cries through the simple expedient of biting down so hard on my lower lip that blood trickled down my chin.

"Stop him!" shouted Entipy.

I had no idea how I might go about accomplishing that, unfortunately. Slaying the beast was no more viable an option now than it had been earlier. All I could do was clutch on with all my strength and pray to the gods that the stupid thing—if it was indeed coming in for a landing, or planning to try and discharge us as passengers—would do so gently. As with most of my prayers, it was met with resounding laughter from whatever divine beings were looking down upon me and watching me toil ceaselessly to amuse them and their perverse humors.

The phoenix suddenly leveled off, and then the bird flipped me.

Some inner, sixth sense warned me at the last moment. I lunged forward and threw my staff across the creature's throat, praying that the monster's beak wouldn't find my arms and snap them off at the elbows. In an eyeblink I had the staff in place and was gripping it on either side, and then the creature was flying upside down, and I was dangling. Only the strength of my arms was preventing me from tumbling to a bone-shattering fate below. My staff naturally pressed all the tighter across the phoenix's throat, but the beast didn't seem particularly perturbed by this state of affairs. And if it was, then it was at least aware that it was a condition destined to be quite temporary, for both the phoenix and I knew that it could fly upside down for far longer than I could hang on. Time and gravity were solidly in the phoenix's corner.

An additional factor, however, immediately weighed in to toss the odds even more greatly into the creature's favor. For Entipy had nothing to grab on to save for some feathers off the phoenix's back. Rather than a means of support, these served only as a handy souvenir of her trip, for they came loose in a heartbeat and then there was nothing between Entipy and the ground save air. By that point it was sufficiently dark that we couldn't see what was below us, but the odds were spectacular that it wasn't going to be something we'd wish to encounter while plummeting.

Entipy let out a shriek and, as she tumbled, grabbed on to the only thing around that offered the remotest hope of support: my legs.

I had tried to bathe a cat once, back when I was a child. The wretched thing was wandering the streets, and nuzzled up against me. So I cradled it in my arms, and it looked so filthy—beyond the animal's ability to groom itself, it seemed—that I found a tub of water and endeavored to immerse it. The cat yowled and wrapped itself around my lame leg. It took me damned near an hour to disengage the thing, at which point it took off for parts unknown, never to be seen again. Pets, whether they be bird or cat, and I don't seem to get along.

Entipy's grasp on my leg reminded me of the feline, as did the high-pitched yelping that she was giving off. She was holding on to my left leg, immobilizing it. That was fortunate for her; if she'd been holding on to my right leg, I'd have used my good left one to kick her loose. I knew that my situation was hopeless, but I had no desire to expedite the disaster that was looming beneath us.

And that was when the creature got the bright idea of tilting its head backward toward its own spine. Basically, the phoenix's own beak and head had been holding my staff in place. In angling its head downward, it allowed my staff to slide straight down and off. And then we were falling.

I would like to say that, even at that point where death seemed imminent, I kept a stoic and manly silence. I would like to. The truth is that I uncorked a scream of terror that probably deafened the phoenix, which certainly didn't bother me greatly. Entipy might have been screaming as well, but I definitely drowned her out. The only upside to the entire situation was that she had come loose from my leg, without my even having to try to bathe her.

I have no idea if you have ever fallen from a great height. Certainly everyone has had dreams of such a thing now and then. I can assure you from personal experience that there is no more horrific sensation than being in free fall. The thing is, when you're experiencing something awful—a battle, an illness, a bad marriage—you can draw some measure of comfort from the knowledge that sooner or later the experience will be terminated. The depressing thing about falling is knowing that the termination is not going to be an improvement.

Impressively, as I fell, I still managed to hold on to my staff. I had no idea why this might be any sort of a good thing; certainly after I was dead, it wasn't going to be of much use to me. Then again, one doesn't tend to think rationally at such moments.

I tumbled end over end, having no idea how long I fell, certain that it was for ages when very likely it was only for seconds. And then I hit.

I heard something loud snapping and for one delirious, insane moment I thought I was hearing the breaking of every bone in my body. My mother had once told me that once a broken bone heals, it becomes much stronger. If that were the case, then I would be a virtual superman if I ever managed to walk again.

But then I realized that the ground was giving way beneath me, and—comprehending by degrees—I further realized that I had not in fact struck the ground. Instead I plunged into the midst of what was clearly an assortment of branches, and I understood immediately that I had fallen into trees. The branches served to slow down my descent, although not by much. They crackled and splintered around me, tearing at my clothes, ripping my skin. I tried to grab onto some for support but none of them were large enough to singly support my weight.

And then I was through the forestry. The air whirled around me and I saw tree trunks hurtling by, and then I crashed into a thicket of bushes.

With thorns, naturally.

Fortunately enough, I was by that point so dazed, my body racked with such pain, that the thorns barely made an impression on me. I simply lay there, amidst the brush, looking around in a daze, waiting for my eyes to adjust to the darkness, and for my brain to adjust to the reality of my not being dead.

That was when I heard a yowling from overhead.

I knew who and what it was before I even craned my neck to look up. I could see Entipy's legs thrashing about in the upper reaches of the branches. Apparently, with her being somewhat lighter than I, the trees had actually managed to slow Entipy's fall so that she didn't penetrate the greensward. She was hung up high above me, uttering a series of most unprincessly imprecations.

"The more you jostle about up there," I called up to her, forcing my voice above her shouting, "the more likely you are to break loose, fall, and injure or kill yourself."

That stopped her.

For a long moment I seriously considered just walking away, abandoning her altogether. The princess was no walk in the woods, and that was apparently just what I was going to be stuck with. I was reasonably sure I could survive in a forest indefinitely. I didn't need her. Nor, for that matter, did I really need to return to the castle. At that point in time, if I never saw the place again, it would suit me just fine.

But I had embarked on a course. I had to see it through, because . . .

. . . because the truth was that I had never seen anything through.

I make no bones about it to you. I have sworn utter honesty, after all. In truth, there was no one in all the world whom I held in greater contempt than I myself: he who came from nothing, aspiring to be something, who had not only surrounded himself with hypocrites, but was the greatest hypocrite of all because he was trying to gain their favor and beat them at their own game. And that self-loathing radiated from me and determined how I viewed all those around me. Part of that inwardly directed anger stemmed from the fact that I had never truly managed to stick with anything and see it through. Every plan in my life had come to an unfortunate end, either due to shortsightedness on my part or character flaws that simply prevented my being able to conclude it properly. So there I was, having embarked on an endeavor to usurp destiny and see through the role of "hero." Which meant that I was going to have to get the damned princess back to her damned palace. As tempting, then, as it might be to melt into the woods and never be seen again by the eyes of man, the inescapable fact was that I was going to have to retrieve the little shrew from her perch and get her home safely.

"I'm not going to jostle or break loose up here," her voice floated down after a time.

"Oh really? How do you know that?"

"Because I'm stuck," she said with obvious annoyance. "The branches are so thick they're snagged in my hair, my clothes . . . everything. Get up here and cut me free."

My getting too near her with a sharp object probably wasn't the brightest idea. "With all deference, Your Greatness, I'm not exactly built for scaling trees. I'm rather lame of leg, as you must have noticed."

"And brain as well, I'd wager." Obscured by the branches, she must have been considering the situation a moment, for there was blessed silence. Finally she commanded, "Throw your blade up here. I'll do it myself."

"As you wish." I wasn't thrilled about the notion of hurling my sword into the shadows of the foliage. Since I wasn't able to see exactly where she was, there was a possibility that the sword might impale her on its upward flight. A pleasant thought but, as noted, counterproductive. So I removed the sword and scabbard, braced myself, and then hurled the sheathed weapon upward. It vanished into the branches and then there was silence. "Have you got it?" I called.

"Yes. Hold on." For a moment more there was no sound, and then I heard the noise of hacking and slashing. She was whacking away quite handily. Bits of leaves and branch spiraled down. I stood there, leaning on my staff, waiting for some indication that she was close to finished.

I got a far more profound indication than I could possibly have hoped, for suddenly there was a quick rustling of the leaves and then the blade plummeted from overhead, straight toward my upraised face. I threw myself out of the way, just barely avoiding it, and it thudded point down right where I'd been standing. The scabbard flopped to the ground a moment later. I lay there, gaping at the still-quivering blade, and then saw the princess—looking rather tattered but otherwise undamaged—easing herself down the tree trunk. I called up with unfettered annoyance, "You might have warned me!"

"Oh. Look out," she said, and continued her descent.

"That was amazingly stupid, Highness." I picked myself up, dusted myself off, and yanked the sword from the ground. "It may not have come to your attention, but you have a much better shot at getting through this in one piece with me at your side."

"Indeed?" She dropped the rest of the way to the ground, landing in a crouch. "At my side, until such time that you see fit to abandon me yet again."

"I told you. I was—"

"—going to get a phoenix to save us." She shook her head and dislodged the leaves from her cloak. "Squire, you are either extremely duplicitous, or extremely lucky, or a combination of both. I haven't quite decided." Then she took a moment to look around, to examine her surroundings in a rather imperious manner. I felt a chill in the air and wasn't sure whether it was because the woods seemed oppressive or the temperature was dropping. Evening was drawing closer, however, and I did not like the fact that we had no shelter.

"We need to find somewhere to take cover," I said. "I don't want us out and exposed this way."

She seemed about to say something in rebuttal, but I think she realized that in doing so, it would only be a knee-jerk reaction. Disagreeing with me on principle, which was a foolish notion and a waste of time. So she said nothing, which was a refreshing change of pace.

I looked around and perceived that, in one direction, the terrain seemed to be turning a bit more rocky. Without explaining why (and, at that point, not really caring if she followed or not), I sheathed my sword and started off. I didn't have to look over my shoulder to see if she was behind me; I could hear her boots scraping on the rocky ground. Despite my lameness of leg, I was making reasonably good time; fear of being stuck out in the woods with no shelter and at the mercy of whatever happened by was always a good motivator. She did not, however, huff or puff or ask me to slow down to accommodate her, which either said a great deal for her ability to keep up or not much in terms of my ability to set a rapid pace.

As I hoped, the ground had a rocky cast to it because it was serving to lead us to a small series of caves. I looked for something reasonably small and insinuated myself within, then looked up at her expectantly.

"Why don't we find something bigger?" she demanded. She was regarding me with tremendous suspicion. "Are you trying to put us at close quarters on purpose?"

"Not especially," I replied. "If you climb in here or don't, it makes no never mind to me. But I was endeavoring to avoid anything substantially larger so that we don't find ourselves sharing facilities with a bear or similar beast that might take issue with unwanted guests."

She seemed to want to toss off a smart remark, but then she closed her mouth and nodded. The fact that she was willing to accept something I said at simple face value gave me some measure of hope, as meager as that hope might be. Without another word she slid into the cave beside me, drawing her tattered cloak tighter around her as if it could serve as a shield. "Shouldn't we make a fire or something?" she said, and then added with a touch of her customary derision, "Or don't you know how to?"

"I may not be on par with you when it comes to crafting infernos, Highness," I said pointedly, "but I have enough woodcraft to begin a blaze. However, I have to assume that the Harpers would likewise have enough craft to track us if we provided them with a convenient means of locating us . . . such as a fire."

"That . . . sounds reasonable," she said with what sounded like reluctance. Then she added, "But don't we need something for warmth? Or to protect us from wild animals?"

"I'll settle for this as protection," I said, indicating my sword and sounding much braver than I felt. "As for warmth, we can always depend on your sunny disposition to suffuse the cave with sunshine-like radiance."

"You don't have to be like that, you know," she snapped, glaring at me. She had pulled her hood up so that practically the only thing I could see were her eyes. "Always so nasty."

"I'm not nasty," I said nastily. "I'm worrying about a

dozen things at once, and having you question me about everything simply adds a thirteenth thing."

"I have a right to question. I'm your princess. I will be your queen."

"Not if I don't get you back alive," I reminded her.

That shut her down. I was, I admit, surprised. She generally struck me as someone sufficiently feisty to continue arguing until she had no more energy to do so. Instead, she was silent for a time, and when she next spoke, it was less challenging and more of a direct inquiry. "So . . . how do you plan to get me back? Alive or dead?"

It was a reasonable question. "I don't rate our chances tremendously high in making it all the way back to your parents, just the two of us, on foot. Probably the best thing to do is find a commweaver and have him or her message your parents."

There were two major methods of long-distance communication in Isteria and the surrounding lands. Sending birds with messages tied upon them was that most favored by those of limited funds. But that was a fairly unreliable proposition. If the bird wasn't well trained enough it could go astray, and even if it was perfectly trained, it could fall prey to predators. Far more reliable were commweavers, spellcasters who were able to utilize magical threads to send messages cast-to-cast. It was a highly specialized form of weaving, however, second only to farcasting in rarity, and it was not inexpensive. I said as much, pointing out that that might prove a drawback.

Entipy looked at me as if I was out of my mind, displaying some of the old attitude that had been mercifully absent for a time.

"Money? Money is an issue?" She snorted derisively.

"Only when you don't have it. I have very little on me; certainly not enough to purchase the skills of a reliable commweaver. Do you have any?"

"We don't have need," she said.

"We don't?"

"No."

"Then what would you suggest in its place? Perhaps you could offer the weaver sexual favors . . . ?"

She slapped me.

I suppose I deserved it. This was, after all, a princess, and my remark was nothing short of crude. Nevertheless, deserved or not, it was all I could do to refrain from smacking her right back. Instead I simply sat there, my right cheek red from where she had hit it. She didn't appear the least bit contrite over having done so, her eyes burning at the very suggestion.

"Your problem," she said, "is that you are accustomed to thinking like a peasant. That's what you were, after all, wasn't it." It was not a question. "I can tell. I can tell nobility from a mile off, and you've none about you. You're some sort of . . . of charity case my parents took in. They do that on occasion, probably to make themselves feel important and less guilty about having everything while others have nothing. Well? A charity case, am I right? That they took in?"

"At least they took me in," I said heatedly, "instead of shipping me away because they couldn't stand me."

Her hand swung again, but this time I caught it at the wrist. I held it there for a moment, Entipy pitting her strength against mine, but this was a contest even I could win. Her arm trembled with the strain and then I pushed it away. I remained alert for a another round, but she lowered her arm and settled for glaring at me.

"We will find a place . . . a civilized place," she said haughtily, "on the morrow. There's certain to be somewhere like that nearby."

"Oh, is there," I said with obvious sarcasm.

"Yes. And once there, I'll simply order a commweaver be brought to me. It will be a royal decree."

"And it's going to be just that simple."

"Yes, Apropos. Just that simple."

"The last simple plan you had," I pointed out, "involved Tacit coming to get you and whisk you away so that you could live happily ever after. And as I recall, I claimed that you should never count on such cheerful conclusions. Considering how right I was, and how wrong you were, you might want to add more credence to what I tell you. And what I'm telling you now is that your scenario—while pleasantly convenient—is taking a hell of a lot on faith. Faith may be fine for the Faith Women, but it can have somewhat dire consequences in the real world if that's what you're counting on to carry you through. Do you understand what I'm saying here, Highness?"

She made no reply, instead preferring to glower. But that was an improvement, I supposed, on listening to her talk, so I said nothing. Instead I leaned against the cave wall, reaching back to pull out my sword. She looked with silent surprise at me as I did so. "Just in case," I explained. "If something surprises us in the night, I'd rather have a weapon in my lap than behind me."

We lapsed into silence, simply sitting and watching the night roll in. I reached deep into myself, pulling up all the old techniques. I sniffed the air, listened as carefully as I could. I sensed things moving in the night, but they were small, insignificant. Nothing that would pay us any heed; indeed, things that would be more afraid of us than we of they. I hoped that cave would provide us sufficient insulation from the night air.

I was so busy listening for the slightest noise that I jumped a bit, startled, when she spoke. There was a bit of weariness in her voice; I could tell she was tired, but something was preying on her mind, and the growing fatigue was enough for her to voice her concern.

"Did you see him?" she asked.

"Him?" I had no idea who or what she was talking about.

"Tacit. In the woods. He should have been easy to spot. He's tall and strong and handsome, and has an eyepatch."

"Ah" was all I said, stalling for time. Not for a moment did I consider telling the truth; instead I was simply trying to figure out which lie would be the most effective. "But . . . you heard the Harper. They killed him."

"No," she said firmly, shaking her head. "I don't believe that. I don't."

"Why not? It is possible, isn't it?"

"No," she told me. "He is a great hero, destined for great deeds. I know it. I just know it."

The thing was, she was right. That didn't make it any easier to hear. In fact, it made it harder.

Opting for a tack that would support vagueness instead of specific duplicity, I said, "Princess, if he *was* there, in the woods . . . if he was alive . . . wouldn't it be much likelier that he would have been the one to rescue you instead of me?"

She had no immediate reply to that, probably because she knew I was correct. Fortunately, she did not make the leap that perhaps the reason he hadn't taken a hand in the situation was because I had thwarted whatever intentions he might have had to do so. "He could still be alive," she said softly.

"True," I admitted.

"And . . . he is a hero . . ."

"Well, you know, Princess, that's part of the problem."

She looked up at me, clearly puzzled. "Problem?"

"Yes, well . . . that's the difficulty with heroes, isn't it. They're very much in demand. People are always seeking them out to go on quests or lead rebellions or such. Their time isn't really their own. It's possible that Tacit became distracted by something, or pulled into some other adventure and was unable to attend to your situation."

"I'm a princess. He was to rescue me. That's the most important thing a hero can do," she said petulantly.

"With respect, Highness," I said, trying my best to sound apologetic, "heroes have a funny way of deciding for themselves what is or is not the most important thing they can do. And then, of course, there are the tragic heroes . . ."

"Tragic . . . ?"

"Yes. Heroes who fail in their quest. It happens sometimes. Look at Orpheus. What a disaster that was. His love remains trapped in the underworld because he couldn't keep eyes front, and he winds up being torn to pieces by Harpies." I shook my head and, coming across as the most conciliatory person in the world, I said softly, "It's all well and good to imagine oneself as the center of a great and epic adventure story, where good triumphs and evil is defeated. But the simple truth, Highness, is that you're a young woman, on the cusp of adulthood, and you have to come to terms with the fact that life simply isn't like that. Those who are evil have virtues; those who are good have flaws. And the outcome of the 'story,' if you will, isn't predicated on high-flown morality, but instead on who's smarter and better armed and luckier. That's simply the way of it and the truth of it, and not all the starry-eyed romantic notions of your beloved savior are going to change that."

She said nothing for a good long time after that, but when she did speak, it was with quiet conviction.

"He'll come for me, Tacit will. And I will have my happy ending, squire, whether you like it or not, or believe in it or not. I will have my happiness."

"May you have all the happiness that you deserve, Highness," I said, and with that I leaned against the wall, keeping my hand wrapped around the hilt of my sword, and allowed myself to drift into a very light sleep.

Chapter 16

When morning came, I found that she was leaning against me in her sleep. Not only that but, instinctively, she had wrapped her arms around one of mine. I looked down at her and, in repose, I found that she was in fact much prettier than I'd originally thought her. In fact, she bordered on lovely. There was something about the way her face was trapped in a perpetual sneer when she was awake that ruined her features.

"You're staring at me," she said. Her eyes were still closed. I had no idea how she had known. "Obviously you think I'm attractive."

"I once spent an hour watching maggots crawl through the corpse of a boar," I replied. "There wasn't any aesthetic value to that; just a kind of morbid fascination."

"You are a pointlessly vicious and mean person, and when we get back, I'm going to ask my father to behead you."

"*If* we get back," and I made a point of emphasizing the conditional word, "your father will be so bloody grateful to me that he'll probably want to make me a knight."

"My father will do as I ask."

"Did you ask to remain at the castle instead of being sent away to the Faith Women?"

She looked down, giving me the answer without a vocal reply. "I want you to stop bringing that up," she said with obvious irritation.

"As you wish, Highness," I said. The Prince of Obedience, that was me.

There was a chill fog hanging over the woods, which on some level was a good thing. Anything which would make it problematic for the Harpers Bizarre to spot us from overhead weighed in our favor. On the other hand, the chill carried with it more than just a feel of early morning. I had the distinct feeling that we were experiencing a definite climatic shift . . . not surprising since we had gone so far north. As I stood, stretched my legs, and swung my arms around to restore circulation, I considered our options and didn't like what I was coming up with.

"What's wrong?" she demanded. She could obviously see the concern in my face.

"I'm worried about how far north we are," I said. "The north is renowned for its early and fearsome winters. If the cold is truly moving in . . ." I didn't finish the sentence. I didn't have to. Even the princess, still caught up in her dreams of the heroic Tacit and happy endings, had to see the danger inherent in such a situation.

"I'm hungry," she said abruptly.

Truth to tell, so was I. I looked around at the vegetation; there seemed to be some plants that appeared edible. Mushrooms and such. But then I saw something stirring in the brush nearby.

Without a moment's hesitation, I pulled my dagger from its sheath on my leg and threw it. It thudded into the brush and, a moment later, a reasonably sized rabbit tumbled out.

"Breakfast," I said.

If the princess was appalled by the notion of feasting on something as relentlessly cute as a rabbit, she gave no sign of it. Instead she sat quietly and watched as I skinned it, never averting her eyes. My estimation of her climbed ever so slightly.

But then my estimation promptly dropped off again as she said petulantly, "You have no plans to cook it?"

"I told you; I don't want to light a fire if I do not have to."

"I think," she said very deliberately, in an obvious attempt to egg me on, "that you're afraid to light it . . . because Tacit might then locate us, and you figure your life is forfeit."

"You can think whatever you wish."

"Then perhaps I'll light my own fire."

"Yes, you obviously have a great deal of experience at that. Aiming to burn down an entire forest this time?"

She glared at me once more. Endeavoring to look as nonchalant as possible, I carved a piece out of the rabbit and extended it to her. Blood was still dripping from it. She looked at it distastefully. "You first," she said, perhaps thinking that I believed the entire matter to be some sort of "dare" situation.

Shrugging, I reversed the knife and popped the piece

into my mouth. I chewed happily; not because of the taste of the raw rabbit, which was chewier than I would have liked, but from the look on the princess's face. I felt blood trickling down the side of my face. I didn't bother to wipe it off. Something in me took delight in causing her to react in disgust.

"Well? Aren't you going to build us a fire?" I said. "Using your considerable experience?" I carved off another piece.

"You really think I burned down the Faith Women's retreat, don't you."

"Yes."

She shook her head, and there was that same smirk. "What," I inquired, "are you saying you didn't?"

"I think I'd rather not tell you," she replied. "I somewhat prefer the notion that you don't know what to expect of me."

"You mean you would prefer that the person who is supposed to be your protector should be afraid to turn his back on the woman he's protecting, for fear that she's so unstable that she might knife him at the first opportunity? Oh yes, Princess, by all means, that sounds like a superb way to travel." I cut another piece. From a few feet away, the rabbit's head—which I had naturally cut off and discarded—looked at me in silent accusation. He got off lucky. At least he didn't have to put up with Entipy.

But something in her expression changed and then, very softly, she said, "Thank you."

I was caught off guard. Part of me thought that that was what she was trying to do. "For what?" I asked.

"For referring to me as a woman. I don't know that

anyone's ever done that. Even Tacit always called me his 'beautiful girl.'"

"Yes, well, I'm not Tacit," I said pointedly. "For one thing, I'm here, and he's not."

"But he will be."

I shrugged. Privately, I sure hoped that she was wrong. Because if he did show up, he wasn't going to be any too pleased with me.

Imperiously, she gestured to the rabbit's remains. "Let me try some. And wipe your mouth. It's disgusting."

I obliged by dragging a sleeve across my bloodied lips. "Change your mind?" I said. I jammed the knife into the remains of the animal's carcass, giving it a "handle" by which it could be held, and then tossed the entire thing over to her. It landed on the ground a foot away from her, and she picked it up delicately. "Sure you're up to it?"

"If you can take it, I can take it," she said defiantly. I'll say this for her: Once committed to the idea, she didn't take it in half measures. She bit forcefully into it, tearing a piece away with her teeth. She chewed it and almost managed to swallow it before she retched up the entire thing. I tried not to laugh, but was only partly successful. She glowered at me. I don't think I was particularly her favorite person in the world at that moment. Determined, she bit off another piece and actually managed to get it down. Before she could take another, her stomach revolted, and this piece exited with even greater force than the previous.

"I see how you manage to maintain your girlish figure," I observed.

"Shut up" was her weary response as she continued

to try and keep some portion of the "meal" down.

I should have felt sorry for her. Surprisingly, I even wanted to. But I didn't. Because let us be candid: If it weren't for her, none of those knights would have died, because if she hadn't been such a loon, her parents never would have sent her away in the first place.

After a few more attempts, a couple of which were actually successful, she slid the carcass off the dagger blade and tossed the dagger over to me. I would have expected that she would hurl it at my chest. Instead she simply lobbed it and it fell to the ground in a most unthreatening manner. I picked it up, cleaned it as best I could, and we started off.

I wasn't even going to try and retrace the path that the phoenix had overflown. I knew what lay in that direction: considerable forest, the remains of the Harpers Bizarre, and a revenge-driven Tacit. I had no clue as to what waited ahead, but it was the classic case of the devil you know versus the devil you do not.

Our journey passed with a minimum of conversation, which was fine by me. At least Entipy did not complain about things that couldn't be changed, such as her feet hurting or her dress being torn and snagged by the brambles and brush. I kept hoping we would stumble upon a road, which would be a sign of civilization, not to mention much easier to navigate, but none seemed forthcoming.

She had to be getting thirsty, though; I was confident of that because I was myself. Every so often I saw her licking her lips, and once I noticed that she was looking to me in a sort of hopeful manner. I, however, was too busy being a nervous wreck over our surroundings. Every time I heard the slightest rustling from around us, I worried that the Harpers had picked up the scent, or Tacit was going to come springing out at me like a great, wounded monster, or maybe the Journeymen were back, or maybe it was something else entirely that was going to have a go at us.

The sun moved overhead without seeming to have much interest in us. At one point, we came across a river, moving briskly but not particularly deep. It provided us our first fresh water in what seemed like a millennium. Entipy crouched on the edge of the bank and sipped from it, but I waded in. If she hadn't been there, I'd probably have stripped down. I'd've done it even if she was there, just to get a reaction out of her, but I was rather certain that the reaction I'd get would simply be derisive laughter and therefore saw no point to it.

I stuck my head under the water, refreshing myself. I came up, opened my mouth, drank deeply, went under again. I liked paddling around. When I was in the floating environment of water, it helped ease the frustration of my lame leg. I felt almost like a . . . there's no other way to put it . . . normal man.

I lost track of time as I enjoyed myself, feeling relaxed for the first time in ages and thinking that maybe, just maybe, things were going to work out.

I had no idea how much time had passed before I realized that she was gone.

"Entipy!" I shouted, took a step forward, fell and submerged. I splashed back to the surface and waded to the shore. Quickly I surveyed the surroundings. My staff

and sword were where I'd left them, and there was no sign of a struggle. That answered my first and most immediate worries. Apparently the brainless little twit had gone off on her own. Still, maybe it was nothing to be concerned about. She might just be going off to seek out some privacy in order to attend to nature's call.

That was when I smelled smoke.

Oh my God, she did *decide to burn down the forest* was my first panicked thought.

I clambered onto the water's edge, nostrils flaring, trying to pinpoint precisely where the smoke was coming from. It took me no more than seconds, because my sight backed up what my nose had already told me: It was coming from the north, not more than half a mile by my guess. I saw a plume of smoke wafting into the air, but even as I set off in that direction, I realized that I was not dealing with a raging fire. It was too controlled. Not only that, but I was starting to detect—ever so faintly—cooking meat. It was a fire coming from some sort of pub or tavern. Apparently my young charge had decided that that place was better than this place, and headed off without so much as whispering to me that she was leaving.

As I made my way through the forest, I began to shiver so fiercely that my teeth started to chatter. Mist was rising from my mouth. As incredible as it seemed, the temperature had dropped precipitously in the past half hour. Considering that my clothes were sodden, obviously that was something of an inconvenience. Memories of how I had fallen ill when I was subjected to varying elements upon my arrival at the castle flooded back to me. I had no desire for a repeat performance, for

I have little doubt that I wouldn't get off quite as lucky should such a thing recur. Naturally, though, I had left my cloak behind when I'd gone in, so it was bone dry. I drew it more tightly around myself, my breath coming in ragged and cloudy gasps.

The woods were thinning out, and I realized that the smoke had inadvertently brought me to the place that I'd been seeking all along: the outside of the forest. I drew closer and was able to make out the structure that was the origin of the smoke. It was belching out of a chimney, situated on top of a building that was rather unremarkable. In many ways it reminded me of the pub in which I grew up, and for an instant I felt a sudden surge of horror. What if, through insane happenstance, I had wound up right back at Stroker's somehow? I didn't know for sure where I was, but I would have bet that it was a geographical impossibility that I could have wound up there. But then cold reason (along with cold air, which seemed to have dropped even more in the last seconds) took hold. Stroker's and my old life were miles away. It was simply that such roadside places were somewhat generic in their construction.

I saw a sign hanging off the edge, swaying in the stiff wind that was cutting through the air. I caught the name of the place as it swung. Apparently I was about to visit the Forest's Edge Pub and Inn. Considering the place was at the edge of a forest, I wondered how many long minutes it had taken the genius who'd named the place to come up with that one.

There were other structures as well. Weapons shops, a butcher, weapons shops, a baker, weapons shops. As you might surmise, the abundance of weapons shops left me a bit concerned that we had wandered into a territory that was less than friendly. People were wandering about on their errands, dressed in heavy and ragged furs, barely nodding to one another as they passed. They were far more interested in dealing with whatever business they had to attend to than engaging in social niceties. Apparently all social congress was reserved for the inn, from wherein I heard rough and raucous laughter. It seemed a bit early in the day for drunken revelry, and that indicated two possibilities to me. Either the people hereabouts were hard and heavy drinkers . . . or else they had found something that was particularly hilarious to engage their attention.

I had the sick feeling that I knew exactly what that source of hilarity might be, especially when my sharp ears were able to detect a raised female voice. My every instinct told me that the only intelligent thing to do was turn around and get the hell out of here, and leave the little fool to whatever situation she'd gotten herself in. But I had gone too far, had thrown far too much of what I laughingly referred to as my self-esteem into the bargain. Like it or not, I was committed to getting her home.

A notice was tacked up on the door that said HELP WANTED. I made a mental note of it as I opened the door to the inn carefully. The noise from within practically blasted me back. I saw therein the scene that I had suspected I was going to see. There was Princess Entipy, standing in the middle of the inn, and assorted roughhewn men were at their various tables, laughing their collective asses off. Entipy was trying to talk above them, but they were chortling so loudly that it was difficult to make out anything she was saying. The only person in the pub not laughing was a heavyset woman behind the bar. She had a glare as hard as coal, and a heart to match by the look of her surly face. She was cleaning a mug and seemed most unamused by the proceedings.

"This is the last time I'm going to say this," Entipy fairly shouted, her fists clenched and quivering with barely restrained anger. "We want you to bring a commweaver to us immediately. It is a matter of utmost urgency! And we require your best accommodations while we wait for the weaver to be brought." Since she'd entered without me, I could only assume that she had reverted to using the royal "we." Unsurprisingly, the men—about a dozen in all—didn't seem the least bit stirred to action by her demands.

"All right, girl," the woman from behind the bar called. She walked around it carrying a mug in either hand and set it down near two behemoths at the table nearest Entipy. "Enough foolishness for one day."

"Our commands are not foolishness," shot back Entipy. "Do you have any idea who we are?"

I started to move across the tavern as quickly as I could at that point, but several men got up at that ill-timed moment, pushing back their chairs, and I was temporarily blocked.

One of the behemoths looked up at her in amusement. "Who are we?" he asked, the phrasing of his question alone getting peals of laughter from his companions and the others in the tavern.

"We are royalty!" Entipy informed him.

"What you are is a royal pain," said the bartender/server. "Now get you gone."

"Ohhhh, Marie, don't be so hard on the girl," the behemoth said. "She's a comely thing, and might provide passing amusement. I've never had royalty before." And he drew back a hand and slapped Entipy on the rump. The smack was resounding and there was more laughter.

Entipy did not hesitate. She grabbed up the mug of ale that had just been set down and hurled the contents into the behemoth's face. It hit him square on, the contents cascading all over his face, down his thick, bristling beard, and down into his breeches.

Oh, my gods, we're dead, I thought, and even as I did, the words *What do you mean "we"?* came to mind.

The behemoth started to rise, letting out a grunt of anger. Entipy windmilled her arm around, still holding the solid metal mug, and slammed it into the top of his head, knocking him back off the chair and sending him tumbling to the floor with a crash.

I would have thought a roar of fury would have arisen as a result, but we had a small fragment of luck, because the sequence of events instead struck the rough men as remarkably funny. In retrospect, I can see why: This slip of a girl comes in, tosses orders about, and when a man twice her size and three times her width takes liberties with her, she promptly gives him what-for.

The victim of her attack, however, clearly failed to see the humor of the situation. He was on his feet, towering over her. If she'd tried to swing the mug at his head she would have missed.

"Let's try that again," he snarled.

"Simon!" snapped the bartender, whom he'd addressed as "Marie." "She's not worth wasting time on! She can't hurt you—"

The words had barely left her mouth when Entipy swung the mug again. This time she was aiming at his crotch. Not a bad change in tactics, except he was ready for her and caught her by the forearm. She let out a screech of rage as he shook the mug loose from her grip, and it was at that moment that I started seriously considering backing out the door and distancing myself from the whole mess. Naturally that was the moment that her gaze fell upon me.

"Apropos!" she shouted. "You are my protector! Protect me!"

All eyes turned to me, and never had I wanted to be someone else, anywhere else, as I did at that moment. I was hoping to get out of the situation on the strength of my not inconsiderable charm. I waved. They seemed determinedly uncharmed.

My mind racing for inspiration, it nearly froze up as the gargantuan Simon took a step toward me, bristling with fury. Suddenly, inspiration seized me. Ignoring the staff in my hand and the sword strapped to my back, instead I grabbed a long spoon off the table next to me, dropped my voice to as deep a level as I could, and bellowed in a purely comic style, "I'll save you, my lady! I, your valiant knight, am here!"

Well, naturally I looked nothing like a knight. Wild-haired, sopping wet, lame of leg, I came across as much like a knight (or a hero, for that matter) as Entipy did a princess. I continued to advance, waving the spoon as if it were the most lethal blade in the land, and declaring, "I am coming, Your Highness! Ho, varlet! Knave! Wretch! Have at thee! Ha! Yah! And yah again!" I stomped on the floor and thrust forward again, maneuvering around Simon, who was simply staring at me, stunned, since I offered about as much practical threat as a pile of leaves. I heard some initial chuckling from nearby, which was exactly what I was hoping for. I got to Entipy, grabbed her by the wrist, and swung her unceremoniously behind me.

"What are you doing?!" she whispered sharply in my ear.

Simon was still watching me, and the laughter was starting to build. Marie, the bartender, still looked suspicious.

I grabbed her by the back of the head and brought her ear to my mouth. I spoke very quietly and very quickly. "Now listen to me, you little git," I whispered right back. "I've got one blade and I count a dozen in potential opposition . . . plus Simon here could kill me bare-handed. The only way we get out of this alive is pretend we're playacting, and if you don't go along with this, we're dead. We've one chance at this; don't muck it up," and with that I raised my voice and cried out again, "One side, varlet, for a princess of the realm! Hah! Double hah!"

For just a moment, Entipy's instinct for arrogance warred with her interest in self-preservation, and suddenly she cried out, "Ha! Arrogant knaves! Now thou shalt know the wrath of my true man-at-arms!"

Pushing it as far as I could, I lunged and jammed the spoon against Simon's massive chest. I made a mental note of the fact that it was like pushing against a stone wall, but simply acting as if I'd scored a hit, I shouted, "Ha! He is down! Let no one else muck with a knight and his lady!"

Simon still didn't make a move against us. He had never seen any display quite like it. In this manner, we "hacked" our way through the crowd, shouting and making as much brouhaha as we humanly could. Laughter began to build, feed upon itself, and I heard people saying "They're mad!" and others countering with "No, don't you get it? They're performing fools!" In reality, it might well have been a bit of both.

We made it all the way to the door, and I threw it open.

Snow was falling.

I don't mean some light, gentle display; it was cascading, a solid white wall, coming down fast and furious. A fearsome wind was cutting through it. Snow was already accumulating at a horrifyingly rapid rate. If we went out into that, we'd be dead in no time.

Without even a second's hesitation, I slammed the door back, turned and threw my arms wide so quickly that I almost smacked Entipy in the face in doing so. "My good friends!" I shouted, dropping the bombast, "we are the Royal Players! Let us have a round of applause for Simon, who's been a terrific sport! Simon, take a bow!" and I limped toward him, grabbed his hand, and raised it up.

There followed thunderous clapping from all around. The confusion slowly seeped from Simon's mien, to be replaced by an appreciative smile and a chuckle as if he was in on the "joke" the entire time. I grabbed up a napkin and helped him dry himself off, saying "Well done!" the entire time.

Entipy was glaring at me. I couldn't have cared less. My concern was our survival, not winning her approval. And I could only assume that she shared that sentiment to some degree, because although she was glowering, she was doing nothing to pierce the veil of our little charade.

The crowning touch was Simon buying us two mugs of mead and treating us as if we were his new best friends. As astounding a development as that was, on some level I could almost understand it. Men like Simon didn't exactly get a great deal of acclaim, so a roomful of people singing his praises for a job well done was heady stuff for him.

The mead felt terrific going down, suffusing me with inner warmth while the fire I huddled near helped to dry out my clothes. Entipy sat a few feet away. She was gulping the mead down. Say what you will about her; at least she could hold her liquor. She was not, however, giving me any favoring looks. That didn't bother me.

A shadow loomed over me. For one frightening moment I thought it was Simon, thinking better of his generosity and moment in the sun, and deciding instead that what we really needed was a good pummeling. But I looked up and saw instead that it was Marie. She pulled a barrel over and sat upon it, bringing us to eye level.

"I'm not so certain that you're traveling players, no matter what you've convinced these fools of," she said in a low voice. "I saw the prideful haughtiness in her eyes, and the panic in yours when she looked to you. No one walking this planet is that good an actor. Whatever you are, you disrupted my customers and put my place at risk of having a brawl." I noted the words "my place." So she wasn't just an employee; she was the actual pub owner. "I'm not going to bring that to their attention because it might prompt the very thing I want to avoid," she continued. "But I want you out of here, immediately."

"It's snowing, madam," I said, "and rather fiercely. We'll surely die . . ."

"That is of no consequence to me."

At that moment, Simon, our most unlikely benefactor, raised a mug and called out, "To our players!"

"Our players!" echoed the others.

Someone else shouted, "And to our Marie!"

"Marie!" came the call. She bobbed her head in acknowledgment, forcing a smile so that she could get back to the business of preparing to send us out to our deaths.

And then a third man shouted, "To our noble liege, the dreaded Warlord Shank!"

"To Warlord Shank!" came the call.

If I hadn't been cold before, I froze then.

Warlord Shank. The lord of the so-called Outer Lawless regions, who had risen against King Runcible and been driven back, but only at great cost.

I glanced at Entipy, but there was no registering of recognition in her face. The name meant nothing to her. No reason it should have, since Shank's incursion and the subsequent war had happened long after she'd been shunted away to the Faith Women and sheltered from news of the outside world. But it meant more than enough to me for the both of us. As incredible as it seemed, we had actually had a major stroke of luck. If these men were loyal to Shank, the acquisition of Runcible's daughter would have been invaluable. Shank could have blackmailed the monarch into practically anything. Either that or the king would have told them to go ahead and kill her, for which I wouldn't entirely have blamed him, except that it would have meant my demise as well (since she was quick to finger me as her "protector").

"So . . . this would be the Outer Lawless regions, then," I said slowly.

Marie looked at me oddly. "Know you not where you are?"

"We . . . became separated from our troupe, and have been somewhat lost recently," I said. "I wasn't quite certain. And if this is the Outer Lawless regions . . . then what I saw outside would be the start of the famed Outer Lawless winter . . . ?"

She nodded, grimacing in a resigned manner. She didn't seem any more enthused about it than I. "Seems more intense this year. Earlier. But that would be it, yes."

Well, we were well and truly screwed. When snow was dumped in the Outer Lawless regions, it came fast and fierce, and then it stayed. The natives of the land managed to get around on the snow-sodden roads, but neither Entipy nor I were natives. Nor did we have the requisite furs, snowshoes, or boots, or any sort of survival equipment. There was simply no way that we would manage to get any significant distance. We were, in effect, stuck there. Except the "there" wasn't being particularly hospitable.

"A commweaver," I said with growing urgency. "Do you know where there is one?"

"Down the road, straight east, about twenty miles. She serves the various nobles and feudal lords. Goes by the name of Dotty, which is apt enough since she is a bit dotty. But she's been around forever; so long that folks hereabouts sometimes call her 'Ma Spell.' Charges a pretty sum for her services, from what I hear."

With the snow on the ground, twenty miles might as well have been twenty hundred. Walking wasn't an option. I would have not hesitated to steal a beast to carry us, but even if we got there, the situation was exactly as I thought: Such weavers charged mightily for their services, and we didn't have two sovs to rub together.

Our predicament didn't garner a scintilla of pity from the hard-eyed Marie. "Now, as I was saying, out you go . . . unless you've money to pay for food or lodgings, which I strongly suspect you don't, since you didn't even have the brains to go around and solicit money for your 'performance' . . ."

I kicked myself mentally. I'd been so relieved that we were alive that I had missed an opportunity for profit. I was losing my touch. Inspired, I said, "We could stay here, be players in residence—"

"Dump alcohol on my patrons? Pick fights on a regular basis? And how long before I wind up the worse for it." She snorted disdainfully at the thought.

I remembered the sign on the door. "You need help. I know taverns. I grew up in one." The truth out of my mouth; God, I really was losing my touch.

"I don't need you two. Her, in particular."

I looked in Entipy's direction once more. She had downed the contents of the mug and was wavering slightly from side to side. I felt one good push would send her tumbling to the floor. "She is something of an annoyance, I'll admit . . ."

"I'll say," she grumbled. Nothing brings commiseration like mutual resentment for others. "A regular prima donna, right? So used to playing noblewomen that she thinks she excretes gold."

"Actresses," I sighed. "What can you do with them?"

"I know what I'd like to do with one of them."

My eyes narrowed and I leaned forward conspiratorially. "And just think what you could do . . . with one in your employ. Lugging water. Cleaning tables. Hauling garbage. Slinging ale."

Marie looked at me thoughtfully and then at Entipy. A slow smile spread across her face. It looked rather odd there, as if it was an infrequent visitor and had no idea what to do having arrived. "You are a schemer, aren't you," she said.

"I have my moments."

She chewed on her doughy lip as she gave the matter some thought. Outside the wind was starting to howl. The prospect of stumbling out into that was not one that I relished.

"Very well. The both of you, then, but I'll pay you as one and feed you as one. And if she so much as drips a drop of ale or mead on one of my customers, by accident much less in a fit of pique, then out you both go. Understood?"

I bobbed my head eagerly, relieved.

"There's a storage room in the back that the two of you can use for sleeping."

"The . . . two of us . . ."

She looked at me oddly. "I assume that you two are lovers. I mean, no man in his right mind would stay with her, so I conclude that you are besotted with ardor and therefore not thinking clearly."

"Why would I be in love with her?"

At that she laughed, and it was not a kind noise. "If there's one thing I've learned, it's never to wonder why men do the things they do."

"Very wise," I said diplomatically.

She looked me up and down. "You've only the things on your back?" I nodded. "There's old clothes you can change into in the storage room as well. Clothes I've taken off the backs of patrons who tried to run out on their bills. Some of them should fit. Get changed and get to work. No time like the present." She rose and waddled off to the bar.

"Are you out of your mind?! You are! You're out of your mind!"

We were standing in the back room. The shelves were piled with assorted supplies, including the aforementioned clothes, plus mugs, plates, cleaning implements, and other things. Entipy was making clear to me that she was less than enthused with the bargain I had struck. "Me! Entipy, Princess of Isteria, a serving wench!"

"Keep your voice down!" I whispered.

"I will not keep my voice down! I am a princess of Isteria, and I—!"

She got no further because I grabbed her, shoved her against the wall with a thud and clapped my hand over her mouth. Several mugs clattered to the floor, but that was the least of my problems. My major difficulty was that Entipy, not taking particularly well to being ham-handedly shushed, was biting down hard on the fleshy part of the hand covering her mouth. I fought back a pained shriek.

"Before you force me to release your mouth and get us both killed, listen to me!" I said between gritted teeth. "You heard them swear fealty to Warlord Shank! He warred with your father and would like nothing better than to get his hands on your father's little girl! Declare your identity to all and sundry and you as good as bring down your father's kingdom! Does that matter to you at all?"

She shook her head furiously and bit down harder. I grunted deep in my throat.

"And while he's holding you prisoner," I managed to say, my voice jumping higher in pain, "he will keep you in a deep, dank dungeon that will make this place look luxurious in comparison, and subject you to all manner of torture. And if and when your beloved Tacit comes to save you, you'll be a blind, tongue-seared, disfigured thing barely recognizable as yourself, that Tacit would just as soon kill to put out of your misery as love you. Is that what you want? Because if it is, keep biting my hand, I'll release it, you convince these bravos of your identity, and that is what will happen to you!"

She stopped biting me. She glared at me poisonously, but she stopped biting.

"*We have* . . . no . . . *choice,*" I said, my hand still stinging. "And we are damned lucky besides. If they had believed you were more than a loon, you'd be on your way to a dungeon. If they had tossed us out into the snow, you'd be on your way to oblivion. This way we have shelter, clothes on our backs, some degree of sustenance, and, most important, a means of earning money so that we can go to this 'Dotty' and have her convey a message to your lord father. This is not only our best chance, it is our *only* chance. I wouldn't give us a hope of lasting an hour in that snow, and with the gods dropping this opportunity in our laps, they might not be so generous if we throw it back at them. Now . . . can I safely remove my hand with the confidence that you won't send us spiraling to perdition?"

She didn't nod, just continued to scowl. But I took that as consent and slowly—timidly—I removed my hand. She pushed me away roughly and I stepped back.

"You expect me," she said very slowly, in an affronted tone, "to earn money by working for it?"

"Believe it or not, Highness, the vast majority of the world has very little problem with the concept. The Faith Women had you working, and there was no money involved. Think of this as a step up in your fortunes."

"This is not just . . . not equitable . . . not right . . ."

And I lost myself.

Looking back, it's difficult to believe that I reacted the way that I did. I advanced on her. She did not take so much as a single step back but instead stood her ground, and I snarled in her face. "Not right? *Not right?* I was born with nothing, the product of my mother being brutally raped! She sold her body to make ends meet and keep us with a roof over our head, and when a passing brute murdered her for sport, the worth of her life was reduced to a handful of coins by your father's court! *Work?* I've worked since before I could walk, which I was never able to do properly anyway! I've scraped for every sov I've ever held, only to see it taken away from me by the first and only woman I've ever let myself feel anything for. I've never known anything resembling rightness or justice in my entire life, so don't you *dare* stand there and complain to me about what's right, *do you understand me? Do you?*"

She made no response. I didn't expect her to. I turned away from her, flushed and humiliated that so much had come spilling from my mouth, and only relieved that I had not—in the heat of emotions—said even more than I should have.

"How are we supposed to share this room?" she asked.

It was such a mundane concern that I was surprised she even asked. I glanced around. "It's not large, but we'll both fit."

"I don't permit it," she said.

"I don't care," I replied, suddenly feeling drained.

She opened her mouth, then closed it, considering. "If . . . I let you reside in here as my bodyguard . . . you will not—"

"Try something untoward?" I guffawed at the notion. "Highness, with all respect . . . I wouldn't touch you with a ten-foot staff."

She was silent for a moment, and then said, "Oh." That's all. Just "Oh."

I wasn't quite sure what to make of that.

Chapter 17

I have never so desperately wanted to take joy in another person's misfortune before, and I have never been so miserably thwarted as I was during those long months at the Forest's Edge Inn.

Most of my time was spent washing dishes or doing relatively benign menial work. For some strange reason, Marie actually seemed to take a liking to me, which I found disconcerting enough. But her dislike for Entipy only intensified and, I have to say, it certainly wasn't because of anything that Entipy was doing. In fact, it might have been because of what Entipy wasn't doing. To be specific, she wasn't complaining.

The princess, for all her . . . princessiness . . . was also apparently something of a realist. I had expected, as had Marie apparently, that day after day Entipy would find something new to complain about. That she would lash out at customers, or snarl at them or in some way do something that would wind up getting her kicked out into the nearest snowbank. We were, however, both destined to be disappointed. Marie bore down on Entipy, working her as hard as she could.

And Entipy said nothing.

I don't mean that she didn't complain, or was reticent. I mean that, from daylight to nightfall, she didn't speak. She would move from customer to customer and take orders without comment. She was able to write the orders down to keep track of them, which made her something of a curiosity considering that most tavern wenches depended upon their memory and repeating the orders back to get it in their heads.

And it's not as if the men were gentle with her. They would shout at her, or speak in "gentle" tones laced with the crudest words and suggestions they could come up with. They would slap her on the backside, pinch her on the cheek, haul her onto their laps as if she were a child's plaything, and laugh as she struggled free.

All through it, she spoke not a word.

I watched all this, and every so often she would glance my way, but I couldn't quite tell if she was genuinely seeing me or not. It was as if she had withdrawn into herself. Either that or she reasoned—probably quite correctly—that if she traded words with them, matters might escalate. As it was, assorted customers would invariably find it a challenge to get her to say something, and then become irritated when their endeavors met with lack of success. Sometimes they became surly or belligerent over it, but invariably they'd just grow bored and mutter amongst themselves.

Entipy's muteness annoyed Marie no end. "You're supposed to make the customers feel at home! That way they'll drink more," Marie had told her one time.

It wasn't as if Entipy *never* spoke. On rare occasions she voiced her opinions, and this was one of those times. "Engaging me in small talk takes up time," Entipy had replied in a monotone, speaking as a woman already dead. "By eliminating that wasted time, it leaves them only to occupy themselves by drinking." I overheard that particular conversation, and had to admit that she had a valid enough point.

Still . . .

. . . it disturbed me. It disturbed me because I had no idea what was going through her head. That should be enough to be of concern to just about any man who valued keeping his skin intact.

She did not speak to me. I think she was disappointed in me. Either that or she was disappointed that Tacit had not yet mysteriously arrived to rescue her from the life of drudgery. In any event, she looked to me less and less as time went on, until the cuffs and abuse she received at the hands of the customers didn't prompt her even to glance momentarily in my direction. She had given up any hope, apparently, that I would be of any use to her as a protector. Part of me was relieved in this. Part of me . . . wasn't.

Marie worked her all the harder, extending her hours and paying us as minimally as possible, and even taking out an unfair percentage from our wages to accommodate the lodgings she had provided and the food we ate. Considering our "lodgings" consisted of a half-empty storage closet, and the food we ate was invariably either leftovers or food of insufficient quality to sell to the guests, the money being apportioned from us was definitely not on par with what we were receiving.

And Entipy continued to bear up under it. I kept wondering if she was like a volcano, momentarily corked. Such efforts are naturally stopgap, and will blow sky high given sufficient time and provocation. I hoped I would not be around when the blowup finally occurred.

Every night we shared that cramped room. I would always wrap myself in a blanket so as not to risk coming into any sort of physical contact with Her Worship. And, suspecting I knew what form her vengeance would take, I always said the exact same thing before going to sleep:

"Thank you for not burning the pub down."

She never said anything. Night after night, month after month, not a word.

The princess became thinner, and I would have thought that such a thing would have made her look nearly skeletal. But I was wrong. Her chin became sharply rounded, her cheekbones more angular. And through it all, she continued to carry herself with something that I can only call quiet dignity.

I did not want to admire her. Absolutely did not. And I certainly didn't want to pity her. I wanted to feel nothing about her or for her. Unfortunately, the world does not always act in a manner consistent with one's plans for it.

Matters came to an unexpected turn one night that was particularly bitter cold, although the calendar claimed that the winter was approaching its end. It was the usual raucous crowd in the tavern, and there was one man in particular who seemed to be more annoying than anyone else. He was a burly man with an eyepatch. Indeed, when he'd first walked in, I'd had a momentary flash of panic when I saw the patch because I thought it was Tacit, but an instant later I relaxed as the rest of the bruiser followed his head into the pub. His name, so I heard people shout in greeting, was "Ripper," although I presume that to be his nickname. He had a large, curved blade hanging from his belt, which seemed to indicate that he took the name rather seriously.

I saw Marie stiffen when he came in, and that alone should have tipped me there was going to be trouble, since Marie was normally the unflappable sort. Ripper was a trapper; I could tell because of the mountain of furs he had tucked over one shoulder that he was likely taking to sell somewhere. Trappers have that certain arrogance that is usually possessed by those who are self-congratulatory about making a living outsmarting creatures with brains the size of walnuts. He swaggered to the middle of the room, flopped down at a table with men of a similar ilk, and ordered up ale in a loud voice.

Entipy, as was her custom, remained silent. She was new to Ripper, though, and he seemed hell-bent on getting a response out of her. He cajoled, he laughed, he poked and prodded, and Entipy took it all. Every so often she would glower at him, but nothing beyond that. Ripper became more and more impatient with her, but whereas others had simply gotten bored, he became even more abusive. He groped at her, fondled her, tried to get her to yelp or curse or do *something*. Still she was close-mouthed. It was as if she didn't trust herself to speak; that if she opened her mouth, she knew that something would come tumbling out of it that would tag her for who she was, and result in an extremely unpleasant series of events.

I was washing a skillet back in the kitchen, a big, heavy iron pan. But as the noises became louder and louder, I peered through the door and watched the scene unfolding. I watched him try to grab a fistful of her breast and, when she turned away too quickly for him to succeed, he grabbed her ass through her dress. She shoved his hand away, and even Marie seemed put out with him as she shouted, "Ripper!"

"No interest in keeping customers happy?" he called out.

And all I could think of was that this was the kind of lout who had harassed my mother all those years. I had witnessed men treating her in such a manner for so long that in my childhood innocence I had thought of it as normal, even acceptable. But I felt the rage starting to build in me, the sense of possessiveness. Perhaps it was motivated by the outraged child I harbored in my bosom, or perhaps the months of being stuck in this place had simply driven me mad with cabin fever. But a brute like this one had taken Madelyne from me, the only person who'd ever really cared about me. The only thing that was genuinely "mine." Entipy was quite a different animal. She wasn't mine, nor did I want her, because I didn't trust for a second the dark brain that dwelt behind those darker eyes. She was mine, though, in the sense that she represented my ticket to fame and riches, provided I could get her back to her father, the king, in one piece.

Was I worried that Ripper would kill her, as a ruffian had taken Madelyne's life? I wasn't sure. I knew that it could lead down that path if left unchecked. And besides . . . he was starting to aggravate the hell out of me. This thuggery, this loutishness . . . I'd seen it for so long, tolerated it for so long, and my tolerance level was dwindling.

And then Ripper grabbed the hem of Entipy's skirt, raised it, and shoved his hand right up it. Involuntary as it might have been, it got him what he'd been seeking: a yelp of protest from the girl as he groped with his rough hands around her privates.

I didn't give myself time to think it through, because if I did, the odds were that I would have thought better of it. I strode (well, limped briskly) from the kitchen, the skillet at my side. Ripper didn't see me coming, because he was distracted, and I instantly saw why. Entipy had whirled to face him, her lips constricted in a rictus of fury, and her fingers curved into what could only be described as claws. She was clearly ready to leap at him and tear the skin off his face. Had I just been emerging from the kitchen at that point, I probably would have stopped and watched her go at him, placing even odds on her. But I was too caught up in the fever pitch of the moment to think rationally.

I pushed through the laughing throng, blood pounding so loudly in my ears that I barely heard any of it, and just before Entipy made her move, I grabbed Ripper's eyepatch from behind and shoved it. The patch slid over his good eye, leaving him momentarily blinded.

Ripper let out a startled yell, his head snapping around

instinctively. There was a blackened hole where an eye had once resided. He reached up to clear the patch from his good eye so that he could see what was going on, and I swung the skillet as hard as I could. The bottom of the skillet slammed into his face, and I heard a satisfying crunch of bone. The skillet made a "clonging" sound as if it were metal striking metal. I drew the skillet back only far enough to get enough of an arc, and I saw blood fountaining down his confused face, and then I hit him again. And again. And again. I didn't give him so much as a moment to compose himself or launch a counterattack. I must have been some sight. My red hair, grown long and uncut, my red beard having grown in somewhat dark since I'd stopped shaving, my eyes wild and furious, seeing the abuses heaped upon my mother and my helplessness to stop them, all incarnated in this one oaf whom I was pummeling with a kitchen utensil.

Ripper tumbled off his chair, tried to sit up, and I hit him as hard as I humanly could on the back of the head. He had never managed to get the eyepatch clear, so I have no idea whether his eye rolled up into the top of his head. But he slumped forward, unmoving.

There was a stunned silence in the bar. I didn't so much as glance in Entipy's direction as I reached down, grabbed Ripper firmly by the back of his shirt, and dragged him toward the door. It goes to show how stupid I was: I didn't care just then what Marie did, or whether she threw us out into the snow. For one moment, one fleeting moment, I had some measure of satisfaction in my life, and it felt damned good.

I threw open the door. Cold air blasted in so forcefully that the still-stunned patrons shivered and huddled against it, and then I sent Ripper's unconscious body rolling off into the snow. I shoved the door closed, which was no mean feat considering the force of the wind pushing against it. I took a few steps forward and saw Marie standing behind the bar, watching me impassively. I looked in Entipy's direction to see what she was doing, but she was just standing there, silent as the tomb, inscrutable. Her fingers were still curled into claws.

The door suddenly burst open and Ripper was there, in the doorway, bruises already swelling on his face. He had his curved blade in his hand, and I mentally cursed myself for not having taken it off him when I'd had the chance. I faced him, not moving from where I stood. Of course I didn't move; the thunderous rush of energy that had prompted me to intercede in the first place had deserted me, and now I was rooted to the spot in absolute terror.

"You little bastard!" howled Ripper, not knowing how apt the description was. A skillet wasn't going to do me a bit of good against an infuriated brute with a blade. I braced myself, wondering in an oblique manner what it was going to feel like to be gutted like a fish, and then a crossbow bolt thudded into the door, not half an inch from Ripper's head. He froze and turned toward the bar.

Marie was standing there, cradling a crossbow as if she'd been born with one. There was another bolt already loaded into it. "Leave, Ripper," she said quietly. "You're banned for six months. If I see you come in here again, I don't miss again. Clear?"

He stared at her sullenly, like a great animal knowing

that it was caught. Then, without a further word, he turned and walked back out into the snow, pulling the door shut behind him.

No one said anything for a time. We simply stood there in a frozen tableau, and then Marie said, "Apropos . . . may I speak to you, please." She lowered the crossbow, storing it behind the bar where apparently she kept it for times of emergency, and headed into the kitchen. I followed her, still clutching the skillet, listening to a rising buzz of voices as the remaining patrons talked among themselves, casting glances toward me as I passed them. I looked in Entipy's direction, but she was looking away from me. All the while I was silently berating myself. I had acted on foolish impulse and it was going to cost us. Not only were we going to lose our lodgings, but Ripper would likely be out there in the snow waiting for us. We were going to be dead before the next sunrise, all because I had forgotten my credo and thrust myself into harm's way. Well, if I was so stupid as to do that, maybe I deserved what was coming.

I stepped into the kitchen. Marie was waiting for me. She pulled me forward and kissed me on the cheek. I gaped at her.

"Ripper used to be my husband," she said. "He dumped me with this bar and a mountain of debt and went off to be a trapper and dally with young and good-looking wenches . . . which I used to be one of, believe it or not. Thank you for rearranging his face. He deserved it."

"You're . . . you're welcome," I said in surprise. I couldn't quite believe it. I kept waiting for some sort of follow-up that would bring my momentary sense of elation crashing down.

What she said next didn't do that at all. "How would you like to earn some serious money?" she said. "Beyond the pittance I can afford to pay you."

My first impulse was to point out that the reason it was a pittance was because she kept extracting sizable portions of it, but for once my brain outraced my tongue. Instead I said, "Will it be enough to pay a commweaver?"

"Probably not, but it will bring you a lot closer."

"Will I have to kill anyone?"

She laughed coarsely at that. "No. No, it's a serving job, actually. Helping to cater a rather lush banquet being sponsored by one of the nobility. They're a bit short on staff help, you see, and the word's gone out to all tavern and pub owners in a thirty-mile radius to send whatever help they can. Job pays nine sovs a head. If both you and your woman go, that's eighteen. It'll leave me shorthanded for an evening, but I can manage. It's the least I can do," and she half-smiled, "just for the joy of seeing Ripper's nose mashed somewhere into the back of his head."

I couldn't believe it was happening. Genuine luck was being tossed my way. I, who was the foremost advocate of the philosophy that no good deed goes unpunished, was actually benefiting from stepping in to help someone else, even though my motives were purely for my self-satisfaction. "All right . . . all right, definitely, yes," I said. "Definitely, I'm in. When and where is it, and what's the occasion?"

"It's a week from Sunday, at the castle of the dreaded Warlord Shank."

I felt my throat close up. "It . . . is?"

"Yes. It appears our beloved Warlord is preparing to take himself a bride, and he is throwing a gathering for all the local nobles to introduce her. The Countess of Pince-Nez, I think her name is."

"How . . . nice," I managed to say. "Although I'm . . . a bit surprised. You'd think that someone of the, uhm, warlord's stature . . . wouldn't be wanting for staff."

"Well, he does have a tendency to kill those whom he finds wanting, so he can be a little shorthanded at times."

"We can't pass it up," said Entipy.

We had retired for the night to the wretched little storage room that we shared, and I was staring at her, goggle-eyed, in the dimness. "Are you insane?" I demanded, and then reminded myself that I knew the answer to that one already. "Walk straight into the den of our enemy?"

"My father's enemy, not mine," she reminded him. "He doesn't know me, or you. We'll be perfectly safe. And the money is too good to pass up. Eighteen sovs is almost halfway to a duke."

"I don't care if it's almost halfway to a king. The risk is—"

"The risk is minimal," Entipy said, "and worth it. I'm going. Whether you go or not is entirely your own affair. But consider that there's an element of risk the longer we stay here. The sooner we get back home, the better, and eighteen sovs will get us there sooner than later."

I glared at her. "I liked you better when you weren't talking."

"Yes, I'm sure you did. So will you go with me?"

I let out a long, exasperated sigh. "It's madness . . . but all right. Just, for pity's sake, keep your head down, don't look anyone in the eye, and stay out of trouble."

She nodded, and lay back on the blankets spread on the hard floor. As always, I positioned myself as far from her as I could.

And then she said something that made my blood run cold.

"You could move closer, if you want."

Oh dear heaven, I thought, *the last thing I want is for her to form an attachment to me.* Out loud, I said, "I'm . . . fine right here."

"Very well," she said, her voice sounding a bit chillier, which was just fine by me. I had no interest in upsetting the status quo between us.

As was my custom, I said, "Good night. Thank you for not burning the pub down."

Every night that remark had been met with silence. Tonight, however, she replied, "You're welcome." And before I could say anything else, she added, "And thank you for handling that . . . man. I would have done it, you know. I was going to . . ."

"Yes, I know. And you probably could have."

"Thank you. But what you did . . . it was very brave."

"Is that what it was?" was my only response. I guess it really had been brave . . . because it was so bugger-all stupid, and if there was one thing I'd come to realize, it was that bravery and bugger-all stupidity went hand in hand.

Chapter 18

I stood over the corpse of the fallen dreaded Warlord Shank, a bloody sword in one hand and his head—still dripping from the severed neck—in my other. "That," I crowed, "is what happens to the enemies of King Runcible of Isteria!"

Everyone in the great room gasped in amazement and fled before my burgeoning wrath. The only one left there was Entipy, who made loud fluttery noises about how wonderful I was. Then the phoenix flew in through the window, its great wings stirring the tapestries on the wall and knocking over candlesticks and flowery ornaments before settling down in front of us. Then we climbed on its back and flew home.

It was a very pleasant dream, and one that I awoke to with startling regularity over the next several days. I wondered if my "destiny" was calling to me, but then came to my senses and decided that it was insanity tempting me instead. There was absolutely no way that I was going to stick my neck out at the banquet and make some sort of strike against the warlord. First, the odds were that I would fail. Second, if I did succeed, I'd never make it out alive. And third . . .

Well, there wasn't a third, really. I hadn't seen much point in dwelling on it beyond that.

I did feel the need to caution Entipy, somewhere in the neighborhood of a hundred times, that we had to be as cautious as possible. Just because we had agreed there was risk involved, that didn't mean we couldn't find ways to minimize that risk.

"You may hear them say things about your father," I warned her, "or your mother. Or even about you. Insulting things, false things. It's not uncommon for people who are celebrating to curse the names of their enemies, since it's something they all agree upon and it gives them a degree of satisfaction that they can 'get away' with it since the person being discussed isn't present."

"I know," she said.

I continued as if she hadn't spoken. "You cannot let anyone notice that this bothers you in any way, shape, or form. It will attract attention, and that would be bad. Not bad as in inconvenient, or naughty, but bad as in fatal."

"I know," she repeated more forcefully. "Apropos, of the two things in this world that I do not care about the most, the first is my parents, and the second is what people say about them. As for what they might say about me—they don't know me. And even if they did, well . . ." She shrugged. "What do they matter?"

It seemed a fairly positive attitude to take. I could only hope that she abided by it.

The only other thing that made me nervous, as I'm

sure you can surmise, was the comment about how the warlord tended to dismiss members of his staff rather permanently. Still, if I managed to keep my head low and not dispatch a guest with a skillet, I had no fear that I could avoid any serious problems. I only hoped that Entipy could be counted on to do the same. She was basically something of a wildblade, and having such a person guarding one's back is more than enough to make one very, very edgy.

Marie's disposition had improved not only toward me, but also toward Entipy. The princess maintained her usual reticence around the pub, but Marie eased up on her somewhat as well . . . probably because she believed that Entipy and I were lovers and therefore the new air of courtesy she was affording me extended to the princess. To that end, on the Sunday of the job, she even lent us a Heffer . . . an extremely long-haired horse that was specially bred for the harsh climes of the Outer Lawless regions. Having been given directions, we set off for the castle of the dreaded warlord.

I sat up front on the horse, Entipy behind me. She had her arms draped around me casually in order to hold on. She wasn't doing anything untoward beyond that, which relieved me no end. Her affections were not something I particularly wanted to deal with.

"I didn't burn it down," she said abruptly. The castle was visible in the distance, or at least the upper towers were. The rest of it was obscured behind a great wall ringing the entire structure. We weren't anywhere close to sunset, but there was a gentle red glow suffusing the horizon.

At first I didn't know what she was talking about. I thought she meant the castle, and then I figured she was referring to the pub. I said nothing, and the only sound to be heard (other than the distant noises of revelry) was the steady clip-clop of the Heffer's hooves.

"The retreat. Where the Faith Women lived. I didn't burn it down."

I wasn't sure which was more surprising to me: that she'd brought it up out of the blue at all, or that she was claiming not to have done it.

"You didn't," I said, sounding skeptical.

"No, I didn't," she repeated.

"The Faith Women seemed to be under the impression that you did." I didn't even bother to mention the demented smile that she had flashed, which came across—to me, at least—like someone who was extremely dangerous and certainly capable of torching anyone or anything that offended her.

She did that little shoulder shrug of hers. "I can't help what they think . . . or what you think."

"You can tell me what happened."

"Why do you care?"

"I don't. I just . . . wanted something to pass the time."

She was silent for a time. I guess she was considering it. Finally she said, "I didn't cause it. I just . . . didn't stop it. I hated the Faith Women."

"Why?"

"Because they hated me."

"Why did they hate you?"

"Because I'm better than they are. People always hate people who are better than they are."

That one struck a little closer than I would have liked, but I tried not to show it. Instead I said gamely, "Then by that logic, you hated the Faith Women because they were better than you. At least, that's one possible interpretation."

She shook her head with assurance. "No. Sometimes you just hate someone because they're cretins."

"Ah. I see. And you can distinguish one kind of hatred from the other?"

"Of course. Can't you?"

"All right," I said, not wanting to get much further into a topic that made me quite that uncomfortable. "You hated each other. But you didn't burn the place down."

"No. Instead I prayed to the goddess for help."

"Which goddess would that be?"

"Hecate."

I knew the name instantly and was not especially cheered. "Hecate. Isn't she a sort of goddess of dark magic?"

"She's been known to be," Entipy replied in a calm, neutral voice that only chilled me more.

"Have you an interest in weaving?"

"No. Just in making people suffer."

I couldn't quite determine whether she was serious. What I did know for certain was that I didn't want to ask.

She seemed to be waiting for me to make a further inquiry. When I didn't, she continued, "I prayed to Hecate that she would deliver me from the Faith Women. She answered me twice. First she sent me Tacit. He could have taken me out of there. But Hecate found a cat's-paw with too pure a heart, because he urged me to remain until the proper time. He kept saying he had a sense of destiny." She said those last words with what I could only term as "disdain." It was the first time in our somewhat odd association that she had spoken of Tacit in less than glowing, even reverent terms. I took silent pleasure in that, even though I knew in my heart that Tacit had been correct, and the only reason he wasn't fulfilling that destiny was because I had interceded. "But then Hecate chose to answer my prayers a second time," Entipy went on. "I was in a study, deep in prayer. There were candles by the window, and suddenly a strong wind came in, blew the shutters wide, and knocked the candles onto the floor. The wind came from nowhere, the shutters should have held, and when the candle fell, it should have gone out. But none of those things happened. What else could that be but divine providence?"

"Coincidence? Bad luck? I've had a ton of it and it wasn't at the hands of gods."

"Are you quite sure about that?" she asked.

I started to reply and then fell silent. Truth to tell, there'd been quite a few times where I felt as if the gods were out to get me.

Taking my silence for assent, she said, "I stood there and watched the flame from the candle start to spread across the carpet. I watched the winds fan the flames, and watched as they leaped to the drapes. If I shouted an alarm, the Faith Women could likely have stopped it. But I didn't. I simply let nature take its course.

"The Faith Women eventually smelled the smoke, felt

the heat. They ran in, saw the entire room being consumed, and saw me standing there. One of them looked at me and kind of shrieked, 'Gods . . . the flames are in her eyes.' Which they probably were, reflected there, but I certainly must have looked nicely demonic.

"To this day, I'm not entirely sure why they didn't just leave me there. One of them grabbed me, slung me over her shoulder, while the others scrambled to find water and bring the blaze under control. But it was much too late; the flames were already licking at the second story of the building, which just happened to be the library. When the books went up, well . . . between those and the dried wood of the structure itself, it was just a matter of time."

"And they just assumed you'd started it."

"Of course."

"And you did nothing to change their minds."

"If there's one thing I've learned, squire," she said lightly, sounding more cheerful than I'd ever heard her, "it's always best to let people think you're more than you are than less. Give people a reason to like you . . . and they'll take advantage of you. Give people a reason to fear you . . . and they'll fear you."

"I see. So when you become queen, you plan on a reign of terror."

"Oh yes," she said matter-of-factly.

"Has it occurred to you that those who reign in terror usually die in pain from the blade of an assassin?"

I felt her shrug behind me. If she had considered it, it certainly didn't trouble her especially. "If things become too dire, I can always pray to Hecate. Although there are some who say that, in one person's lifetime, she'll only answer prayers three times. And she's answered mine twice so far. So I'll continue to worship her, just to stay in her good graces. But if I'm looking for her to actually grant me something—like the death of enemies or something like that—then obviously I'll have to save it for something very special."

I didn't even want to consider what someone as twisted as Entipy might consider "special." Then a thought occurred to me. "Why did you tell me? Aren't you worried that I might wind up liking you?"

"No. You hate yourself too much to like anybody."

I was glad she said that, because it removed whatever danger there might be that I might start to relax my guard or like her a bit more. The only reason I didn't knock her off the horse and leave her behind was because we needed the nine sovs her presence was going to bring at the castle.

The event was already in full swing when we got there and reported, as we'd been instructed, to the castle steward. The contrast between the cold outside and the warmth inside was most impressive. From the upper halls where the celebration originated, we could hear laughter and merriment, and the thrumming of musical instruments and the sound of dancing feet. It was curious. In hearing the dreaded Warlord Shank described, I'd heard him made out to be a virtual incarnation of evil. In fact, all of his followers were likewise ostensibly irredeemably evil. But apparently one can be evil and yet, when celebrating, be indistinguishable from everyone else.

Sometimes I wondered which category I fell into. And oftentimes I stopped wondering because I didn't really want to know.

The steward looked me up and down disdainfully. "Yer uh cripple!" he said in disgust.

"Yes," I said. There didn't seem to be any other reasonable response.

"Ken yuh work?"

"As long as the work doesn't entail extended jaunts, or flashes of dazzling footwork necessitated by complex choreography."

He stared at me blankly. "Wha'?"

"Yes. I can work."

"Fine. Upstairs wi' yuh, then. And no eatin' enny of th' serious food. Yeh can have some bread if yuh want."

The noise from the main hall become almost deafening as we drew closer. We stood outside the main double doors a moment, as I steadied my pounding heart. We were walking into the heart of enemy territory for the princely (and princessly) sum of nine sovs each. Somehow I always thought my life would be worth more than that. On the other hand, somehow I always knew that it wouldn't. I pushed open the doors and a virtual wall of sound slammed into us. People were talking with one another at dazzlingly high volume, most of them—by my guess—with serious amounts of alcohol already in them. A band consisting of pipers, drummers, and a harpist was in the center of the room on what appeared to be a section set up for dancing. And dancing there most definitely was, people grasping each other's hands and spinning in a circle. That certainly seemed the most pointless kind of dancing to me. All that work, just to wind up back where one started? One might simply have stayed there in the first place and saved the exertion.

But all of that was secondary. What struck me most about the great hall was the décor. It was furnished in a style that I could only term "Early Atrocity."

Bleached bones, presumably of former enemies, decorated the walls and, not only that, had been incorporated into much of the furniture. The legs of the main dining table were genuine legs; the armchairs, I'm sure you can guess. There were tapestries, but they consisted mostly of depictions of slaughter, slaughter everywhere. Women being raped, children being tossed onto fires, men being crucified. All of it, a celebration of the worst sort of brutality. Suddenly the line of demarcation between the festivals of good and evil became that much clearer for me. When good is celebrating, you don't have an overwhelming urge to run screaming into the night. Well . . . unless a mime is performing.

I became more panicked than ever over the notion of being found out, because I could have no more pronounced reminder of where we were than the furnishings of that place. I kept imagining being discovered as a squire for King Runcible, in service to his daughter, who was standing to my immediate right. If that happened, my buttocks would likely be pressed into permanent service as an end table. Unfortunately, the hall was quite brightly lit. Would that it had not been so, for I would have liked nothing better than to have my vision of this chamber of horrors severely limited. I looked over at Entipy to see how she was handling it.

Nothing. Face impassive. She was studying some of the tapestries, assessing them with considerable dispassion.

"If someone gets butchered that severely," she finally said, "there's much more blood than they're showing here. These aren't terribly accurate."

"Oh, of course, and maidens cavorting with unicorns is accurate," I muttered.

"Yes, it is."

"There are no unicorns," I told her, "despite whatever Tacit may have told you about his upbringing. And if there were, they'd try and skewer you just as surely as any other creature of myth." I pointed toward a table at the far end that appeared shorthanded. "I think they need help there. Come on."

We started to thread our way through the dance floor, and I have to admit my fantasy life took an upswing. For some of the noblewomen, you see, were considerably drunk and even more considerably liberal in their . . . willingness, shall we say. Naturally I would have been happy to take advantage of them in a moment, but I had other matters to attend to.

We stepped behind a food station that had a ham the size of a two-year-old child, and I started carving it. In slicing it, I envisioned the throat of every person who had ever done me an injustice. Unsurprisingly, the cutting went very briskly. Entipy then served out the newly cut meat to anyone who wandered by.

I have to say, the ham smelled delicious. At one point I looked at Entipy, who—as we'd been told was permissible—was eating two pieces of bread, one atop the other. But then I saw juice dribbling down, soaking through the bread slices a bit. "What are you doing?" I demanded.

"I stuck a few small slices of ham between two pieces of bread in order to hide it," she said cheerfully, obviously pleased with herself.

My taste buds recoiled at that. Taking something as juicy and palatable as meat and sticking it between two pieces of bread seemed a rather repulsive way to eat anything, not to mention an insult to the meat. At the very least it was highly abnormal. But if there was one thing I'd learned about the princess, it was that she was blissfully untroubled by such things as abnormality. Still . . . the ham was tempting . . .

Glancing left and right to make sure that no one was paying attention, I followed suit and moments later was also munching on ham between two slices of bread. There was something to be said for the convenience, but I can say with certainty that—as a means of consuming food—it's never going to catch on.

It was interesting to watch the guests becoming rowdier as the drink flowed even more freely. I looked around and tried to figure out which one might be the dreaded Warlord Shank. Naturally I sought the largest, most forbidding of them, and there seemed several likely candidates. For a time I became concerned that one of those bruisers, in his cups, would begin to harass Entipy, and we would have a whole mess all over again. But I needn't have worried; there were lusty wenches aplenty to sate the ardor of even the most drunkenly passionate of men. Next to those panting fillies, Entipy looked like little more than an awkward two-day-old colt.

And so matters went on for a time, until suddenly there was an ear-shattering flourish of trumpets. At the far end of the hall was another huge set of double doors, similar to those through which we had entered, but bigger, and they had crests with dripping swords upon them. Slowly, ponderously, they swung open, and everyone in the place sank to one knee. For a number of the men, I suspected, that was no great trick; the major difficulty for them had been managing to stay on their feet for as long as they had.

I could only assume that the man who was entering was the host of this evening's festivities, but I have to say that the one who came through that entranceway seemed, well—less than impressive. I do not mean by any stretch that he appeared weak or helpless; but certainly he was not the behemoth, the walking engine of destruction, that I would have expected from someone of his rank and reputation. It was most definitely he, though, as shouts of "All hail Shank! All hail the dreaded Warlord Shank!" filled the air, and everyone slapped their fists against their hearts in fealty. Automatically I did the same, and glanced toward Entipy. She did nothing; just stood there with her hands at her sides. I mouthed to her that she should do as the others were doing, but she just stood there. I could have strangled her and I prayed that no one noticed. Fortunately enough, no one did.

What he lacked in physical stature, he made up for in sheer presence, I have to say that much for him. He was of moderate height, dressed mostly in black. His arms were bare but swathed in tattoos of equally black dragons intertwining 'round one another. At first glance the arms themselves looked unassuming, but closer inspection revealed corded muscle that indicated considerable strength. He had long black hair and dark, deep-set eyes, partially obscured by an overhanging brow, that seemed to take in everything that was happening in the hall with one sweep. He had a mustache so long that either end dangled significantly below his chin, and sported his arrogance like a newly acquired ermine cape.

"Greeting . . . my friends." He held out the "s" in "friends" in a snake-like, sibilant manner. His voice was low and gravelly, and when he spoke it was in a very deliberate, unhurried manner. It was not a bad way of talking; it indicated that you were so important that everyone had to stand around and wait for you to take your time getting to whatever point it was that you were going to make. "I thank you for coming to join me in my time of celebration."

"All hail the nuptials of the dreaded Warlord Shank!" one person called out, and others took up the chant. Shank smiled as he sauntered to a large chair covered in skulls and sat in it. There was another chair next to him, composed of smaller skulls—those of children, by the look of it. I felt the ham and bread heaving in protest in my stomach, repulsed by the notion . . . and repulsed even further when I noticed that the skulls looked very freshly polished, indicating that the chair was quite new. I couldn't help but picture helpless children being hauled off somewhere, to be beheaded and skinned for the purpose of adding new furniture to the warlord's abode. I could practically hear their screams ringing in my ears. Entipy, for her part, remained detached from the entire thing. Sometimes I wondered if she even truly knew where she was, or if she had somehow separated herself from it all just so she could deal with it. If it was the latter, I envied her and wished I could do the same.

The name "Shank!" had been taken up in a chant, repeated steadily as the warlord smiled in acknowledgment of his popularity. He allowed it to go on for some brief time before putting up his hands and indicating that they'd best calm themselves.

"Until now," he continued, "I have sated my legendary lusts in the violation of my victims, with no interest in a wife since my concerns lay elsewhere." He began to walk the room, and it was only at that point that I noticed the sword strapped to his back. The thing looked huge, with a small skull shape visible at the pommel. At least I certainly hoped it was just a shape, rather than the skull of a child ripped from its mother's womb at a tender age in order to provide ornamentation for Shank's blade. "My priority has always been my corps of soldiers. I have trained them, disciplined them, worked them until they were ready to drop and then continued to work them. I have had very little concern for my own time upon this world, for one does not become a warlord and expect to die of old age. Instead, my soldier corps was to be my legacy when my life is done. You all know my motto: Live fast. Die young. And leave a good-looking corps."

There were nods of assent from all around, and more reflexive cries of "Hail the Warlord."

"However . . . however!" he called several times to get his voice over the chants, until they died down. "Recently, in my pillaging and plundering . . . efforts that had met with triumph in all lands except Isteria . . ." He said that last with enormous disgust, and immediately cries of "Down with King Runcible! Runcible will die! Runcible will fall!" were taken up throughout the hall.

Entipy was busying herself slipping more meat between two more wedges of bread. The shouts didn't seem to register on her at all, or at least paled in interest compared to the food.

"In my pillaging . . . I met a woman. Not just any woman, mind you . . . *the* woman . . ."

"A woman who can keep up with your lusts, my lord?" shouted one noble, and there was raucous laughter from all around, whistles and cheers.

The warlord smirked at that. "She comes close. Do not think that I haven't tried her out. One doesn't purchase a Heffer without taking a few rides."

More shouts, more guffaws. Apparently a man's worth in these parts was measured by the size of his "lusts." Well, it certainly seemed more practical than honor or bravery, and certainly more entertaining during its practice.

"She is nobility, of course," he continued, and his smirk widened. "She has pleasured no man before your warlord, for no one has been man enough to seize her interest. Her beauty is unparalleled and, not only that . . . but I suspect she will provide me the son that even my closest advisors have told me I owe my people as a symbol of our continued success.

"My fellow lords and ladies . . . may I present to you . . . Stela, the Countess of Pince-Nez!" And he swept his arm theatrically toward the door behind him.

She entered then, and my heart came close to stopping.

She had on a dress of crushed purple velvet, a glittering necklace that could only be diamond, and an assortment of golden rings and other pricey baubles. She had thick blond hair piled upon her head. She had a lovely smile. She had an ample bosom. And she had all my money in the world.

It was Astel, the tavern bitch who had nearly caved my head in and spread my mother's ashes all over me.

And fate had handed me the opportunity to make an ash out of her in return. Because I was the only person in the room who knew that the warlord's beloved bride-to-be was nothing more than a fraud. There was no question that I was going to take advantage of this knowledge. The only thing at issue was how I was going to do it.

Chapter 19

"What's happened? Something's happened."

Entipy was looking at me very closely. I have to say, not much slipped past her. She was able to intuit, just by my manner, that a new dynamic had been introduced into the mix.

"Nothing," I said in a low voice.

"Don't lie to me." There, for just a moment, was that famed sharpness and snappishness that I'd come to associate with her. Her eyes seemed to bore right into me. "Something's going on. Is it bad?"

"No. It's good, actually. It's very good, providing I play it right. And you're going to have to trust me to handle this. Understood?"

"Now listen, squire—"

I rounded on her then, speaking in a voice that was both soft and yet filled with warning. "Are you out of your mind? Don't address me that way, even if you're whispering . . . even if you're mouthing it. It's not enough that the walls have ears; in case you haven't noticed it, the furniture has bones. And I don't know about you, but I've no intention of being added to them. Now shut up!"

She looked as if she wanted to say more, but instead she silenced herself. I couldn't have been more grateful. "Now stay here," I told her as I made my way around the table. I glanced around, saw a large open bottle of wine, and snatched it. As I did so, I draped a cloth over my arm so as to give an impression that I was a wine server.

"Where are you going?" she whispered.

I didn't respond because I couldn't think of a reply that might not endanger us. This game had to be played very, very carefully.

Slowly I made my way across the room. As I did so, I stopped every few feet, smiled, bobbed my head subserviently, and poured refills from the bottle for any guests of the warlord who looked as if they were in danger of becoming remotely sober. The entire time I never took my eyes off Astel. I couldn't hear anything that anyone was saying to her from where I was, but I could see that she was greatly enjoying herself. She was not standing right by the warlord's side, but she always remained in range of him. That meant that I was going to have to get very, very close in order to achieve my goal.

It was not something that I was looking forward to. The nearer I got to the warlord, the more aware I became of just how brutal and vicious he could be. I could see it in his eyes . . . or rather, I couldn't, because he had cold, dead eyes, like a shark is reputed to have. The kind that shrivel your soul if they happen to light upon you. The closer I drew, the more I felt as if I were not at a celebration . . . but a wake. A wake being held for the attendees themselves. Yes, that was it. Everyone around me . . . was already dead. But no one wanted to acknowledge it. They were too afraid to. So I was surrounded by walking corpses, celebrating their dark god, and no one wanting to admit that they were all damned and doomed. And if I didn't get out of here, I would be one of them.

But it didn't stop me from getting closer still, all the time pouring wine and nodding and acting as if I lived only to bring half-empty mugs up to their proper, filled state of being. Fifteen paces from Astel, then ten, then nine. She still hadn't noticed me. Why should she? No one notices the help.

I was taking a tremendous risk. Everything hinged on my catching Astel off-guard, of maintaining the upper hand emotionally. If somehow she gained control of the situation, I was undone. Part of me scolded me, telling me that if I had any brains at all, I would back off this mad adventure. But if I gave it the slightest moment's thought, I was able to conjure up for myself what it felt like when she sent the urn smashing into my head. I could still taste ash between my teeth and stinging my eyes, still recall the sense of humiliation and frustration as I slumped into unconsciousness, all because of her. I had made peace with myself that I was not brave or honorable, but if I turned away from this, I would never be able to live with myself.

Eight paces, seven, and she was laughing at something her dead-eyed husband-to-be was saying. Casually, ever so casually, she turned and her gaze took in an assortment of people, including me. I froze exactly where I was, concentrating all my focus upon her, as if I could drive a message into her brain by sheer willpower alone.

She looked through me and past me. In truth, there was no reason that she should have recognized me immediately. I was older and scruffier than when she'd last seen me, not to mention hundreds of miles away. It wasn't as if she was scanning the crowd to prepare herself lest Apropos show his face; there was no earthly reason for me to be on her mind at all.

And yet for all the reasons she had for not recognizing me, I still felt a flicker of doubt. What if . . . I was wrong? What if this was not Astel? What if she had a previously unknown identical twin, or this woman was simply a look-alike? It could be, after all, that it was my memory that was faulty. That I was so eager to gain a measure of retribution upon Astel that I was ready to see her face damned near anywhere if it meant I might have the opportunity to get back a measure of the pride I'd lost that stormy night long ago.

At the exact moment that doubts were surfacing, leading me to think that I was mistaken, that was when her head snapped back around and she looked right at me. I had the great good pleasure of watching every bit of blood drain out of her face, her makeup now looking incredibly bright red against the lack of color in her skin.

I had her, then. I knew I did. I said nothing, did nothing, didn't even acknowledge her with a nod. I just stared at her, hard, as if I was capable of blasting her brain out the back of her head with the power of my eyes alone.

Suddenly she started to take a deep breath, and I knew instantly that she was reflexively getting ready to scream. I didn't act the least bit perturbed. I simply shook my head very slowly, and then nodded with a slight tip of my head in the direction of the doors she'd originally come through.

Her hand fluttered to her bosom and I was close enough to her to hear her say to Shank, "My . . . apologies, husband-to-be . . . I feel unwell."

The dreaded Warlord Shank did not seem perturbed by this. "Mayhap you have the child sickness and are already carrying my heir." It was all the more chilling to hear words of amorous, even loving affect issuing from a face possessing eyes that pitiless.

"Anything is possible, milord," she said with a glance in my direction that seemed to indicate that my very presence there was proof of the sentiment. "I would . . . retire . . . if that would suit Your Lordship's pleasure."

His face darkened, and I suddenly found myself wondering if he was as hard on fiancées as he was on the serving staff. "It would not. This gathering is for my nobles to meet you. If you depart so early, it will make you seem weak . . . and, by extension, me as well."

"For a brief time, only," Astel said with more urgency, looking my way surreptitiously. "That is all, my lord. Tell them . . . tell them whatever you wish. You are their warlord. They will listen to you."

Appealing to his overweening instinct was definitely the proper move to make. Shank considered what she said and nodded. "You do look a bit . . . pallid. Do you need help to get you to your chambers . . . ?"

"Oh, I . . ." And she looked at me even as she addressed Shank. "I think this . . . server should be able to attend to me."

"Server!" barked Shank, and I immediately moved to just in front of him. He focused those dead eyes upon me, and suddenly it was all I could do not to shake violently. I felt as if he was capable of picking apart my brain, plumbing it for its secrets, just with a look. Reflexively I looked down, telling myself that it was a normal thing for a server to do rather than an obvious attempt to cover my fear. Shank paused a moment and an eternal afterlife of my rib cage transformed into a musical instrument flickered through my imagination. He was staring at the staff on which I was leaning. "I have a server who is lame of leg?" he demanded.

"I am but temporary help, milord," I said humbly.

"I had people on my staff who thought they were permanent, who discovered that they likewise were temporary," he guffawed, prompting similar amused grunts from his associates. I said nothing, merely tried to look humble. Then he continued, "My fiancée has a brief . . . personal need to which she must needs attend. You seem harmless enough. Perhaps she feels pity on you. Attend to her."

I bobbed my head, still not looking up. "As you command," I said, and turned to her.

She spun on her heel and headed for the large double door. I kept close behind her and a moment later the heavy doors swung shut behind us. We were in a huge hallway that seemed to go on forever, and here it was quite cold indeed. Cold as the grave.

She whirled to face me, her eyes wide. "Pallid" indeed. Her wan face floating in the dimness of the poorly lit hall, she looked positively spectral. *"What are you doing here?!"* she demanded.

"Joining the party," I said mildly. "I heard there was a masquerade: Come as you aren't. I'll have to admit, though, that the identity I've assumed can't begin to compare to yours."

"You can't be here . . ."

Apparently the reality of my presence had not yet fully registered upon her. I had the advantage and I was going to do everything I could to press it. Telling her that my stumbling upon her was merest happenstance might give her some degree of comfort. So instead I said to her, in a voice that was deep with threat, "Of course I'm here. I'm everywhere you are."

Her hand fluttered to her throat. "Wh-what?"

Laughing coarsely, I said, "Do you believe yourself to have been unobserved all this time? That I did not have eyes everywhere? My dear 'Countess' . . . you may have temporarily managed to fool Shank, but my associates and I are quite a different matter."

She almost seemed to have forgotten where she was, and then her vision cleared. "What do you mean?" she managed to say.

"You made a very serious blunder, Astel. You assumed that because I was out of your sight, you were out of my mind. But you have never strayed far from my thoughts . . . or my mind. You trusted the wrong people."

"That bitch!" breathed Astel. "I *knew* there was something about her! She was one of yours, wasn't she!"

I smiled enigmatically. Naturally I hadn't the faintest idea what she was talking about or who the "bitch" she was referring to was, but it didn't matter. All that mattered was driving a stake of pure paranoia through her wretched little heart.

"Or was it . . ." She suddenly looked more suspicious. ". . . or was it . . . somebody else? How far does your influence go? Tell me that, at least. The way you showed up here, now . . . it's almost . . . supernatural . . ."

Ahhh . . . apparently our little Astel carried a bit of the superstitious within her. My smiled widened as I said softly, "Let us just say that in addition to mortal allies, I have friends in . . . high places." My gaze flickered heavenward and then I added, "I assume you've heard of . . . Hecate."

I thought her legs were going to give out. Thank you, Entipy.

"So you know everything then," she whispered. "That I used the money I took from you . . ."

"And that you stole from my mother's mattress. Her earnings, too." It was a guess, but it seemed a reasonable one.

She nodded, unknowingly confirming that which I had only intuited. "I made a few investments, and used it to acquire finery, trappings . . . all the outward appearances of a great lady. That I created the identity of the countess because I knew no nobleman would have interest in a commoner. And came here to Shank's court, seeking a noble husband, and caught the fancy of the warlord himself . . . aided initially by purchased charms. Told him I had vast estate holdings in the west . . ."

"And that you're planning to tell him that there's been an unexpected fire and everything is burned down, lost . . . but since you'll be married by that point, obviously he won't throw you out because of it." That last, naturally, was pure guess on my part, but I figured it was worth the gamble in order to cement, in her mind, the belief that I knew everything that she was about.

It worked perfectly, because her eyes widened and she nodded, unwittingly affirming what had only been surmise on my part. "And you could have stepped in at any time," she said with mounting incredulity. "But you let me put the whole charade together . . . create the countess identity for myself . . . let me get right to the cusp of pulling this off . . . and now, *now,* is when you step in. Ohhhh, I'll admit it, Apropos," and she shook her head in wonderment, "you have a spider's patience. You are fiendish beyond imagining."

"I have my moments," I allowed.

Her eyes narrowed, something glittering in there as if she was trying to determine how to snatch triumph from tragedy. "But you've left yourself vulnerable. It's just you and I. Why . . . I could suddenly shout for help right now and summon half a dozen guards. Tell my beloved fiancé that you tried to molest me." She smiled, showing her teeth, which looked far whiter than I'd remembered them. "He'd lop off your head himself, right in the middle of the court. And you would tell him . . . what? That I'm a fake? Who do you think he'd believe? You? Or me?"

But my thoughts were already ahead of hers. "He

would believe you," and before she started to speak, I continued, "right up until I tell him about the tattoo of a butterfly you have on your inner thigh."

She blanched at that, but then tried to rally. "I . . . can tear at my skirt right now. Obviously you saw it when you . . . tried to ravish me . . ."

"Really?" I said coolly. "Odd. Most women, when they're ravished, don't make noises like a hoot owl when achieving passionate climax. Nor are they noted for crying out, 'Ride me, stallion! Ride me, you stallion you!' The warlord has already made clear in his blustering way that he had his pleasure with you, so he'd be familiar with your habits. Did you do with him what you did with me? Will I be sealing my fate, or will I be lending credence to my version of things? It is possible that he will indeed have me executed for my publicly making a fool of him . . . but if he does, my dear, I strongly suspect that your head will be rolling right on the floor alongside mine."

She swayed slightly, and for a moment I thought she was going to pass out dead away. She leaned against the wall to steady herself, took several deep breaths, and unconsciously put a hand to her throat as if she could feel a blade slicing viciously through it. I knew I had her then. She fixed a level gaze on me and said the four words I had been waiting to hear: "What do you want?"

"What do I want?" I said thoughtfully.

"You obviously want *something*. You didn't go to all this endeavor so that we could chat about old times and then you depart empty-handed. What do you want?"

"Very well," and my voice hardened. There was such

barely controlled rage in it that I almost surprised myself. "I want my naïveté back. I want back the ability to lose myself totally in a woman's passion without always wondering if and when she's about to slip a knife between my ribs. I want to be able to think that when a woman opens her legs to me she's also opening her heart, instead of just finding a way to use me until it suits her fancy to take advantage of me or betray me. I want to have a last memory of my mother as something other than a large pile of ashes covering my face and being washed away by the rain, along with the last fragments of my ability to trust. I want to be able to think back to my first sexual experience without the words 'What an idiot I was' resounding in my head. Can you do that for me, Astel? Can you give me that?"

She looked down. She couldn't stand to look me in the eyes. "No," she said, so softly I could barely hear her.

"Then riches will have to do instead," I told her.

"I'll get together whatever money I can . . ."

"Some coinage will be fine for the local area, but that won't be enough," I said flatly. "Sovs and dukes in this realm have the warlord's face on them. They'll be useless to me anywhere outside of the Outer Lawless regions, and I do not plan on overstaying my welcome."

"Well, it's too late for that," she snapped . . . but not, I noticed, too aggressively.

"Gold," I said flatly. "And silver. And jewels. As much as I can carry out of here without being noticed."

"And how often will you be making such visits to me, eh?" she asked. "How often will you be making return engagements, seeking more from me?"

"Believe it or not, Astel, if I never see you again, it will be too soon," I told her. "The very sight of you stirs such fury in my heart that I can barely contain myself. I'd sooner muck out stables with my tongue than have further intercourse—social or sexual—with you."

She looked skeptical, as if she couldn't quite believe she was getting off that easily. "All this time you've been watching me, scheming . . . and this one confrontation is enough to sate you?"

"I am interested in dealing purely with your monetary theivery, Astel. With evening the scales on that score. Everything else you took from me cannot be replaced, ever, so I won't even try. And more than anything else, I want you to know that, all this time—even now—I could have brought you down, so that it will help to diminish whatever sense of accomplishment you may have. You'll always know that you got as far as you did . . . because I allowed it. That's sufficient vengeance for me, Astel, and I'm interested purely in revenge . . . not overkill. Now . . . let us see how fares your generosity."

"Generosity under threat of exposure is hardly genuine."

"Nor is lovemaking under the pretext of thievery. But if I can survive the experience, I daresay you can, too."

Her jaw twitched, but she said nothing. Instead she turned and started walking. I followed directly behind her, my staff clicking on the ground.

"I have thought of you, from time to time, you know," she said softly. "Believe it or not, Apropos . . . I was not evil. Just desperate."

"How kind of you to clarify that." I was not impressed.

"I mean to say . . . I never meant you any ill. And . . . it didn't happen as you believe."

"Indeed."

"When you and I . . . when we . . . that was sincere. Spontaneous. I had no plans beyond that. It was only when I saw all the money there, and I . . . I gave in to a weak impulse. I am a weak woman, Apropos."

"I see. You're not evil. Just desperate and weak . . . much like the story you're spinning for me now. A desperate and weak one."

"But true nonetheless."

"Astel," I said tersely, "I don't think you know what the truth is anymore."

"And you think you do?"

"No. I just don't care what it is."

We walked the rest of the way in silence.

Entipy, standing behind the table, looked at me with open curiosity as I hustled toward her. "We've leaving," I said as soon as I got within whispering range.

"But the party is still going. We won't be paid our—"

"Devil take the sovs. We're going. Now."

I realized that her eyes were wandering toward the front of my breeches. I looked down and saw what she was looking at. There was a bulge there, more noticeable than I would have liked. She looked up at me, her face a question.

"Jewels," I said in a low voice.

"Family?"

"No. Real." I glanced around, made sure no one else

was watching, and then shifted them around so that the "package" was less obvious.

Then she comprehended, and with conspiratorial shock she whispered, "You *stole* them?"

"No. Extorted. Let's go."

She didn't understand, but she didn't have to. The party was still going in full swing and as a result our hurried departure drew no attention. I was walking as carefully as I could, trying not to jingle or send anything else out of position, considering I had jewelry and money secreted all over my person, and in the hidden compartment of my staff.

The sounds of the party receded into the distance as we made our way toward the servants' exit. Down a curling flight of stairs that seemed to take forever to navigate, down, and then toward the door that would put us out into the night and freedom. It was at the end of a long hallway that felt as if it was a hundred leagues away. I had never felt so frustrated over my lame right leg as I did at that moment, since I was in such a hurry to just put as much distance between us and the castle as possible. To hurry out of there before someone could shout . . .

"You!"

I recognized the voice instantly as the steward, summoning us from behind. We were ten feet from the door, from freedom, and before I could turn I heard the steward continue, "There he is, milord! Apparently he's trying to sneak out."

"Servant!" came a gravelly voice, and I knew at that moment that we were dead, because it was Shank's voice.

Entipy sucked in her breath sharply; she likewise knew that matters had taken a decided turn for the worse. I had been trying to reposition the bag of jewels that were among the riches the unwilling Astel had provided for me; they'd been slipping again in our hasty departure. But it didn't seem to matter now. I gripped my staff with both hands because I felt as if I was going to faint.

Close in my ear, Entipy whispered, "Should we run for it?"

"Why bother?" I returned. True, there was a remote chance we would make it out the door. But it wasn't as if there was an invisible barrier that would prevent Shank from following us the additional three or four feet we might manage to put between ourselves and the castle. Better to surrender now with what little dignity remained to us . . . especially considering that any claims to dignity I might have had would soon be lost in screams of agony as Shank did . . . well, whatever he was going to do.

"Where are you off to in such a hurry?" demanded Shank.

Slowly I turned to face him. Even at this moment of utter doom, I couldn't help but try to stammer out a lie. "Milord, I . . . my . . . partner here," and I indicated Entipy, "has need of a . . . uhm . . ."

Shank looked below my waist and grinned, and then laughed. "Hah!" he said. "I see what she has need of . . . and you appear only too eager to provide it. Go and argue with the lusts of youth, eh, steward?" And he clapped the steward on the back. The steward staggered slightly, but righted himself and nodded gamely. Then the dreaded

Warlord Shank turned back to me and reached into the folds of his tunic. For a moment I was certain that this was it—that he had finished with games and was about to pull out a dagger and simply slice my throat. Instead he pulled out a glittering coin: a duke. "I realize I am remiss in not having given you a gratuity for aiding my wife. Here." And he flipped it to me. I caught it and stared at the coin, astounded, resting in my open palm. The face of the warlord scowled back at me from the coin's surface. "They are newly minted," he said. "You are one of the first to have one. See the reverse." I obediently turned the coin over. Astel's face smiled back at me.

"Once upon a time," he growled, "I would not have cared about such niceties. But if I am to husband a countess, one must observe certain social . . . traditions."

"As you say, milord." I could barely keep the astonishment from my voice.

"Steward? Have they been paid for this evening?"

"N-no, milord, but it is not customary to pay those who have not worked the full evening . . ."

Without a word the warlord yanked his sword from his scabbard and lopped the steward's head off. It rolled across the floor and bumped to a halt against the wall before the body had time to realize it was headless and flop, obediently, to the ground. Entipy and I stood rooted to our places.

"I despise excuses," said Shank. He pulled out a second duke and tossed that to me as well. "This will attend to it, I take it?"

"More than, milord."

"Smile, young ones!" bellowed Shank, and I realized

at that point that he was more than a little inebriated. "Smile on an evening of rejoicing! And know that you have been honored by providing service to the future wife of the dreaded Warlord Shank."

"Milord," I said extravagantly, "believe me when I say . . . that I took no greater joy in this life than when I was servicing your bride-to-be."

And we got the hell out of there.

Chapter 20

Considering the circumstances under which we'd come there, I was surprised to realize that Marie was actually sad to see us go.

I was somewhat concerned over the fact that—even though the calendar indicated that the fierce Outer Lawless winter should be subsiding—it still seemed unseasonably cold and nasty. Nevertheless, the roads were merely inhospitable rather than impassable, and my every instinct was telling me that now was the time to get on our way. As successful as I had been in obtaining an impressive bounty from Astel, I did not want to count on the notion that I was impervious to retribution. On the one hand, she might not want to take any chances mucking with me, since she had no idea how deep into her inner circles my "agents" ran, or even whether I was indeed backed up by the gods themselves. On the other hand, she might sooner or later get up enough nerve to hire someone privately to dispatch me. Make it look like an accident or some such. It all depended upon how comfortable she was with the fact that I was wandering around with full knowledge of who and what she was.

So it seemed incumbent upon me that we vacate the area sooner rather than later.

Naturally I didn't trust anyone in the area, but of all the people I didn't trust, the burly Marie was the one that I didn't trust the least. I felt it would be better to have someone act as an intermediary if at all possible, and so I prevailed upon her to arrange for the purchase of two Heffers for us. Heffers were fairly useless for traveling off the beaten path, but it was my intention to try and stay with the roads, and there they would do just fine. It was a calculated risk, of course. Staying to the main roads might make us prey for highwaymen. But endeavoring to penetrate the woods would make us prey for all manner of predators, and—all things considered—I'd rather take my chances with human thieves.

Marie openly scoffed at the notion of purchasing two Heffers outright until I presented her with enough funds not only to obtain the animals, but also to leave something for herself to cover her efforts. When she demanded to know how such riches had fallen into our hands, I simply smiled enigmatically and said, "The Warlord and his bride-to-be were most pleased with our efforts." She seemed interested in inquiring further, but decided to let the matter drop.

So it was that, early one morning, with no clouds in the sky, the sun creeping up in the east, and a sharp nip in the air, we set out on the main road that would lead us to the commweaver known as Dotty.

"Wait," I said. "How will we know Dotty's home when we get there?"

"Oh, believe me," she laughed, "you'll know it a'right. It's a bit . . . unusual-looking." She wouldn't say anything beyond that, though.

Marie saw us off, and as we prepared to ride away, her gaze took us both in as she said, "I know for a time there I was hard on ye. But I think you're both the better for it . . . especially you," and she pointed her stubbly chin toward Entipy. Entipy shrugged slightly, which for her passed as conversation. "You make a good couple," she added.

"Do we?" I inquired, inwardly amused.

"I see it in the way ye look at each other. Anticipate each other's thoughts and words. A good couple and a good team. Good luck to the both of ye."

Then she drew her wrap more tightly around herself, turned, and headed back into the inn. Entipy and I looked at each other . . . and laughed.

It was the first time we'd actually shared such a thing, a laugh. It felt . . . surprisingly natural.

We headed off down the road, keeping the Heffers at a brisk trot. We didn't exchange any words, but somehow the ensuing silence felt different from such previous instances. It was not an uncomfortable or angry silence such as we had known before, but instead a comfortable one. As if we had become so at ease in each other's company that there was no need to try and fill the void with useless verbiage.

The ride to the commweaver's home was pleasantly incident-free, and I could only hope that it was a good augury for things that were to come. As the Heffers trotted along, I kept dwelling upon what Marie had said, and her apparent confidence that we would know when we had arrived at the weaver's home. Well, when she's right, she's right, because about midday we turned a corner in the road and I knew, beyond question, that we had come within range of the commweaver's house.

In many respects it was ordinary-looking, almost mundane. All the shutters were closed, and I could swear I saw multicolored lights dancing within that might have been fairy lights. What made it clear that this was the home of an unusual individual was the large structure situated atop the roof.

The only thing I can say is that it was akin, in its shape, to an enormous cup. It lay lengthwise along the roof, the open end facing the road. The cup was sufficiently large that I could easily have climbed into it, and had room for Entipy to join me therein. I couldn't begin to conceive what such an odd structure and object could possibly be used for. It seemed to be constructed out of some sort of hammered sheet metal, which meant that it was likely heavy as hell. I wondered how in the world Dotty could possibly have gotten it up there, and realized that it would probably be better if I didn't know.

It wasn't just the sizable gleaming metal cup that caught my interest, though. It was what was behind it or, more precisely, attached to it.

I didn't spot it at first. The thing with magic is, you have to look at it indirectly. Catch it just out of the corner of your eye so that you have an idea of what it is you're going to be looking for when you stare at it straight on. At least, that's how Tacit explained it to me once, and considering that he claimed to have been raised by unicorns, I had to go with the assumption that he knew what he was talking about.

That was exactly what happened in this instance. I'd been staring at the cup, then looked down at the house itself and—as I did so—caught a quick glimpse of something that I hadn't seen before. I looked back at the cup, holding in my mind the image of what I'd thought I'd seen and, as a result, was able to see it more clearly.

It was what I can only describe as magical thread, the type that weavers use. It was gleaming red, and it was attached to the far end of the cup, floating gently in the breeze although it was hard to believe that something as pedestrian as wind could have an effect on something so magical. It was drifting lazily, like extensions from a willow tree, and even though I was looking directly at it, it would vanish from sight every so often before returning to my view once more. There was something that appeared to be a steady pulsation that was running along the thread's length. I had absolutely no idea where the thread might have been anchored at the other end, because the thread extended above and beyond the trees and out of sight.

Entipy noticed I was staring. "Strange cup," she commented.

"Do you see it?" I whispered.

"Of course I see it. The cup's right there," said Entipy, obviously a bit impatient. Her horse shook its head and whinnied in impatience. It had no idea where it was going, but this simple standing around on the road was not to its liking. The other Heffer started following suit, displaying similar impatience.

"Not the cup . . . the thread."

"Thread?" She frowned and tried to see what I was referring to. Finally she shook her head. "Sorry . . . I just don't see what you're talking about."

"It's all right," I said after a moment. "I'm probably just imagining it."

"Well, don't start imagining things," she said tartly. "That way lies madness, and if you're going to be of any use to me, you're going to have to be sane."

Now, that sounded more like the Entipy of old, and I couldn't say I was especially glad to have her back. I bowed with a look of mild annoyance on my face, and then snapped the reins of my horse briskly. The Heffer let out a brief whinny of annoyance and started forward, followed by the other.

When we arrived at the small house, we dismounted and tied the animals up to a hitching post conveniently set up outside the house. There were other hoofprints around; clearly she did a brisk business. I walked up to the door and then hesitated before knocking. I still wasn't thrilled about having any sort of business with weavers, and knocking on the door of one seemed ill advised, as if we were begging for trouble.

"Well?" Entipy prompted impatiently.

Having no ready answer to "Well?," I rapped with what I hoped sounded like authority.

At first there was no sound, not even the noise of feet scuffling across the floor to answer my knock. I wondered what the hell we were going to do if, for some reason, Dotty was unable to help us. What if she was ill or, worse, dead? She'd hardly be in a position to provide us aid then, and I didn't have the slightest idea where to find another commweaver in these parts. Before I could decide what to do, however, the decision was made for me. The door swung open and there was no one standing there. For a moment I assumed it to be some sort of magical door, but the far more earthbound answer presented itself when a woman stepped around from behind it, obviously having been responsible for pulling it open. At least, I think she was a woman. She might have been a toad or frog with delusions of humanity. Gods knew the resemblance was there. She had a wrinkled face, and eyes that darted around as if searching for passing bugs that she could lay claim to. Her hair was little more than white straw, and her skin was leathery and cracked like an old boot. Her tongue stuck out suddenly and, with the toad imagery in my head, I took a quick step back lest that tongue lash out, wrap itself around me, and yank me into her expanding jaw.

"Who're you?" she said.

"I'm Apropos."

"Of what?"

"Of nothing."

Her voice sounded both nasal and shrill, and I was getting a headache just listening to her for ten seconds. I couldn't begin to imagine what prolonged exposure to her would be like. Her gaze flickered to Entipy. "And who's this one?"

"Marie," said Entipy, glancing in my direction, and I realized instantly that Entipy was being wisely cautious.

This was a weaver, after all. They were not to be trusted, because their priorities were always a mystery to mere "norms" such as we ("norms" being the occasionally contemptuous term weavers were heard to mutter under their breaths). Entipy's name was unique, and we didn't need it ringing a bell with the commweaver and suddenly finding ourselves beset by Shank's troops, alerted to a royal hostage in their territory.

The old woman looked from one of us to the other and back again. I wasn't sure if she believed Entipy's quick lie, but after a moment she shrugged and I realized she simply didn't care. That was fine by me. "What d'ya want?" she demanded.

"You're the commweaver called Dotty?"

"Mayhap. What d'ya want?"

"Well, obviously," I said, trying to rein in my impatience and only partly succeeding, "we want to send a message to someone."

"Really. Where might they be?"

"Isteria."

"Isteria. Long distance." Her lips puckered and unpuckered several times very fast, as if blowing a succession of kisses.

"Can you do it?" asked Entipy.

"Henh." It was not so much a word as it was a noise, sounding like a gargling of phlegm. "I could . . . if I were a commweaver . . . which I haven't said I am yet . . . haven't said I'm a weaver at all . . ."

"If you're not a weaver, why do you have a magic thread connected to that great bloody cup on your roof?"

That sure caught her attention. Entipy might not have been there at all for all the attention that the commweaver was paying to her. The old woman's full attention was on me; she looked at me with dark, unblinking eyes. "So . . . you saw that, did you?" she said with a hiss. "What color did it appear to you?"

"Well . . . it was red . . ."

She shook her head impatiently. "Purple. In actuality, purple. Still . . . seeing it as red . . . you've something of the adept about you, it seems. Who did you say you were again, boy?"

I was starting to be uncomfortable that I'd told her my real name, but there was no going back on it now. "Apropos," I said again.

"Henh. Come in. Come in, Apropos, and . . ." She paused and looked Entipy up and down as if she knew the princess was hiding something. ". . . Marie."

We entered. The main room, when all was said and done, looked relatively normal, or at least more normal than I would have expected it to look. It seemed more like a large kitchen than anything else. There was a falcon crouched on a stand. Unlike others of its kind, it was neither hooded nor anchored to the spot. Instead it hopped around at will, glancing here and about at whatever snagged its interest. At one point our eyes met, and I couldn't help but feel that it was sizing me up and trying to determine whether I would provide an interesting meal. Apparently not, since it quickly lost interest in me and turned away. There was a small attachment to its leg that instantly made the creature's use clear: It ran airborne messages for Dotty on a purely local basis.

She saw me studying her hawk, but said nothing.

There was a pot bubbling in the corner, which the old woman shuffled over toward, and she took down a ladle as she removed the lid. I clapped my hands to my ears as a cacophony of high-pitched noises—which sounded like chimings of bells as incarnated in the throat of children—filled the room. Entipy was likewise discommoded, but the old woman seemed utterly nonplussed. She stirred it two, three times and then covered it again, the heavy lid cutting off the sound. She looked back to us, saw the confusion on our faces. "Baby Spells," she said by way of explanation.

"So you would be Dotty, then," I said.

"Henh. I would be, yes. And would you be someone who can actually pay for my services? The middle of the day is more expensive than evening. The most casts are going through at that time, so it's the most effort."

"I don't think we especially want to wait, so now would be the best time," I said. Entipy nodded in agreement. "As for remuneration . . ." I reached into my purse and pulled out a fistful of coins, and placed them on the table in front of her. She regarded them with raised eyebrow.

" 'Tis enough. 'Twill serve" was all she said. "And what would your message be, pray tell?"

I resolved that our phrasing had to be careful. I had no desire to broadcast that the princess was with me, since I had no idea how trustworthy Dotty might be, nor did I know for sure that no one would be able to tap into the lines of communication. Apparently, however, Entipy was thinking exactly along the same lines, for she spoke up before I did. "Inform Queen Beatrice," she said slowly, "that the package Apropos was supposed to deliver her is intact here in the Outer Lawless regions, but travel conditions indicate an escort would be preferred to avoid thievery. A rendezvous is highly desirable."

I nodded approvingly. For no reason my mind wandered back to the Lady Rosalie, whom I'd had to brace myself for every time she opened her mouth. Entipy, on the other hand, was a very different animal. Very different. I was actually finding that she was somewhat reliable when it came to matters requiring wit or quick thinking or pressure under fire. At first I had considered her to be so unpredictable that she was dangerous, and there was still some element of that. But of all the women I'd met in my life, she was rapidly becoming the only one that was remotely akin to dependable in a pinch. Not that I trusted her implicitly . . . but then, who in the world could I say that of?

Dotty nodded, jotting down a few notes with a quill pen. "I assume you wish to receive an answer. Could take a day or more."

"Is there somewhere we can wait?" I asked.

"I have a small barn out back. Unless that's not good enough for you," she added with faint disdain.

"Ohhh, we've gotten quite used to making do, thanks. A barn will be fine," said Entipy.

We unhitched the Heffers and brought them around to the barn. Night came early in these parts, so although there was still significant daylight, the shadows were already stretching their dark fingers. The animals seemed happy for the shelter, and I looked at Entipy thoughtfully. She saw me studying her. "What is it?" she asked.

"I'm just surprised that you accepted such humble lodgings so readily," I admitted.

She shrugged. "It's nothing."

"No, it's not 'nothing,'" I replied. "You've made it very clear what you feel you're entitled to as a princess, and shelter inside a barn certainly seems outside that entitlement."

She laughed softly at that. "Yes. I suppose it does, all things considered. I guess to someone like you, who thinks you know me so well, it's confusing."

"It is a bit, yes."

There was a bale of hay in the corner, and she sat on it, stretching her legs. "If you want to know the truth . . . although I don't mind tossing my rank around to annoy people . . . I've actually very little love for the status of 'princess.' Of royalty in general. It's one of the reasons my parents sent me to the Faith Women. We would meet other royalty or nobility, people with title brought to me with an eye toward future marriage, when I was no more than eight or nine years of age. Can you believe that?" She made a contemptuous, dismissive noise. "Eight years old and they wanted to circumscribe my future for me."

"Most people of limited means—peasants and such—have their futures circumscribed at younger ages than that. Circumscribed by the circumstances of their birth and the nature of their station in life," I pointed out.

She pursed her lips and studied me thoughtfully. "You're probably right. I hadn't considered that."

My gods . . . she sounded more and more human. It was beginning to make me nervous.

"Anyway," she continued, "in would walk these princes or young lords or young dukes or whomever, each one filled to the brim with his own importance. Each one acting as if I should be thrilled that they were even considering me for a possible bride. Each of them so mannered, so smug. I came to revile them, each and every one. And perhaps the most repulsive thing was that I was seeing male reflections of myself. If they were so repulsive . . . what did that make me?" I didn't answer her; the question seemed rhetorical. "So each suitor I treated with the increasing disdain I felt not only for them . . . but for myself as well."

"Causing havoc every time such an encounter was made."

She nodded. "My parents felt that I didn't appreciate all that I had. They had it wrong, though. I appreciated it for what it was . . . a sham, an arbitrary accident of birth. I was no more deserving of all that was handed to me than anyone else. My vision in the matter was clearer than theirs. They just wouldn't acknowledge it. So they sent me to the Faith Women, hoping that I would come to be happy for what I had through the simple expedient of taking it away from me."

"And did it work?"

"What do you think?"

I sized her up. "I think you understood all the reasons your parents did what they did, but still resented them for it. And that resentment became as hard as stale bread, and you took it out on the Women, even though you didn't really mind the hard work since it eased your conscience."

"Ah. So you'd credit me with having a conscience then. Not all that long ago, I don't think you would have."

"You're probably right."

"And now?"

"Now?" I shrugged, a gesture that she seemed eminently comfortable with. "Now, frankly, I don't know what to think of you."

"Good." She smiled at that, and you know what? When she was making no effort to be an arrogant little shrew, she had a genuinely lovely smile. I didn't tell her that, of course. I'd have been insane to say something like that to her.

Then her face clouded and she looked down at her boots. Immediately the old apprehensions started to return. "What's wrong?" I said.

"Tacit's not coming, is he," she said. Despite the phrasing, it was not a question. "I thought he was a hero. He said he was a hero. But a hero would have come for me. A hero would have been there for me."

I shifted uncomfortably, suddenly feeling ill-at-ease in my own body. "I'm sure he would have come if he could. Just because he, uhm, couldn't . . . doesn't make him less a hero . . ."

"Yes. It does," she said simply. "When you promise things and then don't come through on them, when someone was counting on you . . . it makes it harder to count on anyone in the future. Makes it harder to trust anyone."

"I can certainly sympathize with that view," I said.

Her gaze fastened on me. "Why?" she asked.

"It's not important."

"It is to me," she said, and from her tone of voice I could tell it really was. "Why do you say that? Does it have anything to do with how you managed to acquire all that money? I saw you go out of the room with that countess. Did she betray you somehow, and you extorted the money from her in exchange for silence?"

Gods almighty, she had a brain sharper and better targeted than an arrow. I made to deny it, but I looked into those eyes and realized that, for some reason, I couldn't.

So I told her.

I had no idea why I was telling her. It really wasn't her business. I didn't have to spin some lie off the top of my head; I could have just said, "It's none of your business," and left it at that. But something in me . . . *wanted* to tell her.

I didn't go into my entire history, of course, and I certainly didn't make any mention of my connection to Tacit. But I told her of how Astel had taken not only my virginity, but whatever rudimentary ability I might have had to trust anyone. Of how she had left me with the literal taste of ashes in my mouth, penniless, with no resources.

Entipy took in every word, and when I stopped talking—after what seemed an age—she said in amazement, "If I were you, I'd hate the world."

She really did understand me. The concept frightened me.

"It's amazing," she continued, "that you're as heroic as you are."

Then again, maybe she didn't understand me all that well.

I'd been sitting on the floor of the barn, and she climbed down off the hay bale and sat next to me. And we continued to talk for quite some time after that. I was still guarded, and I suspect that she was as well. But we spoke of many things, most of them involving our cynical view of the world at large. I sensed within her a kindred spirit, someone who was capable of perceiving the dark underbelly that those in power seemed incapable of seeing no matter how clearly it was pointed out to them.

"Sometimes," Entipy said, "I think the only person in the entirety of my father's court who makes any sense at all is the jester. He, at least, is capable of treating the world the way it deserves to be treated: with humorous contempt. And the real joke is, as often as he points it up, my parents and the courtiers all laugh as if it's some great jest with no deeper meaning. They don't understand that their inability to understand that they're all shams is the biggest joke of all. They are the butt of all the humor of the jester and they blindly snicker about it. Fools."

I couldn't help but agree.

I also noticed, though, that the more we talked, the closer she seemed to edge to me, until—as the evening hour drew late—she was within bare inches of me. As chill as the barn was getting, she was so close that her body heat was warming me. I found it . . . disconcerting. We had lapsed into momentary silence and this time it was an uncomfortable one, because I sensed that there were things she wanted to say, and I didn't want to hear them. "Princess . . ." I said after a time.

"I hate that," she said abruptly. "I hate when people call me that. Don't you call me that."

I blinked in surprise. "But . . . it's your title."

"Yes, I know. And that's what people see me as, and that's all they see me as. My title is me, I am my title. The title says everything that I'm supposed to be, except it's a title given anyone of that birth, so we're all supposed to be alike. Except I don't want to be like anyone else."

"Trust me: You aren't."

She didn't seem to have heard me speak. "I'm so defined by my rank," she said softly, "that I feel as if no one knows the real me. I even start to wonder . . . if there's any real me left anymore."

"There is. I'm sure there is."

She looked to me and smiled that dazzling smile again. I felt a warm stirring in my loins, and shoved the thoughts away immediately.

Understand, I wasn't being bound by any prudish concerns. A female is a female is a female. But there were two major problems. First and foremost, as much as I was beginning to feel some rudimentary connection to her, I couldn't help but remember that it wasn't all that long ago that I had considered her borderline insane. That I would look into her eyes and see an ocean of madness in those orbs. I was not ready to set aside the notion that she was a loon, and the last thing I needed to do was couple with such a mad creature.

Second, and just as problematic: This was no bored

wife of a knight. This was no tavern maid. This was a princess. One does not form the beast with two backs with such an individual and then expect that it ends with a shake of the hands and a "See you later." When one engages in such horizontal activities, one had better be damned ready to make a lifetime commitment or be prepared to lose one's head, or other body parts.

You might think me mad to flinch from an alliance that would wind up making me consort to a future queen. Not so. It was simply not my way to rush into anything. Not until I had the opportunity to consider every possible angle and determine the potential negative aspect of a situation. I had given in to impulse before, remember, and had nearly had my skull caved in by my mother's funeral urn because of it.

"It's getting cold," said Entipy. She got up and took a large blanket piled in the corner, then brought it back to the two of us. She draped it around herself and then held it up, indicating that I should join her under there.

"I think," I said slowly, "that it would be best if you wrapped yourself up in that, Highness. I can sleep next to you to provide warmth, but . . . within the blanket, well . . ."

For a moment, just a moment, she looked hurt. Then the hardness of rejection was reflected in her eyes. "Is there a problem?" she said, her voice suddenly sounding much colder than the air around us.

"Entipy . . ." I said, deliberately not making use of her title. "As you yourself have observed . . . I have every reason to have a difficulty with the concept of trust."

"Are you saying," she asked with incredulity in her voice, "that you don't trust me?"

"No," I corrected her as politely as I could. "I'm saying I don't trust myself."

At that, the corners of her mouth turned up again, ever so slightly. "Oh. I see" was all she said. Whereupon she wrapped herself up in the blanket, tightly cocooned, and presented her back to me. I lay next to her. Somewhere during the night, I draped an arm over her, and that was how we slept, while the Heffers looked on and doubtless thought we were ridiculous.

They were probably right.

"Get up."

Dotty was prodding us with her foot. Immediately I snapped awake, worried that we were under some sort of attack. Entipy was slower than I to be roused, but only slightly, as we both blinked against the early morning sun streaming in through the door of the stable. I could still smell the dew in the air. Whatever time it was, it was damned early.

It was at that point that Dotty drew back her foot and gave me a swift kick, hard enough to send me rolling. "I was awake!" I yelped in irritation.

"I knew you were," she replied tartly. "That was payback for my inconvenience."

"Inconvenience?" Entipy was rubbing the sleep from her eyes. "What inconvenience? What did we—?"

"I received a return on your message," she said. She was looking at the two of us with renewed suspicion. "Never got one back so fast and so early. Whatever your package is, someone obviously considers it to be extremely important. The spell landed in my cauldron, shrieking its blasted head off. Wouldn't shut up until I transferred it to parchment for you. Here." As she leaned forward to hand it to me, I saw that there was still some slight gunk in her eyes. She'd really only awoken a minute or so before.

I unrolled the parchment and studied it. Entipy looked over my shoulder. She seemed to be breathing in my ear, but I chose to ignore it.

"We are quite pleased, as you can probably surmise, to know that your package is safe" (said the note). *"For obvious reasons, coming into the Outer Lawless regions is not practical. We will trust you, Apropos, to get the package to the fortress outpost called Terracote. There you can turn your package over to its rightful owners."*

Very carefully worded. The reasons were obvious, all right; unexpected and unprompted troop movements over the borders into Outer Lawless would certainly attract the attention and interest of the dreaded Warlord Shank. It might make him wonder just what it was that had so sparked the king's interest that he would undertake such an endeavor. I couldn't say that I was thrilled to think that we were, in essence, still on our own for as long as we were in Outer Lawless. But I suppose I shouldn't have been surprised that there were not going to be easy answers.

"Terracote," I said, looking up at Dotty. "Where is—?"

But she was already reaching into her robes and extracting a map. "Thought you might be needing that," she said. "It's about a two-, maybe three-week ride from here, just beyond the Outer Lawless borders, at the outskirts of Isteria."

"A hazardous journey?"

"In places," she said. "Some is well traveled, some . . . less so. It's hard to say for sure. The makeup of the land is changing. Don't know if you've noticed that or not."

"Somewhat. I wasn't sure what to attribute it to."

"These are dangerous times," she said darkly . . . which is what weavers usually say when they've no idea what other answer to make. "Now . . . get off with thee so I can return to sleep. Usually I don't waken until noon. I need my beauty sleep."

Privately I thought that there weren't enough hours in the day for her to sleep through to help her in that score, but I saw no reason to voice the opinion.

"Madam," I said abruptly, just before she was out the door. She stopped and looked at me balefully. I thanked what gods there were that her specialty was communication. If she had any knack for transformation, I'd most likely have been a raccoon or some such by that point. Gamely I said, with a slight bow, "I cannot thank you enough for you service. I was hoping that I might be able to impose on you for one last—"

"No," she said, and started to walk away again. I knew her type, however, and when I made a significant enough jingling while pulling out my purse, it stopped her in her tracks right enough. She regarded me with a suspicious, but accepting stare. "I'm listening."

"I hope I did nothing to give you the impression that you would not be well compensated for your—"

"What is it, what is it?" she said impatiently, making

a hurried gesture that indicated I should get to the point.

I reached into my tunic and pulled out a folded parchment that I had carefully prepared the night before. "I would like you to wait seven days . . . and then see that this gets to the dreaded Warlord Shank. It is to be delivered directly into his hand." I reached deep into my purse and said, with carefully constructed nonchalance, "I'd say two dukes should cover your services in that regard, wouldn't you?"

Her eyes widened. She was so startled by the amount that she didn't even bother to haggle. She held out a clawlike hand and snatched the coins. Then she took the parchment from me and startled to unfold it.

"Pardon me . . . that's intended to be private."

At that she gave a contemptuous laugh. "You want me to walk up to the most formidable individual in our land and hand him a message sight unseen? And if it said something about me that would prompt him to put me to the sword? They kill messengers, boy."

She read it over, frowning, and then her eyes widened. She looked straight at me. "If you think I'd give this to him and be anywhere within the vicinity, you're mad. I'll send it by bird or by nothing."

"Bird. You mean that great falcon I saw?"

She nodded.

Well, it would have to do. The falcon looked formidable enough, and I doubted anyone could stop it if they had a mind to. "Very well," I said with a curt nod. "I believe it will suffice. And thank you f—"

She didn't hear what I was about to thank her for, which was all well and good in that I don't think she especially cared either. Instead she just walked out of the barn. The loose flaps of skin under her arms waved like twin pennants in the breeze as she lurched away.

"That note," Entipy said with interest. "What did it say?"

"Oh. That," I said with a feigned blasé attitude. "That was simply a note giving the good warlord some background information about his new bride. Things that she would be too modest to mention."

"The commweaver acted as if they were bad things."

"They were true things. I leave good and bad to be judged by others."

She smiled at me, genuinely smiled, and it was utterly devoid of the faintly demented looks I'd received from her before. "You told Shank about his fiancée's background. Didn't you. And he's not going to like it."

"True. But they're to be married within the week, so by the time he finds out, she'll be his wife. So I've given her a sporting chance, you see."

"But she paid you for your silence."

"I never promised to remain silent. I simply said I'd go away. I'm keeping my word. However I also owe her a debt from the past . . . and make no mistake. I always repay my debts."

Chapter 21

The Heffers we had obtained were worthy beasts, and we made reasonably good time with them. I was still not pleased over the fact that the weather had not become as temperate as we had hoped, but it wasn't as if I had any choice in dealing with it. Other than the weather, things went fairly smoothly.

We did the best we could in our journey to draw no attention to ourselves, and for the most part we were successful. Entipy cut her hair reasonably short so that, at first glance, she would appear somewhat boyish. We then did all that we could to make certain that no one gave us a second glance. We made eye contact with no one and, when addressed by other travelers, would mutter several indecipherable words to give the impression that we didn't speak any tongue known to civilized man. It was enough to encourage people not to bother with us.

At night we would pick extremely busy inns to stay in. The money that Astel had provided us proved to be more than sufficient to get us quite nice lodgings. Not only that, but it was enough for Entipy and I to have a room each to ourselves, and that much was an extreme relief indeed. You see, I couldn't help but get the feeling that Entipy was becoming more and more attached to me, and that was a circumstance that simply was not going to benefit anyone.

And yet, much as I am loath to admit it, I found her increasingly easy to talk to. The first thing to make conversation livable was that she had stopped mentioning Tacit with every other breath. At this point she had stopped mentioning him at all. She had totally lost faith in him, and that was not surprising. When one is put on as high a pedestal as Tacit was, one makes a very loud thud when one falls off it. The second thing was that she seemed to want to find out all about me. She found me interesting. I was not, she said, like any other squire or even knight that she had ever encountered before. I'd wager she was right.

For obvious reasons, I wasn't about to tell her chapter and verse about my life. There were certain aspects that were far better kept close to my vest. So the specific circumstances of my conception, for instance, were omitted. I did tell her of my mother's sense that I had a great destiny, and I further mentioned to her the immortal phoenix bird incident my mother had described so often from her pre-Apropos days. Entipy's eyes widened at that point in the recitation. "So she saw one even before you were born! That's impressive. You might have even greater auguries for your future than . . ."

She stopped. I knew that she had been about to say

"Tacit," but she stopped herself before mentioning the name. Instead all she said was "Go on."

I described the brutality of her death and the circumstances which had resulted in my coming to Runcible's castle. One of the things that I discovered Entipy liked to do was speak contemptuously of those who weren't there, and I was able to give her plenty of fodder for it. She was lukewarm on Sir Justus, despised Sir Coreolis ("He's not at all trustworthy," she said several times), and almost oozed disdain for all of the squires . . . particularly the self-absorbed Mace Morningstar.

She didn't seem to have much use for her parents, either. She seemed to find the queen tolerable if naught else, but she had no patience for the king at all. "He's a sham. I know he is," she said with a snort. She wouldn't go into detail about how she knew this. Apparently she felt that details and facts were unnecessary. If she said it, it had to be so. End of discussion.

Day became night, which became day and on into the night again. On the third day, after she'd found yet another triviality to complain about, I asked her point-blank. I said, "Is there anyone or anything in this world that doesn't upset you? That brings you pleasure?"

I had a feeling that she was going to bring up Tacit, but instead she surprised me. "I like sunrises. They make anything seem possible," she said.

I blinked in surprise. "I've always felt the same way," I said.

"Well, of course," she said matter-of-factly. "I mean, even *you*, squire, can't be wrong all the time." It was typical of the snide and arrogant comments she had made to me when we'd first met, but she said it without any heat or vituperation. I caught her eye as I looked at her with open curiosity . . . and she winked at me.

That wink said more than anything else thus far, and once again I felt apprehensive.

My ambition was at total war with my common sense. I had, after all, seen the "real" Entipy: the sullen, arrogant, somewhat dangerous young woman whom we had picked up from the Faith Women. And Mace Morningstar had likewise seen her . . . and almost got his skull cracked for his efforts. Whatever I was seeing now was some new, flirting creature that had been applied to the surface like a cake of mud that some women believed removed wrinkles. She was not remotely genuine. Let us say, as a matter of insane speculation, that we wound up together. Sooner or later the demented Entipy would return, and I would be stuck with the creature for the rest of my life . . . which would probably be foreshortened as a result.

Except . . .

. . . how did I know that? Really? What if . . . what if the Entipy that I had seen before . . . was the "impostor"? That the one I was seeing now was real? What if she really was as easy to talk to as she now seemed? What if . . .

Gods. What if she really was my ticket to everything?

Just imagine it. Just imagine the faces on the knights, on Morningstar, on all of them, if the king announced that the princess had affianced herself to Apropos. Imagine the sputtered indignation from Justus and Coreolis and the rest. Imagine the look of pure horror from Morningstar and his ilk, knowing that I would eventually be in a position where they would have to bend knee to me, attend my commands, go where I told them they had to go. The joys of honor and obedience: I could instruct Morningstar to strip naked and ride into combat single-handedly against the dreaded Warlord Shank . . .

. . . and he'd have to do it!

"Apropos, why are you smiling in that slightly demented way?" Entipy asked, bringing me back to reality.

A steady chill wind was blowing against our faces, the Heffers treading along the path as best they could against it. We'd been on the road for some days. I glanced at her as she spoke and, pulling my thoughts back to focus, said coolly, "Just imagining the joy on your parents' faces when I bring you back, Highness."

"They never liked me, you know," she said with sullen petulance. "If they had, they'd never have sent me away."

"All parents have to do what they think is best for their child."

"Would you have done it?" There was both curiosity and challenge in her voice.

The easy, facile answer would have been to say no, protesting that she was much too charming to do such a thing. But she'd see right through that, and it had suddenly become of great interest to me to court the princess's genuine affections. Whenever my resolve wavered from that, I'd picture the helpless Morningstar riding into battle and that would help me back onto the correct path.

"You are speaking to one," I said slowly, "who never

knew the normal trappings of father and mother. My father, as you know, died before I was born" (the story that I had given her to cover the truth of my origins) "and my mother worked such long and hard hours that she rarely was able to give me any attention. And then she was taken from me. Because of that, I would never want to—in any respect—deprive any child of mine of the immediacy and relationships that I was never able to have. So, no, I would not send you away. Perhaps that makes me selfish . . ."

"No, no, not at all. It makes you a good father."

"It reflects my own upbringing, is all. Frequently, Highness, that's all one sees in one's parents: how they themselves were raised. For all you know, your father and mother were likewise sent away, or by other means kept distanced from their parents. For them, what they did was simple normal behavior. On that basis, it would be no more fair to condemn them for their actions than it would to accuse a bear of laziness because it sleeps away the winter. It simply does what comes naturally."

She nodded thoughtfully, processing the notions. I, in the meantime, continued to let my common sense war with my ambition . . .

"Apropos . . ." and she reached over and took my hand, reining her Heffer to a stop. "Thank you. Maybe you're right. Maybe . . . you're actually providing a reason for me not to hate my parents. And that's not a bad thing to have at all."

I squeezed her hand tightly, returning the gesture . . .

. . . and she started to pull me toward her, clearly intending to kiss me.

And as I was faced with this outward, physical display of her affection, an entirely new dynamic entered my mind. I automatically flinched back, and she knew it. I saw the disappointment, the surprise, and even the faintest flutter of anger in her eyes.

The problem was, I knew where it was going to lead. One kiss becomes a second, then a third and so on, and the next thing you know, clothes are everywhere and other parts of you are places they shouldn't be. Places where, I was reasonably sure, Tacit had already been.

That's what it came down to, really. It had taken me a while to realize it, but that was the truth of it. If matters went in that direction, if we became engaged, married, well . . . sooner or later, I'd have to make love to her. And if I made love to her . . . she would compare me to Tacit. It was only inevitable. And there was no question in my mind that, as in all things except the one time I caught him totally by surprise, I would come up short in measuring up . . . so to speak. She would hold me up against his performance, find me lacking, lose all respect for me . . .

None of which I could say to her, of course. But I had to say something, and fast, because I had a hurt and angry princess on my hands, and such a creature is wildly unpredictable. And here, entering a somewhat mountainous and potentially treacherous region of the Outer Lawless realm, I didn't need unpredictability at my side. It could get us both killed.

"Highness . . . as flattered as I am . . . it . . . it wouldn't be right."

"Why wouldn't it," she said, sounding quite icy.

"Because," I said, sounding as reasonable as I could, "anything you might be feeling for me, Princess . . . might be from the intensity of the moment. Unusual alliances, such as what we have forged, cause all sorts of emotions to become more . . . heightened . . . than they ordinarily would be. They give rise to feelings that would not be there if circumstances were more normal. For me to take advantage of what you might be feeling for me right now . . . it wouldn't be right. The impulses might not be genuine. Once we are to safety and you can think rationally . . . then we shall see what's what. I wouldn't want to risk taking advantage of you . . ." and then, as a masterstroke of inspiration, I added, "as others may have, finding you vulnerable and saddened."

A direct hit. A perfect score. Her eyes widened and she nodded in understanding, and I knew exactly what was going through her mind because I, Apropos, master of subtlety, had planted it there. She was starting to wonder whether her involvement with Tacit had truly been the grand romantic adventure she had thought it was . . . or whether he was simply taking advantage of her. And if he was . . . while here, Apropos was refusing to do so . . . how noble did that make Apropos, and how much of a cad did that make Tacit? Apropos, who had been here and come through for her, and Tacit who hadn't? My mind soared with joy.

And that was when it hit me.

It wasn't anything bad, actually; in fact, it was very surprising. It was a gust of warm air, so unexpected and so out of place that its sudden appearance struck me almost like the blow of a hammer.

What was even the more surprising was that the general area we were in was somewhat colder than before, probably because the road was going on a steady upward slope, which meant we were going higher, where altitude was less and the air was chillier. In the near distance I could see mountain peaks, thick with snow. So a sudden gust of warm air truly seemed to come from nowhere.

I pulled out the map that Dotty had provided us. The fortress at Terracote truly didn't seem all that far . . . another few days at most. However, it was going to become more difficult before it became easier, because I saw more mountains dotting the path. They seem to be fairly low by comparison to others on the same map, but it still was going to be an effort. So I certainly didn't want us to become distracted by things that were off the path.

Yet that was what was happening, because Entipy felt the same gusting warmth that I did. "Is it from a spring, do you think?" she asked. "Or some sort of sulfur caves?"

"For all I know they left the door to hell ajar. Whatever it is, it's none of our concern." Even as I spoke, though, I felt another wafting of warm air and, more, the whiff of lilacs. I hadn't a clue to what was going on.

The Heffers, though, did not seem pleased. They whinnied uncertainly, and mine started to back up slightly.

Entipy, however, would have none of it. "I want to see what's causing that. If it's a warmer path than through the mountains, we should take it."

I looked at the wall of trees which was lining the edge

of the road. There were no leaves upon them, but instead thick green needles . . . not sharp, but enough so that we couldn't have a clear vision of what lay past them. "There's no path here to take," I said in what I hoped was my most reasonable manner.

She didn't reply. Instead she dug her heels into the sides of the Heffer and urged it off the road. "Princess!" I said in annoyance, but she ignored me. The Heffer made one more noise of protest and then reluctantly went where it was led.

My own Heffer angled its head around at me and seemed to look me in the eyes as if to say, *You're not thinking about going in there, too, are you?* But I had no real choice. I couldn't let the little fool just wander off by herself. So with a resigned sigh I snapped the reins and guided my own beast off the path as well.

Fortunately enough, Heffers were even more surefooted than ordinary horses, so I wasn't all that concerned about riding one off the beaten path. I would not have essayed a gallop, of course, because that would likely have resulted in a broken leg in short order.

At first their hooves crunched through the thin layer of ice and snow on the ground, but then I realized that the crunching noise had stopped. The reason was quickly obvious: The ice was gone. The air was getting warmer the farther we went. A few minutes ago there had been mist coming out of our mouths when we spoke, but now there was nothing. And the aroma of lilacs was becoming stronger than ever.

Entipy kept glancing at me, clearly puzzled, apparently hoping that I would come up with an explanation.

But I just shook my head, as bemused as she was.

The going was becoming increasingly easy, the trees thinning out. It was as if we were literally crossing seasonal lines, traveling directly from winter into spring, with summer a few yards ahead. The Heffers, however, were becoming increasingly agitated. They slowed to a crawl, and all the rein snapping on both of our parts was not getting them to move any faster. "What's wrong with them!" Entipy demanded in frustration. "Stupid animals! Don't they want to go where it's warm?" And she dug her heels into the belly of her Heffer, who didn't seem particularly pleased by the gesture.

"I'm getting the impression they don't," I said, "and I'm starting to wonder if they know something we don't."

"How could they? They're just dumb animals."

"Animals can sometimes sense problems before humans. I think we'd better go back."

"Why?"

"Because my horse isn't going forward."

And it was true. The Heffer had come to a complete halt. No matter how much I urged it to do so, it wasn't budging. As a matter of fact, it was trying to back up. Entipy was in the same bind, her horse not moving an inch. Not taking to this particular development in the least, Entipy dismounted, grabbed up the reins, and tried to pull the horse forward. She shouted at it, informing the horse just exactly who she was and precisely the kind of trouble it was going to get in if it ignored the royal decrees of a princess.

The Heffer suddenly let out an ear-curdling cry of

protest and reared up, thrashing the air with its front hooves. That was about all the warning I had before my horse did likewise. Unlike Entipy, however, I was still on its back. I tried to hold on, but I had no chance, and I tumbled backward off the horse. As I fell I snagged the saddlebag, more for the purpose of trying to hold on than anything else, but the saddlebag tore free and went with me to the ground. "Stop them!" Entipy shouted, as if I were remotely in any sort of position to impose my will on two bucking horses. I lay stunned on the forest floor, and suddenly I saw the Heffer's hooves pounding straight toward my head. Sheer panic galvanized me and I rolled out of the way just as the beast pounded past me. Its associate followed directly behind it, ignoring the princess's shouted curses and threats.

"What's got into them?!" she cried out. She looked down at me as I lay there, gasping at how close I had just come to being a splotch on their hooves. "Are you all right?" she inquired, sounding vaguely solicitous.

"Ohhh . . . fine," I managed to say. I sat up slowly and looked behind us. There was already no sign of the horses. "Wonderful," I muttered, and then turned just in time to see Entipy heading not back after the Heffers but forward toward whatever the hell had just sent them dashing in the other direction. "Are you daft?!" I called after her. "Where do you think you're going!"

"I want to see what caused them to run off," she replied. "If we're going to lose the horses over it . . ."

"We're not going to lose anything of the kind," I protested, using a tree to pull myself up. I picked up the saddlebag, breathing a sigh of relief; the majority of the riches I'd taken from Astel were in there. I redid the straps and tied it off around my waist. Between the jewels and the sword I still had strapped to my back, I was getting a bit loaded down. "We'll go back out to the road. They're probably waiting for us there."

"Or they've run away. Besides, I want to see what's up there."

"No, you don't, and I'm going back for the horses."

"Fine. You do that." And without another word she turned on her heel and set out in the opposite direction from where I wanted to go.

I muttered a string of profanities under my breath as I started to head back to the road. I got about twenty feet and then envisioned what it would be like to face King Runcible at the fort and inform him that the last time I'd seen his little girl, she'd stomped off on her own into a forest and I'd done nothing to stop her. Immediately after that, the next thing I'd likely see would be a headsman's axe. With a moan I turned around and started off after Entipy.

She wasn't difficult to follow, leaving a trail that a blind man could track. The warmth had evened off, fortunately, because if it had kept up, the weather around me would have become positively scalding. "Entipy!" I called up ahead, hoping to get her to slow down since, even moving as fast as I could, my lame leg was slowing me up. "Entipy! Get back here! This is madness!"

I saw Entipy just ahead, standing on what appeared to be a ridge. Apparently there was a valley of some sort just ahead. "Entipy!" I called to her. "Enough games! Enough foolishness! It's time to—!"

She turned to look at me, and I stopped where I was, taken aback at the sheer wonderment in her eyes. It wasn't me she was reacting to, that was for sure. She saw something in the valley ahead that had completely stunned her. Cautious and uncertain, I made my way up the narrow incline until I was by her side, and then looked where she was looking, the smell of lilacs so thick in my nostrils that it was almost suffocating.

I gasped. You would have, too.

Unicorns.

Not a couple. Not a handful. A herd.

In the near distance, snow-covered mountains towered. But here, in this valley, it was spring, and would always be so for as long as the unicorns chose to graze there. There was an endless supply of food for them to consume, because the grass continued to grow at an amazing rate. It was impossible to tell how long they had been there—a day, an age. To such creatures, time truly had little meaning.

They were not entirely what I had expected, not precisely what I had seen as depicted in tapestries. They were, for one thing, smaller. Not a one of them was much larger than a pony. Yet there were so many of them at that size that I could only conclude that that was how big they got at maturity, rather than that we had stumbled upon a herd of young ones. Some of them were white, yes, but there were others who were deep brown, and some that were—incredibly—green. Green that was as green as the forest. I thought of the times when I would be in the Elderwoods and think that I'd seen something move, just out of the corner of my eye, but when I'd looked straight on I'd seen nothing. Perhaps the "nothing" I had seen had been a unicorn standing against a bush and blending in perfectly.

The fabled horns were not quite as long and pointed as I would have thought; they were shorter and curved upward, appearing more like tusks than horns. Their second most noticeable feature was their tails, which were long, thin, and almost snake-like, a small tuft of hair at the end. And they were shaggy beasts. Their manes were long and unkempt, and their fetlocks were thick to the point of almost being furry. However, I quickly noticed something, and that was that the manes and fetlocks seemed to be glittering as the sun hit them. Sparkling, even, in a rainbow of colors that made it seem as if the light was dancing along them. And their eyes . . . their eyes were the deepest blue I had ever seen. Such blue that I could have stared at it for hours, forever. Such blue that it hurt to look away, even for an instant.

As scruffy as the creatures appeared on the outside, they seemed to glow from within. I understood why someone weaving a tapestry would depict them in such a manner; it was because it was a rendering of the glorious souls these animals possessed. I knew that I was going to start crying as soon as I walked away from them, which I would obviously have to do eventually. I could not, after all, live among them. Although even that seemed possible at the moment. Anything did.

"Gods," I whispered because, really, what else could one say?

Entipy was looking at me with wonder. "It's because of you," she said.

"Me?" I had no idea what she was talking about. In fact, it took effort for me to force my attention back to the fact that she was there at all. "What's because of me?"

"In all my life," she said in wonderment, "I've never seen a single magical beast. Not a one. I've read about them, thought about them. But never seen one. Then along comes Apropos, whose mother witnessed an omen of a phoenix. Here you come, riding on the back of one, just as it was shown in the tapestry back at my home. And now I come upon more glorious creatures while in your company. There's something about you that intertwines your fate with such animals."

I didn't bother to point out that I tried to head away from the creatures, not toward them. She was so caught up in the magic of the moment that she was already reordering events to suit the new worldview. Fine. Let her. If it was going to benefit me, I wasn't about to argue. "I suppose anything is possible," I said.

I glanced over my shoulder to see if there was any remaining sign of the Heffers. Nothing. I hoped my guess was right and they had decided to wait for us by the side of the road. I turned back to Entipy.

She wasn't there.

My heart leaped up into my throat, for I could see the top of Entipy's head disappearing beyond the edge of the rise. She was climbing down into the valley where the unicorns were grazing. "Princesssss!" I hissed. "Get back here!"

Either she didn't hear me or she simply acted as if she didn't hear me, but in either event she dropped from sight. Immediately I scrambled to the edge of the rise and looked down. She had already reached the bottom; it was only about ten feet down, and on an incline rather than a straight drop, so it had been no great challenge for her to get down there. "Entipy!" I called to her again in a desperate low voice. She looked up at me, her eyebrows knit, as if she couldn't possibly figure out what I might want to talk to her about. "Get back up here!"

She put her hands on her hips and said with obvious impatience, "How am I going to be able to ride a unicorn if I stay up there?"

I felt a pounding starting in my temple that I had become all too familiar with since making the princess's acquaintance. "Are you insane!" I demanded, already knowing the answer. She did not bother to make a response, instead simply walked away from me with a shrug of her shoulders as if I was not worth a moment of her time.

I had no choice. I swung my legs over the edge of the rise and slid down as quickly as I could. Dirt and small pebbles tumbled around me and I halted my fall using my lame right leg because the last thing I wanted to do was risk damaging the good left one. I used my staff to haul myself up and made off quickly after her. She was approaching the herd with a bold stride, her chin upraised and her eyes sparkling with excitement.

"Princess," I said with a desperate urgency that I did not remotely have to fake. "Princess, this is ill advised. Unicorns or not, they remain wild animals, and such creatures tend to be rather territorial. A stranger marching into their midst—"

"I am no stranger," she said airily. "I am a princess of

the blood royal. My place in the world of the unicorn is assured." She slowed ever so slightly to allow me to catch up. "We are going to do something that will be the stuff of legends, squire."

"We will?" I liked the sound of this less and less.

"Yes. I am going to find us the right unicorn. And I will mount it and ride it straight to Fort Terracote. It will carry me there on its pure white back—white, Apropos, it has to be white. None of these brown or green ones."

"So noted. Entipy—"

"And it will hold its beautiful head high, and its horn will glow," she continued, caught up in her fantasy. "And all will see me coming, and my father will feel ashamed that he ever thought to send me away."

"That's a charming scenario." We were drawing uncomfortably close to the herd. Some of the unicorns were taking note of us, their tails whipping around in what I feared was agitation. "Now allow me to offer an alternative: You walk up to a unicorn, try to exercise your influence, and the skittish animal runs you through with its horn."

"That could never happen. Unicorn horns have the power to cure."

"So I hear . . . provided you grind them up and use them properly. Having neither a grinder nor knowledge of proper procedures, I'd rather not take my chances."

"You are a squire, Apropos. If you are ever to become Sir Apropos, you will have to learn to take chances."

"Not with the life of the princess," I said tautly. Which was true enough. I reached for her, ready to sling her over my shoulder and haul her out of there if necessary, but she increased her speed and dodged my efforts. She even let out a curt laugh, as if the entire thing were a game. "These things are unpredictable, Entipy!" I reminded her. "They could kill you . . . !"

"To die . . . at the hooves or horns of creatures as beautiful as these . . ." Her eyes widened at the exciting thought. "How glorious would that be?"

Such words as these did nothing to lighten my mood. There was nothing romantic about suicide, and that's where I was worried this was going. "Not as glorious as living to tell people what we witnessed here today. Let's go, now. N—"

"Apropos," she said, her voice firm, "I'm going to do this."

"But you have to be a—" I stopped.

She looked at me, curious. "I have to be a what?"

I licked my lips, my voice suddenly feeling very raspy. "Well . . . you have to be . . . you know . . ."

"No, I don't know." I wondered if she was going to make me say it just to watch me be uncomfortable.

Taking a deep breath, I said, "Well . . . you know . . . a virg . . . a virg . . ."

"Virgin?" There was thick sarcasm in her voice. "Number one, that is an old wives' tale. And number two . . . what are you implying?"

"I'm not implying anything."

"Yes, you are. You're saying I'm not a virgin."

"No, I'm not." I was trying to cover as fast as I could. "I was just, uhm . . . reminding you that you had to be one."

"Why would you have to remind me of that? If you

believed me to be one, then you would think that my status would guarantee safe passage. The only possible reason you would feel the need to bring it up is a belief that I am not. And I am, frankly, a bit insulted."

"I'm just suggesting caution, that's all. I—"

"You think I can't do it." There was rising ire in her voice. I felt as if the ground around me were turning to sand, sucking me down, even though it was beautiful and green and harmless. "You think I'm not a virgin and that I'm not up to the challenge. Well, I'll show you . . ."

"You don't have to show me anything!"

Obviously, though, she felt she did, because she quickened her pace all the more. She was making a beeline toward one particular unicorn. She certainly had picked out a remarkable-looking one. It was indeed purest white, and the sparkles in its mane almost made it look as if light was pouring out from the creature's immortal soul. It was watching her with those soulful eyes. I wondered how many sights the unicorn had seen in its lifetime, how many foolish maidens had tried to approach it. It tilted its head slightly, watching Entipy as if she were a mad little thing . . . which she was.

She slowed ever so slightly as she drew near. The unicorn took a step back and gave a faint, musical whinny that sounded more than anything like a warning. It had not lowered its horn as if to charge, but it certainly didn't seem enthused about seeing her. Entipy was making soft "chuk chuk" noises as she got within range of the beast. I noticed that Entipy and the one unicorn were not exactly operating independently of the rest of the world. Every unicorn in the vicinity was now watching the scenario play out. I wondered how they were going to react if it didn't play out in a manner to their liking.

"Hellooooo," said Entipy softly. She kept both her hands flat and open, palms up, so that the unicorn could see for itself that she was unarmed. "Apropos . . . what do you think it is? A girl or a boy?"

"Neither. It's a damned horse, and I mislike this whole thing. It stinks of magic and I'd sooner we were anywhere but here."

"We will be, I told you. We're going to ride them to Terracote."

Now that I was a bit closer (already closer than I liked) I could see that there was even hair on the horns themselves. It was such a light color as to be almost invisible, but it was there nevertheless.

I was getting a very uneasy feeling about the entire business, because a number of the unicorns were looking at me, or at least it seemed as if they were. All I could dwell upon at that point was Tacit's saying that he had been raised by unicorns. What if he'd been telling the truth? Not only that . . . but what if it had been these unicorns? What if one of them had actually suckled him? What if . . . what if they knew what I had done?

I could feel those stormy blue eyes burrowing into me, and the more I wanted to clear my mind of my assaulting Tacit, the more it seemed to rise to the forefront. Could they read minds? Smell guilt feelings? I had no way of knowing; these were magical creatures, to be sure. They were capable of just about anything.

"Entipy," I said slowly, not taking my eyes off the great beasts who were not taking their eyes off me, "these are not captive show creatures in a traveling circus. These are wild animals, out in the wild. We are on their turf, in a very uncontrolled situation, and anything can happen. And a goodly number of those anythings would be counterproductive to our continued health."

She wasn't listening. Part of me was hoping that one of them would just run her through and get it over with. The suspense was killing me. She was almost up to the unicorn that she had selected for the questionable honor of being her mount. The horse wasn't backing up at that point. Why should it be? It had a sizable number of friends to serve as support against a single unarmed girl. Entipy was continuing to make those clucking noises, causing her to sound like an overlarge chicken, interspersed with such useful comments as "Here, unicorn. Nice unicorn. Pretty pretty unicorn."

Then, with an extremely credible display of horsemanship, Entipy snagged a handful of the unicorn's mane and swung herself expertly onto its back before it could offer protest. She straddled it, looked triumphantly over at me, and started to call out "See?!" right before the unicorn threw her into the air.

I should have let her just hit the ground. It might have jolted some sense into her. Instead I stupidly bolted toward her and lunged for her. She crashed into me, sending us both to the ground in a tangle of arms and legs. I felt a soreness in my chest and fingered my ribs, hoping that the impact hadn't broken one.

"I'm all right! I'm all right!" Entipy said, disentangling herself from me.

"I don't care!" I shot back grumpily, sitting up. "That was a damned fool thing to do."

"I am a princess," she said haughtily. "I do what I like."

"If what you 'like' is to get your fool neck broken, keep right on doing it because you were well on your way. You'd probably have done it by now if I hadn't caught you."

She regarded me thoughtfully and crouched beside me. Her face softened. "Yes. You did, didn't you. That was sweet."

The smell of lilacs was making me feel light-headed. I wondered if it was having the same effect on her. Then, before I could stop her, she wrapped an arm around the back of my head and kissed me passionately. I felt myself being carried away by the moment, and I returned the kiss with passion of my own, taking her into my arms. I felt giddy, intoxicated. For just a moment, all my concerns about her being unpredictable and untrustworthy faded away, and I felt something deep and profound within me . . . as if, impossibly, in this hard and cynical world, I had found a genuine soul mate. A part of myself I didn't even know I was missing. All that from one ardor-charged kiss.

The unicorn let out a whinny, and it was not musical, and it was not alone, because the lot of them chorused in.

We broke off and I looked at them, my eyes wide with alarm. I could no longer make out which unicorn had been the one that Entipy had been endeavoring to mount, because they were now clustered together. More and more of them were coming in from all sides, advancing. Their tails were no longer swishing back and forth in leisurely fashion. Instead they were straight back or straight down, tense and quivering with what I could only interpret as rage.

Oh, gods, they do *know,* the frantic thought went through my head. *They know what I did . . . they know that I shouldn't be here.* Unicorns were, as noted, magical. They were true creatures of destiny and, therefore, must have had some clear idea of how destiny was to be shaped. And here came I, Apropos, who had usurped the rightful place of the unicorn-bred hero of the story, flaunting that craven triumph in their faces. Little wonder they weren't exactly happy with me at that moment.

Entipy didn't understand any of that. "It was just a kiss, you horned prudes!" she said in irritation as we got to our feet. "He saved me! He's . . ." Caught up in the moment, she took my hand in hers. "He's my hero."

And then went up a sound of pure fury such as I'd never heard and hope never to hear again. The sea of white was advancing on us like a great wave. I looked in the direction from which we'd come, but we were cut off, the herd having moved across it. It seemed that every single unicorn in the herd had now made us the complete and undivided focus of their attention.

From directly behind us I felt a gust of cold air. It was an area more toward the mountain passes, bereft of grass, and so the unicorns had focused their energies, or charms, or whatever you would call it on that particular piece of land. The path to it seemed clear, which was fortunate, because if we'd been surrounded on all sides we wouldn't have had a prayer. As it was, I wasn't giving our chances great odds.

Even Entipy was now fully aware that we were in serious trouble. Those blue eyes of the unicorns, as beautiful as they'd been to look at while they were relaxed, were terrifying to see in anger. Entipy's gaze was riveted by them, and all her high-flown words about what it would be like to die at the hooves of the mythic beasts flew right away. "I think . . . we'd better leave," she said slowly.

I was already backing up, not removing my gaze from them. "I couldn't agree more. On the count of three—"

"No," she said sharply. "Don't run."

She put an arm around my waist. This gesture seemed to incense the closest unicorns, and they actually reared up and pawed the ground.

"I think they want us out of here as quickly as possible," I told her.

"I read in a book about unicorns: Never run from anything immortal. It attracts their attention."

"We've already got their damned attention."

"Just . . . do as I do." She took a deep breath to steady herself and then turned her back to the unicorns and proceeded to walk in a calm, unhurried manner. As much as I wanted to bolt, I couldn't bring myself to flee and leave her behind. Besides, with my lame leg, I don't know how fast I could have gone anyway.

So I walked next to her, maintaining as much dignity as I could. The way ahead of us, toward the mountains, remained clear. The herd had converged behind us, apparently not trying to cut us off from departing. We weren't going the way I wanted to go, unfortunately. We were leaving the road behind, heading toward a far more hazardous path, but I didn't see much choice. Still, we weren't completely out of options. We might be able to double back around the unicorn grazing area. And, at the very least, I had the map, so I might be able to locate us again provided I could find a decent landmark.

One step after another, and even though we weren't looking at them, I could sense the eyes of every one of the beasts upon us. But at least it seemed that they were going to let us go. I thanked the gods for that, and even began to chide myself that I'd let my imagination run was wild as I had. Thinking that somehow they were able to read my mind and know what I had done to their favorite son. It was, really, the height of absurdity to attribute that much insight to dumb animals, magical or no.

"That," I breathed, once I started to feel that we were a safe distance, "was close. Good advice there, about the walking."

"Thank you for trusting me," she said. "I know it's not easy for you to trust anyone. I'm honored."

"You're welcome."

"And by the way . . . you kiss very well."

And she reached over and actually grabbed my ass, giving it an affectionate squeeze and causing me to jump slightly.

The unicorns went berserk.

As one, an infuriated bellow was ripped from their collective throats like damned souls in hell. Our heads whipped around just in time to see that the lot of them had lowered their horns, and they were charging.

Obviously, they'd noticed us.

"Run!" I screamed. Suddenly all the lameness of my leg was completely forgotten as Entipy and I bolted. The unicorns were a fair distance behind us, but they were closing the gap rapidly as we ran as fast as we could down the mountain pass. The incline was sharp, the footing uncertain, but the need to flee was great. Entipy was clutching my free hand tightly as I used the staff as never before to propel me along.

The ground rumbled beneath the pounding hooves of the unicorns, and we ran like mad. We ran as if our lives depended upon it, which they most certainly did, because the unicorns were not stopping, and if they caught up with us, we would be pulp beneath their hooves in no time at all.

Part of me viewed the scene almost as if my spirit had left my body. I could see, in my mind's eye, the sea of white, with dots of brown and green, converging upon us and, in many ways, it was a thing of beauty. No, of joy. Creatures of myth, creatures of legend, creatures of power, moving as one, their manes shimmering, their hooves flashing. If one was able to see it perched safely atop a mountain, one would find oneself weeping in joy at being able to see such a sight.

As for me, I was weeping in terror. I could practically feel the horns running me through, the hooves trampling me. The ground trembled all the more, and Entipy and I took turns, her dragging me, me dragging her. *"Run! Run!"* I kept shouting unnecessarily. Entipy stumbled, her dress ripping, and I yanked her to her feet as if she was weightless and kept going.

The unicorns were closing. We had no hope. For one wild moment I entertained the notion of trying to leap to one side or the other, to get out of the way of the stampede, but there was nowhere to go. We were deep into the pass, the mountains looming on either side of us, the rock face too sheer for us to have any hope of getting away. Even the mountains themselves seemed to be trembling in fear as the unicorn herd descended upon us. And worst of all, they were bringing that same damned smell of lilacs with them. I was going to be gored and crushed while sniffing flowers. I didn't know whether to laugh or cry, and settled for shrieking in terror. It was a most unmanly sound and probably would have lost me Entipy's respect, had she been able to hear me over the deafening pounding.

That was when a huge chunk of ice and snow struck the ground directly in front of us. We dodged around it, and then another struck, and another, and we were leaping to one side and the other automatically, without thinking about what was happening. The thunder of the unicorns had not abated, and then more pieces of ice fell, and more, like a great rain, and then I thought, *It can't be,* because it sounded to me as if the stampede was slowing. I chanced a glance around and yes, it was true, it was gloriously true, the unicorns were breaking off their pursuit.

"We're saved!" cried out Entipy, who had seen the same thing.

Except . . .

. . . except the rumbling hadn't stopped.

. . . except it had . . . but had been replaced. What I

was hearing and feeling now was not the concentrated thudding of hundreds of hooves. Instead it was something deeper, even more profound, as if we were trapped inside of a thunderhead. The rumbling was no longer originating from behind us; instead it was all around us, above, below, and the chunks of snow were getting bigger, one of them striking me a glancing blow.

I looked up.

The snow on the mountains was breaking loose, descending toward us at horrifying speed and velocity.

Instantly I realized what had happened. The pounding hooves of the unicorns had jarred loose the snow from the mountains. "*Avalanche!*" I shouted. Entipy looked up as well and gasped. There was nowhere to go but forward, and that we did as fast as we could.

It wasn't fast enough.

The snow came crashing down, filling in the gap between the mountains. A sea of white of a very different sort from the equine sea that had been pursuing us, but no less deadly.

The path ahead of us suddenly dropped off. We ran as fast as we could and then the snow caught up with us. The frosty tidal wave lifted us off the ground, tumbling all around us, and I held on to Entipy's hand for as long as I could, but then I was torn away from her. I heard her cry out my name once and then her voice was lost in the crashing of the snow.

Gods, how could this get any worse? I wondered, right before we hit the cliff.

I wasn't aware of it until I was over it, nor did I have any true picture of how high it was. All I knew was that suddenly there was no sense of solidity beneath me aside from the huge pieces of snow that were endeavoring to bury me. I thrashed at the air as if I could somehow use the airborne ice chunks as stepping-stones to keep me aloft, an endeavor which worked about as well as you can probably suspect. Amazingly, I managed to hold on to my staff, wrapping my arms around it, and it was raining snow all around me. I resolved never to wonder how things could get worse, and then I hit bottom—or whatever it was—so hard that it knocked all the breath out of me. That was unfortunate, because more snow piled on top of me from overhead. I curled up, bringing my arms over my head to try and afford me protection, and waited until the rumbling—which seemed to go on for an eternity—ceased.

I was entombed. Buried alive in white.

I had no definite idea which way was up or down, but I took a guess and started digging as fast and as frantically as I could. For all I knew, it was a futile endeavor. If I was under twelve feet of snow, there was no way I was going to be able to break surface before I suffocated. But that wasn't going to stop me from doing my damnedest to survive.

There was a small pocket of air around me, and I clawed for the surface, trying to dig my way through it. It was everything I could do not to let sheer panic overwhelm me. I knew that if that happened, I'd be finished. I'd thrash around so much that I'd use up my air before I even came close to escaping.

My fingers dug into the snow as I shoved and pushed, trying to burrow out. Right above me, the snow seemed so packed in that I couldn't get through it at all. I snapped open the bladed end of my staff and shoved it in, prying at it, jarring it loose. It fell in my face and there was more right above it, but at least it was loose enough that I could push it away and keep going.

My breath was coming in ragged gasps, my eyes filled with dirt and moisture so that I could barely see. My feet and hands were completely numb. I wasn't scooping or pushing the snow away at that point; I was clubbing it with fists that weren't feeling anything anymore. Once again I felt light-headed, but this time it wasn't from the scent of lilacs; it was from the scent of my own death. I was going to be buried alive there, and my body would never be found. Runcible's people would be sitting there in Terracote, waiting in futility. I wondered how long they would remain there before they gave us up for lost; before they decided that that bastard whore's son, Apropos of Nothing, had bungled the job of returning the "precious cargo" and my name was entered into the lists of the greatest failures in Isteria.

Had Entipy made it out? Had she survived somehow? Was she nearer to the surface, on top perhaps? Or was she buried even farther below? She could be within inches of me and I'd never know. So much I would never know. My life was going to end there, a series of questions with no answers . . .

The world was hazing out around me, my efforts to clamber upward becoming less and less emphatic. I tried to tell myself that I had to keep going. To make it for Entipy . . . for my mother's sake . . . for . . .

For yourself. That's the only thing that's really important to you. Don't try to pretend otherwise.

It was the voice of Sharee . . . the voice of the weaver whom I had rescued a lifetime ago . . . and she was right there next to me, in my mind's eye, looking at me with open scorn. *That's really all it's been. You. You can fool others, but not me.*

"Go away," I muttered between swollen lips as I kept pushing upward, if for no other reason than to get away from her.

Do you want some free advice?

"No."

She's not worth it, she went on as if I hadn't spoken—which, considering my state of mind at that point, I might actually not have done. *The princess, I mean. She's going to bring you nothing but heartache. Trust me on that.*

Trust a weaver. Fat chance.

If you get out of this, you head off and never look back. Carve out a new life for yourself. Stay away from knights. You were never meant for that life. Live within your reality, not your dreams.

"All I have are my dreams, because the reality is a nightmare."

Your reality is what you make it.

I moaned. Not only was I going to die, but I was going to die having to listen to homilies.

Her face was floating just above me. *And another thing . . .*

"Shut up," I growled in my delirium, and I shoved the frozen meat-and-bone thing called my fist through her face. It punched through the snow overhead . . .

. . . and touched nothing.

I couldn't believe it. My flesh was so numb, my mind so frozen, that it took a few moments for the significance of what I wasn't feeling to set in. The surface. The surface was just above me.

There was still no sensation in my legs, and yet somehow I managed to muster enough strength to push my way up and through the snow. It was like being born again as my head crunched through the hoary crust, and I gasped in great lungsful of air. I struggled like mad, throwing aside caution, pushing and shoving and clawing the rest of the way until I had pulled myself completely clear.

I looked up. The edge of the cliff we'd gone over looked hideously high. I couldn't believe I'd survived the fall.

Then I saw that the snow around me had a large area of red on it, and I wondered about the source of that until I touched my forehead and saw my hand come away stained with a dark red. The snow had actually benefited me as the chill had slowed the blood loss. Still, I felt dizzy, the world beginning to spin around me.

Then I saw her hand.

It was sticking out of the snow not three feet away.

She's not worth it, came Sharee's warning unbidden to me, but I ignored it and lunged for Entipy. I grabbed the hand; it felt frozen solid. For one moment I was actually worried that it might snap off the wrist. "Entipy! I'm up here! Don't you die on me! Don't do it!" I shouted, knowing that I might already be addressing a corpse. I had set my staff on the ground next to me and shoved aside the snow as frantically as I could. The towering mountains looked down upon us, uncaring of whether we lived or died.

I kept calling her name, trying to let her know that I was there, trying to get some sort of response out of her. She was giving me absolutely no help. If she wasn't dead, she was most certainly unconscious. Fortunately, the one benefit I had was that my arms were strong, almost tireless, especially with the goal so close. It took me seconds to clear away enough snow to expose her head and shoulders and then pull her clear of her snowy entombment.

Her eyes were closed, her face and clothes covered with frost, her skin slightly blue. She looked terrible, and I can only imagine how I must have looked. I shook her violently, trying to bring her to wakefulness. Nothing. I put my head to her chest, tried to hear some sign of a heartbeat. I thought I detected something faintly, but couldn't be sure. What I knew beyond question, though, was that she wasn't breathing.

"Breathe! Breathe!" I shouted at her. She didn't respond. I shook her again. Still nothing. I did the only thing I could think of: I opened her mouth, brought my lips down upon hers, and blew into her mouth. Her lips were frozen solid; it was like sucking on ice. I tried to keep my breath slow and steady, tried to simulate normal breathing. Her chest rose up and down, but not on its own. I kept going, despair clutching me and chilling me as thoroughly as the snow had. I lost track of how long I breathed into her mouth. I lost track of time . . . of myself . . . of everything . . . the world was swirling around me, and I fought desperately to hang on, to push back the blackness.

And I failed. Failed as I had at so many things in my life.

I slumped forward onto her body, unable to keep my mind functioning anymore. My head lay on her chest . . .

. . . and rose slightly . . .

. . . and settled down slightly . . . and rose again .

She was breathing.

Son of a bitch, I thought, right before I passed out.

Chapter 22

I awoke slowly and painfully to find myself on the floor of a surprisingly warm cave.

As caves went, it was quite sizable. Not only that, but it was clear that someone had gone to a good deal of effort to transform it from a simple shelter into something that was actually rather homey. Several torches were mounted on the walls, the flames flickering pleasantly and providing both light and warmth.

I was lying on what appeared to be a bed of hay. Someone had lined the floors as well. I glanced to my right and saw the princess lying a short distance away. A similar layer of hay had been laid down for her as well, and she appeared to be resting comfortably.

Then, from the corner of my eye, I saw someone, or some thing, huddling just beyond the glow of light that the torches were giving off. He (if it was a he) was crouched over in a corner, and he appeared to be watching me. I sat up slowly, feeling the creaking in my joints, and blinked against the dimness. "Who's there?" I called.

The figure in the darkness slowly stood. Actually, he didn't stand so much as he seemed to uncoil. He took a step forward, then a second, and emerged into the pool of light.

My breath caught in my throat.

Tacit glowered at me with his one good eye.

I let out an ear-piercing scream and jolted, waking from a horrible dream. Except when I looked around I was saddened to discover that I had not, in fact, awoken, because I was not dreaming. The cave, the torches, the bed of hay, and Tacit were all still there, and my shriek of alarm was just starting to fade in its echo. Tacit said nothing, but simply titled his head slightly as he stared at me. I looked to the princess. She stirred slightly but otherwise continued to slumber.

My sword was to my right. My staff was to my left. He'd left both of my weapons within easy grabbing distance. But Tacit was not the type who was sloppy or forgetful; if he'd done that, it was because he didn't care whether I reached them or not. That showed a remarkable degree of confidence. Would that I had possessed some.

Still he did not speak. I said nothing either. I was actually somewhat curious, even as my heart hammered against my chest, who would break the silence first.

Tacit did so.

"How could you?" he asked.

Except I didn't quite understand him. It came more along the lines of, "Howcudoo." I frowned and said, "What?"

He rolled his eye slightly, the other obscured by the patch, and when he spoke again he did so very meticulously, moving his tongue slowly over each syllable, repeating the question.

"How could I what?"

Tacit shook his head, as if astounded that I would even have to ask. In retrospect, I suppose it was pretty obvious. He was asking how I could possibly have betrayed him the way that I had. In fact, it was so obvious that he apparently didn't feel the need to repeat the question, probably going on the assumption that he wouldn't get a straight answer out of me.

Now that I saw him closer, I could make out the residual damage from our last encounter months ago. There was a fearsome scar where I had laid open his forehead. It had healed, but irregularly, almost zigzag. There was some disfigurement to his nose as well, and his jaw seemed a bit askew. I could see where the teeth were missing on the side. When he spoke, not only did he have to fight to make his words clear, but there was a faint whistling sound through the space. His hair was wild and matted, his beard scraggly. He didn't look remotely heroic.

He looked insane.

"I had to reset my jaw on my own," he said as casually as if we were sitting at a table in a pub knocking back drinks and he was looking back on a portion of his life that had provided him some mild inconvenience. "You did quite a thorough job, Po." He paused and then said again, "How could you?"

I tried to find an answer. After all this time, I felt I owed him one. Nothing came to mind, and finally I shrugged and said, "I had to."

He nodded. In a bizarre way, it seemed to be an answer that made sense to him. "We all do what we have to," he said philosophically. "We cannot help ourselves Just as now: I'm going to have to kill you, Po. Nothing else for it. Hope you understand. No offense."

"None taken," I said hollowly. I paused and then said "Are . . . you going to do it now?"

"Oh, no!" he said with astonishment, as if the very idea was unthinkable. "No, why would I do that? While Entipy is unconscious? No, Po. No . . . first we have to wait until she wakes up. Then you have to grovel. That's very important. She has to see you grovel."

"Why does she have to do that?"

"Because she's fallen in love with you by now. Am I right? You can tell me; I won't get upset."

"Won't get upset?" I yelped. "You just got through telling me you're going to kill me!"

Tacit came toward me and knelt a few feet away. He focused his one eye on me, and when he spoke—again, carefully caressing each word—it was as if something had died in his throat. "Yes. I am going to kill you. But there's no upset over that. There was at first. I would like to tell you that, as a true hero, I rose above such petty concerns as anger . . . or revenge. I would have liked to, truly. But I did not. When you ambushed me, left me lying there . . . then I wanted to kill you with a passion hotter than a thousand suns."

"That's . . . very hot," I said, not knowing how else to respond.

"Then when I had to reset my jaw, when I felt that agony that lanced through my skull as if it had been cut in half, it just inflamed my fury all the more. A thousand suns? Say a hundred thousand and you'd be closer to the mark. But you know what, Po?"

"No. What."

"It is most difficult to maintain that level of intensity of hatred. Not when you're expending energy to try and survive at the same time. One has to pick and choose. To decide where one's priorities are going to be. And I had to set my priorities on healing . . . on surviving . . . on hoping that somehow, in some way, we would meet up again. Following you wasn't difficult. The phoenix was newly hatched; as a result, he left a small fire trail behind him when he flew. It singed the tops of trees. Left a trail of burnt wood that most others could not have followed. But I could. You know what I'm capable of, don't you, Apropos."

I nodded. Strength had surged back into my limbs, possibly a giddy rush of energy coming from the fact that I was still alive. But I made no motion. What motion could I make, after all? I was on his terrain, under his control.

"Actually, I might not have been able to survive at all . . . had I not met my friend."

"Friend?"

He puckered his lips, putting his front teeth against his lower lip, and blew a sharp whistle of a note. I heard a faint clip-clop approaching, and braced myself for another onslaught by unicorns. And then a large, equine shape glided into the cavern. I could scarce believe what I was seeing.

"Titan!" I said in astonishment. For indeed it was;

gods knew that I had combed down that coat so many times, I could likely have recognized the steed of the late Sir Umbrage even if I were blindfolded. I could see scar tissue on the horse's magnificent coat, but otherwise it appeared unharmed.

Tacit looked mildly surprised, but only mildly. "So . . . Ulysses, as I called you . . . or Titan, as you were formerly known . . ." He looked at the horse. "It appears that you did, indeed, recognize him at that. Take a long look at him, Apropos. This noble beast may well be the only creature in the world, walking on two legs or four, who feels any loyalty to you whatsoever."

"But . . . this is impossible . . ."

"I found the mighty beast after the caravan transporting my beloved Entipy had been assailed by the Harpers Bizarre. Oh, yes, Apropos," and he smiled at my obvious confused surprise. "Between the scents, the broken branches, the bodies . . . I was more than capable of figuring out what had happened. Ulys—my apologies—Titan . . . had been gravely wounded. I took it upon myself to attend to the horse, to nurse it back to health. Thanks to the burn trail, I knew which direction you had gone in . . . at least in general terms. Titan was too magnificent a creature to leave to the untender mercies of the forest. So I aided him."

As if knowing that he was the topic of discussion, Titan let out a little whinny and bobbed his head up and down.

Entipy was starting to stir. I heard a low moan from her. Tacit cast a glance toward her before turning his focus back to me.

"We came as far in this direction as we could before the winter set in. Unfortunately we traveled somewhat slower than you. After all, we did not have a phoenix upon which to ride . . . thanks to the intervention of my erstwhile friend, Apropos. We took refuge here, and it is here that we have been residing for some time now. All this time I have been hoping, praying that somehow I would catch up with you, Po. And then . . . then . . ." and he sighed softly, blissfully. "I smelled the lilacs. I smelled the unicorns. My olfactory senses are not what they once were; the damage done to my face by my good friend, Apropos, attended to that. But even though I was not what I once was, I knew a herd had come to the area. I was going to go to them, find a way to them . . . when I sensed that they were disturbed. The next thing I knew, there was an avalanche, cutting off the mountain passes that would have enabled me to join them. I cursed my fates once again, as I have a great deal recently. And then . . . then Titan here seemed to scent something. He insisted on going out into the snow, in searching out something that he was sure was there. And he was right. He found you, Po. Nor did he protest in the slightest at the additional weight when I loaded both you and Entipy onto his back so that you could be brought here. His loyalty to you knows no bounds. That sort of loyalty is very touching, don't you think? And so rare . . . so rare . . ."

"Your jaw must be exhausted, considering you're using it so much," I said. I was beginning to tire of the snide remarks, the backhanded insults. "If you're going to kill me, then be done with it."

"I told you . . . she has to witness it. She has to understand, to know, to . . ."

Entipy was sitting up, her eyes bleary, her attitude confused. She was trying to make out the interior of the cave, and was looking directly away from us. "Apropos . . . ?" she called out in a gravelly voice.

"He's right here, my beautiful girl."

Naturally she knew his voice in a heartbeat, as she looked at him and gasped. "Tacit!"

"The one and the same. My beautiful girl, I'm here for you, as I said—"

He reached for her . . . and she flinched back. She squinted at him in the darkness.

"You look terrible," she said.

"I have . . . looked better, I admit," he said. "But—"

"What did you say? It sounded like, 'I have . . . look becker, dammit.'"

My heart was leaping with delirious joy as inwardly I chortled at Tacit's discomfiture and frustration. Entipy was not reaching out and falling into the arms of her long-lost hero. Instead she was looking at him like a squashed bug, and with about as much affection. She seemed confused as to why he should even be here, as if . . . as if his time was already past. This was just getting better and better, provided I could survive it.

Tacit displayed a momentary flare of impatience, but he quickly stifled it. Instead he went back to speaking very slowly, very carefully, and once he'd repeated the first sentence, continued—just as precisely—"Entipy . . . I know that you are someone who has always been capable of seeing beyond the surface.

When you first met me, you were able to see through the exterior of a young cutpurse . . . and your belief gave me the strength to pursue my heroic undertakings. You have been my strength, my support, my—"

As if she hadn't heard a word, she commented, "No, you don't understand, you *really* look *terrible.* You're not handsome at all anymore. You're disfigured, you're unkempt."

"It's what is inside that—"

"And you smell ghastly. . . ."

"What would you have me do?! Bathe in snow?!" he shouted. "It's been freezing! I could barely find enough fresh water to drink, much less—"

"Don't yell at me. I'm a princess. You've no right to yell at me."

"I'm sorry," he said quickly, steadying himself. It was all I could do not to laugh out loud as I watched. "You're right. But you have to understand . . . everything I've done of any note has been for you. For you, I accomplished the three tasks of the Elder Giant. For you, I sought the Ring of Poseidon, which enabled me to command the loyalties of the Naiad . . . which wound up saving me from certain death when the Harpers Bizarre sent me hurtling into—"

"That's all very nice," Entipy shot back, "but in the meantime, while you were off gallivanting from one epic task to the next, I was being made a personal slave of the Faith Women, and then I was attacked by the Harpers, and then I wound up cleaning tables in a tavern in the Outer Lawless regions. Did you think I enjoyed being up to my ass in menial tasks while you were out adventuring? If it weren't for Apropos . . ."

"*If it weren't for Apropos?!*" He looked on the verge of having a seizure. "Entipy . . . they've written songs about me! Epic poems! You compare me to him? What have they written about him to celebrate his 'great deeds,' eh?"

I leaned forward and offered, "I heard one of the squires came up with a couple of obscene limericks. . . ."

"*Shut up!*" he snapped at me. "It was a rhetorical question! Entipy, you would turn your attentions, your loyalties, to him? Him! Virtually all of the troubles you've encountered were because of his actions!"

"What are you talking about?" she demanded.

I braced myself, not daring to interrupt considering that Tacit looked ready to take my head off if I said another word. Tacit proceeded to tell her everything. How his epic journey and series of adventures had led him to the birthing place of the phoenix. How he had witnessed the creature's death and rebirth. How he had been about to reach the culmination of his personal crusade . . . only to be blindsided by the wretched and scheming Apropos. How his phoenix had been absconded with while he'd been left to suffer owing to the unworthy and cowardly attack.

In short, he told the truth.

Entipy took it all in, listening without interruption, nodding in places. When Tacit finally stopped speaking, she did not answer immediately. She turned to look at me . . . and then back at him. Her face was unreadable.

"Tacit," she said softly.

"Yes, my love."

"That is, without question," and her voice hardened,

oozing with contempt, "the most appalling set of fabrications I have ever heard."

"F-fabrications . . . ?" He could barely believe she was saying it. No, not barely. He really couldn't believe it.

"How dare you," she continued. "How dare you try to foist off blame for your own shortcomings upon Apropos . . ."

"Shortcomings! Foist off blame!" He seemed to have lost the ability to do anything other than repeat what she had already said.

"Here Apropos was resourceful enough to find the phoenix after you had clearly failed . . . and then he risked himself to come back and rescue me, and watch out for me all these months . . . and now you have the temerity to sit there and tell me that this brave squire—"

Oh gods, I did it. I actually pulled it off.

"—that this brave squire mounted some sort of sneak attack on you, just for the purpose of stealing your glory!"

"He did! That's exactly what happened!"

"Have you considered, Tacit, that maybe it wasn't your glory to have in the first place?"

His mouth moved. It made a sound; a sort of clicking where the jaw had been forced back into place. I think it was top and bottom teeth clicking against each other because they were out of alignment. Otherwise no words emerged at first. "Not . . . my glory?" he finally managed to get out. "Of course it is! All the tasks I had to accomplish, the quests I performed! All the work that I went to in order to track down a mythic creature that was to take me on the final leg of my grand undertaking! A creature snatched from my hands by that . . . that ingrate! That nothing! You are asking me to believe in a world that does not recognize merit, or striving, or a heroic ideal, but instead rewards duplicity and sneakery and whoever is fastest to watch out for their own self-interest. A world where there is no justice! What sort of world is that!"

"The real world," I said softly.

His jaw twitched, which probably hurt him. Then he said tightly, "I refuse to accept that world. Po . . . tell her. Tell her what happened. She will believe it if it comes from you."

"You expect Apropos to admit to your demented view of things?" she asked contemptuously, as if the very notion was laughable.

"There is nothing demented about it! Apropos," and his voice sounded very dangerous, and his eyes were glittering with near madness as he said, "tell her. If you value your life . . . tell her."

And that was when I opted to roll the dice.

You see, I had slowly become convinced he wasn't going to hurt me. Not really, no matter what he'd said earlier. Oh, he would have no compunction about making me *think* he was going to hurt me, kill me, whatever. Try to trick me into blurting the truth to Entipy. But the Tacit that I had always known would never simply cut someone down, murder them in cold blood. And Tacit, for all his annoying traits, remained a hero. Heroes didn't do things like that . . .

Which meant I was safe. Which further meant that I didn't have to play his game if I didn't feel like it.

But I decided to be diplomatic about it.

"I regret to say," I said carefully, "that Tacit's view of things . . . is how he sees them." Then I settled back on my bed of hay and sat there complacently.

"What the hell is that supposed to mean!" Tacit fairly shouted, which was naturally the reaction I'd been hoping for. It was entirely to my advantage to get him to lose control. "You make it sound as if I'm deluded."

"Couldn't imagine why anyone would think that," Entipy said caustically.

He turned back to me, and he actually sounded pleading: "Apropos . . . putting your own life aside . . ."

"Something I am loath to agree to do, obviously," I interrupted.

He spoke right over me. "The bottom line is, we both know the truth. Lying to her is doing her a disservice. You cannot let your ego get in the way. She deserves the truth. She deserves the person destined for her. She deserves—"

"*You,* is what what you're saying. She deserves you."

"More or less," he admitted.

"Rather more the former than the latter," she said. "And have you considered, Tacit, that I'm quite capable of deciding for myself just what I do and do not deserve?"

She stared at him challengingly. He was slowly shaking his head back and forth, apparently still unable to believe what he was being confronted with. "This can't be happening," he was saying, over and over in a quiet voice. Ironically, I knew exactly what the problem was. How long had he thought about this moment, dreamt about it? It was probably what kept him going. And he had had much time to decide just exactly how the entire confrontation was going to play out. Entipy was going to believe him, of course, because he was the hero. He was Tacit. If he tried to lie his head would likely explode. She would believe him, and recognize me for the thoroughgoing bastard I truly was.

Except that wasn't happening.

For a joyful moment as I watched him muttering to himself, I thought his mind was gone. In that event, we could simply slip right out of there, ideally without his even noticing. But apparently it was not going to be as easy as all that. Then again, what aspect of my life ever was?

Tacit suddenly refocused himself on me, and his voice dropped lower. In a tone that carried with it the unspoken message *I'm not joking about here,* he said, "Po . . . tell her. Now."

"I don't know what you mean," I said, trying to sound sincerely sorry for him.

"Tell her now."

"I wish I could help you, old friend, but I'm afraid that it's beyond my—"

That was when he grabbed me by the arm in a grip that could probably have torn my arm out of its socket and he started to drag me to the cave mouth. I tried to pull free but realized that, even in his fallen state, Tacit still had a grip of iron.

"Now, let's discuss this—!" I tried to say, but he wasn't listening.

"Go to, squire!" Entipy shouted encouragingly.

"Show him! Show him he cannot spread lies about you in that manner!" If this was designed to inspire me somehow, it failed utterly.

Tacit dragged us out into the sunlight. The air was biting again, the kindly influence of the unicorns not spreading to this relatively forsaken clime. In the brightness of the day, Tacit swung me around and released me so that we were facing each other. I stood on unsteady leg and blinked against the sudden light.

"Your sword," Tacit said. It was at that point I saw that he had picked up my weapon when he proceeded to haul me out into the morning air. He tossed it to me and I caught it smoothly. He reached behind his back and pulled out his own sword. It was gleaming and pure and I could swear I heard a musical chime as it sliced through the air. It probably had a story behind it. Everything about the damned man had a story behind it. "Use it, Apropos."

"For what, trimming my stubble?" I demanded.

"Use it to try and kill me, for God as my witness, if you don't I will certainly try to kill you. And I will succeed."

More and more, I was sure he was bluffing. It just wasn't Tacit, to threaten and then annihilate someone, especially me. The Tacit I knew would hold out hope unto the very end for some fundamental good in another person. He was a humanitarian, someone who just never gave up hope in the human race.

"The only thing you're going to succeed at, Tacit, is to show what an unfortunate specimen you are," I informed him. "Admit that it's over. Turn around and—"

He did not turn around. He came at me.

The thing was, he had no idea of the training I'd undergone. How I'd been taught, night after night, thanks to Sir Umbrage, the manly art of knightly battle. No longer was I the desperate urchin he had once known. I was more than capable of defending myself. As a matter of fact, there was nothing to say that I might not even be superior to him. Yes, that was quite possible.

It was a pleasant enough delusion, and lasted me for the three seconds it took for Tacit to cover the space between us and swing his sword. It sang through the air and I barely got mine up in time. When they came together, I felt a crash so violent that my arms vibrated furiously from the impact.

He came at me again and, by luck as much as design, I deflected the second blow as well as the first. But then he stepped in fast and slammed the hilt of the sword itself against the side of my head. Stars exploded behind my eyes and I wavered in place, and that was when he swung the flat of the sword and took me in the back of the head, sending me to the ground.

"Tell her," he said tightly.

Determined to overcome my momentary feeling of surprise, I came at him again. I swung the sword so quickly I felt as if it was a blur. He blocked it with no effort, and seemed to be moving in a most leisurely fashion. For a moment our hilts locked, and then he shoved me back several steps. I almost toppled as my weak leg nearly betrayed me, but I shoved the sword down into the snow-encrusted ground and steadied myself.

"Out of consideration for our past . . . and for your

last moments . . . I'll let you make a good showing," Tacit said. I could see Entipy emerging from the cave a distance away, blinking against the brightness of the sun. "But you will tell her, even if I have to chop you apart one limb at a time, like a tree."

"Get away from him!" shouted Entipy, and she started to charge toward us. But I put up a hand and cried out, sounding as heroic as I could, "No! This is my fight, Princess! If you have any respect for me whatsoever, you'll allow me to see it through!"

To my utter astonishment, she actually came to a halt and nodded. Her face was alight with excitement and there was genuine bloodlust in her eyes. She was completely caught up in the moment, anxious to see a hero and villain battling it out with, naturally, the hero triumphant in the end. The problem was, lines had become so blurred that I was no longer sure which of us fit into which category.

Tacit looked at me in momentary confusion, but then his face cleared. "Of course," he said, understanding. "You want to keep her far enough away so that she doesn't hear anything we say to each other."

I didn't bother to nod. He knew he was right.

"I'm impressed, Po. You actually care what the princess thinks. I didn't believe you cared what anybody thought of you. You've changed."

"So have you," I shot back. "And only one of us has changed for the better."

His easy smile thinned into a frown and then he came at me again.

I tried to remember everything that I'd been taught. I

watched his sword less than I did his body movement, looking for signs that would telegraph which way he'd come at me: a twist of the hip, an angle of the shoulder. At first it seemed as if I was doing an excellent job. I felt my confidence building as his preliminary attacks did not get through my defenses, and I was actually contemplating launching an offensive of my own when his sword suddenly slashed across my right thigh. I'd blocked his first five thrusts, but his sixth had gotten through. It was just the tip, a light scratch at best, but there was a thin line of blood where the point had cut across.

"Tell her," he said.

"Tell her yourself if you think your diction's up to it," I suggested.

He charged again. Once more I defended myself, but again after initial success, he scored, this time across my left thigh, and just a touch deeper than the first. Again a series of engagements as he drove me back, back across the ground, and at one point I almost slipped but then quickly recovered, and again his sword flashed, and again I had a cut, this time across my upper shoulder.

Then I realized: He was scoring every sixth attempt. It was like clockwork. I wasn't truly defending myself. He was toying with me, striking at will, allowing me to block five times before hitting home with the sixth. He was in complete control the entire time. He must have seen the dawning realization in my eyes, because he nodded and smiled grimly, and of all the bastards that I had encountered in my life, I swear to you I have never seen such an evil expression in my life as I saw on the face of Tacit One-Eye at that moment.

"Tell her," he whispered, and I could see from his face, hear in his tone, that he was approaching the point where he was going to stop fooling around. "You don't seem to understand yet, Po. I'm going to kill you no matter what. No less a fate can be left for you after what you did to me."

He was bluffing.

"The only question at issue here is," he continued, "do I kill you cleanly and quickly with your limbs attached . . . or do I hack you apart and leave you to bleed to death from four stumps, sobbing for mercy. It depends upon whether you tell her the truth, and how quickly you do it."

He *had* to be bluffing.

"Well? Your decision, Apropos. The last one you'll have the luxury of making."

"Get him, Apropos!" shouted the princess.

"Go to hell," I said tightly.

His face darkened like a thundercloud. "You first," he said, and he came at me. And this time there was no stopping him. He continued to hammer me back, back, his blade scoring at will, cutting here and there, wherever he felt like it. I backed up until I could go no farther, the wall of a mountain face stopping me, and he swung hard and I ducked under it. I think that was the only true moment when I actually saved myself, because his rage was building so greatly that it was that anger which made him miss me rather than my clumsy evasion. I tried to circle back but he cut me off. In the distance I could hear Titan's whinnying combined with Entipy's desperate pleadings that I should stop fooling around with him, giving him a false sense of security. Would that it had been the case; his sense of security was quite, quite genuine.

Back and back more, and despite the coldness of the air, sweat was cloaking my face, running in rivulets down my chest. My breath was heavy in my lungs, my vision starting to become blurred as all the little cuts continued to bleed, and I felt my strength ebbing. And Tacit wasn't letting up, and when he lunged forward and actually stabbed me, I cried out in agony. The blade glanced off one of my ribs, but it was a deep cut, and I clutched at it as best I could to try and stanch the bleeding.

He stopped a moment to survey the damage, and that was when I gathered all my waning strength and lunged at him with my sword, giving it everything I had.

He caught the blade with one gloved hand, disdainfully, held it for a moment, then pushed the blade aside, my thrust so inconsequential that it didn't even merit his sword to deflect it. He lashed out with one foot, catching me in the chest, right where the stab had gone in, and that sent agony ripping through me. I fell back, hit the ground heavily. He slammed his sword down and I just barely rolled out of the way. I tried to get up and he shoved a foot down on my chest, his swordpoint right in my face. His other foot was practically crushing my wrist, keeping my sword pinned. Not that it would have done me any good.

"Tell her," he said, "or I swear to God, I'll kill you right now."

I looked into his eye.

He wasn't bluffing.

"All right," I said, the words more a sob torn from me than anything else. "All right, I'll tell her."

"Everything," he said firmly.

"Everything . . . just . . . just . . ." Tears, unmanly tears, hot and humiliating, streamed down my cheeks unbidden. "Just don't kill me . . . please . . . please don't . . ."

"No promises. I'll still kill you, like as not . . ."

"Tacit, please, don't . . . it's . . . it's not fair . . ."

"Not fair!" he practically bellowed. "After what you did, you dare speak to me of fairness!"

The princess was far enough away that she couldn't hear us. "Yes, not fair! You, Tacit, born brave, strong and true. Raised by unicorns, at one with the forest! Born to be a hero! Look at me, bastard son of rape, born lame of leg! I did the best I could with nothing! You had everything . . . everything so easy . . . !"

"Easy? You have no idea what I went through these past years, Po! No idea! Do you seriously think I went into the dangers I faced confident of my success? Do you think I didn't know stinking fear every time some ogre tried to step on me, or some great beast prepared to rip me apart if I didn't answer its damned riddle? But I overcame my inner weaknesses!"

"And so did I! You just don't like the way I did it!" And then I cried out as he increased the pressure of his foot on me.

"Tell her everything . . . and perhaps . . . perhaps . . . I'll let you live," he said.

"What if she doesn't believe me?"

"Convince her. Your life depends on it."

"All right . . . all right, I'll find a way." There had been any number of times in my past that I had hated myself for my weakness, but never more so than that moment. "Call to her . . . tell her to come here . . ."

Tacit nodded and, never moving either foot, turned to shout to her. And I knew that somehow, I would be able to convince Entipy of the truth of it. She'd see me bawling like an infant, see that I wasn't remotely heroic, realize that someone who would go to such lengths to save his own miserable hide was just some craven poseur who wasn't worth the time of day of the meanest of the king's subjects, much less his daughter. I had managed to make my cowardly actions before the Harpers seem like some sort of grand scheme, but I'd had to pull a phoenix out of my hat to make that even semi-believable. This she would never, ever go for. She would see all that I was, and hate me for it, and for reasons I couldn't even begin to understand, I was saddened beyond measure.

Then I heard what sounded like a high-pitched buzz, ending with an abrupt thump. Tacit's mouth was still open to call to Entipy, but there was blood trickling from it. He looked down in surprise at the arrow that had thudded into his chest. And then, before it could fully register on him, a second arrow joined it.

Tacit lost his balance and fell off me. I lay there, stunned, as he tumbled back into the snow. It might have been my imagination but I was sure that somehow, from in the distance, I could hear discordant, shrieking music . . . like an orchestra gone mad . . . or a herd of unicorns crying out in hysterical grief as if from one throat.

Blood was pouring copiously from where the arrows had struck him. Tacit struggled to his knees, broke off the shafts, shaking his head, trying to comprehend what had gone so wrong. He looked at me as if trying to see how I was holding a bow, and then another arrow struck him, this time from behind, and then more arrows. He shuddered each time they hit, and still he wouldn't fall. He just kept shaking his head, all the color draining out of his skin as the blood left his face to gush out his chest.

"Tacit . . ." I whispered, seeing the only link to my youth which had any pleasant memories dying before me. I looked around . . . and saw soldiers advancing. They were wearing light armor, with the black and silver trim of the court of Isteria, and several of them had purple banners fluttering from their tunics. Soldiers of the king. Several bowmen had more arrows nocked, ready to let fly.

I looked back to Tacit. A dozen emotions warred for dominance in his face, and confusion won out. Despite the blood gurgling in his throat, despite the twisted jaw, I was still able to make out what he said.

"But . . . but . . . *I'm the hero . . .*"

And then one more arrow flew, struck home and pierced the mighty heart, and Tacit fell over, and died with the snow pooling red with his blood, and the mournful cries of unicorns fading over the mountaintops.

Chapter 23

I have no idea how long I remained there, crouched in the snow, staring at his unmoving body. The first one to reach us was, naturally, Entipy. She half-ran, half-slid over the snowy ground until she got to us, and she looked down at Tacit's mortal remains. I had absolutely no idea how she was going to react. I didn't know how to react myself.

She started to laugh. It was high-pitched and chaotic-sounding and even vaguely familiar, although I couldn't figure out why. Her laughter continued as she circled him, staying just outside the pool of blood that was spreading across the snow.

"Stop it," I said hollowly. I felt as if I had no more fight left within me.

Somewhat to my surprise, she did stop. She looked at me with astonishment and said, "He's dead and you live. Don't you think that's funny?"

"I hadn't . . . thought about it in terms of humor." His eyes were still open, staring up at the sky, perhaps watching where his soul was departing to. I reached over and closed his eyes for him.

Entipy was now looking at me very oddly. "You're crying," she said. "I've never seen a man crying." Her voice hardened. "What's wrong with you?"

I realized she was right. The tears were still flowing. My face was so cold I hadn't even realized it. I wiped them away as best I could and said, "I weep . . . for the waste of the warrior he could have been. For the young man who saved me from beatings or worse, back when I had what few tatters of innocence ever graced my spirit. And I weep for joy that you are safe from him. That . . . is all. If that makes me less the man in your eyes . . ." I let my voice trail off because at that point I didn't care what she thought of me.

She was quiet for a moment and then—surprising me even more—she knelt down next to me and put an arm around my shoulder. Naturally I did not tell her that, most of all, I wept for myself . . . and my betrayals.

We remained that way until the soldiers got close enough. They were looking at us very tentatively, almost as if afraid to believe that they had found whom they were apparently searching for.

"Apropos?" the lead man said to me. I nodded slightly. "I am Captain Gothos, of the king's men. And this . . . ?" He turned to Entipy and his voice dropped to a whisper. "Princess?"

"Aye" was all she said.

That was more than enough. Gothos and the others immediately dropped to one knee and lowered their heads. Entipy rose, looking very regal indeed despite her haggard appearance and the oddness of the situation. "Rise, Captain," she said softly. She didn't sound imperious. Perhaps she, too, was tired.

Gothos and the others rose, and one of the bowmen had come near Tacit's body to inspect the handiwork of himself and his fellows. "Tacit One-Eye, right enough," he said in approval. "The king's been looking for this bastard since the Pell uprising. And just think, we got here barely in time to stop him from slaying a gallant squire."

"Just think," I echoed.

"Bring his head and his balls for the king as trophies Leave the rest to carrion eaters," Gothos said authorita tively, and one of his men moved forward with his sword to do his bidding.

Before I even knew what I was doing, I had interposed myself between the soldier and Tacit's corpse. I had picked up my sword and I was holding it with utter confidence. "So help me gods," I said very quietly, and very dangerously, "you try to mutilate this man, and I'll kill you myself."

"Squire! Stand aside. This is the king's business!" said Gothos, choosing to pull rank as if I cared about such things at the moment.

"The princess has her own business," Entipy abruptly said, which promptly captured all attention. She glanced in the direction of the cave that we had been in. "Take the body and place it there, in that cave. Seal off the entrance with rocks and debris. It was his home. Let him stay there."

"But princess . . ."

" 'But' and 'princess' are not two words that should keep each other's company, Captain," said Entipy frostily.

Apparently that was all the incentive the "gallant" soldiers needed. They gathered up Tacit's corpse and brought him to the cave. They disappeared within for a few moments and then emerged. They began to hammer at the rocks above, and at other debris and rubble nearby. It was not easy work, covered as it was with hoarfrost. But within about two hours or so they had managed to completely entomb Tacit into what would be his last resting place. Naturally by the time they had finished I had long since managed to compose myself, and had gone over to Titan to try and calm the great horse down. The poor beast seemed very confused, uncertain of what had happened, and frustrated that two of the individuals to whom he had felt the most loyal had come to blows. But explaining matters to a horse is no easy trick, and I did not even try. Instead I simply patted him on the side of the head, whispered niceties to him, and fed him some oats that one of the mounted soldiers happened to have in his saddlebag.

"The princess looks quite fit," Gothos said to me. He was watching Entipy, who was standing a distance away, watching the laboring knights finishing the entombment of Tacit. "The king and queen are most grateful that, thanks to your efforts, she is alive. And what of the other knights? Those others who served as the escort? What of them?"

I told him, as quickly and straightforwardly as I could, of the circumstances of how the Harpers had descended upon us. His eyes widened as I recounted it. "The Harpers Bizarre are real?" he said in unbridled surprise. "I thought them merely creatures of myth."

"Oh, they're very real. And we had the fatalities to prove it," I said.

"And what happened then? How did you escape? How did you come to be in the Outer Lawless regions?"

I began to reply, but somehow felt as if I simply didn't have the energy for it. "It is . . . very complicated. Tell you what, Captain. Buy me a few mugs . . . no, a barrel . . . of ale one night, and I'll tell you the entire tortured narrative. Dare I ask where the king is?"

"At Fort Terracote, awaiting our return. We're one of several advance guards sent to sweep the area and see if there was any sign of you. Obviously there was." He shook his head. "Tragedy about what you've had to endure up until now. But worry not. You're with us, now. You'll be safe."

"Funny. That's just what I thought months ago before the Harpers attacked and put me into this position in the first place."

He had no answer for that.

As it turned out, though, the balance of our journey to the fort was sublimely dull. I couldn't have asked for better than that. I rode upon Titan and the princess sat astride the great horse behind me. She leaned her head upon my shoulder and her arms were wrapped tightly around my middle. Some of the other soldiers and knights noticed and nudged each other with amusement or winked at me in a manner that seemed to indicate I was doing quite well in courting the fancies of a princess.

Me, I couldn't get my last image of Tacit out of my mind. That powerful body being carted off into the cave like so much refuse, tossed in and then entombed. It was better than being decapitated and left for scavengers. But on the other hand, it was far worse than still being alive. Which is what he would have been, if not for his "erstwhile friend."

I wanted to feel relief . . . joy . . . rage . . . something. Instead all I felt was empty. The bleeding from the wounds he had inflicted upon me had stopped, but when Entipy held tightly on to me, they hurt like the devil's own lashes. I said nothing, though. I felt as if I deserved to be in pain. I cannot think of many times in my life when I have felt quite as sorry for myself as I did during that long, slow ride back to Fort Terracote. I would hear the knights talking among themselves in low voices, and sometimes my name would be mentioned. I ignored them all.

We didn't stop the entire way to the fort. We ate while on horseback, Gothos riding over to us to hand us provisions, including a large cooked leg of some sort of bird. Part of me grimly wished it were from the phoenix, considering all the aggravation that the damned bird had cost us. If it had only flown in the right direction, we wouldn't have had all the problems to begin with.

It was getting late in the day. The terrain, while still chilly, had become more forested once again. There were no leaves in the trees, although the branches stretched high. It made me nervous, and I was constantly on the lookout for signs of anything that might come leaping out at us. Nothing was forthcoming, which was a relief.

Then the trees began to thin once more and we found ourselves in a gorge that stretched around the corner of a small set of foothills. "Just around this bend," Gothos called. I couldn't have been more relieved. I was tired, weary of being on horseback, weary of having the princess's arms around me as she would continue to tell me about how brave I was. I didn't feel brave. As I said earlier, I didn't feel anything. And more, I was wondering if I ever would again.

We came around the bend and, sure enough, there it was. The fort was on a rise, providing a good view in all directions. It was a good, solid stone fort, made all the better by the fact that its back two walls faced against a sheer cliff, unscalable by anything short of a gargoyle with clawed fingers. So although retreat out of the back of the fort was a practical impossibility, no one could get up from behind, either. The outer wall was at least fifty feet high. The main door appeared to be solid oak, huge and reinforced. It would take a heavy-duty battering ram quite some time to pound through, and during that time archers on the parapets would be picking off assailants with relative ease. All in all, it seemed a rather safe place to be. Not far off was more forest area, with a wide path heading into it that I assumed (correctly, as it turned out) to be the main road called the King's Road, which would lead us back to the capital city of Isteria and, ultimately, safety.

I saw dark clouds on the horizon. I hoped they weren't more storm clouds. I'd had enough of bad weather for the time being.

Several knights atop the fort started pointing and

waving when they saw us approaching. One of them pulled out a large ram's horn and blew into it, and clear, beautiful notes pealed out from it. The large doors to the fort slowly opened and I was able to see groups of knights on either side pushing their shoulders against them. It underscored just how heavy the doors were. And there, standing in the entranceway, arms draped behind his back, was King Runcible. He was dressed for traveling, but he had the imperial crest on the front of his tunic. He was the image of restraint. I could see from his face, even at this distance, that he recognized Entipy, but he did not run toward her. Instead he remained exactly where he was, not saying a word. He nodded slightly to the incoming soldiers, but his eyes never left Entipy . . . except for one brief moment when they strayed toward me. He nodded to me as well, and I returned the gesture. Once the blast from the ram's horn faded out, there was no noise except the steady clip-clop of the horses' hooves.

We drew within a few feet of the king and I dismounted. Then I reached up a hand to help Entipy down. She glanced at my hand a moment . . . and then abruptly swung her legs back and vaulted off the back of the horse in a perfect rear dismount. She did everything except spread wide her arms and say something along the lines of, "Ta da."

She faced her father, and he her. The several feet between them seemed like a chasm, and I knew that she still hadn't made up her mind as to whether to forgive him and the queen for sending her off as they had.

Then the king took one step toward her. Just one, and

no further. She looked at him in puzzlement as he regarded her, one eyebrow cocked in a slightly amused fashion. And then she understood (before I did, certainly), and she likewise took a step toward him. Just one, and no further.

Then he toward her once more again, and she toward him, and in this way they met each other halfway.

"Gods," he said, so softly I could barely hear him. "You're the image of your mother. You've nothing of me in you at all. Count your blessings."

She smiled, and it was a very warm one, with nary a hint of insanity about it.

He started to put his arms out to her, then paused. "Dare I?" he asked.

"What?" She looked confused, but then he tapped his forearm, and obviously the gesture meant something to her because she chuckled lightly and said, "I think it would be safe, yes." He embraced her then, and I felt a great deal of relief. She was so unpredictable, I'd been thinking that maybe she'd pull out a knife and commit regicide and patricide with one stroke. But no, she actually seemed pleased to see him.

"I've missed you terribly," he said.

She took a step back. "You never came to visit," she said evenly.

"No."

"But you could have."

"Yes."

"Why didn't you?" There was enough of an edge in her voice that I was beginning to get wary again.

"Because," he said sadly, "had I done so, I suspect I

never would have been able to leave without you. And your mother and I felt it best . . . well," and he tilted his head slightly. "There you have it."

It was the most conversation I'd heard out of the king at one time, but Entipy didn't seem satisfied by it. She seemed about to respond again, and suddenly feeling a touch of concern, I broke in. This was, of course, a horrible breach of protocol. One simply did not interrupt two royals in the middle of a conversation, but I'd been through enough that I was beyond caring about social niceties. "Your Highness," I said. Naturally both of them looked at me. "Perhaps it would be best if this were continued inside, in privacy. Certainly that's more appropriate for such royal discussions."

I heard gasps and a bit of muttering from the knights, who were more than aware of my discarding etiquette, but the king did not seem the least put off. "Yes . . . yes, I daresay you're correct, squire. Come, my dear. We will speak further on this." He gestured for her to enter the fort, and as she did so, he turned to me and regarded me most appraisingly. "And you . . . Apropos . . . I will speak further on this with you as well."

"I await Your Highness's pleasure," I said suavely.

At that point I was feeling extremely tired, not to mention extraordinarily hungry. Suddenly I heard the pounding of hooves behind me, and whirled Titan around instantly to see what new danger was descending upon us. "Get inside!" I shouted even as I did so.

But the other knights were looking at me as if I were insane, and quickly I realized why. It was another squad of Runcible's knights, these coming in from the north-east. Gothos had indeed said that several groups had gone out as advance scouts, and this was obviously one of the others. I saw them approach, and recognized the one in the lead almost immediately, and with appropriately sinking heart.

It was Sir Coreolis. Following just behind him was the easily recognizable Mace Morningstar. There were a handful of other knights behind them, but naturally these were the two who caught my attention. Morningstar had grown a rather impressive and neatly trimmed beard since last I'd seen him, and Coreolis still looked as massive—and belligerent—as ever. Both of them realized who I was almost immediately, and seemed duly impressed (or disappointed) upon the realization.

They rode straight up to me and Coreolis reined his horse around. "Well, well . . . Apropos. Still not dead?" he said with a considerable amount of false cheer.

"Not for want of opportunities," I replied easily.

"You wouldn't be on the lookout for one more, would you, Apropos?" Morningstar spoke up in that singsong, musical voice of his.

"I'm always on the lookout, Morningstar. That's why I'm still alive."

Coreolis merely "harrumphed" to himself, snapped his reins, and guided himself and the rest of his squadron into the fort. Morningstar took up the rear, presumably so he could sidle over to me once the others were almost within the perimeter of the fort.

"Well, Apropos?" he inquired.

He offered no follow-up to that comment. "Well . . . what, Morningstar?"

"Is she everything I told you she would be?"

I remembered then the rather colorful stories that he had spun about Entipy. I decided to lie a bit, just for fun and old times' sake. "Actually," I said, looking as contemplative as I could, "she was charming. Quite, quite charming. We hit it off rather well, we two."

His face fell. "Charming? *That* little monster—?"

"Tut tut," I cautioned him in a most arch tone. "It would not serve you well to be so outwardly critical of the princess. I doubt her father would take very kindly to that."

"And who's going to tell . . . him . . ." His voice trailed off as he saw the sadistic smile upon my face. "Apropos, you . . . you wouldn't . . ."

"Not enough that you call her a monster. But you told me you spied upon her, while she was in her chambers. I somehow suspect that will get her father even angrier. . . ."

He drew himself up, endeavoring to remember where he was in the pecking order of society as opposed to me. "Say what you wish. Who will the king believe: You? Or me?"

"Me, most likely, when his own daughter vouches for your lack of proper behavior."

He went deathly pale, but then composed himself rather quickly and nudged his horse closer to mine. "Don't think for a moment, Apropos, that you are in substantially a better position than you were before. In the final analysis . . . you're still no gentleman."

"Why, Mace!" I said with genuine cheer. "That's the nicest thing you've ever said to me." And with that I urged

Titan forward and entered the fortress, happy that—for a moment at least—the image of Tacit lying in the snow could be replaced by the scowling visage of Mace Morningstar wondering just how much trouble he was in.

It didn't surprise me that it was decided we would stay in the fort overnight. Darkness and cold were coming rather swiftly, and surely it made sense for us to remain so that we could get an early start the following morning. I couldn't say that I was looking forward to the ride home. I had, after all, been luckier than I deserved to be in surviving the previous deadly encounter with the forces that roamed in the woods. I didn't think I was going to get quite that lucky again. But there really wasn't any alternative, unless the king chose to declare Fort Terracote as his new castle and set up a permanent home there.

The fortress itself, I learned, was fairly sparsely manned. In point of fact, it was somewhat ancient, built so long ago that the names of the original craftsmen had been lost to antiquity. Runcible had "captured" the fort many years ago, mostly because no one else was particularly interested in the place. Reportedly there had been some freelances who had been squatting there when Runcible made his move to take it, and that battle had lasted for as long as it took the squatters to say, "We'll get packed and out of your way."

At the time it held no strategic value at all, and it still didn't, really. It was a convenient resting stop and not much beside that. The garrison stationed there—under command of Captain Gothos, as it turned out (hand-picked by the king for the assignment, which made me wonder what Gothos had ever done to deserve the honor)—was fairly small and had become used to its relatively quiet life. That's not to say they weren't necessarily brave men, stout and true. I had, after all, witnessed their bravery as they heroically picked off a swordsman using bows and arrows from fifty paces away. You couldn't ask for more boldness than that.

I didn't see much of either the king or the princess that evening. That suited me just fine, since my mind was in a turmoil over all that had happened. I could see from the way the princess looked at me that she was falling, or had fallen, in love with me. At least, I think she had. I was still uncertain how I felt about that, or how I felt about her. What I did know I liked, though, was the way the knights and soldiers were treating me. They were extremely intrigued to find out all that I knew, all that I had experienced. It made me forget my lowly status and even more lowly birth. I knew on some level that that way lay danger, because it was the knowledge of who and what I was—and the quietly burning fury that I maintained because of that—that remained my best hope for survival. As much as they might treat me like one of them, I was not, and never would be, one of them. Forgetting that fact could have serious consequences. And yet . . .

I have never had camaraderie. Not ever. It was an uplifting feeling and, selfishly, I didn't want it to end. As we sat around the cookfire in the small but comfortable barracks, I discovered that the best way to impress them was to sound as offhand about my experiences as possible. To simply toss off the facts, or at least the facts as I chose to present them, and then treat their wide-eyed responses quite casually, as if such matters were purely routine. *"You rode a phoenix?!"* they would say to me, and I would shrug and act as if it was not much different from riding any other steed. *"You had your way with the dreaded Warlord Shank's betrothed?!"* I smiled enigmatically and waggled my eyebrows. There was much laughter and chortling and elbowing of ribs, which caused me to wince since I was still suffering from the wounds that Tacit had inflicted upon me. But I endured it and maintained a forced smile.

Sir Coreolis had absented himself from the festivities, but his squire was there right enough. Mace Morningstar simply sat and listened to it all, and when there was a lull in the festivities he said quietly, "Some rather tall tales you're spinning there, Apropos."

I looked at him indifferently. "It may surprise you to learn, Mace, that I don't especially care if you believe me or not."

"Oh . . . I don't."

The silence in the room promptly became something else, something more hazardous. If Morningstar was to outright call me a liar, that might very easily be construed as a challenge to my honor. That way lay madness . . . not to mention duels and probably further ugliness.

I smiled in my most charming manner and said, "As you will, Mace. I know the truth . . . as does the princess. Even as we speak, she is no doubt conveying the same tales to her father. You remember her father: The king." I feigned shock. "Are you . . . calling the princess a liar,

Morningstar? I would hate to think you were. Such accusations could carry very nasty consequences."

Whereas a moment before, all attention had been upon me, it now shifted back to Morningstar. He squirmed under the sudden scrutiny. "I would never say the princess was lying. But it is possible that she was . . . deceived . . ."

"Unlikely."

It was not I who had spoken, nor anyone else grouped around the cookfire. As one we turned and saw the king standing there. Next to him, in his usual crouch, his jaw slack and his eyes twinkling with quiet lunacy, was Odclay the jester.

Immediately we all went to one knee, although I moaned slightly in doing so from the pain.

"They bow to me!" chortled Odclay. "They know, they know, they make it so, no one can fool 'er, I am the true ruler!"

The king wasted no more than a sidelong glance at Odclay before he turned his attention back to the others. "Squire," he said in a summoning voice.

Immediately Morningstar was on his feet, still bowing deeply. "Yes, Highness."

"Not you," he said dismissively. "Apropos."

Morningstar's face went three shades of red as he went back to kneeling, and I rose and also bowed. "Highness?"

He said nothing, but merely gestured with his head that I should follow him. I did so, not even casting a glance back at the others.

We walked across the small courtyard of the fortress,

Odclay gibbering and capering about, until the king said curtly, "Stop that." The jester promptly did so and instead walked silently behind the king, hanging his head slightly and looking a bit crestfallen.

We entered a small building which I took to be, under ordinary circumstances, the quarters of the garrison leader, Gothos. But naturally he had vacated it in order to accommodate the king. So it was not exactly regal, but it remained the best rooms in the place.

"Sit," said the king.

I sat.

He sat opposite me, gathering his cloak around him. It was black trimmed with silver, but lined with purple.

"Umbrage is dead." There was a hint of a question to it, a vague hope, but in truth he knew the answer before he asked it.

I nodded.

Even Odclay seemed saddened by it, his mood reflecting the king's.

The king absorbed this information, and then said, "Tell me. Everything."

So I did. Even in this recounting, there were certain things I customized in order to make myself sound better. For instance, my pleading with the Harpers for my life became a cunning delaying tactic because I had scented and sensed—with my unparalleled woodcraft—the nearness of a phoenix, and determined that I would enlist the beast's aid in combating the Harpers. Nor did I mention, of course, the details of my final conversation with Tacit right before he was made into a human quiver. Little things like that.

The king listened to all of it, without interruption, occasionally nodding slightly. Finally, when I finished my narrative, a silence fell over the room.

"Did you know," the king said after a time, "that there is a tapestry which hangs in the throne room . . . showing someone riding a phoenix who is destined to rule over Isteria?"

"Yes, Highness."

"One might almost think that your description of your endeavors caters to that."

I didn't look the king in the eyes. "If His Highness is implying that I am fabricating it, he need look no further than his own daughter—"

"Entipy has given an account not dissimilar from yours, actually," said the king.

"Well, then—"

"My daughter," the king said almost cheerily, "is quite mad."

"There are worse fates," the jester piped up, but then fell silent once more.

I didn't know what to say and, for once in my life, said nothing.

"Then again," and the king half-smiled, "we're all a little mad in our own ways. Are we not, squire?"

I nodded, unsure of how else to respond. When in doubt, agree with a king. Good words to live by . . . if for no other reason than that they will help you to keep living.

"My daughter is quite fond of you," continued the king. "There was once a time when I would have thought her incapable of being fond of anything save causing trouble, bringing us to the brink of war, and driving tutors into asylums. Do you believe that people can change, squire?"

"I would like to think so, Highness."

He looked at me askance. "Have you changed? Squire?"

I glanced down. "I . . . do not know, Highness."

"An honest answer. Perhaps you have changed at that."

I wasn't quite sure what to make of that comment, and somehow didn't want to know.

"I have asked Captain Gothos to prepare guest quarters for you," said Runcible. "Not as fine as this, of course. But suitable to one who single-handedly kept my daughter alive. We shall speak more anon. Odclay will lead you to your room."

There was a fire burning in the fireplace nearby. The king rose and went to it, stood in front of it to warm his hands, and appeared lost in thought. Odclay rose without his usual capering and gestured that I should follow him, which I did. In silence we walked back across the courtyard. The jester kept looking me up and down, as if trying to figure me out. He could spend as much time attempting that as he wanted; heaven knew that I hadn't managed it yet.

"Thank you," I said finally, "for showing me the way to the king's liquor supply."

Odclay studied me with obvious curiosity. "Was that you?" he said distantly.

"Yes. Yes, of course it was. Why, don't you remember?"

"I remember so many things," sighed Odclay. "The

problem is, only half of them are true . . . and the half which is true keeps changing places with the half which is false."

"Thank you for sharing that," I said diplomatically and spoke no more to him. I didn't see the point; by tomorrow he'd probably have forgotten we'd chatted at all. On the one hand I felt contempt for him; on the other hand, in some ways he didn't seem so different from me. Simple creatures with infirmities and weaknesses (mine of body and breeding, his of mind and body and who-knew-what in his own background) doing everything possible to survive in a world that had no care for whether they lived or died.

I glanced over to the jester, feeling sympathy, and saw a long trail of drool trickling from his jaw, and decided that maybe we were less alike than I was first thinking.

The room was indeed more than adequate. I enjoyed the relief for the first time in hours, not having to recount stories that I wasn't comfortable with, or keep up a front or appearances.

I lay back on the bed—a genuine bed—and thought about Entipy. Did the king really think she was mad? Why shouldn't he. I did. Or did I?

I was beginning to get impatient with my life. Everything had been so simple, so clear, when I burned with quiet hatred for everything and anything. But now I was starting to develop loyalties to things other than my own self-interest, and I was uncertain as to whether that was a good thing or not.

What if she came to me now? If, as I lay there, the door opened and the princess entered and slid into the bed with me? If she insinuated her naked body against me and begged me to take her? With the ghost of Tacit hanging over me, what would I do? I had no idea. And I disliked having no idea. If you were unable to decide what to do about any given situation before it happened, that left open the opportunity for events to overtake you. That was how people got themselves killed, and I had every intention of living as long and full a life as possible.

Still, I lay there on my side, watching the door, waiting to see if it would creak open, and in short order my eyes closed and I fell into a deep sleep.

I was suddenly shaken to wakefulness and Entipy was looking at me, her face inches from mine.

Oh gods . . . this is it . . . she wants me to mount her like a stallion . . .

And without preamble she said, "The sun has risen, the troops of King Meander, the mad wandering king, are heading this way, and we are completely helpless because the fort is empty save for you, me, my father, and the jester."

There are some mornings where not only do you wake up badly, but you just know the day isn't going to get any better.

Chapter 24

I dressed quickly and emerged into lightly falling snow. "This weather is driving me insane!" I raged.

Entipy, who had been waiting outside my quarters, replied, "You won't live long enough for it to make any difference if Meander gets his hands on you."

"How can the fort be empty? Where are the soldiers? The garrison . . . ?"

We were moving across the courtyard toward the main battlements. Entipy was walking so quickly that, because of my lame leg, it was difficult for me to keep up. I held my staff securely, taking some measure of comfort in its heft as well as in the sword strapped to my back. But if Meander and his Journeymen had really returned to the vicinity, my meager weapons wouldn't last me long at all.

"I have no idea where they are," she said tersely. "I woke up, found the main doors ajar, and when I climbed up onto the ramparts, I saw the Journeymen in the distance."

"Are you sure it's them?"

"They fly the flag of Meander. At least that's what the jester says."

I stopped dead. "The *jester?* You're listening to Odclay now? The king's fool?"

She frowned at me. "Far better to believe he's right and try to prepare for it than assume he's wrong and wind up captives."

I couldn't argue with that either.

The doors were still open. I wasn't surprised; the things were so damned heavy that it had taken several burly men all their effort to shut them before. We were completely vulnerable. Looking up, I saw that the king had joined the jester on the parapet. They seemed to be having an intense discussion as the jester pointed, and then danced about a bit for good measure. Runcible was nodding, looking very solemn and very serious.

"And you've looked everywhere for the rest of the troops?" I asked.

She nodded briskly. "Checked all the barracks, everywhere. Everyone's gone."

The light snow continued to fall, slicking up the ladders that led up to the ramparts. I almost slipped as we clambered up. The king looked down at us with mild eyes and said dryly, "Pity I can't wish you a good morning, squire, but it doesn't appear very good."

I looked where he was looking, and couldn't quite believe what I was seeing.

In the distance, there was heavy snow falling to the left of the King's Road, thick and fast. The tops of the trees in the forest were already abundant with white. It was exactly the same to the right. As for the road itself . . . nothing. A few stray flakes fluttering in from the wind that was whipping through, but otherwise nothing was obstructing the path of the Journeymen.

And Journeymen they most definitely were. I remembered their uniforms of black and white, and that emblem of theirs—the globe with marching feet around it. I was too far to see it on their shields, as I had that time in the Elderwoods with Tacit, but it didn't require the eyes of an eagle to see the symbol emblazoned on banners being held high that were fluttering in the wind. With the snow whirling on either side of them, it was as if Meander had brought the spirit and climes of the Frozen North along with him.

"That," Entipy said slowly, "is unnatural. It's as if the snow is his very friend . . . it . . ."

"Oh . . . gods," I whispered. "Of course. *Of course.*"

"Of course what?"

"It all makes sense . . . I mean, a warped kind of sense, but sense nevertheless . . ."

"It all makes sense, makes sense, makes sense," chanted the jester, "I sense, the scents of sense incensed . . ."

"Shut up," I said.

"Speak, squire," said the king, his eyes narrowed. His demeanor was quite calm; you would have thought we were simply chatting about niceties rather than being faced with the impending arrival of an army, who couldn't have been more than an hour away.

"The weather patterns. They've been out of whack. It's been because of Meander. He may have left the immediate area of Isteria, but apparently he hasn't gone far from these parts. And he's been using a weather-weaver to re-create the climes of the Frozen North for him. It's the environment that he's most accustomed to. So when the mood suits him, he has the weatherweaver manipulate the cold to benefit him, when he's going on the offensive, or whenever he's simply feeling nostalgic for his homelands."

"I knew that other kings were fighting him," Runcible said, shaking his head. "I advised them against it . . . told them the foolishness . . ."

"As foolish as ignoring him, Father?" demanded Entipy. As cold as the air was, there was genuine heat from her. "Is that how ruling works? To sit about on your royal throne with your royal thumb up your royal ass, while others do whatever they wish to whomever they wish? Apropos told me how one of Meander's people killed his mother, and you sat by and did nothing."

The jester immediately started to chant. "Blue is ground, brown is skies, King Meander is so wise, knows he to avoid a fight when the timing is not right . . ."

"Shut up!" This time Entipy and I had spoken in unison.

"We all do what seems right at the time, Entipy," the king told her.

"And what seems right this time, Father?" And she pointed in the direction of the oncoming army. "Face facts: You have been betrayed. Your whereabouts offered up to Meander, and he's coming for you, and we're defenseless . . ."

"I have a cunning plan!" declared the jester. I moaned inwardly, and Entipy audibly. "As cunning as the good king's brilliant outflanking maneuver at the Battle of Ralderbash! As outstanding as the way in which he outthought the evil hippogryph of Collosia. As clever as the way in which he managed to obtain the Veil of Tiers from the very heart of the Land of Wuin! As—"

"Is this a cunning plan or a résumé?" I asked in exasperation.

But the king seemed genuinely interested. "What would that plan be, Odclay, pray tell?"

"I will stay here, perched in plain view, and distract Meander and his men when they arrive. In the meantime, the three of you can flee."

"We do not run from danger," Entipy snapped.

"The hell we don't," I shot back, and then quickly added—to sound noble—"Not when you and the king are at risk. The problem is, there's no place to run to. If we head north, away from Meander, we wind up back in the Outer Lawless regions. If we head east, he'll catch up with us, and besides, the terrain is too daunting for us to put any serious distance between us. West is problematic, considering there's a thousand-foot drop in that direction, and south takes us right into his arms."

"I said it was a cunning plan, not a perfect one," retorted the jester.

They were still approaching, taking their own sweet time. They knew they had us.

"If only we knew for sure that we were helpless," said the king. "If only we knew where our troops had gone . . . whether they would return in time . . . there's so much that's uncertain . . ."

"Yes, but we don't know for sure," said Entipy.

And that's when it hit me.

"No," I said softly, "we don't know. And neither do they." Suddenly I turned to them, seeing the confused expressions on their faces. "Highness . . .what do you know of a siege? When an army lays siege to a fortress such as this. What do you know of what happens?"

"Well," the king said slowly, "you secure the gateway, lower the portcullis if you have one. Man the battlements. Get boiling liquid or heavy stones to be dropped through the machicolations if you have any. Ready the archers, keep behind the merlons to present as minimal a target as—"

"Right. Right. And they know that, too."

"Of course. Everyone knows it."

"All right. Here's what we do." My mind was racing down the slippery slope of inspired madness. "Highness . . . change clothes."

He looked at me blankly, as did the others. "You consider this an inappropriate ensemble in which to be captured?"

"Not with something else you brought. With him."

And I pointed at the jester.

"Are you crazy?" asked Entipy, genuinely curious.

"No," I said. "But they're going to think your father is. Crazy as a fox, as the saying goes."

And I laid out my plan for them, as quickly and efficiently as I could. When I finished they were still staring at me as if I'd grown a third head.

"It won't work," Entipy said flatly.

"Do you have a better idea?" I asked.

"She's right, it won't work!" said Odclay, sounding

pleasantly lucid. "The moment they see him up there, a perfect target, they'll put a hundred arrows in him!"

"No, they won't. They'll want him alive; he's far more valuable that way."

"Are you sure?" asked Runcible doubtfully.

"Reasonably so."

"Reasonably so?"

"Look," I said in exasperation, "if they want you dead, then we're finished no matter what. If they want you alive, then this can work. But we have to decide now, because if I'm going to get into the forest and accomplish my part of the plan, we have to get started."

Entipy and the jester looked to the king, who instead looked at me as if hoping that I might somehow suddenly transform into a great wizard and simply spirit the lot of us out of there. The snow was coming down harder around us.

"All right," he said finally. "We will trust the squire's plan."

"Father—!"

"You should not be complaining, Entipy. Think: If it doesn't work, you have the questionable joy of seeing your father making a total ass of himself in his final moments. Not quite the compensation for the years you feel you lost with the Faith Women . . . but hopefully it will provide some small amusement. All right, Odclay . . . let's get started. Apropos," and he clamped a hand on my shoulder. "Good luck."

You'll need it, I thought privately.

"And Apropos . . ."

"Yes, Highness . . . ?"

He smiled. "If this works . . . and we live to tell the tale . . . I shall make you Sir Apropos."

The king and Odclay climbed down off the parapets, and I prepared to follow . . . and suddenly Entipy caught me by the arm and swung me around, looking at me hard in the eyes. She seemed to be searching for something in there, something she could hold on to and believe in.

And then she kissed me. It was as firm and deep and passionate a kiss as I'd ever received, and she didn't seem the least bit insane at all. She broke off and looked at me with wide eyes, and she whispered, "I trust you."

What was I going to say? *More fool you, I'm out of here, because this demented plan will never work, even though it's mine.*

"Thank you," I said.

Understand: When I first started outlining the plan, I actually thought it was workable. The further I got into it, though, the more I became convinced that I was suggesting sheer idiocy. If the king had smiled patronizingly and said, "We'll have to try some other course of action, squire," I would have nodded and been glad for the out. The only thing that made me get defensive about it was that Entipy dismissed it out of hand, and for some reason the fact that she was the one who had done so prompted me to rise to the occasion.

So now they were stuck with it.

They. Not me.

I was getting the hell out of there.

The moment I had seen Meander's Journeymen

approaching, I began assessing the odds—not where the royals were concerned, but where I was concerned. And from where I stood, it didn't look especially promising. I was reasonably certain that I could escape into the woods, make my way through them silently, slip away like a ghost. Lame of leg or not, I had still learned my woodcraft from the best, and even though these were not the Elderwoods, I was willing to take my chances on my own. I was not, however, enthused about the prospects of evaporating into the woods if I was dragging along the king, the princess, and the court jester. The king, possibly. *Possibly.* But the princess had the woodcraft of a diseased wombat, and the court jester was so unpredictable that he might start singing eighteen choruses of "My Crumpet Was a Strumpet," getting the attention of not only Meander's people but probably a wandering regiment of Warlord Shanks's men as well. I did not think that the king would be willing to leave either of them behind . . . although of the two, he might just take his chances with the jester. The only possible way I could manage to survive was to know everything that could go wrong, and bringing the unholy trio with me simply offered too many unknowns.

Furthermore, I wasn't all that worried about Meander's capturing them. I truly did believe that the king was going to be of more value to them alive. The princess would likely fall into that same category. The jester they would probably keep around for amusement value, and if they didn't, well, small loss. They would all fare perfectly well in Meander's care. Perhaps they'd get on so famously that they'd all take up a house by the shore together. But a lone squire, lame of leg? They'd chop me for kindling in a heartbeat.

No, my resolve was solid and reasonable: I was departing as fast as my good leg would carry me.

In the fort's storehouse, I found a supplies belt that was ordinarily used for carrying rations. I opened the pouches, dumped in the jewels and money from my saddlebag, and closed it up again, leaving the coinage in the hidden compartment in my staff. I shook the belt violently several times to make certain that there was no telltale jingling. There wasn't. I had it packed in too tight. I tightened the belt around my waist and allowed my tunic to hang loosely over it, covering it quite well. I rolled my cloak up tightly and tied it over my waist. By that point I was bulging there, but it was better than trying to make my way through the woods with my cloak snagging on branches. I would probably need it later, though, as proof against the cold, particularly if the snow didn't let up. My scabbard remained on my back, my staff firmly in hand.

I took a deep breath and made my way to the front. The king didn't see me; he was heading toward the battlements. He was jingling, attired in the fool's motley. Yes. Definitely an insane plan. Thank the gods I wasn't going to be around to see it. Entipy had secured herself in the barracks, although I suspected that she was going to be trying to watch from there. I couldn't blame her. Who would pass up an opportunity to watch a king make a complete jackass of himself? Well . . . who besides me, that was.

I exited the front of the fortress through the doors

that remained wide open. Meander's men were still a distance away, and I covered the distance between the fortress and the forest in no time. As opposed to the ludicrousness of the plan I had hatched for the king, my personal plan was simplicity itself: Stay the hell out of Meander's path.

The moment I was in the forest, all my doubts melted away. I felt as if I was truly back in my element. This was where I was meant to be. Not posturing about in castle halls, pretending I was something I wasn't. Instead my place was living a life of freedom, unencumbered by all the demands that society put upon one. The trees seemed to say "Welcome back" to me, even though I had never been there before. I had enough money in my belt to live life in any manner I chose. I could build a house, build a business . . . or even just live in the woods and emerge only when I felt like it, buying what I desired and vanishing again. It would bother no one. If you're penniless, you're mad, but if you're rich, you're eccentric. I would owe nothing to anyone, buy what I felt like, and even take what I felt like, because when you have money, you can do anything you want.

I looked behind me, the fort already lost to sight. There was snow upon the ground. There were no footprints upon it. That was how smoothly, how lightly I had passed over it. I felt like a great fish finally and gratefully returning to the oceans that were his home. I felt like a liberated soul. I felt . . .

. . . I felt . . .

. . . I felt . . . the warmth of her lips upon mine. I felt the sincerity with which she said, "I trust you." The last person to trust me had been Tacit . . . and look what happened to him.

I felt a clear, vivid recollection of the sensation that passed between us. I felt the pride, however fleeting it had been, however misplaced it was, when Runcible had accepted my plan and resolved to try and make it work.

You will not do this to yourself! You will not! You will not turn into some mewling, smitten creature! My mind was fairly screaming at me, the same inner voice that had warned me to just take the money Justus had offered me to compensate for my mother's death. If I'd listened to it then, think of all the problems I could have avoided. *You must not forget who they are, and who you are! He is the king who oversees the knights that raped your mother! She is an unstable little creature whom even her own father says is insane! And a jester? The jester is the only one in the bunch worth saving, truth be told, and you're certainly not going to risk yourself for him! You will never be Sir Apropos of anything! You liked the feeling of her kiss? Women's lips are a sov a dozen, and you've got enough riches on you to purchase the affections of a hundred women far more voluptuous, and far less trouble, than Entipy.*

I slowed.

Listen to me, Apropos! This is not who and what you are! Tacit really was *the hero, and you saw how he ended up! How much worse will it be for you? You owe them nothing . . .*

I slowed more . . .

. . . nothing, do you hear me? Wipe your mouth! Get the taste of her lips off there right this instant! Flee! Flee, right now! You do not want to do this! You cannot want to do this!

She trusted me . . .

Damn you, Apropos! ***Can you do nothing wrong right?!***

I stopped.

I looked behind me.

There were tracks now. I was sinking into the snow. Sinking into my own frustration and confusion.

And that was when the Journeyman came at me.

His woodcraft was impressive, admittedly. He was keeping downwind of me so that I couldn't possibly scent him. Still, I would have heard him if I hadn't been so busy arguing within my own skull. He was not a behemoth by any stretch of the imagination, but he was larger than me. He had a heavy brow and a mashed-in nose, and the rest was covered by a chain-mail coif. Disdaining a hauberk, which oftentimes accompanied a coif—probably because chain-mail hauberks made an unholy racket when moving through the forest, and this was apparently a light- infantry man—he wore thick black leather armor with white trim, and a cloak of similar colors dangling off his shoulder. The only thing that tipped me to his presence, at literally the last moment, was his trailing cloak snatching a branch and causing it to crack. I spun, my staff in my hand, but he had his sword out and was not wasting any time.

"Wait!" I said, throwing up a hand. He halted, a wolfish smile on his face. "Why kill me? Meander once extended hospitality to an entire regiment! I'll . . ." My mind raced. "I'll join him. Join you. I have no difficulty with that."

He looked at me askance. "Would you be 'Apropos'?"

I blinked in surprise. "Why . . . yes."

He sighed. "Sorry. Can't help you."

And with that halfhearted and utterly puzzling apology, he came at me, swinging his sword high, fast, and down, like an axeman chopping wood.

He wasn't giving me a chance to pull free my sword, but I didn't need to. I yanked either end of my staff and it came apart at the middle, as it was designed to. With a baton in either hand now and acting entirely on reflex, I swung one side of it up and around even as I darted inside the downward arc of his swing, pushing off with my good left leg for more speed. The baton caught the sword on the flat of the blade, shoving it aside and sending it to the ground just to my left. On the other baton, I pushed the triggering device and the blade snapped out, even as I lunged forward and stabbed upward.

The four-inch blade sank into his right eye and angled up into his brain.

His remaining eye widened in surprise as he dropped his sword, and he would have let out a shriek right then that would have alerted the damned in Hell, except that I let my momentum carry me forward and I slammed into him. We both went to the ground, and I clapped a hand over his mouth, stifling his agonized screams. I think he had no clear idea what was happening at that point; all he knew was that he was half-blinded and could no longer control his body. He spasmed wildly and I held him down, staying atop him as if I were trying to break a wild horse. Blood spurted from his ruined eye socket all over my gloved hands, and I tried not to think about the fluids that were pumping out onto me.

And slowly . . . horribly, horribly slowly . . . the frantic twitching stopped. His head slumped to one side, and for the second time in two days, I watched someone's lifeblood turn the snow crimson. Except this time . . . I was the one who had done it.

The full impact of it had not yet settled in on me. I pulled out the half staff and stared at the blood-tinged blade on the end of it in wonderment. I had taken the life of a man, with my own hand. Granitz had fallen on his sword, the Harper that I had killed had been more beast than human, and Tacit had been annihilated by the archers. But this time, this time . . . I had fought a man, a soldier, who was trying to kill me, and I had killed him first. My first true kill.

I didn't even know his name.

And as I watched the life light vanish from his one remaining eye, I let out a choked sob and then retched violently, my stomach seized with dry heaves. I knew he had been trying to kill me. I had beaten him fairly . . . well, as fairly as one can when one is pulling a surprise weapon on an opponent. But still . . . I had killed him . . .

I felt no elation. I only felt cold and empty . . . and a sick sense of irony. Because this soldier over whom I had stumbled was actually the first piece in my utterly preposterous plan. The plan that I had known, beyond question, could not possibly work, required that I find one of Meander's men in the woods and overcome him.

Step one in the chain of idiocy had been accomplished. And at that point, I couldn't think of a single good reason not to proceed to step two.

You're going to get yourself killed! They know you're coming for some reason! It's a death trap! It's—

Allow me to rephrase: I simply didn't want to think of a single good reason not to proceed to step two.

It was only a matter of minutes to don the man's armor. The most disgusting thing was donning the coif. His blood still tinged the inside. But I wanted to cover myself up as much as possible, and so I pulled on the chain-mail headpiece and tried not to dwell upon the stuff within that was sticking to my hair. I found a sizable downed tree with a goodly part of the trunk's interior rotted away, and I stuffed the man's corpse into it. Then I retched again, and this time allowed it to keep going until it ran its course, rather than fight it. I wrapped the man in my cloak; I figured it was the least I could do. Besides, his cloak was nicer.

This is madness, this is madness, my inner voice kept chanting, over and over. I stopped listening to it, because I knew that it was right and therefore there wasn't much point in arguing about it.

I made my way through the woods as carefully as I could. Even if I had possessed no craft at all, I would still have been able to catch up with Meander's men. They were, after all, trooping down the main road, making no effort to hide their presence. The main thing I had on my side was that Meander's troops were somewhat fluid in nature. Soldiers tended to come and go as they saw fit. Indeed, "soldiers" might have been too generous a name for them, since the word carries with it careful training, a military command structure, and sense of order. Meander, on the other hand, was the antithesis of order.

Naturally he believed in obedience to he himself, but beyond that, he was—shall we say—flexible. It would probably have been more accurate to term them "warriors." No matter what you called them, however, they tended to get the job done. But because of that fluidity of nature, my hope was that I would be able to insinuate myself into their ranks without being noticed.

By the time I arrived, the head of the procession—where Meander presumably was—had already gone by. I chose my spot behind a nicely large tree and watched them pass. I heard them making comments about Runcible, about ransoms and such, which settled for me beyond any question that their goal was to go to the fort and take the king captive. I waited until there was a brief break in the procession, where the men ahead were engaged in conversation and the men just behind weren't paying attention, and I simply stepped into place and started walking. No one paid me the least bit of attention. For all I knew, if someone had seen me stepping out of the woods, he might well have assumed that I was answering nature's call and now falling back into line.

The most fantastic aspect of all this was to be at the heart of the insane weather conditions that accompanied Meander's advancement. Snow had been coming down on me in the forest mere seconds ago; I shook out my newly acquired cloak to try and get as much off me as I could. And snow continued briskly on the other side. But here, on the road . . . nothing. It was a truly eerie sensation, like standing in the middle of a downpour and not getting wet.

Subtly, I managed to catch up to the men who were

discussing Runcible. ". . . hasn't a prayer," I heard one of them saying, a burly man with beady eyes. "'Runcible the Crafty.' There's a laugh. We have the crafty one cold."

I piped up, "Yes, he's caught with his jerkin off this time," and this prompted a rousing guffaw from the others.

"Well said!" the burly man commented, apparently not caring who I was as long as my views were along his lines.

And then I added, almost as an afterthought, "Although . . ." I let it hang there for a moment and then said, "No . . . never mind."

"Never mind what?" The burly man had fixed those beady eyes on me, and the attention of several others trudging along had also been caught.

"Well, it's just . . . I heard that there was an entire army who thought they had Runcible cold. I mean, absolutely pinioned, no way out. Turned out that they'd fallen into the middle of an elaborate scheme of his. A handful of them escaped with their lives . . . the rest, put to the sword. But that's just what I heard," I added dismissively. "Very likely nothing to it. I suppose that's how legends get built . . . by the constant repetition of deeds to the point where you don't know if they're true or not."

"That's valid enough," said the burly man, but he was looking slightly uneasy.

Which was exactly what I wanted.

I started picking up my pace. Considering my physical limitations, that might not have been possible were it not for the fact that the troops were taking their own sweet time. I smelled alcohol on the breath of quite a few as I made my way past them. Yes, by the gods, this was a group that was entirely too relaxed. Still, what they lacked in sobriety, they made up for in numbers. They stretched as far back and ahead as I could see. And every so often, I would stop and have a conversation along the lines of the one I just had minutes before. Each time I would then move on, leaving the Journeymen with food for thought and the smallest seed of suspicion planted within them.

I moved forward, ever faster. I had to try and get to Meander himself, or at least get near him, so that I could be in the proper position to have some sort of impact once we reached the forest itself. My inner voice had stopped talking to me. I think it decided that it was wasting its time and was going to go off and be an inner voice for someone who actually paid it some mind.

Several of the soldiers grunted or mumbled, "Watch where you're going," as I shouldered my way past. I kept my head down and my feet heading ever forward. I knew I was getting closer to the front, though, when I heard voices saying "Your Highness" every other sentence. Everyone was being properly obedient, subservient and obsequious. Would that I had brought thicker boots for wading through all the bullshit that was being tossed about so freely.

I didn't hear Meander's voice much. I heard others asking him questions or firing opinions at him, and he would say "Hmm" or "Ahhhh" or "I see." In that respect, he reminded me of King Runcible a bit. Except in Runcible's case I wondered whether or not it was subterfuge to cover a slow mind, whereas with Meander it was a different story. I had no doubt that Meander was genuinely brilliant. Who else, after all, would have come up with the entire "movable feast" concept. As near as I could tell, though, he did not like to volunteer much beyond that in the way of instructions or even jobs. Then again, I was not a big one for listening to, or accepting, rules, so I certainly couldn't condemn him for that.

We rounded a mild curve and I took the opportunity to speed up a bit more. I did not want to draw too much attention to either me or my staff. Even so, I was a bit apprehensive about being recognized somehow . . . particularly since that one soldier I had killed had blurted out my name.

And then I saw Meander, from the back. I was positive it was he, because he had the largest circle of advisors and they were all babbling contradictory information simultaneously. That and the fact that he was in a throne. The chair was mounted on a litter and was being carried by four men, two in front, two behind. It was certainly the best way to travel. Finally I was relieved to see him clap his hands to his ears and declare, "Enough!" His advisors promptly shut up. As far as I was concerned, that was enough reason to become king right there: Being able to tell people to shut their mouths, and make it stick.

I walked faster still, drawing in close, coming up behind, and then alongside, and I cast a glance at King Meander.

His hair was almost solid gray, like ice, and yet I could

see that he was not truly all that old. But he had very old eyes, as if they had seen so much of life—enough for ten lifetimes—that they were all but ready to close for the final time. His eyebrows, surprisingly, were solid black, in contrast to the gray and black beard, neatly trimmed as a contrast to his rough-hewn exterior. His face had a craggy, weatherbeaten, care-filled look . . .

. . . and four scratches down the left side . . . nasty, ugly vicious marks . . . such as might be made by an attacking animal . . . or like a woman might have made struggling in her last moments before death . . .

Chapter 25

My world reeled around me and I hadn't even realized I'd stopped walking until an irritated Journeyman pushed me from behind and muttered an imprecation that I should move my ass or he'd cut it off for me. I was in motion before I even realized it, walking numbly, casting repeated glances in Meander's direction, looking at those marks on his face as if they were calling to me from beyond the grave.

Had it been *he*? Had it been the leader of the Journeymen, riding about, looking for some sport, who had killed Madelyne? Had nothing less than royalty been responsible for striking her down? My mind was whirling, out of focus, and that was extremely dangerous because the only thing that was going to give me anything faintly resembling an advantage was my ability to think. At that moment, though, I could barely string two coherent thoughts together.

I heard the sound of running feet and looked up the road. Two men, dressed similarly to the fellow I had dispatched, were approaching as quickly as they could, and for a panicked moment I thought they had discovered his body. "All stop," said Meander, and the order was relayed back with rapid-fire precision. Within moments the entire procession had halted as the two runners knelt before Meander and I waited to see just how screwed I was.

The throne was lowered to the ground and Meander stepped from it. "How now, good runners?" Meander said. His voice was deep and rough.

"We have seen the fort, sire. It is just ahead, beyond the grove."

A ghost of a smile touched Meander's lips. "And what preparations has Runcible made for us? Doors bolted? Does he have a handful of arrows at the ready, perhaps?"

"No, sire. The doors are wide open and there appear no signs of resistance."

Meander sighed heavily. "Gone on the run, has he? Foolish. We'll have to track him down, then." He turned to a man standing at his side, an older man who reminded me slightly of Umbrage, except without the vacant stare. Indeed, he looked as if he had brought some of the Frozen North with him, except on the inside. "Captain Grimmoir . . . I want you to take two—"

"Begging Your Majesty's pardon," one of the runners said, "but Runcible is not on the run."

Slowly Meander looked back at his two information gatherers, his face a question. "He's not? You mean . . . he's surrendering?" He sounded slightly disappointed.

The runners looked at each other uncomfortably, as if not sure how to best express it. "Not . . . exactly, sire."

"Well, then, what, then?"

"It . . . isn't easy to describe, Highness."

"Give it a whack," said the king icily.

One of the runners, the older of the two, took a deep breath and said, "King Runcible is sitting atop the battlements, dressed in fool's motley, jingling little bells and singing baudy tavern chants, with the front doors wide open and no sign of defenses being made whatsoever."

There was dead silence for a moment, and then a ripple of disbelieving laughter. Meander leaned forward, his fingers interlaced, and he said very softly, "Are you *quite* sure?"

"Yes, Your Highness."

The man he'd called Grimmoir made a loud, scoffing noise. "The man is mad!" he declared loudly, and there were nods of agreement.

Meander turned and looked at Grimmoir thoughtfully. I couldn't take my eyes off the scars on his face; they seemed to cry out to me with my mother's voice. "I've heard the same thing said of me, Captain. Do you concur? Do you follow a madman, Grimmoir?"

"No, Your Highness," Grimmoir said quickly.

Once again that same ghostly smile, and then Meander said, "There are others who might disagree. Well, then . . . let us see this phenomenon for ourselves, so that we may determine how many mad kings are at issue this day. Advance, Captain."

"Advance!" shouted Grimmoir, and once again the order was quickly relayed down the line as Meander climbed back onto his throne and was hoisted once more.

I tore my thoughts away from my mother's final moments, not wanting to lose sight of the plan—as pathetic as that plan might be. I drifted close, not to Grimmoir, but to the man to his immediate right, who appeared to be his lieutenant. Seconds-in-command enjoy attention, since they receive it so rarely. "Do you think him mad, sir?" I asked in a low voice. "Runcible, I mean."

The lieutenant shrugged. "No other explanation for it."

"That's quite true. Such a reputedly crafty king would never engage in such actions unless he was truly bereft of reason. Unless, of course . . ." Once again I stopped. "Fie. 'Tis of no consequence."

He looked at me oddly. "Speak, soldier. What is on your mind?"

"I said, sir, it is of no consequence—"

"And I said speak. That's an order." He liked saying that, I could tell.

"Well," I said, glancing around as if to make sure we weren't being overheard, "what if it's . . . a trap . . ."

"A trap? How could it possibly be a trap?"

I shrugged. "If I knew such things, sir, I would be an officer."

"But his troops have left him!"

"So we believe. But if we allow for a moment that it is, in fact, a trick . . . a deception . . . anything is possible. An ambush. Hidden reinforcements of which we knew nothing. Anything. I mean, Runcible does have a considerable reputation for craftiness. Certainly it must be based on *something*. Maybe it's precisely this kind of trickery, catching armies unaware and annihilating them, that has led to it." Once more I shrugged. "But I probably imagine these things simply because I am but a lowly trooper, and not as experienced in the ways of war as others. Certainly if there was a chance that this was some sort of deception and we were riding into disaster, the captain or the king would have thought of it. I have overstepped myself. I apologize."

With that, I took a few steps back as if the conversation was over, joining the rank and file once more.

Then I watched. And waited.

I did not have to wait long. Within less than two minutes, the lieutenant was at Grimmoir's side, whispering into his ear. Grimmoir frowned, shaking his head at first, but then he started to look thoughtful as well. He did not, however, approach the king.

As for me . . . my temptation was to approach the king with a dagger in my hand. But I would probably get nowhere near him. And what if I did? What if I got within range of him and actually managed to, say, kill him? Aside from the fact that there would, in short order, be nothing left of me . . .

Well, actually, there was nothing aside from that fact. But it was a significant enough fact to give me decided pause.

We drew within range of the fort and once again a halt was called. Meander stepped down from the throne and moved beyond the edge of the forest, eyes wide with curiosity. Snow was continuing to descend even more rapidly. Naturally it was continuing to keep clear of us, but it was falling on the fort unabated.

And it was falling upon Runcible, who was in the midst of doing exactly what had been advertised. The runners had omitted the fact that Runcible was strumming a lyre, rather badly, with one hand, while continuing to shake a bell stick with the other. He wore the fool's cap and the badly mismatched clothing, right down to the boots with the extended toes and the bells on the ends. His words drifted through the air to us, sung badly off key . . .

"And then there was Molly
The fattest damned whore
The slut who weighed seventeen stone
She swallowed poor Charlie
And asked for some more,
Since she despised dining alone . . ."

"What the hell does that mean?" demanded Grimmoir.

"I'm not sure," said Meander thoughtfully. "Since it's a tavern song, I would surmise it makes more sense if you are drunk. Well, Captain . . . it appears Runcible has indeed gone quite mad."

"Yes . . . it appears so," said the captain slowly.

The way in which Grimmoir said that caught Meander's attention. So, too, did mutterings from the rest of the rank and file. They were pushing forward to see the supposedly demented king, fully exposed and easy pickings, and they didn't seem happy about it. I heard words like "crafty" and "too easy" and "annihilate" being bandied about. Words that I had been spreading, thoughts that I had been planting. Moreover, they were spreading back down the processional like a forest ablaze, and the uncomfortable murmurings were becoming louder.

I don't know that Meander was especially concerned about insurrection among his men, but he was certainly curious over what the problem was. "Captain," he said slowly, "is there some difficulty?"

"Well, sire . . . may I speak to you privately . . . ?"

"No," Meander said firmly. "If there is a concern, it is apparently shared by many, and so should be heard by all. Speak your mind."

Grimmoir didn't appear happy about it, but he steeled himself and said, "Well, sire, some of the men . . . they're thinking that this might be some sort of trap."

"A trap, you say?" Meander looked back to Runcible, who had moved on to singing about a whore known as the Fabulous Funt. "How now?"

"Well, sire . . ." He glanced at his lieutenant and acknowledged others as well. "They seem to feel that it's too easy. Runcible has earned a reputation for craftiness, not madness . . ."

"Unlike me," Meander said thoughtfully.

"As you say, sire," allowed Grimmoir. "And the reasoning is, which is the more likely: That a wise and crafty king has lost his mind? Or that a wise and crafty king is endeavoring to ensnare us in some sort of brilliant scheme? Trick us as he has tricked others?"

"And you think me capable of being tricked, Captain?"

The question sounded faintly dangerous, but

Grimmoir, to his credit, stayed his course. "Anyone—even a king, such as yourself—can only make decisions based upon the quality of the information presented you by others. If that information is faulty . . ." He let the supposition trail off.

"Hmm," Meander said thoughtfully, looking back at the king. "And you are saying that the information I have received . . . that Runcible is alone and helpless . . . may be incorrect."

"There is that possibility, sire."

"And he is but awaiting an attack in order to spring the trap."

"Yes, sire."

"And that if I send men in, they may well be slaughtered before they get within distance. And that, furthermore, it would signal the moment when additional troops of Meander's are to come in from behind and cut us off, or some such."

Grimmoir nodded. "All of those are possibilities, yes, sire."

"On the other hand," continued Meander, and he began to pace, "he may be taking these actions because he is, in fact, utterly helpless, and wants us to think that it is a trap. That he is hoping, praying, that what seems to be happening now would, in fact, happen. That we will be paralyzed, not by force of arms, but by force of reputation."

"That is also possible, sire."

"So what you are saying to me, Captain . . . is that this is either a painfully obvious last-ditch effort to save himself . . . or else a painfully obvious trap."

"Aye, sire. That would seem to be the case."

"There is a third possibility. Perhaps he is hoping that we will see him and laugh ourselves to death."

"I . . . would not think that last to be terribly likely, sire," Grimmoir said doubtfully.

"Nor I," sighed Meander. "I'm merely trying to consider all the options." He frowned a moment more and then said, "Archers . . ."

Three men wielding the largest composite bows I'd ever seen stepped forward. Meander studied the distance between himself and the castle. "About two hundred . . . two hundred fifty yards, would be my estimate. Well within range. Gentlemen . . . do you think you can hit that madman up there?"

"Aye, sire," and there was a uniform nodding of heads.

My heart went into my throat.

"Very well. I'd like you to fire a volley—"

I started to take a step forward without the faintest idea of what I was going to say.

"—and see how close you can come . . . without hitting him," finished Meander, and I released my breath in relief.

The archers stepped up, took aim, and let fly. I prayed that some capricious cross-gust of wind would not send one of the missiles off course and into the king's head.

Two thudded just below him, and one to his immediate right. There was no way that Runcible could not have noticed them. The king didn't flinch. He kept right on strumming the lyre and singing foolish ditties.

"Damn," murmured Meander. "Well, that solved

nothing. If he had jumped away from them, that would have been a sign that we were not dealing with a madman. But he did not react. So he is either indeed insane . . . or else willing to keep his cards so close to his vest that nothing short of fully committing ourselves to an attack will cause him to show his hand . . ."

"At which point it might be too late," said Grimmoir.

For a long moment Meander was silent.

Then, slowly, he turned to Grimmoir. "Captain," he said, "I do not wish you to take insult at this . . . but you are not a very imaginative man. You are superb at following orders. You can execute any strategy that others have developed. But seeing the situation present here before you . . . it is simply not within your nature to come up with such a means of second-guessing a crafty opponent. I do not fault you for this; you have served me well without imagination, and will continue to do so in the future. I do not believe that this concern—that it may be a trap—was something you intuited. Who suggested it to you?"

"Sire, I—"

"Who?"

Grimmoir apparently knew better than to try and slip something past his king. He pointed at his lieutenant, who stepped forward and bowed.

Meander looked him up and down.

"I know you. You're dumb as a post, as your father was, and his father before him. No offense."

"None taken, Your Highness," said the lieutenant, a bit bewildered.

"Who spoke to you then, eh?"

Suddenly feeling my privates shriveling to the size of peas, I tried to back slowly away without catching attention, but it was too late. Dumb as a post he might have been, but he also had a keen eye. "That man. There," said the lieutenant, and pointed straight at me.

"You. Light infantryman. Come here," said Meander in a voice that was not brooking any dissent.

Slowly I advanced. I was doing everything I could to keep my staff hidden within the folds of my cloak and obscuring my limp. I bowed. "Your servant, sire."

"You speculated to the lieutenant here that Runcible might be setting a trap for us?"

I looked resolutely down. "I . . . may have done, aye, sire."

"Quite an imagination you have."

"I . . . simply do not wish to see you fall into a trap, Highness. I would have been remiss in not voicing my speculations. But they are just that."

"And have you spoken to others of my troops about these concerns? Because there seems to be some uniform discord among the men, and I am endeavoring to trace the source."

"Again, I . . . may have. If I have overstepped myself, sire, I humbly—"

"All opinions are welcome," Meander said. "You are a curious fellow. I do not recall seeing you recently. What is your name?"

I said the first thing that came to mind. "Tacit, sire."

"Tacit? Tacit One-Eye? I've heard of you a'right, but both eyes seem quite intact."

"You have . . . heard of my brother, sire. Not me."

"Your brother. Two brothers, both named Tacit?" he asked in polite bemusement.

My brain had completely frozen. "Our . . . parents were very poor, sire," I said desperately.

"And could not afford more than one name for you?"

I had no reply to that.

Meander laughed softly. I was amazed how soft-spoken the man was. "Well then, Tacit Two-Eye . . . your imaginings have given me much food for thought. Do I commit my forces into a foolish trap . . . or risk being foolish and walk away from it? What would you do, Tacit Two-Eye?"

I gathered my nerve and looked straight into his face. He still looked quite tired, as if the prolonged discussion was dispiriting somehow. "If I were to attack, sire . . . and it was a trap . . . I would be a laughingstock, presuming that I survived. If I walked away . . . and it was not a trap . . . I would never know otherwise. Then again . . . no one is expected to know everything. So not knowing something for sure that leaves us all alive . . . seems to me preferable to knowing something for sure that could leave us all dead."

"And if he truly is helpless and this is all a façade? I am letting a potential captive depart unharmed."

"Not unharmed, sire. He will always know the depths of humiliation to which he had to resort just to survive."

For no reason I could understand, that seemed to catch Meander's attention. "That . . . can be a very terrible thing indeed," he said, sounding very distant. "A very terrible punishment for anyone to carry with them . . . much less a king."

The silence then seemed to drag unto infinity. The only noise to be heard was the distant strumming of the lyre and the wretched singing voice of Runcible.

"Captain," Meander said finally. "Sometimes the game is simply not worth rolling the dice. We are departing."

I couldn't believe it. My legs went weak and I supported myself on my staff to stop from keeling over. It had worked. Son of a bitch, it had worked. Now all I had to do was wait until a propitious moment, fade back into the woods and double back . . .

Or else . . . or else I could stay with the troops for a while . . . wait for an unguarded time . . . and then kill Meander for what he'd done to my mother . . . now wouldn't that be just too, too . . .

"Apropos!"

"Oh, shit," I whispered, as I heard the last voice I would have wanted to hear just then.

Chapter 26

I caught myself just before I started to turn in response to my name. Such an action would definitely be the last thing I'd want to do in that circumstance. And I did everything I could to hide my disbelief upon hearing that voice.

He stomped toward me, as big and burly and ugly as he'd been when I'd first met him and he'd been about to cut me in half with his sword. "What are you doing here? What is he doing here?" And he whirled to face Meander. "What has he been saying to you?"

"What did you call him, Sir Coreolis?" Meander asked.

"Apropos! This is the pissant squire I told the forest men to be on the lookout for! I knew if anyone was apt to try and bolt for it, it would be this little coward." Coreolis looked at me with disdain. "Well? Did you think you'd get away with it, you fear-crazed weasel? Did you? Speak up?"

Keeping the quavering out of my voice as best I could,

I said politely, "My apologies, sir . . . have we met?"

"Have we—?" I thought his eyes were going to pop out of his skull. "Damn you! I should have simply killed you in your sleep! But no, I had to decide that you weren't worth the trouble! More fool I! And more fool you, Meander, for listening to him!"

"Have a care, good sir knight," Meander said with clear danger in his voice. "I am still a king, and will not brook such insolence."

Quickly realizing that he'd overstepped himself, Coreolis bowed. "My apologies, Highness. I let my rage carry me . . . rage directed not at you, but at this little cretin!" and he pointed a trembling finger at me.

"You speak of Tacit?"

"Tacit! Tacit lies dead with a brace of arrows in him! I speak of this creature, Apropos of Nothing, who serves Runcible and has the eye of Runcible's daughter."

"Is that a fact?" inquired Meander, turning to me.

"Sire," I said as patiently as I could, as if Coreolis was a lunatic whom I did not want to offend for reasons of personal safety, "if the good knight claims my brother is dead . . . I am . . . I am taken aback, milord. Grief-stricken. I will need time to deal with his loss. As for the rest . . . I am not certain what sort of madness has embraced him . . ."

"Madness!" bellowed Coreolis. "The only madness is that you're all standing here when I've delivered Runcible to you on a silver platter! He's—" He frowned. "What's that damned singing?"

He looked to the point of origin of the singing and his eyes widened. "Is . . . is that . . . ?"

"Aye. Your king, on a silver platter," said Meander. "Except we believe that it is in fact trickery. A clever plan to entrap us. Which would mean, sir knight, that either you are also tricked by a king who suspected your treachery . . . or else you are in on it with him and have endeavored to lead us into an attack. Neither possibility bodes well for you."

"Don't you see!" howled Coreolis, face purpling, looking as if he was on the verge of a breakdown. "The only trickery here is on the part of Apropos . . ."

"Tacit," I quietly corrected him.

"Damn you and your Tacit!" He yanked out his sword, brandishing it fiercely. "I know who you are!"

"That makes two of us." I was feeling that same sense of empowerment that I had so long ago, what seemed a lifetime ago, when my attitude had sent Sir Justus into fits of fury. I, the lowborn son of a whore, was giving a highborn knight convulsions while simultaneously maintaining my sangfroid.

Meander regarded me thoughtfully. "Well. We seem to have a disagreement as to your identity. And who you are will weigh rather heavily into what is to be done. Tell me, young sir . . . have you any here who can vouch for you? Anyone of long standing in my ranks who knows you to be Tacit, rather than this 'Apropos' who seems to have Sir Coreolis so overwrought?"

Dead silence. I could hear nothing save the snow, and the distant howling of the wind. It suddenly seemed much, much colder, with more ice coming in. Overhead the branches were becoming thick and encrusted with frozen coatings. I looked to Grimmoir, to the lieutenant, to any of the men that I'd spoken to in hopes that somehow they would misremember and think that I had been around for quite some time. Nothing. No responses. I felt my blood running as cold as the ice forming overhead.

And then a female voice floated through the stillness.

"Tacit, my love . . . I thought you would never get here."

I couldn't believe it. Could not believe it.

Before she said another word, before she pulled back the gray hood to reveal her features, I knew who it was. The crowd of soldiers parted for her, as if they were afraid to have her come into any sort of contact with them. If she was put off by that, she didn't show it.

I should have known. A weatherweaver controlling the environment. I should have damned well known.

"Hello, Sharee," I said, keeping my voice as casual as I could.

Coreolis had gone completely ashen. Sharee didn't even bother to glance in his direction. Instead she walked up to me and draped an arm around the back of my neck. "You certainly took your time in arriving," she said with a voice like a winter's sigh. She pulled me to her and kissed me. Her lips were like frost; I nearly stuck to her.

Our mouths parted and I thought desperately of something to say. "Sorry" was all I came up with.

"You know this man, weaver?" asked Meander slowly.

"My beloved Tacit? How could I not know my lover? He who warms me with his very essence?"

"The good Sir Coreolis claims that he is in the

employ of Runcible, and is actually named Apropos . . ."

She laughed at that. "What foolishness. The good Sir Coreolis is misinformed."

That caused him to find his voice. "The good Sir Coreolis is going to kill the both of you!" he bellowed.

Meander froze him with a glance. "Sharee has been in my service for some time now, Coreolis, and served me well. Restrain yourself. Now." Without even bothering to make sure that Coreolis did as ordered, Meander turned back to Sharee and said, in as grave a voice as I've ever heard any man employ, "Sharee . . . do you swear on your oath as a weaver that this man is named Tacit? That he is your lover? That he is not now, nor has he ever been, in service to King Runcible? On your oath, Sharee?"

The wind began to howl. I heard a distant creaking of ice from overhead. It felt as if the wintery winds and fierce weather that had been kept at bay by Sharee's magiks were starting to intrude on our zone of safety. I looked to Sharee nervously, and she, in turn, never wavered in her gaze as she and Meander faced one another.

"On my oath as a weaver, I do swear it to be so," she said.

"She lies!" bellowed Coreolis and, gripping his sword with both hands, he charged.

At that exact moment, there was a massive cracking noise and a huge tree, weighed down by the ice that had gathered in its upper reaches, and pounded by winds so fearsome that they threatened to knock us all over, broke off at its base. It toppled over, massive, irresistible. Everyone in its way scattered . . .

. . . save for Coreolis, who was so focused on attacking Sharee and me that he dashed directly into the tree's path. At the last second the crashing of icicles around him alerted him and he looked up, but too late. He had barely enough time for an abortive scream, and then the tree slammed down and crushed him beneath its weight. His armor did him no good, as it was flattened along with the rest of him.

Once again silence reigned over the scene as we stared at the mishap, Coreolis's body completely obscured by the huge trunk.

And then, the picture of calm, Meander said, "Well. That would seem to be it, then." He raised his voice and addressed his men. "Gentlemen . . . it would appear that the clever King Runcible sent the late Sir Coreolis to us in an attempt to trap us. The supposed alliance he offered to form with us months ago, in exchange for our capturing King Runcible, was apparently naught but a meticulously constructed and elaborate invitation to disaster. Well . . . we will not accept his invitation. Allow the king to sit there in his foolish motley. We will attend to other matters. As for you, weaver," and he turned to Sharee.

"Yes, Highness?"

"Your servitude to me is at an end."

She blinked in surprise. "It . . . is?"

"You have attended to me quite well during this time. And in this instance, your intervention helped to unmask the duplicity of Coreolis and prevented me from tumbling into whatever trap Runcible had set. I believe that it is time to call our accounts settled. Unless you have objections to that . . ."

"No. No objections at all."

"Very well. Tacit . . . am I safe in assuming that you will remain with your lover, rather than with the Journeymen?"

"That . . . is a safe assumption, Highness."

"Yes. Well, I cannot say I am surprised. Then again . . . it takes a great deal to surprise me."

He smiled at me.

I looked at the scars. My mother's handiwork on her murderer's face.

My hand started to go for my knife and then Sharee's hand was resting, gently but firmly, on my arm, freezing it in place.

Moments later the army of King Meander was moving off. I stood there and watched them go, the cloak drawn tightly around me to ward off the cold. Sharee stood close to me, and not a word passed between us for quite some time as Meander's troops disappeared from view. The only thing that was left was the crushed body of Coreolis, somewhere beneath the frost-covered tree. When the spring thaw finally hit—which would happen sooner rather than later, thanks to Sharee no longer interfering with the weather patterns—some lucky scavenging animals would find their first meal, neatly preserved.

"That was interesting," she said.

I turned to her. "I was ready to think we were even now, for the time I saved you," I said. "But because of me, he released you from service to him. Let me guess: Gambling debt."

"You know me too well," she said with mild amusement, which quickly faded from her voice. "But no. We are not even, for reasons you cannot begin to comprehend. Don't you see? The only thing that enabled me to convince Meander of the truth of my words was to swear a weaver's oath. But I lied under that oath. Such actions, while benefiting in the short term, have long-term harsh consequences."

"For whom?" I asked nervously.

"For all who benefit in the short term."

I did not like the sound of that, but I felt that dwelling on it would serve me about as well as dwelling on the fact that I'd just let my mother's murderer walk away. Instead I shifted the subject. "You've been in my dreams. Why? What have you been trying to tell me?"

She stared at me as if I was mad. "Me? I've never been in your dreams. I'm no dreamweaver. You're imagining things."

"Are you willing to swear a weaver's oath on that? Or would you be violating two within minutes of each other?"

She didn't reply, unless you can consider an enigmatic smile a reply. "On your way now, little man."

"On my way? You mean . . ."

"I'm not coming with you, no. Not yet. It's not time. This other foolishness has to play out."

"What foolishness? Dammit, Sharee, can't you stop talking in riddles?"

She looked surprised that I even had to ask. "No," she said. She started to turn away and then, in an offhand manner, inquired, "Oh . . . is Tacit dead yet? Tacit One-Eye, I mean. Your childhood playmate. He who first tried to rescue me and owes his salvation to you and your purse."

Obviously she had not heard Sir Coreolis's bellowed pronouncement of his fate. " 'Yet'? How did you know he was dead at all?" I asked, startled.

"That's easy. You're still alive. I never thought this world was big enough for the both of you."

And with that, she stepped back toward the icy trees. I swore I never took my eyes off her, and yet the next moment, between eyeblinks, she had blended in with the snow and was gone.

I stood there staring, although I had no idea for how long I did so. Although on the one hand I wanted to will her back to me, I nevertheless had the distinct feeling that I might have got off lucky. It was with those precise mixed emotions that I trudged away to the fort, having no idea how I was going to feel when I saw Entipy again . . . especially considering that I had already resigned myself to never seeing her, or her father, again (never seeing Odclay the jester wasn't preying on my mind at all).

As I approached the castle, I smiled and shook my head at the ludicrous sight of the King of Isteria, on my say-so, continuing his nonsensical singing. But I could tell that he was already beginning to suspect that Meander had departed, and when he caught sight of me, I waved to him and nodded. He didn't recognize me at first, clad as I was in the garments of a Journeyman. But when he did he got to his feet and returned the wave, looking somewhat relieved that he didn't have to keep singing. Then he disappeared from view as he climbed down, only to emerge some minutes later—with Entipy and Odclay on either side of him—from the front gate.

Entipy was, I have to say, quite a sight. She ran toward me, her arms pinwheeling, intermingling shouting of my name with nearly incoherent squeals of joy. I suddenly felt very tired, even exhausted, still having trouble believing that such a half-assed plan as I had developed had actually worked. Never in a million years would I have given myself the slightest hope of succeeding.

The princess got within four feet of me and then jumped, literally leaping into my arms. I staggered from the impact, and would have fallen over had not the king arrived quickly enough to brace me. I should say, though, that if there was one man even more ludicrous-looking than the king, it was the jester, attired in the king's own raiment. Yet even the jester rose to the occasion as he pumped my hand firmly and said, "Well done. Very well done," with absolutely no trace of insanity to his voice. If the man was capable of staying lucid for longer periods of time, we might actually be able to be friends.

"I never doubted you! Never!" said Entipy.

She had no idea, of course. No idea that, save for the timing of my encountering the scout in the woods, I would be far away from this place, while she and her father would be captives of Meander. Nor did she ever need to know.

"Nor did I, Princess," I replied as suavely as I could, "for I knew that I had you to come back to."

She held me tightly, and I winced because I was still

aching from the wounds Tacit had inflicted. But I tried to keep a stoic face.

"Tell us what happened, Apropos," said the king as we walked slowly back to the fort. "Tell us everything."

Well, obviously I didn't tell them everything. Somehow I didn't think I would be doing myself any favors by telling them that I'd been looking to flee when fate had taken a hand. So obviously I gave myself a slightly more . . . willing . . . role in the proceedings.

The king looked both surprised and saddened to learn of Coreolis's involvement and duplicity. When Coreolis's name first came up, he stopped walking so that he could give the tale his full attention. Naturally we all had to stop as well as I told him everything, up to and including Coreolis's curious demise at the hands—well, limbs—of a tree.

"I have known for quite some time that he was discontent," murmured Runcible. "But that he would do this . . . it is tragic. Truly tragic. How someone can aspire to greatness and do so with no sense of honor at all . . . I do not understand it. Do you, squire?"

Desperate to move on, I simply gave a quick shake of the head and then managed to say, "So . . . what do we do now, Highness?" I was most anxious to do anything to draw attention away from myself.

The king frowned, considering the question. Surprisingly, it was the jester who spoke up, sounding as if he was sliding back into his comfortable lunacy. "No matter where they go . . . here we are," he said cheerfully.

I didn't pretend to understand, but the king promptly said, "That is a good observation, Odclay."

"It is?" Entipy said, surprised.

"Yes," said the king, cheerfully. "What he's saying is—"

And a voice, cold as ice, interrupted, "What he is saying is that you should remain here for a time to see if your escorts and knights return."

We stopped and looked ahead of us.

King Meander was leaning against the great front door of the fort, with a wry smile upon his face and a long sword in his hand.

Chapter 27

Naturally we froze.

"Hello. I'm King Meander—also known as the Keepless King and the Vagabond King. Although since it is just us few, I tend to think simply 'Meander' will do. I am not often one for standing on ceremony." Meander looked at each of us in turn, and then pointed the long sword at each of us, one by one. I was amazed by the fact that, even though it was a two-hander, he held it with one hand as if it weighed nothing. "The true jester . . . ?"

"Odclay, yes, sir," said the jester, trembling as the point was aimed at him. He probably thought that Meander was going to run him through simply on general principles. I thought as much myself.

But Meander just nodded slightly and turned the point to Entipy. "And . . . the princess?"

Entipy said nothing. She just looked at him defiantly, chin slightly upturned. But to her obvious surprise, her father said quietly, "You are being addressed by a king, my dear. Even an enemy king. As a princess, you are obliged to respond in a suitable manner."

She spit at Meander. The glob landed squarely on the front of his armor.

That's it, we're dead, I thought.

But to my shock, Meander simply laughed. "There are many," he said with obvious amusement, "who would concur that that response was appropriate. But they would not have the nerve to see such a sentiment through. Well done, Princess." He paused and then added as an afterthought, "Do it again and I will leave your neck longing for your pretty head."

She puckered her lips, preparing to let fly again. Immediately I clapped my hand over her mouth. The result was a large wad of saliva in my hand. I was rarely more thankful that I was wearing gloves.

"And 'Apropos,' I take it?" Again the Keepless King chuckled. "Alas, poor Coreolis. To die confused about matters is a sad enough state . . . but to meet your demise knowing beyond question that you are right and everyone else is wrong . . . ah well. Your fortunes were clearly in ascendance over his. Although you managed to enlist a weaver who willingly swore a false oath on your behalf. Aside from still being alive, that may be the single greatest accomplishment of your life, squire. How did you do it? What hold do you have on her?"

"I've no idea," I said honestly.

"Her?" said Entipy.

"Well . . . whatever it might be, learn from it and learn how to exploit it, for it is a most formidable thing.

And when you next see her, in this life or the next . . . do give her my best wishes."

"Her?" Entipy said again.

"Quiet," I said between gritted teeth.

And then Meander turned to Runcible. His sword was still unwavering. The amount of strength in his arms must have been considerable. "And you. Runcible the Crafty."

"Meander the Mad," replied Runcible. He wasn't looking at the sword at all; instead he was staring straight into Meander's eyes. I wondered what he saw there.

"An honor."

"The same."

"Did you craft this little strategy?"

"My response depends upon yours," Runcible said thoughtfully. "If you wish to kill the one who conceived it . . . yes. It was I."

Meander considered this for a moment, and then turned back to me. "A very clever plan, Apropos."

He said it with such flat conviction that I couldn't even bring myself to try and deny it . . . which, for me, was a hell of an admission to make. "Thank you, Highness," I said. "Personally, I thought it was rather an insane proposition at best. So you flatter me."

"It takes no imagination to conceive a plan that everyone is expecting. You think outside of the box, Apropos. That may take you far . . ."

"'May' meaning . . . if you don't kill me here and now."

He sighed heavily. "Such talk of killing. Is that all the world exists for? Killing?"

"I should like to think not," Runcible replied. "I would like to think that other, softer emotions and interests provide beauty and charm to us all."

I couldn't quite believe the conversation that was occurring. I scanned the area, looking for some indication of the rest of Meander's forces. Were they hiding? Had they doubled back and taken up positions in the fort? But no . . . such actions would have left tracks all over the snow, and the only ones I saw at this point were Meander's. So they had to be waiting in the forest nearby, arrows undoubtedly trained on us. Why, then, was Meander prolonging this business? He had us . . . appropriately enough . . . cold. What was his game?

"Softer emotions?" He seemed to consider that, then looked back to me. "Is that what motivated the weaver, Apropos? Softer emotions? Feelings for you?"

Entipy was looking extremely annoyed at repeated mentions of a female weaver who apparently felt something for me. Desiring to move on, I suggested, "I saved her life on one occasion. Perhaps she felt indebted to me."

Meander scoffed at that. "Weavers feel no debt to any except themselves," replied Meander. "Although, like all humans, they excel in self-deception. Much as you do, young squire. I was young once . . ."

"Highness, with all respect . . ."

But he wasn't listening to me. Instead he looked as if he was gazing into a time and place very, very far away. "Would you like to hear a tale? That I . . . heard in my youth?"

Entipy turned to me. "Give me a sword. I'm going to throw myself on it just to end this."

"Quiet, Entipy," Runcible said firmly.

"Once upon a time . . ." began Meander.

"Oh my gods," Entipy moaned. But Runcible fired her a severe look and she silenced herself.

" . . . there was a king," Meander continued. "He was not the wisest of kings, nor even the bravest of kings. But he was the coldest of kings, for he was of his land, and his land was a cold and barren place. It was a place that the sun had forgotten about.

"In this place was a great, cold castle and he lived there with his great, cold heart. And rarely did he smile, or frown, or give any indication that he had any interest in the frozen world around him. Entire days would pass and he would simply sit in his throne, like an ice statue, and stare at nothing. His courtiers would walk gingerly around him, wondering if he was even alive. Only the occasional blinking would inform them of such, because he was so cold within and without that even his breath would not mist up. That is how cold he was. He came to be known in some circles as Old King Cold, even though he was not all that old. And as Old King Cold would stare into nothingness, he would be looking for something. And the oddest thing was, he had no idea what he was looking for.

"And then, one very cold day—as they all were—he found it.

"Her name was Tia. She was a jewel of the North, but where the cold king was frozen ice, she was a frozen diamond. She had many facets, and when Old King Cold would look at her, he would see small flames jumping about within her. It was the first time that Old King

Cold was able to approach flames while feeling some measure of safety in doing so.

"And the people of the frozen land loved their Tia, who became the brightest star in their cold northern sky. And they loved the effect she had on Old King Cold, whose great ice face cracked with a newly etched permanent smile. And even though it remained cold in the frozen lands, still there was newly discovered warmth. For the king had finally found what he had had no idea he was looking for. He gave her his love. He gave her his kingdom to share. And he gave her a beautiful dagger that had been in his family for generations, made of a metal so fine it could almost be seen through, and yet cut purely and cleanly. It was called 'Icicle,' and she accepted it proudly and kept it with her always.

"And Old King Cold stepped out onto the balcony of his ice palace, and he said, 'I have everything! I am all-powerful! I am the ultimate ruler of the Frozen North, for I no longer have any weaknesses!'

"Well . . . one should never say such things within hearing of the gods of the North, for they are sorely jealous creatures and dislike others claiming superiority. So they decided to put Old King Cold in his place. To remind him of who, precisely, truly ruled the Frozen North.

"And Old King Cold and his beloved Tia embarked on a journey. The skies were clear, the weather calm. So Old King Cold, in his confidence, believed that there would be no danger from the elements. It was exactly this attitude that the gods chose to punish.

"They sent a fearsome storm, the likes of which no

one had ever seen. It snowed and it snowed and it snowed, a mighty blizzard, and the gods laughed, with laughter that sounded like the howling of the wind. And Tia and Old King Cold were separated from the rest of their group, driven in different directions, until even the king—who had lived his entire life in the frozen climes and knew every glacier and every bit of frozen tundra as if it was his own body—even he had no idea which way was east or west, or even up or down.

"They were driven away, away, and eventually they found shelter inside a cave. But the gods were angry that the king had escaped, and so they maintained the fearsome storm until the small entrance to the cave was literally buried behind snow and ice. Air filtered through a small frozen hole, but so little light as to be insignificant. Darkness settled in, a darkness like unto a grave.

"They had no idea how long they lay within there. They had no food to sustain them. They were able to obtain water, of a sort, by consuming the snow and sucking on the ice, but as day passed into night and into the next day, and as the wind and storm continued to howl mercilessly, they grew weaker and weaker.

"They spoke to each other at length during their entombment. They spoke of times past, and times to come. They spoke of their love for each other. They spoke of the children that Tia would bear him. Sons, big strapping boys, heirs to the Frozen North. And all during that time, they continued to grow weaker still. Old King Cold thought of trying to push through the snow and ice that entombed them, but to what end? The terrible storm was still out there, and they would not survive long at all.

"Finally, after more days and nights had passed than he could count, the king said, 'We have no choice. We must brave the storm.'

"'I am too weak to move,' she said, and what she said was indeed true. Her face was wan, her body shrunken beneath the furs. 'I would not last. Nor would you. You must at least wait for this storm to abate.'

" 'I cannot wait,' spake he. 'We are famished. If we do not find nourishment, we are finished.'

" 'Not quite, my love. If I do not find nourishment, I am finished. But that is a small thing, husband.' The only part of her that still had that cold fire in her was her eyes, which seemed to dance with light even more so in the confines of the cave. 'If you do not find nourishment, however, that will be most tragic. You have a great destiny, husband. Your people need you. My loss is a minor matter . . .'

" 'Not to me. To me, it would be everything. I could not go on without you,' he said.

"And the famished queen actually seemed to grow stronger when she heard this. She drew herself up to a half-sitting position and said, 'Stuff and nonsense. Do not insult me with that which I know is just pretty words. You would go on without me. You would be a great leader, a great king, of a great place. A place others call Wasteland. But what do they know of it? Of us? What do they know of . . .' Her voice seemed to catch a moment. 'Of the glory of a sunrise reflected from ice canyons? Of the perfect formation of a snowflake? Of the blissful stillness of a frozen tundra? They do not know of these things. They do not know of us. But you, my king, will tell them. You will let everyone understand us.'

" 'We will do this thing. Get up,' said he with a voice so firm that it was clear that he would not brook stubbornness. But it was also clear, at least to her, that he had no means of enforcing his will. He himself could not rise and, within moments, he would likely fall over.

"The queen refused to allow that to happen. As gently as an early evening snowfall, she said to him, 'You are fading, my love. You do not realize it quite yet . . . but you are starving to death. Fading from life. I will last longer than you, I believe, but not by much. I cannot allow that to happen. Too many people need you.' She gave a smile . . . her last . . . and said, 'Have I ever told you how much I love you?'

" 'In a hundred ways.'

" 'Then here is the hundred and first. Women's bodies are designed to give life to infants. But I shall use mine to give life . . . to you . . .'

"And the weakened Old King Cold cried out as his beloved wife pulled out the blade called Icicle and slit her own throat with it. The movement was quick and efficient, and Old King Cold shouted at Tia, and called her all manner of foul names (for which he later repented) followed by a string of loving ones (which he never recanted). A warm vapor rose from where she had exposed the inside of her throat to the open air. And as he watched that fire die from her eyes, he said to her, 'I know what you want me to do to survive. But

I will not do this thing. I will never do this thing.'

"She mouthed her reply: 'If you love me . . . live.'

"He did love her, more than anything else.

"For so long, she had given him emotional nourishment. Now she provided him physical nourishment in response.

"He stared at her body lying there, unmoving. He stayed that way for another full day to the point where he was ravenous beyond any hunger he had ever known. He felt so weak he could barely lift his arms. The knife remained there, next to her body. A knife that could be used for stabbing, or killing . . .

". . . or cutting . . .

". . . not unlike a slab of beef.

" 'No!' spake the king. 'I would rather die!'

"But in the end . . . in the end . . . he did not die.

"And as he cut into her, he told himself it was because it was her final words and final desires. As he peeled the flesh from her, he told himself it was because she wanted him to live, and that it was of such importance to her that she had made this sacrifice. As he consumed her flesh, still warm even though her inner fire was extinguished, he told himself he was doing it in order to honor her. But he knew in his heart, in the place wherein all truth dwells, that he did it because he was afraid to cross over into the abyss and join her. He wanted to live, and in the final extremity, would do anything—did do anything—rather than stop living.

"At the last, he consumed her heart. One would have thought such an emotional organ to be soft and delicate, but it was tough and hard-muscled. And from that grisy dessert, all of his previously lost strength, and more esides, was in his limbs. The storm was abating, but till fierce, but Old King Cold did not care at that point. He hammered his way through the obstruction, faced he storm. As he stood there in the cold and the ferocity f the hostile clime, he heard the gods in the wind say-ng, 'Such arrogance as yours, King, left you with no oubts as to your superiority. That is not right. That is ot the way of mortals. All mortals must possess doubts, nd be aware of their frailties and limitations. You ndeavored to leave them behind. We could not permit hat. And so you will carry the knowledge of your basic ears in your belly—along with the heart of your true ove—forever.'

"The king found his way back to his great ice castle, nd his people concluded that his beloved Tia had sim-ly perished. There was great sadness in the land. As for he king . . .

"At night, he could feel her stirring within him. taying with him. Haunting him.

"He wanted to run away. It is impossible, of course, o run away from yourself. But Old King Cold decided o attempt to do that very thing. For the king, you see, ad crossed a great line in order to survive and, in doing o, lost the belief in any lines, in any restraints. orderlines of any sort became meaningless to him. And o he declared to all his people that he would be a king ithout borderlines. A king who would go anywhere, do hatever he wished, wherever he wished, as the mood ruck him. Those who wished to accompany him could o so. Most of them chose to come with him.

"He left behind the place that had been his palace, destroying it in his wake, for he had no need of it.

"He left behind the great Frozen North, and the gods of that forbidding place, for he had no need of it.

"He left behind his sanity, for he had no need of it.

"The only thing he did not leave behind—could not leave behind—was the voice of his beautiful Tia, residing forever within him. He could feel her warmth, feel her soul, trapped forever within him, trying to console him, but serving instead to give him only guilt no matter how far he wandered. That . . . and this . . ."

King Meander reached into the folds of his cape and pulled out a dagger made of a metal so sheer that, at certain angles, we could barely see it. "The dagger . . . Icicle . . . that he knew he would use one day, under the right circumstance, when he finally had sufficient bravery . . . bravery on par with his beloved Tia . . . to end his miserable existence and join her in the afterlife. Beautiful Tia. And poor Old King Cold . . . the most unmerry of souls."

There was a long silence then. Runcible, Entipy, Odclay, and I looked at each other, our faces pallid, our souls shriveled within us. Finally it was Entipy who spoke.

"Are you . . . are you going to kill yourself now?"

"Me?" Meander seemed confused for a moment, and then he chuckled. "Ah. I see. You thought I was speaking of myself. You thought the narrative genuine. I will take that as a compliment, girl, to my storytelling. No, it was . . . it was . . . it was quite fabricated. After all, if such a thing had truly occurred, the poor bastard to whom it happened would be the most wretched creatur who ever strode the earth, would he not? Certainly not fit to live . . ." He stared at the dagger point. "Not fit to live at all."

Again he was silent for a time and then replaced the dagger in his cloak. In a distracted voice, he said, "Your escorts and retainers should be back before too long, I think. Coreolis was quite clever in his maneuvers. In the night he came to his own troops and told them you had ordered night maneuvers, and he sent them in one direction . . . and then went to the permanently stationed garrison, told them the same thing, and sent them in the other. But they will figure out the trick sooner rather than later, and be along. Once they've returned, they will escort you home."

"Home?" Runcible couldn't contain his surprise.

"Yes. Home. You still believe in such quaint things, do you not?"

"But . . . I thought you . . ." Entipy couldn't even get the words out. "It doesn't make sense."

Meander shrugged. "That, child, is one of the glorious advantages to being a madman. I don't have to make sense. It's very liberating. You should try it sometime. You might find you have a taste for it. You would be amazed what people discover, in this lifetime, they have a taste for." His attention swiveled to me, and his voice was singsong and chilling as the north wind. "Young love. What the weaver has for you, what the princess has for you . . and what you have for you . . . and perhaps for them. I'm not certain of that quite yet, young Apropos. I will probably never know the outcome . . . but I'd rather there be an outcome. And besides . . . no one knows, better than

I, what it takes to survive in this world. You have that same sort of knowledge. I can see it in your eyes . . . just as I see it in mine. In any event . . . I wish you better luck in this world than Old King Cold had. And in the final analysis . . . I'm not entirely coldhearted."

He rose and started to walk away from us. And despite my better judgment, I suddenly said, "The scratches on your face. How did you come by them?"

He stopped, turned, and looked at me coolly. "I do not recall."

"You don't recall."

He shook his head. "Each day . . . I do not recall much of what happened the previous. Each day is a blankness for me . . . a sheet of snow, a blizzard, coming down and cutting me off, leaving me to wander. I have not remembered much, you see, since I . . . heard . . . the story of Old King Cold. Instead, every night, I work to expunge my brain of all memories, so that I can leave that particular story behind. In telling it to you, I hope that that might have cleansed it from my thoughts and recollections. But somehow . . . I suspect it won't. There are some things, you see, that you carry with you . . . no matter how far you wander."

And with that, the man who might or might not have murdered my mother sheathed his long sword and walked away into the forest. And somehow, although it might have been in my imaginings, I could swear I heard the voices of gods laughing in the distant howl of the winds.

Chapter 28

It all happened precisely as Meander had foretold. The confused soldiers who had been sent hither and yon by the scheming Coreolis returned, in fairly short order, to the fort. Upon learning of Coreolis's treachery and their unwitting participation in it, ohhh, there was breast-beating, and ohhh, there was second-guessing, and ohhh, there was groveling. And I have to admit: I was loving every moment of it.

The most glorious aspect was the look on Mace Morningstar's face. Too long had I had to bask in the reflected lack-of-glory of Sir Umbrage. Now it was Morningstar's turn. And for him, it was much worse. After all, I was simply the landless bastard son of no one remotely noble, attached to a knight who had been perceived as once great, now incompetent (at least until the joust). But here was Morningstar, titled, proud, even arrogant, suddenly discovering his lord and master knight was a traitor to the crown. It immediately made Morningstar suspect. After all, if one is being trained by a knight who sought to usurp the king, doesn't that likewise make the squire a possible co-conspirator?

That, at least, was the question that King Runcible raised as the returning knights presented themselves for inspection and groveling at Fort Terracote. In the case of most of them, Runcible accepted their apologies and oaths of fealty with aplomb. But when it came Morningstar's turn, the jester suddenly started to jump around and chant, "The squire of a traitor, does he betray sooner? Or later?" Morningstar looked like he'd been poleaxed when Odclay said that. I'd never really been fond of the jester's japes until that moment, but suddenly I was starting to like him a lot.

Runcible frowned, as he often did. "There is something to be said for that," he said slowly.

"Highness, no!" Mace debased himself, looking very little like the swaggering, posturing peacock he normally was. "No, I swear! I knew nothing of Sir Coreolis's hidden intentions! If I had known, I would have informed Your Highness immediately! Please, sire! Do not tar me with that same brush!"

And then Runcible—gods bless him—after giving the matter some thought, said the best five words I could possibly have heard:

"Apropos . . . what do *you* think?"

I've never seen someone's clothes turn pale. But that seemed to be what happened with Mace. Certainly there was no more blood left to vanish from his skin.

It was as if Mace was running the sentence through his head several times before he could actually dare to accept that it had been spoken. He was aware that I was standing off to the side; after all, the king had looked right at me when he'd asked my opinion. But he obviously couldn't bring himself to look at me. Perhaps the sight of a triumphant grin on my face would have been too much for his titled heart to take.

I carefully weighed my responses. Truthfully, I was fairly certain that Morningstar in fact knew nothing about Coreolis's duplicity. Traitors' stock-in-trade is untrustworthiness, so their inclination is to trust as few people as possible. Coreolis's plan would have been strictly on a need-to-know basis, and Morningstar simply wouldn't have been in on it. If nothing else, Coreolis would have been concerned that Mace would have gone straight to the king in hopes of getting something out of halting a treasonous plan. And he might very well have.

But truth did not necessarily have to have anything to do with my response. For I had not forgotten Morningstar's taunting of me, his high-handedness. There was the entire debacle with the joust, and his leading the others into the intended pounding of me that only Umbrage's last-minute intercession managed to stop. Indeed, one could make an argument that Morningstar was responsible for Umbrage's death. If Mace hadn't taunted me and pushed me into that misbegotten bet, I never would have arranged for Umbrage to win the joust and none of this would have happened.

Shut up. It was your fault and you know it.

I was surprised. My inner voice usually came up with ways for me to avoid responsibility, not force me to own up to it. Perhaps even that nonexistent conscience of mine was impressed by the fact that Runcible had turned to me and inquired what I thought should be Morningstar's fate.

I dwelt on it a moment more. The bottom line was, Mace had made me suffer. There should be equity for that, a quid pro quo. If I said that I thought Mace was a part of Coreolis's schemes, Runcible would likely exile him, or perhaps even execute him. If it was the former, I wouldn't have the opportunity to see Mace suffer. If the latter, then his suffering would end too quickly. Where was the fun in that? Where was the satisfaction for me?

If, on the other hand, he became indebted to me in some fashion, why . . . that would be the greatest suffering that could possibly be inflicted upon him. Better still, that annoying sense of nobility to which he aspired would hold him in its iron grip, affecting all his subsequent dealings with me.

And so, reasoning that the truth would be of benefit to me, I said, "I firmly believe, Highness, that Morningstar . . ." I paused, watching with delicious pleasure as Morningstar involuntarily trembled in anticipation of the worst. ". . . had no idea whatsoever of what Sir Coreolis was up to."

Mace's head snapped around so fast that I'm surprised it didn't fall off. He gaped at me, and I continued, sounding infinitely reasonable, "I am familiar with Morningstar's character, sire. I simply do not believe that he would have cooperated with such an endeavor. It would not be honorable."

"I would have thought the same of Coreolis," replied the king. It seemed as if he was challenging me. Mace's apprehension was growing.

Utterly calmly, I said, "But I never trusted Coreolis, sire. You are asking me my opinion. I never would have spoken against Coreolis, of course, because it was not my place to do so. But since you ask what I think of Morningstar now, I say again: I think him trustworthy." I then bowed slightly. "Of course, it is Your Highness's opinion that holds sway, not mine."

Slowly he nodded and then turned his thoughtful attention back to Morningstar. "Squire . . . since the noble Apropos, to whom I owe so much, has vouched for you . . . consider your position safe."

"Although," I suddenly said, as if thinking out loud, "it is a pity that Morningstar was not able to perceive that duplicity. After all, of all of us, he spent the most time in Coreolis's company."

"A good point," said the king. "Morningstar . . . once you are reassigned, you will continue your term as squire for an additional year beyond the others. Obviously your senses require a bit more honing."

Morningstar choked slightly, but he knew there was nothing he could possibly do. He knew, in fact, that he had got off extremely lightly, considering that the king could have—purely based upon suspicions—sent his head rolling across the ground with a word.

He made a point of avoiding me much of that evening, but as we prepared to set out for Isteria the following morning, Mace finally screwed his courage—not to mention pride, and humility—to the wall and approached me.

"Apropos, I . . . don't know what to say," he said.

"That's never stopped you before."

For a moment his face darkened, but then he fought

the annoyance back as he remembered who he was talking to and why he was doing the talking. "All right . . . I . . . suppose I deserved that," he said, his voice falling into that musical up-and-down manner he had. "You've . . . you've done me a service, there's no denying that. I'm . . . wondering why . . ."

"As I wondered, when you 'warned' me of the princess. Do you know what I've discovered in all of this, Morningstar? That sometimes a little wonderment can be a good thing."

He looked at me uncertainly, then glanced around as if to make sure that we were unobserved. Then he leaned in closely and said in a low voice, "What do you want?"

"Want?"

"You heard me."

"Yes, but I don't understand you."

He sighed. "After all that has passed between us, Apropos, don't think for a moment that I don't know you want something."

I considered a moment, and then said, "Knowledge."

"Knowledge?" He couldn't have been more puzzled. "What do you want knowledge of?"

"Not knowledge for me. Knowledge for you. The knowledge that I held your balls in my hand . . . and didn't squeeze the last bit of juice out of them. Keep that knowledge with you, Mace. Let it warm you to sleep at night and awaken you in the morning." I smiled and turned away, not even bothering to see the expression on his face. Whatever it was in reality most likely paled compared to what I was imagining.

We set out for Isteria, and quite the little procession

it was. For the king made certain that I rode as near to him as possible, Entipy at my side (or I at hers, depending how you look at it). Every so often I would glance back at the knights and retainers who rode behind us, and it seemed to me that they were always looking at me with reverence, or respect, or just plain terror. I couldn't entirely say that I blamed them. My lowly background was no secret. The thought that one such as I could rise to a position where I was being accorded respect by no less a personage than the king himself was enough to throw their entire worldview into a positive tizzy. Who knew what might happen as a result of my elevated stature? Could it be that . . . that the poor would come to be regarded as something other than a means of providing luxuries for the rich? Could it be that the downtrodden would actually be seen as worthy of help, rather than something simply provided for the amusement and service of those at much higher stations? I could snap the link of the entire chain of society.

And they had to be nice to me. Not only because of the way the king seemed to regard me, but also because of the princess. Her fondness for me was rapidly becoming evident to all. She certainly made no effort to hide it. She would ride near me and constantly be bending my ear. Although I had to admit that her conversation was most entertaining, since much of it consisted of making a series of cutting remarks about not only everyone who was riding with us, but the entirety of the king's court, whom she remembered very unfondly from the time that she was in residence there. There seemed to be no one who was spared the fierceness of her tongue, and her insults were gloriously scathing.

"Ah, good Sir Austin. A man who is to intelligence what flatulence is to dinner conversation." "If my well-being depended on the good right arm of Sir DeBeres, I'd be better off riding naked through the streets of Isteria shouting, 'Free tea biscuits for the first ten customers.'" And so on.

The fact that she was as highborn as those she held in contempt didn't seem to enter into it. She certainly didn't seem to feel that she was one of them, and heaven knows she certainly didn't act like it. In a way, it almost felt as if we were developing a quietly subversive relationship.

Nevertheless, my inbred distrust still ran deep. As entertaining as she was, I still could not erase from my mind our earlier time together when she had seemed on the border between insane and completely insane. The notion that she had transferred her fixation on Tacit over to me didn't necessarily put me at ease. After all, she could in turn shift it to someone else, and where, then, would that leave me? Furthermore, she was, at the end of the day, still a princess, while I was . . . what I was. Every time I had lost sight of my background and my goals, it had gone badly for me. There was no reason to assume that if I let down my guard with Entipy, it would go any differently. Indeed, there were damned good reasons to think that it would play out just the same.

Whenever we stopped to rest, Morningstar or one of his associates would come by and endeavor to engage me in chat. Their reasons couldn't have been more obvious: They were trying to get on my good side, concerned that I might wind up someone of power who could do them harm. I was consistently cordial to all of them, which was more than I needed to be, but that was all. They came away from time with me knowing no more about my mind than they knew when they first approached, which is how I preferred it to be.

We made camp when night fell and I went to sleep convinced that I'd be awoken by the screeching of the Harpers or some new disaster descending upon us. Instead the only thing that happened was a very vivid dream reliving the unicorn stampede. Except this time Entipy and I were being pursued through the halls of the great castle. The walls were shuddering from the pounding hooves, bricks tumbling all around us, and the screeching of the unicorns was so deafening that I thought my head would explode. There was a window just ahead of us, and standing next to it was Sharee, her arms folded, her expression self-satisfied. When she spoke, no words emerged from her mouth, but I could hear them in my head. *The unicorns have spoken. A pity you don't speak unicorn,* she said, and laughed, and then we were out the window and the courtyard was hurtling up toward us.

I awoke, bathed in sweat. It was not yet sunrise, but I did not go back to sleep. Instead I just sat there, clutching my knees tightly to my chest until dawn.

Runners had been sent on ahead to inform the castle of our arrival, and they had obviously done their jobs. The place was alive with celebration. I regarded the entire thing in a rather sour way, feeling that the celebrants had somewhat lost sight of reality. This entire business had, after all, begun as the routine dispatching of a group of knights to bring home a princess so obnoxious that her parents hadn't seen her in years. All the knights and retainers save for one had ended up dead, and the return of the princess had turned into a winter-long endeavor in which she had repeatedly almost been killed . . . mostly because of dangers that arose as a result of her own big mouth. I didn't exactly consider it knighthood's finest hour.

But you certainly couldn't have discerned that from the greeting we were receiving. The streets were lined with people, rose petals being strewn in our path. People were chanting and dancing and singing the praises of the king, and the princess, and most of all—believe it or not—me.

Me.

Apropos of Nothing.

It was the mummers, dressed in oversized puppets, emerging from within the castle walls to meet us and marching alongside us, who truly made me understand just what it was that everyone was getting so worked up about. The mummers were outfitted to look like—so help me—phoenixes. And on the backs of these majestic fake birds rode small dolls that were supposed to represent me. I realized that what I was seeing was a street-level theatrical representation of the tapestry that hung in the great court.

They were associating me with that woven hero. The one who was supposed to be a being of legend, who would come to Isteria, end up ruling over all, and unite Isteria and all the surrounding lands—as Queen Beatrice had said—in a golden age of reason and enlightenment.

These people believed themselves alive at the time of a great, fulfilled prophecy.

They thought I was the great hero, promised them through the vision of a farweaver. Why not? The tales of my riding the phoenix had preceded us. Plus my other escapades, which I had seen as nothing more than desperate attempts to stay alive, were being transformed into great acts of bravery, determination, and whatever other positive view people chose to give them.

Only I knew the truth. Only I knew that the real hero, the "anointed one," the one glimpsed by some unknown farweaver years agone, was actually lying entombed back at the edge of the Outer Lawless regions, with so many holes in him that—were he still breathing—he could whistle in five different keys simultaneously.

It seemed to me that, no matter what endeavor I was involved in, I was to be something of a sham.

But as women looked up at me, their eyes wide, their bosoms heaving . . .

And as knights who had had little patience for me shouted my praises, whether out of appreciation for who I was or stinking fear of what I might become . . .

As all of that was happening, I started to think . . .

You know . . . damn . . . I did accomplish a hell of a lot, did I not? I mean, who would have given two sovs for our chances, considering what we'd been through? A squire, lame of leg, surviving an attack of the Harpers . . . overcoming a phoenix and flying it (badly, but still . . .) . . . standing up for the princess's honor in a tavern . . . obtaining the money to summon help through the auspices of the dreaded Warlord Shank, all without his knowing . . . outrunning unicorns in full gallop . . . battling a known outlaw and surviving long enough for reinforcements to show up . . . preserving the freedom of the king, no less, through quick thinking and a plan that seemed ludicrous at one time but now was being touted as positively inspired, a work of brilliance . . .

It was . . . well . . . maybe not epic. But damned close.

Stop it. You're letting yourself believe that which they say about you. That way lies the greatest danger of all.

It was good advice that I was giving to myself. Nevertheless, it all still felt very tempting. Very . . . very tempting . . .

I had not seen much of Entipy since we'd arrived back in Isteria, which I'd considered a good thing. Heaven knew there were enough others. I was the hero of the moment, the fascination that took people out of their mundane lives and thrust them into something extraordinary. I was given new chambers and, of course, knew them instantly: They had belonged to Sir Umbrage. Yet all of his belongings had already been removed, as if he'd never existed. The problem was that I didn't have all that many belongings. At least . . . I didn't before I'd moved into the room.

It was one of the most disconcerting moments of my life. When I'd been brought to my new rooms, I went straight for the only thing of interest to me at that moment: the bed. I flopped down upon it. It was the most majestic, the most glorious piece of furniture I had ever experienced. After years of beds composed of straw, or wafer-thin mats, here was bedding that I almost sank into. I had never known that slumber could be had on anything approaching such terms of comfort. I did not even bother to undress; I simply closed my eyes and let years' worth of collective exhaustion overwhelm me. For once, my slumber was dreamless.

When I awoke, hours and hours later, I suffered from that usual disorientation one feels when waking up somewhere new. It was not helped by the fact that the room was suddenly crammed with belongings that belonged to someone else. Wardrobes were there, doors open, and richly designed finery hung within. Long, tapering candles were flickering on tables nearby. A large plate of fruit was sitting on a table, neither of which had been there before.

"What the hell . . . ?" I muttered.

I don't know how long I lay there, and then the door to the chamber creaked open. I saw the face of Queen Bea poke around it.

"I didn't do it!" I immediately said. I struggled to get out of the bed, but had sunk so far into it that my feet were practically above my head. "I didn't take any of these things! I don't know whose they are—!"

The queen laughed lightly at that as she opened the door fully and stepped into the room. "My, my . . . for one who has survived as many dangers and disasters as you . . . you tend to panic rather easily, squire."

"I'm sorry . . . I . . ." I was still utterly befuddled.

"No one is going to make accusations against you, Apropos, for these things are indeed yours. Think of them as tokens of gratitude from a grateful mother and father . . . who just so happen to be royalty."

I looked around as if seeing the finery for the first time. I had never had but two or three items of wearable clothing at any given period of my life. All of this . . . I didn't even know where to begin to figure how I would wear it all. "You could clothe a family of ten with all this," I said.

Once more she laughed. "I suppose you could at that. And if you're so inclined to do that, it's your prerogative. They're your possessions, after all. Now . . . I've been checking on you about every hour or so, and you were beginning to worry me. I was afraid you were going to sleep right through the banquet."

"Banquet?" I echoed.

"Yes. To celebrate your safe return of the princess. Surely you must have expected that you would be feted."

"With all respect, Highness, I've been spending too much of the past months being concerned about my life being forfeited to think about being feted."

"That's understandable," she said. She was kind enough to walk over to the bed and extend a hand. Never too proud to accept assistance, I grasped it and allowed her to help haul me to my feet. "Now . . . a warm bath will be drawn for you . . ."

"A what?" I couldn't even conceive of such a thing. The most I'd ever had was cold water to splash on myself from a basin.

"A warm bath," she said patiently. "A hairstylist to clean you up, I think; the beard is very becoming, but you'll likely want to get that trimmed." She looked at me critically, assessing. "I might as well just get everyone possible up here to get you presentable. The banquet is, after all, in your honor. Oh . . . and this is from me . . ."

She stepped toward me and kissed me on either cheek, and then squeezed my hands fervently. "Thank you," she said, and it looked like she was doing everything she could not to cry. "Thank you . . . for bringing her back to me. Thank you for not letting me spend the rest of my life dwelling on the mistakes I've made, or thinking about how I should have made more of an effort to be a good mother."

"You're welcome," I said.

She did not let go of my hands as she said to me, "And as for what happened between you and Entipy, well . . . given the circumstances . . . it's understandable. I want you to know that neither the king or I is upset . . . well . . . he was a little, but I calmed him."

"Ah," I said, not sure precisely what she was talking about.

"After all, no one knows better than I that Entipy can be quite a handful."

"Well, she *is* a princess," I said diplomatically.

"Yes, but even taking that into account, she can be . . . well . . . somewhat unpredictable. And she's quite excellent at hiding what she truly is." Almost as an afterthought, she added, "She gets that from her father, I suppose."

"Is that the king's secret of success? Misperception?"

"The king. Yes . . . the king," and she smiled. "Very much . . . more than you would think, actually. Well," and she rubbed her hands briskly together, "let us attend to matters, Apropos."

And attend she did. Minutes after she departed, the various groomers, bathers, handlers, and such trooped in and proceeded to undertake the laborious task of transforming me into something "presentable," whatever that might be.

I found out in short order.

The bath was unlike anything I'd ever experienced. Stripped naked as the day I was spat out into the world, I almost leaped out when they started pouring water into the tub. The steward looked properly startled by my reaction.

"It's so you'll be presentable at the banquet, young sir," said the steward.

"Presentable as what?" I demanded, crouching and covering my privates for protection from the steaming water around me. "The main course? You'll boil me like a chicken!"

"We will not, young sir, I assure you," he said in most soothing tones. He then clapped his hands and several young women with scrubbing brushes entered. I was taken aback for a moment. "Worry not, young sir. These are the regular bathers. I promise you that you possess nothing they've never seen before."

"Considering the temperature of the water, I'd wager it's less than nothing," I muttered as the women set to their work. Every so often one of them would giggle slightly. I didn't want to think about what she found so amusing.

After I was dry, then came the groomers. I felt like a damned horse. They cleaned me from head to toe while an outfitter seemed to take excessive interest in figuring out precisely what outfit for me to wear. He kept asking me for my opinion, but I'd none to offer. "Scarlet or flame would be good . . . but there's nothing that matches your hair, so there'd be unpleasant contrast . . ." He muttered comments like that endlessly. He finally settled on a dark blue doublet woven with gold and made of samite. He added to that blue/black hose, and a slate-colored cloak that was lined with fur. The black boots were also lined with fur, and the outfitter insisted I bend over the tops in order to display the lining.

"I look ridiculous," I muttered as I stared into the full-length mirror.

"You look like a noble."

"A noble ass," I retorted. Still, despite the absurdity of my outer appearance, I had to admit that I was rather . . . well . . . taken with it. The outfitter, I suspect, knew what was going through my mind and said nothing, but merely smirked.

And that set me to smirking as well.

I had fooled them. I had fooled them all. If clothes make the man, splendid clothes make the splendid man.

And this was my night to be splendid.

I swept my cloak around me, reached for my staff so that I could affect my most imperious walk, and said archly, "I believe I have a party to attend."

I was escorted to the banquet hall. It was staggering, beyond belief, even more elaborate than what Warlord Shank had put out. Immediately I saw that the phoenix tapestry from the main hall had been relocated to here, undoubtedly so my connection to a great and wonderful destiny could be reiterated silently to all. But that was the least of the spectacles before me. There was food everywhere. I felt a flash of guilt; an entire town could have been fed for a week on what was being consumed there. Odclay was present, of course, jumping about with his folly bells jingling. But this time he was hardly the only source of entertainment. There were jugglers, there were clowns, there were dancing girls, there were mimes, there were magicians (clever fakers and not to be confused with weavers). There was, in short, all manner of purveyors of distractions. Not that the food required that anyone be distracted from it. I could tell just by smelling it that it was superb. Beef, turkey, pork . . . it seemed that anything and everything was being offered by servers to rooms of hungry knights, lords, and ladies.

It was breathtaking and, for just a moment, I found myself with the same giddy reverence that my mother had had for knighthood in her younger days. Remember, the only major celebrational to-do that had been held during my tenure was the one relating to the knights who put down the rebellion of Shank, and I hadn't attended that one because Morningstar and his associates had been endeavoring to beat the stuffing out of me.

That recollection helped remind me of the dark underbelly of knighthood . . . but still . . . this was . . . this was extraordinary no matter how you sliced it.

With Morningstar fresh in my mind, I looked around quickly and finally espied him. He was on the far side of the hall, as far from the royal table as he could possibly be. Apparently he had been assigned as assistant squire to Sir Bollocks, a blockheaded knight who had a capacity for thought slightly above that of a bowl of soup. Mace didn't look happy about it at all; when he spotted me looking at him, he glanced quickly away.

"This way, young sir," the steward said, and he guided me through the banquet hall. I wondered where I was supposed to be sitting, since my knight was gone and the squires' table had already been passed. I saw people looking at me, murmuring and pointing. It was a heady experience.

"Apropos! Join us, will you."

It was the king's voice, not three feet away from me. He was standing behind the head table. He was clad in gold and white, and had never looked more majestic. Standing next to him was the queen, wearing a gown that was the most vivid scarlet I had ever seen. And next to them was a young woman that I didn't recognize. She had stunning blond hair and was ravishingly attired in a purple gown with gold brocade. She sported a white tippet hanging off her right arm and trailing to the floor, except it was silk rather than the standard linen, and a heart-shaped golden chaplet upon her brow.

"Yes, join us, please," said Entipy's voice, emerging from the mouth of the young woman.

I was utterly flabbergasted, and was unable to hide it. I mouthed her name but no words came out. She smiled, obviously pleased at how disconcerted I was.

"You remember our daughter," the king said with mock ceremony. "You spent quite enough time with her. Please . . . do come around and join us. There's a seat next to her."

"Yes . . . yes, of course," I said, finding my voice from

wherever it had momentarily vanished to. I moved to the seat next to her. She winked at me as I eased myself down. "I'm . . . sorry, Princess. You . . . uhm . . ."

"Clean up well?"

"I was going to say something along those lines, yes."

"And may I say the same of you," she replied.

I proceeded to break bread with the royal family.

That, to me, is such a preposterous sentence that I have to write it again: I proceeded to break bread with the royal family.

The food was beyond all previous definitions of superb. The meat was not tough and stringy, as I'd always expected, but instead crafted so perfectly that it virtually seemed to melt in my mouth. I felt as if my tongue were going to pass out from the richness of the tastes moving over it. The wine kept flowing; every time the contents of my glass lowered, a servant would be there to fill it once more. I felt a sort of giddy warmth, and the singing and laughter and all of it melded together into a gentle, hazy buzzing.

We ate. We chatted. We laughed about matters which, at the time, had been moments of life and death, but now became simply anecdotes. The time passed, dare I say it, pleasantly. And yet I never lost awareness of the great tapestry behind me, the image that everyone in the place was associating with me . . . except for me.

"I have to tell you, Apropos," Entipy said with a smile, "that I really liked the way you were looking at me when you first got here."

"Did you?" I think my smile was somewhat lopsided at that point. I tried to rest my chin on my hand and missed.

"Yes. I feel as if I surprised you. That's good. I think you decided that you had me too thoroughly figured out. No girl wants to be that predictable, especially a princess."

"Your hair is what threw me the most," I told her. "Hardly the hue I'd become accustomed to."

"Do you like it?"

"It's very becoming. But how—?"

"One of the conveniences of royalty, Apropos," the princess smiled. "There are weavers who specialize in providing glamour. Weavers for eyes, for mouth . . . weavers for hair . . ."

"Ah. So you had a hair weave done. Very nice."

"I've had them done before," said Entipy.

"Yes, and I'm sure that Apropos would like nothing more than to discuss your ever-changing hair color," commented the king, and he was starting to rise. "But we have other matters to attend to this night."

The king turned to trumpeters who were positioned on the other side of the court and nodded to them. Immediately they blasted a fanfare from their instruments that naturally captured the full and instant attention of everyone in the place. King Runcible spread wide his arms as soon as the silence had fallen.

"My good and dear knights . . . lords, ladies, and retainers . . . as you know, this grand banquet celebrates several happy occasions. First and foremost is the celebration of the coming of age of our beloved princess—Natalia Thomasina Penelope—or, as we lovingly call her, Entipy."

There was warm applause from the assemblage as Entipy stood and bowed to them. I had a feeling that if the Faith Women had been in attendance, they would have been less than lovingly inclined toward her.

"Furthermore," continued the king, "her presence here is due to the rather singular achievement of one squire. Wise beyond his years . . . resourceful beyond his training . . . brave beyond his station . . . her protector, Squire Apropos."

Once more there was applause, and I basked in it. I looked out upon the assemblage, and I wanted to feel contempt for them. I wanted to feel anger. But instead it felt . . .

. . . it felt good.

More, it felt triumphant.

The king had stepped back onto a raised platform, and he gestured for me to join him upon it. I had no idea why, but did as he so indicated.

"This young man, it should be noted," the king said slowly, "saved not only Entipy's life . . . but mine. And he did so through the following means: He convinced me, your sovereign, to dress in fool's motley and put myself across as a jesting madman."

My blood suddenly ran cold. I didn't like the way he was saying that. I glanced over at the queen and Entipy. Their faces were inscrutable.

His tone of voice grew more severe. "He then had me climb up to a high wall and, fully at the mercy of enemy arrows, proceed to sing a series of chants, ditties, and songs, some of them so ribald that I would never dare repeat them in the presence of my wife. And while I was doing this . . . he ran off into the forest."

Oh gods . . .

"In short . . . for the purpose of saving your king's life . . . he thought nothing of asking me to make a total jackass of myself while he vanished into the protective brush. He did not care about how I appeared . . . or how he appeared to me . . . or anything else, except getting out of there alive."

And he drew his sword.

All the feeling went out of my body. The rich meal settling in my stomach prepared to make a return engagement. Stricken with terror, I nearly swooned. As it was, I dropped to my knees in front of him, looking up at that great gleaming blade poised above me.

This had all been a joke, I realized. A horrific joke on me. Every other person in the place must have known that they were gathered together to fatten up the lamb being led to the slaughter. My likening myself to a chicken being served at the banquet had been more accurate than I'd dreamed; I was about to be quartered like a game hen. And none other than the king was going to be doing the honors.

All of this went through my horrified mind in an instant, and then the king brought the sword down gently on first one shoulder, and then the other. And as he did, he intoned, "Putting aside the debt that all of us owe you, I dub thee . . . for your sheer audacity, if nothing else . . . Sir Apropos of . . ."

He blanked and looked at the queen. She shrugged.

". . . Nothing," he said with an amused sigh.

It took a moment for it all to sink in, and what helped was the thunderous applause washing over me. Entipy was helping me to my feet as I looked out upon the assemblage. For one, wild moment I actually thought I saw the shade of my mother. She wasn't looking at me. She was snagging candy from a large dish. Then she vanished. Trust my mother to have her priorities in order.

And from within, my conscience said with utter disgust, *You have become what you most despised. How does it feel, whore's son?*

"Superb," I murmured.

You're an idiot.

"Sod off."

The king took a step forward, resting a hand on my shoulder. "I know some of you," he said, as the applause died and the standing knights took their seats, "may be wondering whether granting Apropos here knighthood—after such a relatively brief time of service, and with such a . . . curious . . . background . . . is truly warranted. My good friends," and he smiled more broadly, "there are some matters in which even a king has no choice. And that includes matters of the heart. For you see . . . my daughter's chosen husband could never be anything less than a knight."

I fell again.

This naturally drew a startled gasp from the assemblage. Runcible looked down at me, slightly puzzled. "Sir Apropos . . . did you so enjoy the experience of being knighted that you desire me to do it again?"

Not necessary. Just stick the sword straight out and I'll throw myself on it, said my inner voice. And this time I was not in disagreement.

Chapter 29

"How could you have done that?"

I was stalking down the corridor, my staff click-clicking on the paving. The pleasant haze that the wine had been instilling in me was long gone. Entipy was walking briskly next to me, trying to keep up.

The banquet was still going, although it was showing signs of tapering off. After the king's announcement I had sat there, stunned, a forced smile plastered on my face, nodding in acknowledgment of the many congratulations I was receiving while simultaneously trying to force myself back to wakefulness. Oddly enough, I wasn't waking up. The only conclusion was that either I was awake, or that I was dead and in hell. I wasn't sure which option I preferred.

"Done what?" She sounded genuinely puzzled.

I whirled to face her. *"Done what?!* Your father just announced to the entire damned court that you and I are going to be married!"

"Yes." The question "So?" was implicit in the tone but unspoken.

"For crying out loud, Entipy, you didn't ask me about it! Never consulted with me! Don't I get to have any say in the matter?"

"Well . . . no," she replied, sounding puzzled that I would even have to ask.

"No?!" I was stunned. "How can you say no?"

"It's not that difficult. Watch." She carefully positioned her lips and teeth and enunciated, very meticulously, "Nooooo."

"You sound like a pessimistic cow."

"And you sound like a total ingrate."

"Ingrate! Entipy . . ." I gestured helplessly. "I should get to have some say in the direction my life goes!"

"Under ordinary circumstances, yes. But you are not an ordinary person, Apropos. You are someone of destiny, and—"

"Ohhhhh . . ." I turned away, not wanting to hear that one again, and headed for my quarters, leaving her behind.

But she didn't stay left behind. I could hear her footsteps following me, and the chances were that wherever her footsteps were, she was likely accompanying them. I turned at the door of my chambers and faced her. "Leave me alone!" I said.

"You do not talk to me that way! I am the princess—!"

"And I'm your 'intended,' which means I'll talk to you any way I like! Or are you going to threaten to chop my head off every day of our married life if you don't appreciate what I have to say."

"Maybe," she said defiantly.

"Oh, well, doesn't that sound like wedded bliss. You're insane!" I leaned against my doorframe, shaking my head. "And even more insane is your parents going along on this mad venture. What could you possibly have said that would have got them to agree to it?"

"They respect my wishes and desires. They know I love you . . ."

"Love! You don't know about love! You know nothing of it! To you it's all a . . . a game! A romantic notion that grabs whatever fancy may be flittering through that newly blond head of yours! What was it before? Blue, green . . ."

"Red, if you must know."

"The color of fire. Makes sense . . ."

"Are we back to that again?" she demanded, looking most agitated. "I told you—"

"How do I know I can trust you! I mean, look at you! Going behind my back, having us betrothed without whispering a word of it. It's wonderful that your parents respect your wishes and desires. A shame that you don't have the same respect for mine. And to be perfectly blunt, Your Highness, if I were your parents, I'd never have given you your way on this . . . this insane match. Just because you said you wanted to marry me . . ."

"Well, there was that . . . and the fact that I told them you and I had made love."

If I hadn't been holding on to my staff, I would have fallen and this time not gotten up. I could barely get the words out. "You . . . what?"

"Told them you and I had made love. Don't worry . . .

I made it clear that it was what we both wanted."

Well, now the solution easily presented itself. I wasn't going to have to marry her. No one would make me marry a corpse, because I was going to kill her with my bare hands.

"Made . . . love . . . ?" I managed to get out in a strangled voice.

"That's right." Her eyes were blazing bright. "Love like two wild stallions, thundering across a shoreline. Love like two great storm clouds, converging to create a thundering crescendo of—"

I heard footsteps approaching. I did *not* need this little lunatic spouting her poetic euphemisms for sex in the middle of the hallway. Things were bad enough as they were. I grabbed her by the elbow and hauled her into my chambers, slamming the door behind us. She seemed startled by the abrupt movement, but then she smiled. I think she liked it.

I ran back in my mind the conversation I'd had with the queen, the one that left me puzzled. About them understanding about Entipy and me, although the king took some convincing. Well, it was all too clear now, wasn't it.

"Love like two crazed weasels—"

"Shut up!" I snapped, endeavoring to keep my voice down. Sounds tended to carry in these corridors. "How could you have told them that? We didn't make love!"

"We thought about it."

"No, we didn't! I never thought about it!" I snapped Which wasn't entirely true, but I certainly didn't want to give her the slightest encouragement.

"Well, I did, and that's all that matters."

"It's not all that matters!" I had put aside my staff and was pacing my room with an agitated limp. "Gods, Entipy . . . what if your father had decided that, instead of wedding us, he was going to execute me for deflowering his little girl!"

"Deflowering. Oh, *now* you believe I'm virginal," she said, arms folded and looking at me with a cocked eyebrow.

"No, I believe you're deranged! I believe you're unhinged! A mentally defective troublemaker who is out to ruin the lives of anyone and everyone who comes in contact with you!" I was waving my arms wildly. "Tacit would still be alive if he hadn't fallen for you!"

"But he did and he's not. And you are here," said Entipy, brow knitting. "What, do you wish that you weren't?"

"Yes!"

"That you were just some peasant, wandering in the streets, begging or maybe stealing?"

"Perhaps," I said, although I admit I sounded slightly less certain about it. Then I rallied. "But that's what Tacit was! And you loved him, or thought you did! And Tacit—"

"Tacit! Tacit! Gods in heaven, Tacit!" Entipy nearly shouted in exasperation, ignoring my imprecations to keep quiet. "Gods, one would almost think that . . ."

Then she stopped and looked at me with an air of challenge.

"What?" I said uncertainly.

"That's it, isn't it."

"What's it? What are you talking about, Enti—?"

"You're afraid that Tacit really was my lover . . . and that if you try to take his place, you're not going to compare to him."

I suddenly had a feeling of what the sensation had been like for Tacit when he'd taken an arrow in the chest. My lips were abruptly very dry. "I . . . I told you you were crazy . . . and now you're proving it," I tried to say.

But she was shaking her head with conviction. "I should have figured it out sooner. You actually feel inferior to him. Even though he's dead, you're still lagging behind him . . ."

"I'm not lagging behind anyone!" I said defensively, almost forgetting to keep my voice down. "This has nothing to do with Tacit! It has to do with . . . with what's right! And respecting my wishes, and—"

She snorted disdainfully. "You sound like a woman. No wonder you're concerned that you couldn't hold a candle to Tacit. You probably couldn't."

A white haze passed before my eyes, my blood pounding in my temples. And then she turned her back on me. "Don't worry about it. I'll tell my father that it was all a lie, that someone as hopelessly inadequate as you couldn't possibly—"

That was when I grabbed her by the arm, swung her around, and kissed her as fiercely as I had ever kissed anyone . . . more so. There was no love in it; instead it was driven by pure fury and a need to dominate this insane creature who was playing havoc with my life.

She pushed away, and there was a sneer on her mouth,

challenge in her eyes. "Is that it? Is that the best you can d—?"

And I saw Astel in those eyes, laughing at me, and Tacit in those eyes, proclaiming that he, not I, was the hero, and I saw the contempt of the knights, the sneers of the squires, the disdain of Stroker, everyone, all encapsulated in this one neat package. And I tore into that package, and I did so with relish.

I lifted Entipy clear off her feet, swung her around and—even with my limp—hauled her toward the bed. The sweep around knocked the candles off the table, and they snuffed out, plunging the room into darkness. But moonlight filtered through the window, and I could still see her eyes, those eyes, looking at me, and the challenge was still there, and the veiled contempt but also the eagerness.

I tore at her beautiful gown and it came away with a rip of cloth. She pulled at my clothing as well, yanking the doublet over my head. We fell upon the bed, a writhing combination of arms and legs, torsos and hips, becoming more naked with each passing moment as the clothes flew from us. Never had I worn such finery; never had I been less caring of what happened to it.

She was covering my face and neck with kisses, and moved down to my chest, biting down on one of my nipples so hard that I cried out. I returned the favor and her body moved against mine.

And for a moment, just a moment, my mind's eye became filled once more with the sight of that phoenix, and the thought that it was Tacit who was supposed to be where I was . . .

. . . and then I thought . . .

. . . what if I was wrong?

It was a glorious, liberating notion.

What if . . . what if I actually *was* supposed to be the hero? What if it really was my story? If my epiphany had moved me in the right direction, but for the wrong reason? Dammit . . . why not? What if Tacit had been wrong? It was possible. Of course it was possible! The idiot had wound up a human target; obviously he didn't have a perfect record for accurately foreseeing every possibility.

"Yes! Yes!" I shouted encouragement to myself. Because in one, heartfelt, perfect moment I had dared to accept the possibility that—despite my lowborn birth, despite the violence of my beginnings, despite the contempt, despite it all—I was actually entitled to reap the benefits of all that I'd aspired to. That I could do what I wished, enjoy the rewards, and not feel guilty about it.

Entipy, not realizing that I'd been talking to myself, cried out *"Yes!"* in return.

Naked, she wrapped her legs around me and I plunged into her, bringing down my lips upon her, and it was as if a final connection was made. Then I kissed the curve of her jaw, her throat, and her breath came in short gasps in my ear, and she was no longer the arrogant and demanding princess. Instead she was mine . . . mine to do with as I wished, mine to fill, mine to pleasure, mine, all mine, and the ghost of Tacit spiraled away, crying out at his banishment.

I thought of the phoenix, going up in flame, even as the heat built within me and in her. And from that searing heat was reborn something new and great. So it was with me, because a wave of burning passion ripped from me, enveloping me, reducing me to the emotional equivalent of ashes as I cried out her name. And she called out mine, and there was a joy such as I had never heard from her, one such as I had never felt.

"Entipy . . ." I practically sobbed, *"I love you . . ."*

"It's about damned time," she whispered in my ear, and then I exploded into her.

The rays of the morning sun caressed us.

I had woken up some little time before to the soft but steady snoring of the princess, who was resting her head upon my shoulder. Her nude body was still intertwined with mine. The sheets were wound around us; during the night the cool air had prompted me, in my sleep, to try and pull the covers over us. I'd been only partly successful; they covered us from the waist down.

There was a trickle of drool from her mouth down onto my chest. I actually thought it was cute. Shows how besotted I was.

Now that I could see them in the daylight, her breasts were surprisingly small, but quite firm. The rest of her body, from the waist up, at least, was quite well muscled, actually. I wasn't surprised; I had a sense of just how much endurance she had from our activities in the night. Gods, the girl was practically insatiable.

There was no doubt in my mind that she was a virgin. The eagerness, the raw need, reminded me of how I had felt that first time with Astel. How, once that floodgate of ardor had been opened, there was no shutting it, and I had wanted to experience it again and again. Entipy had exhibited that same sort of unquenchable lust.

I laughed softly to myself. In her sleep, she must have sensed the rise and fall of my chest in silent laughter, and she smiled as she ran her fingers across my chest hair. I ruffled her hair gently, affectionately.

I dared to dream.

I dreamt of a life together with Entipy. Was such a thing possible? It was hard to say. She was still somewhat on the insane side. How could I trust someone like that? Then again . . . at least I could trust her to be insane. She was most consistent about that. I mean, look at Astel. She wasn't insane, but one moment she was affectionate, and the next, she was trying to smash my head in. With Entipy . . . I could never let down my guard, because her very nature would not permit it. She couldn't be trusted in anything except not being able to be trusted. It made a bizarre, circular sort of sense.

I dreamt of what it would be like to sit upon the throne. Runcible and Beatrice would not be around forever. Indeed, for all I knew, considering their delightfully antiquated and quaint notions of my being this great warrior and ruler they'd been waiting for, the king and queen might actually abdicate. And there I would be, Apropos, with either the greatest power in the land in my palm, or at the very least I'd be alongside Entipy helping her to consolidate her own power base. I could be involved with ruling through her.

I dreamt of sending Morningstar running twenty times around the castle, every day, while wearing full armor. "Exercise. He needs it," I would shrug, even as I stood there with a grin and watched him running about and losing his mind.

I dreamt about being feared. About being powerful. About being the Hero Who Had Been Foreseen. It all seemed intriguing, marvelous.

I had never felt so relaxed. So complete. It was truly as if I was with—not another person—but another aspect of myself.

Entipy let out a soft, contented sigh and drew up one leg to bring it across my hips, snuggling for greater warmth. But her efforts were counterproductive as the movement caused the blanket to slide away, exposing some of her finely shaped ass to the cool air. I looked at it in the light of day and laughed to myself.

If I ever wanted evidence that we belonged together, there it was, right there. She had a birthmark on her hip, in the shape of a small burst of flame, that was identical to mine.

I found that very interesting indeed. Hers was slightly lighter in color, but otherwise, it was a perfect match with mine. One would almost have thought that we were of the same . . .

. . . family . . .

A birthmark . . . identical to mine . . . a linemark, a sign of parentage . . .

My skin suddenly grew much colder than the early morning air as I sat up slowly, staring into her face. I'd never noticed how, relaxed in repose, it looked . . . familiar . . .

And a dozen little things . . . small comments . . .

observations . . . suddenly were viewed in a light that was as different as the morning light was from the moonlight. The queen's instinct that we would get on so well together, my feeling that she was a missing part of me . . . the unicorns going mad whenever we'd touched each other . . . I'd . . . I'd thought it was just because they knew what I had done to Tacit, but it wasn't just that, it was because unicorns knew the way of things, knew that destiny had intended someone other than me, that romance between us was . . . gods . . . she'd had red hair originally . . . red, like mine . . . like a close family member . . . too close a family member . . . like a sis—

I let out a scream so loud that, to this day, I am convinced that Tacit, lying dead in his tomb back in the Outer Lawless regions, heard it and his deceased mouth twisted in a satisfied "I told you so" smirk.

Chapter 30

The agonized shriek not only jolted Entipy to full wakefulness, but it knocked her clear out of the bed.

She looked up at me with a confused face that was like mine, gods, how could I have been so blind? How could I not have seen it? How could others not have? I continued to scream, no longer in command of myself.

Immediately Entipy assumed that I was in the throes of some hideous nightmare. "Apropos, my love, it's all right!" she said as she scrambled to her feet and came toward me. I stared at her, my eyes fair to leaping out of my head, and she put a hand on my cheek and made to kiss me. This set off another round of terrified bellowing as I scrambled backward on the copious bed, grabbing some of the bedclothes around myself and doing everything I could to keep as much distance between us as possible.

"Apropos, wake up, you're having a nightmare!" she cried out. And how the hell was I to explain to her that in the slumber lay the peace while the waking was the nightmare.

Naturally there came a pounding at the door. What else was to be expected? The fiancé of the princess was howling like a banshee; naturally that was going to attract attention. At that moment, though, I was beyond caring. All I knew was that, after a joyous night of screwing the princess, I was now screwed myself.

Entipy gathered up one of the fallen sheets and wrapped it around herself expertly. Impressively, she actually managed to look rather imperious in the makeshift garment as she strode toward the door. That was when I belatedly realized that she was about to open it. *"Stop!"* I shouted, lunging for her, and falling off the bed with the other blanket wrapped around me. "Don't—!"

"It's a little late to be worried about discretion, considering you bellowed loudly enough to wake the dead," she commented as she pulled the door open, "to say nothing of—"

Her father.

Who was standing there, a bleary-eyed look on his face. He had tossed on a robe over his nightclothes. Sir Justus, also nightclad, but holding a sword firmly, was beside him, as were two other guards. I suppose on some level I should have been flattered that the king himself was coming to check on me. As it was, I would happily have forgone the compliment in exchange for a widespread case of temporary deafness throughout the castle.

If there was any slumber left in their eyes, it promptly vanished at the sight of the sheet-wrapped princess presenting herself quite unabashedly in my room. From where they were standing they could easily see me in the background, looking like a fallen ghost . . . an apt description, between the shroud-like sheet wrapped around me and the fact that I was probably so ashen that my pallor was more suited to one dead than alive.

"What's all this then?" demanded Justus in a low voice. The king looked stunned. The guards behind them were grinning. It was probably a good thing that neither of them saw it or the guards' tenure would most likely come to a quick end, along with the guards themselves.

"Apropos was having a nightmare, Father," Entipy said, the picture of innocence.

Remarkably, the king actually managed to sound solicitous. "Were you having a nightmare, Sir Apropos?"

I managed to get out, "I'm . . . still having it, Highness." Of all those rare instances in my life where I had spoken the absolute truth, none was more accurate than that.

His voice ice, Sir Justus said, "Perhaps it would be best if the princess went to her own chambers now . . . ?"

"Yes. Yes, by all means," said the king distantly. I wasn't sure if he was still having trouble coping with what he was seeing, and was thus in shock . . . or if he was so angry he was simply fighting to contain his rage.

Entipy inclined her head slightly in acknowledgment and then glanced back at me. "I'll see you later, my love," she said, and she blew a kiss at me. I felt another small piece of my soul die as I forced a wave. She slid out of the room, angling past her father and the others and padding down the hallway.

Runcible's cold eyes swept the chamber and took in the torn garments lying scattered on the floor. Then he looked back at me. I considered the possibility that he'd kill me on the spot and tried to see the downside of that. None presented itself.

"Apropos," he said slowly, "there are those who take amusement from youthful indiscretion. There are even those who would say that, since you are betrothed to Entipy, that anything you do is completely fine and acceptable. I wish I happened to be one of those individuals, since it would simplify both my life and yours tremendously. However . . . I am not. Nine o'clock, this A.M. My court. Please be so kind as to be on time . . . properly attired, if it would not be too much trouble," said the king.

"Yes, Highness" was all I managed to get out.

The door shut behind them, and the last thing I saw was Justus's scowling and disapproving face.

I flopped back on the bed and stared up at the ceiling.

"I hate family reunions," I said to no one.

I had no breakfast. I was not hungry. Would you be?

As I dressed, my mind was racing. I was thinking back to when the queen was making passing remarks about how Entipy was much like her father. There had been something in her tone, something in the way that she'd said it, that struck me as curious. I had not, at the time, been able to determine what it was. Now, of course, I knew.

King Runcible was not Entipy's father.

I had long ago discounted the possibility that Runcible was one of the men who had brutalized my mother that stormy night long ago. Madelyne would most surely have recognized him, and I could not believe that I would not have learned from someone—her, Astel, Stroker, one of them—that I might indeed not only be a bastard, but a royal bastard to boot. Besides, I had come to the conclusion that Runcible was many things . . . but a raping brute was simply not one of them.

Which meant that the man who was the father that Entipy and I both shared had not only done my mother . . . but the queen as well. And somehow—call me a fool, call me eccentric—but I tended to think that he had not had to resort to having other knights hold her down while he had his way with her.

Considering the state of mind that I had possessed when I first arrived at the castle, angry and bitter and seeking justice for my late mother, I did not think it possible that my opinion of people in general, and knights and royalty in particular, could have sunk much lower than it had before. But I was wrong. Because if there had been one person in the entirety of the court whom I had been certain was a good, true, and faithful individual, it was the queen. Part of me wanted to believe that I was mistaken, that I had misread the situation. That it was, in fact, the king who had transgressed rather than the queen. But my every instinct was telling me otherwise.

What the hell was I going to do?

Marry the princess? Could I do it? Could I possibly climb back into bed with her, knowing she was my sister?

It was my ever-aggressive, ever-ambitious inner voice

that was speaking. *She's only your half-sister. And it's not as if you've been raised side by side all these years. You have no real blood loyalty to her on that score. You're making more of this than there needs to be. And besides, there are some other parts of the realm that not only do* not *abominate incest but, in fact, encourage it, to keep the bloodline pure.*

And then I thought about the realms where such customs applied. The ones overseen by such inbred monarchs as King Rudolf the Dribbler and King Clyde the Numblingly, Mind-Bogglingly Stupid.

No, that didn't seem too workable an option. To say nothing of the fact that I kept coming back in my mind to the legends of the mythic king of the Britons, Arthur. He who had lain with his half-sister, Morgana, and had wound up siring his own nemesis, Mordred. The thought that my own little downfall might, at this moment, be brewing in the cauldron of Entipy's belly was a most unpleasant one.

And, ultimately, what it came down to was the thought of coupling with her again, knowing who she was . . . knowing that the madness I saw and despised in her was simply a reflection of my own . . . simply made my skin crawl.

I went to the window and considered leaping out of it. Escape would be impossible; on the other hand, if I killed myself in the fall, that would certainly put an end to my difficulties. I strongly considered it, even put one leg out the window to try and steel myself for it.

What if you're wrong?

And that stopped me. "Wrong?" I said out loud to no one.

Yes. Wrong. Have you considered the possibility that you're simply jumping to conclusions? Yes, she has a birthmark like yours, and yes, she bears a resemblance to you in a variety of ways. But that alone does not make you siblings, or even half-siblings. What if she is but a cousin? You cannot know for sure. What if her father, whoever he is, is a brother of yours? As long as you don't know whether her father was at the inn that night, raping your mother, you can't say for certain. You may be walking away from the opportunity of a lifetime for no reason. Think! She will be queen! You, her consort, would rule by her side!

"Except she is not the daughter of the king. Queen Beatrice is queen only by marriage; it is from the king himself that the royal bloodline flows. Entipy has no true claim to be the princess; she's just a royal bastard with no rights. If I ruled by her side, I'd be living a lie!"

And your point is—?

Then came a brisk knock at the door to summon me downstairs. Once again I cursed myself for my lack of nerve and resolve, and—after taking my staff firmly in one hand—I opened the door. The guard looked at me oddly. "Is there . . . another here?" he inquired. I shook my head. "Odd . . . I . . . thought I heard you talking to someone," he continued.

"I was talking to myself. It's the only way I'm assured intelligent conversation," I said, and followed him out.

The queen, a faithless trollop, more base than my mother. The king, an ignorant cuckold. Entipy, an unknowing bastard who had no more claim to the throne than I. This was the royal family that was seated before me in the main hall. Other knights were in attendance as well, which I was personally appalled by. Had the king so utterly lost his mind that he was going to discuss indelicacies in front of the entirety of the court?

As it turned out, that was exactly what he was going to do. He did not, however, say so. Instead it was Justus, standing to the king's right, who said gravely, "The king is more than aware of the nature of gossip . . . and knew, since others saw that the princess was in your company this morning, that word of it would quickly spread throughout the castle. He may command hearts and minds, but virtually nothing can stay gossip's swift hand. A truly wise king knows his limitations."

Odclay the jester capered about, his bells tinkling merrily, and he chanted,

"The king today, sad to say, is most completely ruing,
the snickering amongst the knights about his daughter's scr—"

"That's quite enough of that, jester," the queen said sharply. Odclay promptly lapsed into silence after a final, slightly defiant jingle of his bells.

"That said," continued Justus, "the king and queen . . ."

"Mostly the queen," rumbled Runcible.

". . . have decided to be . . ." Justus stopped and glanced at Runcible, who nodded slightly. "Magnanimous," he concluded.

"Magnanimous," I said hollowly.

"Yes. It is clear that you and the princess are—shall we say—a bit overanxious for the union to take place.

Rather than focus on what should not have been done, the king and queen . . . mostly the queen," he added in anticipation of the clarification, "have decided instead to focus on what will be done. So we are here . . . to set a wedding date. The sooner the better. We were thinking something along the lines of . . ."

"Now," the king said quietly.

"Now?" I whispered.

"Do you have another, more pressing appointment?" asked the queen.

"No . . . no, I . . . didn't have anything else planned today. Well . . . I was thinking of reshoeing my horse, perhaps, or . . . or . . . taking a bath, that was nice, a bath . . ." I was yammering. I wasn't making sense to anyone, least of all myself. I rallied and said, "I mean . . . isn't this a bit rushed? A royal wedding, after all. There should be, uhm . . . pomp and circumstance . . . and . . . and . . ."

"Under the circumstances, we can forgo the pomp," said Justus. "The princess has already consented . . ."

"Again," muttered the king.

The queen fired him a scolding look, and there was some quick laughter from the court.

"Apropos," Entipy spoke up, and she stepped down from the raised platform upon which the thrones rested. She crossed to me and took my hand. It was everything I could do not to pull it away. "Apropos, it's all right. Really. The ceremony, the trappings . . . they mean nothing to me anyway. Only you mean anything."

"And besides," the queen said, "what need have we to invite nobles and such from other lands? They likewise mean nothing. The people that matter to us," and she took in the entirety of the court with a sweeping gesture, "are all right here. We are, in a way, all family."

Oh my gods . . .

"So, good sir knight," and Justus clapped his hands together briskly, like a great showman about to proceed with a circus, "the archdeacon is in the next room. I can bring him out and the ceremony can proceed, so that you and the princess can be lawfully husband and—"

"I can't." The words fell out of my mouth and splattered to the floor like eggs gone bad. And it was true. I couldn't. My mind was awhirl, my thoughts conflicted. I had spent my life acting in my best interests, and for the first time, I had no idea what those were. My trusty inner voice was shouting, *Shut up! Marry her! So what if she's your sister? She could be your mother for all you should care! Deal with it and wed the bitch!* My lips tightened. I said nothing further.

There was a deathly silence for a long moment.

"Apropos," Justus said evenly, "it is said that knights do not know the meaning of the word 'can't' . . ."

"Except when it comes to beggars," Odclay piped up. "They utter their beggars' cant. Also, I hear beggars can't be—"

"Not now," the king said sharply, and I had never heard that tone of voice from him. He had risen from the throne. "Apropos . . . I owe you a great deal . . . but you owe me, as well. Another king would have gutted you for your actions. I am choosing to rise above it. I do not suggest you drag us down, or it will go badly for you."

"I . . . have no doubt," I managed to squeak out. I was looking up at the phoenix tapestry, restored to its normal place. In my imagination, the image of the rider—Tacit, of course—was tossing a rude gesture to me.

Entipy was looking at me with wide, hurt eyes. "Apropos . . . ?" she was saying.

I looked into those eyes, and it was like seeing my soul mirrored back at me. This was no cousin, no distant relation. I became more and more convinced with each passing instant. My voice barely above a whisper, I said again, "I . . . I can't . . ."

"How. Dare. You." Never before, and very likely never since, had the king engaged in such a public display of fury. He was rooted to the spot, perhaps concerned that, if he approached me, he'd kill me with his bare hands. What a favor he would have been doing me. "How dare you treat the princess this way. Treat us this way."

Entipy was backing away from me, shaking her head in denial, still unable to believe that I was refusing her. The king took a step down from the throne, still not getting near me, still trembling with barely suppressed fury. "I raised you up! I trusted you! What is the problem here, 'good sir knight'? Mayhap you think that my daughter is not good enough for you, you peasant bastard? Not as good as the . . . the whores and what-have-you that you've consorted with before coming here?"

The single most stupid thing I could possibly have done at that moment was to lose my temper. Naturally that's what I started to do. "At least they were honest whores," I shot back.

The court gasped in unison as if it possessed one throat. The king, royally, purpled. "And to think . . . to think that the queen pled with me on your behalf! To think that my daughter trusted you! To think that we invited you to join us, to be one of us! We should have known! Known that someone whose roots are from so low in our society could not possibly share that to which we aspire! The nobility of spirit, the purity of soul! Here we thought that you would be able to join us in sharing our scrupulous sense of morality, and here you could not pollute it with the daughter of my loins! As if she was not good enough for you—!"

There may have been more ill timed moments for me to completely lose control of my sense of discretion, but in retrospect, none come to mind. "Scrupulous sense of morality!" I bellowed, appalled. "What a joke!"

"*Joke? **Joke?!*** You take advantage of my daughter, and you call it a joke?"

Never had I been less concerned about my long-term health than in that confrontation with the king. Because finally, finally I was going to say that which had been on my mind all that time. Even if he cut me down right there—which he probably would—he would at least hear the truth of it. He would hear about the foundation of sand upon which he had constructed this glorious little fantasy realm which existed—not around him, but instead only within his head. Lowborn bastard I might be, but I would take being a lowborn realist over being royalty trapped in self-delusion any day of the week. And I knew right where I was going to start in the deconstruction of this false world of chivalry and morality. First it would be with his delusion that his queen had been faithful, his daughter his own . . . and then I would move on to the circumstances of my own creation. At last, at last, I finally understood my true reason for existence. It was for nothing else other than to bring this world of lies and deceit crashing down. "Aye, joke, say I," I snapped at him. "And that's the biggest joke of all! Your daughter, you say? *Your* daughter of *your* loins? And your wife, her mother? Why, I'll have you know that your queen—"

And I stopped.

Because I saw Queen Bea's face go ashen.

She knew what I was about to say. She knew that, somehow, I knew. There was panic in that face, like a trapped animal. And maybe it was a case where she had utilized all of her ability to be deceitful on the sheer act of keeping it secret. That, once it was yanked out into the open, she would not be able to resolutely deny it to her husband's face.

All of that, though, was secondary, to the fact that her panicked gaze had reflexively shifted. With her secret about to be revealed, she had not looked at her husband, nor at me, nor her daughter.

Which, of course, made sense. In an instant like that, with your duplicity about to be revealed, you would not look to those from whom you kept the secret.

Instead, you would look to him with whom you shared it.

Without even turning my head, I saw where her gaze went. Saw where it went . . . and saw it returned, from a face as momentarily frightened and desperate as her own. A face that looked like an odd assortment of different parts slapped together. A face topped off by a jaunty fool's cap.

Well . . . of course. I mean, of course. I, who had been

a joke for the entirety of my life . . . naturally, I would have a booby for a sire. Any final doubts that Entipy and I shared the same father were washed away in that instant, because of course, *of course* . . . it was too perfect. It was too cosmically apt, the answer to my long-standing question right in front of me, irrefutable and poetically just: Who else could possibly produce such a fool as I but a royal fool?

Queen Bea, and her clandestine lover, Odclay the jester, father of the princess, and of the princess's former intended, looked at each other in the way that only petrified deceivers can when their deceit is about to be made public.

And I knew at that instant that I was right. That she wouldn't be able to deny it. That I'd caught her too flat-footed . . . her and Odclay. If I kept the momentum going, they'd be sufficiently disconcerted so that the web of lies would come unwoven, the wall of silence and secrecy would crack.

It was right there, all of it, within my reach. With just a few words, I could bring an entire kingdom crashing down. With just a few words, I could avenge myself on my father. With just a few words, I could destroy the hypocrisy rife within the system that Runcible had created. All I had to do . . .

. . . all I had to do . . .

. . . was wreck the life of Queen Beatrice. A pathetic, frightened creature who, aside from her indiscretion, had done nothing. Nothing except be the only person in the castle who had treated me with compassion. Who had nursed me back to health, who had intervened on my behalf with the king. Even her "forcing" me to go on the mission to retrieve her daughter had been motivated by concern for her daughter and a sense that I was the right person for the job, that Entipy and I would share a bond. She couldn't possibly have known.

And Entipy. Gods, the knowledge of what had happened . . . of who and what she was and wasn't . . . of what her mother was and wasn't . . . it would drive her mad. Truly mad. She had been a handful the entire time, there was no denying that. But she did not deserve to see her entire world crack apart around her. Did not deserve to be sent spiraling down into the pit of disgrace. My turning away from her and the future she had built around us was bad enough, but to see her own place in that denied, to suffer the scornful looks and contempt hurled upon all those pathetic creatures who had the heartless label slapped on them—"bastard"—how could I? How—?

Do it. Do it. This is what you've been waiting for. The king is a cuckold, the queen is faithless, the daughter is a loon, and your father is the only jest in the kingdom bigger than you. If you're not going to take advantage of marrying her, then at least have your revenge. Do what must be done. . . .

The king's voice was icier than the Frozen North. "My queen . . . is what," he said. It was not remotely a query. It was a prompting for the words that would, unbeknownst to the king, mean damnation for all.

"—your queen . . . and your daughter . . . and you . . . deserve someone more worthy than a peasant bastard," I said quietly. "There is nothing more to say than that, Your Highness. And if that will not suffice . . . then throw me in the dungeon now and be done with it."

Chapter 31

As dungeons went, it wasn't that bad. There were hardly any rats, the straw was changed daily, and the king—in a burst of generosity—hadn't manacled me to the wall.

I sat there, staring into darkness. The one thing I wasn't wondering was why the king hadn't simply executed me on the spot. The only thing I could think of was that the gods were not through tormenting me yet.

I knew I would never forget the astonishment that played over Bea's face, or the choked sob of betrayal and hurt that came from the throat of the princess. Nor, try as I might, the grinning triumph in the face of Mace Morningstar as the guards hauled me past him and away to the dungeons to await . . .

. . . what?

I didn't know. And at that point, I didn't care. For someone who had spent the entirety of his life caring first and foremost about himself, it was an odd sensation to have stopped giving it any priority at all.

My guess at that point was that the king was just going to leave me in there to rot. He could have me executed, of course. The volunteers would likely be lining up. But the king was less a believer in martyrdom and more a believer in mercy whenever possible, and in the grand demented scheme of things, he'd probably think that letting me live out the rest of my life in this hole was merciful.

I stared into the darkness and tried to figure out how I could have, should have, handled that final moment in a different manner. But try as I might, I simply could not see myself stripping away the queen's secret. Perhaps I saw in her, in some measure, some of the same traits that my mother had possessed. A fundamentally good woman who, owing to circumstances, wound up doing some fundamentally bad things. That was not, however, enough to make them fundamentally bad people who deserved the misfortunes that befell them. That was a far more accurate description of me, when you get down to it.

And that was, ultimately, what it boiled down to. I deserved this. I'd had a good run . . . made some good enemies . . . held triumph in my hand for a brief time . . . and now it was done. I was done. Over. All, all over.

I heard a turning of a key in the lock and looked up. For a moment I thought of trying to attack whoever was entering, but then reasoned that I might as well stay put. I had no idea, after all, what the odds would be like outside. There could be twenty men waiting for me in the hallway, and the person entering was the one who was going to give me food. If I jumped him, and then ran straight into the waiting arms of the guards, all I would have accomplished would have been to anger the person on whom I was depending for sustenance. What would be the point of that?

So I sat there and waited.

Of the four people I most did not want to see at that moment, naturally it was the one I didn't want to see most of all. That was probably because he was the one I'd been thinking about for the longest time.

Odclay stood a couple of steps away from me, allowing his eyes to adjust to the dimness. There was none of the fool about him. "I wouldn't suggest you try to get away; there's guards at either end of the corridor." The door swung shut behind him.

I said nothing, did nothing. Just stared at him. Part of me wanted to launch myself at him, to knock him to the floor, to feel his throat between my hands, to feel the pulse slow and stop beneath my fingers as I choked the life out of him. I would have. I should have.

I couldn't. I just couldn't work up the interest. After all this time, after all that had happened, it seemed . . . it seemed irrelevant to me somehow.

"How did you know?" he finally asked.

I told him. Why not? What did I have to lose at that point? In as flat and steady a voice as I could, I told him everything. The circumstances of my creation, the birthmark, the reason I had come to Isteria, the involvement with Entipy, the realization . . . all of it.

He took it all in, nodding. He didn't reply immediately. Instead he wandered the cell, looking around it as if he were surveying my summer home. Seeing him walk in this way, rather than capering about, I noticed for the first time that—in addition to his other deformities—he had a limp. I never would have thought that I would consider my physical impairment as having gotten off lucky.

And yet . . . part of me wanted him to deny it. After all, if he said he wasn't there, that left possibilities open. Finally he stopped wandering and leaned against the wall. "That night," he said softly, "was the worst night of my life."

" 'That night'?" I asked, momentarily confused. But then I understood. That night. That night with my mother. That terrible, terrible night. "Oh," I said.

"Yes. Oh." There was grim amusement in his voice, and no hint of the madness whatsoever. None. My thoughts flew back to Beatrice, talking about how people hid what they were. She wasn't talking about Entipy so much as she was talking about Odclay. He continued to speak, and it almost seemed as if he wasn't just speaking to me . . . but also to the distant shade of my mother. "Because when the knights insisted on my joining in . . . why, to them, it was the biggest joke of all, you see. A jester having a woman that knights had taken. It was the crowning giggle. I kept . . ."

His voice caught. He looked as if he was ready to cry. Unsurprisingly, my heart didn't exactly go out to him. "I kept . . . kept whispering in your mother's ear, 'I'm sorry, I'm sorry,' even as I kept a grin forced on my face, and there were peals of laughter from all around. A joke. A great joke."

"You are so full of shit," I said coldly. "They were likely half-drunk. They couldn't have been too difficult to fool. You could have pretended, could have mimed it, could have joked your way out of it. Instead, you took her. Took her just like the others did, to prove to a group of men who thought you incapable that you could be as brutish as any of them. And you're sitting here now, years later, telling me that you were reluctant. That you, of all of them, were the man of conscience who didn't want to have anything to do with it, so that I'll feel . . . what? Compassion? Sorry for you?" I snorted. "You claim that you were forced. Gods . . . you'd paint yourself to be as big a victim as she was. Let me say something, jester, that I'm sure very few say to you: Don't make me laugh."

He looked down, but he was smiling grimly. "Believe what you will, Apropos. I can't really blame you for it."

"Oh, good. I truly lived in fear of your blame." I studied him for a moment, thinking about all that had happened, putting the final pieces together. "It's been you, all along, hasn't it."

"I've already admitted to being with your moth—"

"Not that." I waved impatiently, as if the last thing of interest to me was that which I had been dwelling on for nearly two decades. "I mean the brains behind the throne. The craft. The cunning. It hasn't been Runcible at all, has it. It's been you."

He smiled at that. "Very good. I daresay you've inherited a good deal of my wit, along with some of my more," and he glanced at my leg, "unfortunate attributes."

"Shame my mother didn't mention to me one of her 'visitors' had any physical deformities. Might have narrowed down for me who to look at as potential father material."

Odclay shrugged. "It was dark. We were cloaked. And she had stars in her eyes that night, Apropos. That much

I can tell you. To her . . . we were all giants. All of us. I . . ."

Then he saw how I was looking at him, and looked down. "In any event . . . yes, you're correct. As a jester, I've always been appreciative of the ultimate joke. None of them know, none of them realize . . . Runcible has no knack for strategy at all. He's neither wise nor clever . . . well, no more so than the average man. But it takes more than an average man to become king. It's always been me, guiding him in private, telling him what to do. He likes the limelight; I like to run things, try and make the world a better place."

"You've certainly made a mess of it so far," I said bluntly.

"We all do the best we can, in our own way. As you yourself have just done."

"I don't give two damns about the world," I said flatly. "I care about myself, and that's all."

"So you say," and he eyed me skeptically. "Yet you could have said what you knew, or guessed. But you were willing to sacrifice yourself on others' behalf. That's heroic, Apropos. A father could not be more proud of his son."

And that was all I could take. He was crouching near me when he said it, and that was his mistake. I lunged toward him, swinging as hard as I could. My fist caught him square in the face and I heard the satisfying crunch of a very familiar impact. He lay back on the ground, stunned.

"Enjoy your broken nose," I said tightly. "Gods know I've had mine shattered enough times."

I leaned toward him and he put up his hands reflexively to try and ward me off. I think he thought I was going to hit him again. Once upon a time, I would have. Once upon a time, I would have set upon him and strangled him with my bare hands. But now . . .

. . . now I was just tired.

Instead I satisfied myself with looking at the blood gushing from his nose. Copious flow. Good. Nice to know I still had a good punch. Then I leaned back and just stared at him.

"And that's it?" asked Odclay after a while.

"You want more? I can accommodate you . . ."

"No, that's . . . quite all right. Still . . . it's interesting."

The longer he stayed, the more tired I was getting of him. "In what way?" I asked, despite my better judgment.

"Your world has widened, Apropos. I don't think you yet realize how much. Only a few years ago, if you'd known who I was, you'd likely have kept hitting me until I stopped moving, forever. Because vengeance against me was so much a part of your existence."

"Don't flatter yourself," I said.

He ignored me and went on, "But now you're part of a much greater, much grander scheme of things. Compared to that, I've shrunken to insignificance."

Slowly I shook my head. "You," I said slowly, "are a coward who raped my mother and hides his intelligence behind fool's motley. Take my word for it, Odclay: You were always insignificant."

He seemed prepared to argue the point, but instead shook his head. Then he rose and went to a far corner of the cell. I watched him with little interest . . . until I saw him push against one particular brick. Suddenly a small section of the wall slid aside. It was not much; just enough for us to slide through, one at a time, on our bellies. I gaped at it as Odclay turned back to me and gestured for me to enter. "After you," he said.

"You first," I replied cautiously.

He shrugged, apparently uncaring, and crawled in ahead of me. I waited for a moment, glanced around nervously, and then followed him in.

The passageway remained narrow for a time, but in short order it widened out and I was able to stand. Odclay was already standing, and he was holding a torch in order to illuminate the area. He angled it down and I looked where he was pointing. My eyes widened. My staff was there, as were a few of my things . . . including the belt that held the jewels, gold, and other riches I'd garnered from Astel. He must not have looked within the pouches.

"Take them," he said tersely. "Let's go."

"Go . . . ?"

"Hurry up. It wasn't easy greasing the palms of the guards to 'forget' that I came in to see you. I think it wiser not to press our luck by acting as if we have all the time in the world."

Deciding that it would be best to save all questions, I picked up my staff and few belongings, and headed down the corridor. The jester remained close behind me, not saying anything. Indeed, what was there to say?

The flickering torchlight seemed to indicate that the path ahead was ending. Nothing but a large wall greeted us. However, Odclay pushed against another section and this one, too, swung open. I stepped out into the night air, breathing in deeply. It was a warm night and there was no rain, which was certainly a pleasant change of pace.

"I am sorry your mother was killed," he said softly. "You . . . seemed rather focused on the scars Meander carried upon him. Do you think that was her mark upon him? That he did it?"

"I don't know," I admitted. "I may never know. Although I'm beginning to think that knowing things can wind up being as painful as not knowing them."

Odclay stood in the doorway, not emerging. I noticed now that there was a package sitting on the floor next to him which apparently he'd had waiting there. He picked it up and handed it to me. "In the event that it was him, and you seek vengeance . . . or find another blackguard who was truly responsible . . . I wouldn't want you to go against him, or even out into the world, armed with nothing but your wits and a staff."

"It's gotten me this far," I said.

"So has luck. But this might help you make your own luck."

The cloth seemed to be thick, woven. I unwound it and discovered within it a sword. I held it up in the moonlight. It had an odd heft to it, and an elaborately carved pommel in the shape of a screaming bird's head, not unlike that of a phoenix.

"It's called a hand-and-a-half sword," said Odclay. "It can be wielded with either one hand or two, depending upon whether you're holding your staff or not. And it's a particularly appropriate weapon for you."

"Why?" I had to ask.

"Because it's also called a 'bastard sword.'"

"How apropos," I said mirthlessly. Then I realized that the cloth in which it had been rolled had some sort of an image on it. I straightened it, held it up in the moonlight.

It was me. I looked older. There was gray in my hair and—I might have been mistaken, but I appeared to be missing an ear. I was leaning forward on the sword that I was holding at the moment, and I was seated upon a throne.

"What is this supposed to be?" I asked.

"A farweaver did it."

"A farweaver did the tapestry that hangs in the castle. That didn't come true."

"Didn't it?" he said.

"No. It called for a great hero to come. He didn't come. He died. You got me instead."

"People read things into the tapestries that might or might not be there. And don't sell yourself short; you might just be more of a hero than you want to admit. Has it occurred to you that maybe you've spent your whole life doing the right thing . . . and justifying for yourself that it's from selfish motives?"

"It's never occurred to me, no. Probably because it's not the case."

"As you will," he said with a shrug. "In any event, take that with you if you wish. Consider it a gift . . . from the same farweaver who did the tapestry in the castle."

"Really. I'd like to meet him so I can tell him he's an idiot. Although," and I looked at it with a critical eye, "I admit . . . I'm not happy about the missing ear . . . but it's a rather good likeness."

With a wry smile, my father said, "Thank you. I try."

And as I gaped at him in astonishment, Odclay swung shut the wall, locking me out of the castle and giving me my freedom.

I turned, took two steps . . .

. . . and froze as Entipy came around the corner. She stopped, faced me, and simply stood there with her arms folded.

My mouth, my throat, were completely dry.

"Did you think I was stupid?" she inquired. When I was unable to make a response, she continued, "I had a feeling you'd show up right about here sooner or later. I know about the hidden passages in this place. Odclay showed them to me when I was a child. He was the only one in the whole place, aside from my mother, who had any patience with me. He's the brains behind my father's kingdom, you know. Had you figured that out?"

I nodded. She sounded so calm, so conversational, that part of me thought I'd gone mad, because the entire encounter seemed unreal.

"He's not so foolish as he seems," she went on. "In some ways he'd be a better father than my real one is."

I shuddered. I didn't think she noticed it, and she didn't. Because although she was looking at me, I think she was also looking inward as well.

"Am I hideous? Is that it?" she said abruptly.

I finally found my voice. "What? No! No, it's—"

"A bad sex partner, perhaps. You seemed to be enjoying yourself—"

"Yes, I did! You're . . . it's not you. It's me. I can't."

"You still can turn this around, Apropos," she said, sounding quite reasonable. I couldn't tell whether she was bottling her emotions or had simply detached from them. "Apologize to my father and mother. Tell them you were overwhelmed by the moment. And marry me. You know you want to. You know you love me."

"It's not that simple . . ."

"Yes, it is."

"No, it's not. Trust me. Don't you trust me?"

She laughed at that, as if it was the most absurd question in the world. "No. Of course not. I know you better than I know myself. You're a scoundrel, and always will be. That's what makes you attractive to me."

"But back at the fort! You said you trusted me then."

"I lied."

"Were you?" I said sharply. "Lying then? Or are you lying now?"

She didn't say anything. And then something occurred to me. "You keep saying that you know I love you. Do you truly love me?"

"I want you."

"That's not the same thing."

"When you're royalty, it is."

I leaned on the staff, feeling much, much older than I was. "And what would have happened, Entipy . . . once you had me? If you truly didn't trust me . . . and the closest you could come to loving me was desiring me, in the same way that you might fancy attractive jewelry or a fine wine . . . what hope would there have been for the two of us?"

"Apropos," she sighed, as if pitying me greatly, "I thought you, of all people, understood. This is a hopeless world. We would have fit right in."

I let out a long sigh. "I want . . . more than that. I never thought I did until this very moment. I want to be . . . I want to be better than the world that surrounds me. I spent years thinking I was. But now . . . I genuinely want to be. And you should want it, too. And I know, beyond any doubt, that we can't possibly achieve that together, for more reasons than I can go into. And I know you say you can't trust me, and maybe I deserve that, but at least listen to me and believe me when I say this: I've spent my whole life doing what was right for me, even if it was wrong for everybody else. This is the first time I've actually done what I know is right for everybody else . . . even though it might be as wrong for me as it could possibly be. Will you accept that? Please?" And I sank to one knee. "Please . . . Your Highness . . . ?"

Entipy looked at me for a long moment, as if from a very great height. And then, very softly, she said, "Apropos . . . I have to admit . . . you've become the one thing I never really thought you'd be."

"Heroic?"

"No. Dull."

And she drew her cape around herself, raised her hood to cover her features, and walked away. For a moment, just a moment . . . I thought I heard a choked sob from her, but it might well have been my imagination.

I walked as quickly as I could, distancing myself from the castle, but stopped at one point to look back at it. In a high window, framed against a glimmer of light, I was sure I saw Entipy seated there, a single candle burning just in front of her face. I thought, *She's leaving a candle burning for me in the window,* and for half a heartbeat, I almost turned back to go to her. But then she blew the candle out and became one with the darkness.

I made my way to the front gate of the great wall surrounding the city. I drew my cloak tight around me, my hood up and over my face, trying to minimize my limp so as not to attract attention from the guards. Neither of them paid me the slightest mind. It might have been that I simply wasn't interesting-looking or important enough to warrant a glance from them, or perhaps Odclay had "greased" their palms as well. In either event, I passed through the front gates with no problem and increased my speed until I had left it behind me.

I made my way down the main road, then off to a less-used trail, then off to an even less frequented one. I kept moving, straining to hear sound of pursuit, but nothing came. The absence of it, though, did not cause me to fear it any less. I didn't run, not wanting to wear myself out, but I kept up a very brisk pace. Slowly the sun rose, and I, worn out from the constant moving, decided that it would be best to get off any roads entirely. Certainly forests held their own risks, but they were preferable to traveling roads that angry knights could come riding down, looking for escaped prisoners.

It might be that they'd never notice my absence. That the intention was that I would remain in the cell, never to be seen again by the eyes of man. On the other hand, what if the king changed his mind, or the queen implored him, or whatever, and my disappearance was discovered? Best to be far away when and if that happened.

I made my way into the woods and kept going until I found a pleasant-looking glen. I settled against a large rock, getting off my feet, allowing my rapidly pounding heart to settle into a rhythm that was a bit less frantic.

I thought about all that I had experienced and realized that: I had learned who my father was; I had made my enemies' lives miserable, at least for a time; I had avenged myself on Astel; I might have an idea as to who had killed poor Madelyne, and could explore that in the future; I'd had my share of rolls with females, and even though most of them—all right, all of them—had ended in total debacles, at least there had been entertainment in the doing; I'd slept in a fine bed for a couple of nights; and, most of all, I had a small fortune upon me. That was the most important thing of all, the most lasting. The riches which were safely in my belt and staff . . .

I patted the belt.

It felt odd. The weight was correct, but something appeared to be . . . wrong.

I pulled the belt out and opened the pouches.

Pebbles. Pebbles and rocks.

And a note. I opened it, my fingers numb.

Where do you think I got the money to grease the palms to get you out? And the remainder, of course, is in my pocket. My taking risks, after all, has its own price. Best of luck, son. Yours in laughter. —Odclay.

Quickly I unscrewed the top of the staff. That money was still in there . . . except it was sovs from the Outer

Lawless regions, useless for the area in which I was.

I screeched in outrage. I moaned. I sobbed. And finally, finally . . .

. . . I laughed. Laughed long and hard, and kept on laughing at this final joke which had been made upon me.

"Would you mind telling me what's so funny?"

I turned.

Sharee, the weaver, was standing there, as if she'd just materialized out of nowhere.

"I should have known," I sighed. "After all the times you spoke to me in my dreams, I should have known you'd show up now. . . ."

"I don't know what you're talking about," she replied. "You've said this before, and I'll say it again: I did not speak to you in your dreams. Now would you mind telling me what is so damned funny?"

"I am," I sighed. "I am destiny's joke. I was so close, Sharee . . . so close to having it all. Instead, it slipped through my fingers and I'm left with nothing. Sir Apropos of Nothing, just like the king said."

"You're better off," she harrumphed. "If you had something, you wouldn't know what to do with it. Better that you have nothing."

"Not necessarily." I managed a smile as I stood, adjusting my cloak. "I have you."

"You don't have me," she said tartly. "I'm simply journeying in the same direction you are, by coincidence."

"Really. We've met in a glen. You don't know which way I'm going."

"Of course." She hesitated and pointed west. "You're heading that way."

The truth was, I was heading east. Then again, the truth and I had always had a testy relationship.

"Amazing," I said. "It's amazing that you knew that. Well . . . let's be off, then."

We started off west, Sharee matching my stride.

"There's something you should know," I told her after a time.

"And what would that be?"

"This is my story."

She looked at me with open curiosity. "I beg your pardon?"

"We're going to have adventures. And they're my adventures. You're here to provide support for me."

She snorted disdainfully. "I think not. I'm a weaver. I'm magic. You're a lame fool with a staff. You are obviously accompanying me in order to provide amusing comic relief for my adventures."

I stopped where I was. "Then it's not going to work," I said flatly. "I refuse to exist as a side issue to someone else's epic again. That's no way to live."

"My sympathies, but that's the way it's going to be," Sharee said flatly.

"Then it's best that we part company."

"Fine."

"Fine."

We stood there, waiting for each other to turn away. Neither of us moved. To this day, I've no idea how long we stood there.

"We'll alternate," Sharee said abruptly.

My eyes narrowed. "Pardon?"

"Monday, Wednesday, Friday, it's my story. Tuesday,

Thursday, Saturday, it's your story. Best offer I'm going to give you."

I thought about it a moment and then nodded. "All right. That sounds fair."

"All right, then."

"All right."

We started off. And as we walked, I said, "Wait a minute . . . what day is today?"

"Sunday."

I moaned.

"We can switch off Sundays," she suggested.

"Fine. That'll be fine. So today is my Sunday."

"The hell it is," she replied. "Today's my Sunday. I need it more."

"The hell you do. You've no idea of the day I had yesterday."

"It can't compare to mine, I guarantee it," she said.

I stopped walking again. "Tell you what . . . you tell me about your day, I'll tell you about mine, we'll see whose was worse, and the worst story gets today."

"Fine." There were two stumps facing each other. We each sat on one. She pushed back her hood and said, "It all started in the Screaming Gorge of Eternal Madness . . ."

I stood up. "Next Sunday will be fine for me."

And we headed off into the west.

Thursday, Sunday was your stop. [illegible] I'm going to give you.

I thought about it a moment and then nodded. "All right. That sounds fair."

"All right, then."

"All right."

We started off. And as we walked, I said, "Wait a minute. What day is today?"

"Sunday."

I nodded.

"We can switch it around," she suggested. "[illegible] Then I'll be fine. So today is my Sunday."

[illegible] "Today's my Sunday [illegible]"

[illegible]

"[illegible]"

I suppose walking again. "Tell you what — you tell me about your day, I'll tell you about mine, whoever [illegible] the worse story gets [illegible]."

"[illegible]." There were two swings facing each other. We each sat on one. She [illegible] her hood and said, "[illegible]"

I stood up. "[illegible] Sunday [illegible] for me."

And we headed off into the west.

Pocket Books Proudly Presents

THE WOAD TO WUIN

Sir Apropos of Nothing
Book 2

PETER DAVID

Available in Paperback
from
Pocket Books

Turn the page for a preview of
The Woad to Wuin . . .

The One Bad Thing

It is important you understand that I do not like taking people's lives. I have done it several times but derived no pleasure from it. Furthermore it has always been in self-defense, and, as suspect as it may sound, it has usually come about as a result of someone inadvertently throwing themselves on some sort of sharp implement I happened to be pointing in his, her, or its direction. I have never, however, been the sort to start a fight when it could be avoided . . . or, for that matter, failed to run from it if remotely possible. Anyone who has read my previous chronicles of my "adventures," of which this is a continuation, is already rather painfully aware of that.

So you will understand the distress I felt when I was standing there in the middle of an otherwise lovely glade, on a fairly crisp and yet invigorating day, staring in dismay at the hairy-footed dwarf that I had unintentionally killed. A death which would unexpectedly thrust me—in every sense of the word—into an escapade that was alternately the most exhilarating, and most terrifying, that I had ever experienced. And considering what I had experienced previous to that point, that is saying some.

For those who are new to what can only in the broadest and most ironic terms be referred to as my hero's journey, I shall tell you in the simplest terms what you need to know in order to understand me. (Indeed, I should observe that if you are interested in my life, you may very well lack sufficient brain power to comprehend all but the most minimal of explanations.)

My name is Apropos, occasionally referred to as "Apropos of Nothing" due to my lowly birth and lack of . . . well . . . anything, really, that could be considered valuable. Of late I was dubbed Sir Apropos, still of Nothing, an honor which—for reasons I won't go into here—did not quite work out.

Suffice to say that one whose patrimony consists of a group of knights raping my tavern wench mother, providing me an existence of endless betrayal and deprivation which served to give me a somewhat cynical, shall we say, view of the world . . . well, one such as that does not end up living happily ever after. I was foolish enough to briefly entertain the notion, and paid severely for that unbecoming naïveté by winding up tossed in a dungeon barely twenty-four hours after being knighted, which was something of a record at the court of King Runcible in the state of Isteria.

Once I managed to escape the dungeon through means literally too ludicrous to go into here, I hit the road in the company of a rather vexing young sorceress (or "weaver," as her type is also known, short for "magic weaver") who called herself "Sharee," which may or may not have been her true name.

I never found out whether Runcible sent his knights after me to bring me back. On the one hand, his pride was no doubt hurt; on the other hand, he and his queen—and certainly his daughter—might have been well-pleased to be rid of me. If they had been determined to hunt me down, it likely would not have been all that difficult. My ears tended to stick out a bit too much, and my flaming red hair was long and unruly. My nose was crooked from having been broken several times, and although my eyes were a remarkably pleasing shade of gray, the rest of my hodgepodge of features invariably overwhelmed them. Furthermore I was lame of right leg, and got about with the aid of a sizable walking staff that also served as a formidable weapon. In short, I was easy to spot and difficult to disguise.

Sharee was less distinctive. She dressed customarily in black, with ebony hair cut short and curled around her ears, and her rather prominent chin perpetually out thrust as if she were challenging the world to take its best shot at her. There were times when it seemed to me that her prime reason for existence was harassing me and taking great pleasure in the bizarre vagaries of my life. Still, in some ways she was the truest friend I had ever encountered, if one defined *friend* as "perpetual irritant."

Just in case Runcible's knights did happen to be following us, we retreated west and later north, to take refuge in the Tucker Forest. This was not done without a certain degree of trepidation on my part. The Tucker Forest was a nesting area for a particularly vicious group of cutthroat monstrosities called the Harpers Bizarre, with whom I had considerable bad blood. I would far have preferred to take refuge in the Elderwoods of my youth, but the only way to get there was either along roads too heavily traveled for my comfort, or across the Screaming Gorge of Eternal Madness, about which the less said the better. Besides, Sharee seemed rather confident that if difficulties arose, her weather-related magiks could dispose of the Harpers with alacrity, and so the Tucker Forest became our temporary haven while we waited for the name Apropos to fade into the furthest recesses of royal memory.

Fortunately I had considerable proficiency in forestry, one of the few true talents I possessed other than evasion, self-preservation, and rank cowardice. I had developed the forestry skills in my youth, and they had not faded in time as I grew to young manhood. I was reaching the end of my teens when we took up temporary refuge in the Tucker Forest. We found a cave in which to reside, well hidden from casual observation either from ground level (i.e., thieves) or from overhead (i.e., the Harpers Bizarre). We figured we would spend a couple of days there and then work our way farther west in order to distance ourselves more from Runcible's men. I spent time hunting, catching small game, while Sharee preferred to alternate between meditating and acting as if she had something far better to do with her time than remain with me.

Occasionally, though, we had mild fun together. For instance, I commented to her that I would be interested in learning some magic. In response, she started teaching me card tricks. Not real magic at all, and I was quite irritated with her at first. But in short order, I actually derived some genuine amusement from it. I was a fairly quick learner, and also picked up some easy sleight-of-hand, including misdirection and the ability to apparently pluck a card out of the air. Not much of a trick to the latter, really. Simply keep your hand straight, hold the upper corners of the card securely on the back of your hand, between your fingers, and then snap it quickly forward. The card seems to have come out of nowhere. As noted, not genuine magic, but sometimes we measure the quality of life's passage by just how much of an assortment of mindless pastimes we develop to entertain ourselves through it.

In terms of hunting, at first I stuck to small animals. But I tired quickly of a steady diet of rabbit and squirrel. So I redesigned and reconfigured the traps for bigger bait, hoping to snag a small deer or perhaps even a straying unicorn. Immortal or not, such creatures could still die from a quickly snapped neck, and such were my traps intended for. Naturally I set them nowhere near the roads that occasional travelers might use, lest an unfortunate accident occur.

Yet it happened anyway.

I was moving through the forest one day with my customary stealth. It may sound boastful or vainglorious, but when I elect not to be detected in the woods, it is nigh unto impossible to find me. It is one of the few instances, outside of swimming, where my lame leg does not deter me. Stealth does not arise from speed, but from economy of motion. A high-speed marathon would leave me hopelessly abandoned, but if you were seeking someone to move at a snail's pace for days on end, I was your man.

Approaching one of my more crafty noose traps, I suddenly heard a startled and truncated yelp from ahead. It was definitely of a human variety of noise. It took me a moment to realize whence the sound had come—namely from my trap—and but a moment more to grasp, with horror, the likely significance of it.

Disdaining silence, I practically crashed through the underbrush, hoping there was time to salvage the situation. 'Twas not to be. Instead I came upon a scene utterly dismaying . . . and yet also utterly fascinating in a perverse way, and I do mean perverse.

The small pile of food which had served as bait within the snare now lay scattered about. The noose was drawn taut, dangling about three and a half feet in the air. And suspended from the noose itself, its feet clear of the ground by a good six inches, was the aforementioned dwarf.

It was a damned odd-looking thing. Its head was slumped to one side. It was round, with features that looked fairly squashed, as if someone had sat on its face. Its arms were the disproportionate length so common to its kind, but its legs were longer and less bow-shaped than one customarily saw in such creatures. Its feet were odder still. At first I thought it was wearing hairy slippers of some sort, but then realized that it was barefoot and simply had the most hirsute pedal extremities of any creature I'd ever seen that didn't also possess a tail.

It also sported an extremely sizable bulge in its loins which even its loose-fitting breeches couldn't obscure. I'd never been present at a hanging, but had heard that the victims of such incidents usually had themselves a fairly healthy protuberance at the moment of death, which had always struck me as somewhat puzzling. If anything could be deemed a sure killer of arousal, it was having your neck snapped. But here was I, first-hand witness to the phenomenon, and so knew it to be true. Who would have thought?

I still felt some measure of guilt for the passing creature's untimely demise, but there wasn't much I could do about it after the fact. So instead I proceeded to do the most reasonable thing one could under the circumstances: I checked him over for valuables. I didn't bother to cut him down; gruesome as his situation was, it was easier to inspect him while he was upright. While his most noticeable bulge began to diminish, I happily relieved him of another—a fairly decent purse hanging on his belt which I quickly discovered was filled with gold coins the like of which I'd never seen. Still, as opposed to coins unique to specific realms with different faces of monarchs etched in the surfaces, gold was definitely gold no matter whose countenance adorned it.

Then I spotted something twinkling on the brush just beneath the dwarf's dangling feet, shining and winking at me in the rays of the setting sun. I reached down and picked it up. It appeared to be some sort of golden ring, but it was much too large for ordinary wear. I could easily fit three of my fingers into the thing. An earring perhaps, but there was no clasp for it to fasten on. It felt rather warm, and I turned it over and over in my hands, inspecting it carefully. It was then I noticed some sort of writing on the inside. It was not easy to make out and, confusingly, the letters seemed to be fading along with the dissipating warmth. But what it read was:

One thing to rule them all.

I didn't know to whom "them all" referred, or what the one thing might be, so really I was somewhat ignorant of the purpose of the ring. Would that I had remained that way.

It was at that point that I heard something coming toward me through the woods. From the sound of it, it appeared to be a group of men, at least half a dozen. They were making no attempt to move quietly; a deaf man could have heard them coming. Unfortunately they were between me and the cave.

Without thinking, I shoved the ring in my pocket and quickly sought, and found, refuge amongst the underbrush. As I mentioned earlier, when I am endeavoring to hide in a forest, I am almost impossible to detect. I drew my cape around me and huddled low, unmoving in the lengthening shadows of the forest.

The men arrived in short order, and a more motley assortment one could not have imagined. The one who seemed to be the leader was a strong, fox-faced, handsome-looking individual. With him was an astounding array of . . . hell, I'm not sure what they were. A couple more hairy-footed dwarves, a few trolls, some other freakish-looking individuals. I had absolutely no idea where they could have come from; none of their ilk had ever passed through any of the regions in which I'd resided.

They saw at once the dangling dwarf, and oh, the moaning and caterwauling that they sent up then, I cannot begin to tell you. In catching the names they were tossing around, it appeared that the deceased one was called Bubo, and the tall man was Walker. The others had an assortment of staggeringly annoying monikers that were impossible to keep straight: Hodge and Podge, Hoi and Paloi, Hither and Thither, Tutti and Fruitti, So On and So Forth, etc. It was rather cloying, and I could only be thankful I wasn't traveling with the group as I would likely have beaten myself to death after two days rather than die slowly of excessive cleverness.

The tall one called Walker was standing directly in front of Bubo, obscuring him from my sight, and then he turned and looked grimly at the others. "The ring is not here," he said.

There were gasps and lamentations and growls of "Death to the thief!" which naturally didn't sit all that well with me.

"The body is still warm," said Walker. "The thief cannot have gotten far." Now, I have to admit, I bridled a bit at the word thief. Not that I wasn't one, you understand, but in this particular circumstance, it wasn't as if the deceased had any use for his possessions anymore. I figured I was as entitled to what he was carrying upon him as anyone else. "Spread out. Find him," Walker continued.

Moving in smooth coordination, they headed out in all directions. I didn't breathe. One of the dwarfs came within two feet of me but passed me by without noticing me hunkered down in the brush.

I waited what seemed an interminable time there, my legs

getting numb, my arms feeling like lead weights. Night had almost fallen when I finally chanced to rise, my sharp hearing convincing me that I was alone.

Except . . .

In a sense, I wasn't.

I felt an extremely odd tingling in my loins. My little soldier was standing at attention, and he wasn't little. Furthermore, I felt some sort of foreign object down there. Even though I knew I was alone, I still glanced right and left to ensure privacy, then reached down into my breeches to see what was up. Well . . . what else was up, beside the obvious.

To my utter astonishment, I discovered the ring, nestled securely at the base of my member. Apparently I'd had a hole in my pocket, and as if it had a life of its own, the ring had worked its way through and nestled into my loins, wrapping itself around my privates as if it were destined to be there. I pulled on the ring in an endeavor to remove it. It wouldn't come off. I tried again and again, as forceful as I could be while still retaining some delicacy, as I'm sure you can well imagine.

It didn't budge. Here I had been wondering how one could possibly sport such a sizable ring, and now I had inadvertently discovered the answer. Furthermore I was so swollen that it didn't appear capable of being removed until the tumescence went away. Which it did not seem inclined to do. And out here, exposed in the woods, I felt rather too self-conscious to "relieve myself" of the pressure.

I was utterly mortified, but I had nowhere else to go as I headed back to the cave. Fortunately I had my great cape with me, so I would be able to draw it around myself and hide the noticeable bulge, for I certainly did not need Sharee laughing at my predicament. My hope was that if I simply ignored the thing, it would go away. And certainly spending time with Sharee would increase that likelihood, for if I'd had any remaining interest in the opposite sex after my rather disastrous history of liaisons, the weaver was certainly capable of putting it to rest.

I hoped that she might not be in the cave when I arrived, just so I had a few minutes to get myself settled with the cape still around me. Such was not to be, however, for there she was, tending a small fire and looking up at me expectantly. "Did you bring food?" she inquired.

"Bad luck trapping," I said, which was true enough. Hungry we might have been, but I didn't think we were hungry enough to eat a dwarf. I settled down some feet away from her, adjusting the cape. My loins did not seem to be calming. Instead, in Sharee's presence, there appeared to be even more excitement than before. And I thought, Oh, my friend, are you barking up the wrong tree. If there is anyone who is not at all interested, it is—

She was upon me in a flash.

I could not believe it. One minute she was sitting there, looking at me oddly, and the next she was on top of me with such force that I slammed my head against the cave wall. Her hand went straight to the place I'd been trying to keep hidden, as if she knew what was going to be there. Her eyes were wild with a fiery light, and she was smothering me with kisses even as she started pulling both of our clothes off in her eagerness.

Now . . .

I'm not stupid.

I figured out what was going on in pretty short order. I didn't for a moment think that suddenly I had acquired so sensual, so commanding a personality that Sharee felt compelled to savage me in every carnal way imaginable. Obviously it was the ring. The damned thing was enchanted somehow, and it was an enchantment that no one—even a skilled weatherweaver such as Sharee—was able to resist. She was not in her right mind. Under the circumstances, I would have been a cad, a bounder, and an utter rotter to take advantage of the situation. And if you think that I failed to do so, then clearly you have not been paying attention.

Truthfully, although I was not exactly resistant to the concept, I'm not sure I could have kept her off me even had I desired to. She was unstoppable, and thanks to the ring, I was more than up to the challenge.

And later I was up to it again. And again.

And again.

All through the night.

I lost count. By the time the morning came, my head was swimming with exhaustion, my belly practically in pain from lack of nourishment. But my suddenly very public private was still fresh as ever, and Sharee just as enthusiastic. I let her have her way with me again, this time so bone weary that I didn't even move. I just lay there, splayed on the cave floor, and thought about bathing in freezing water.

Finally Sharee felt asleep, and I knew beyond question that I had to get the hell out of there.

Apparently realizing that the joy ride was over, my seemingly insatiable rod slumped a bit, but not enough for me to pull the ring off. Quickly I dressed and bolted from the cave. I figured that Sharee would be waiting for me when, or if, I got back.

I was ravenously hungry at that point. Perhaps Sharee could live on love, but I did not share that capacity. I moved quickly through the woods, counting on my staff—my wooden one, not the betraying member in my breeches—for more support than even my lame leg usually required. Animals seemed to be giving me wide berth, however, and the few nuts and leaves I could safely eat off the trees were hardly enough to keep me going, particularly after the evening of ardor I had spent.

I made my way to the main east/west road which ran through the upper section of the Tucker Forest and cut east. I knew there was an inn along the way. It wasn't much, but I figured that at least they'd have some sort of minimal food there, and I could replenish myself. I also needed to distance myself from Sharee for a time. I assuredly couldn't go back to sleeping in the cave with her; the woman obviously would not leave me alone. Not as long as I had this Significant Other to deal with.

I felt it stirring with renewed life as I approached the inn, and drew my cape even more tightly around myself. Fortunately enough it was a brisk morning, so no one would question why I was keeping myself so covered up.

Once inside, I took a table toward the back, in a corner, with the intention of keeping entirely to myself. The innkeeper, a dyspeptic-looking fellow, glanced at me suspiciously. I held up the money, jingled it slightly, and that seemed enough to satisfy him. He moved away as the serving girl approached me. I'll admit she was a comely thing, which is what made what happened next somewhat tolerable.

"A stein of mead," I told her, "and do you have any decent mutton?"

She looked me up and down. Even though I was covered up, I suddenly felt as if her gaze was boring right to where I didn't want it to go. I crossed my legs, cleared my throat, and started to repeat the question.

"Upstairs," she interrupted. "First door on the right. Now."

"But . . . I haven't eaten."

She brought her face toward mine, and her breath was warm and pleasant. "I'll be your appetizer . . . and your main course . . . and your dessert."

Oh, my gods. "Miss . . . I . . . that is to say . . ."

"Upstairs, now," and there was iron in her voice, "or I'll take you right here."

She meant it. I could see it in her eyes, hear it in her tone, she was quite serious.

I went upstairs, to the room she indicated. There was a bed there with a lumpy mattress. Ten seconds later she was there, and the waitress provided room service.

Five minutes later the waitress's mother burst in on us, shocked and appalled. She threw her sobbing daughter out, slammed the door behind her, faced me, and I knew then what was coming.

I was worried that the tavern keeper was the husband, and figured that he'd be upstairs in short order with an ax . . . or, worse, love in his eyes. But such was not the case; they were simply a mother and daughter who worked at the tavern.

And they had friends.

Lots of friends.

Now I have to tell you, a situation like this had, at one time, been one of my fantasies. I grew up in a tavern, saw whores in action. And I had always wondered what it would be like to be so in demand that people—women, in my case—would throw themselves at me by the cartload, and even be willing to pay me, just for the privilege of melding their bodies with mine.

Well, no one was offering me money, although I have no doubt that I could have fleeced them for all they were worth. I likely would have, too, had any of them given me the chance to talk.

Apparently there was a village nearby, and all I can surmise from the parade of female flesh that marched in and out of my room was that the menfolk were not doing their job. The women came to me in all shapes, all sizes, young and old, pretty and . . . less so. I tried to keep a smile on my face, tell myself that this was the price of fame. I literally, however, lost track of time. Day and night became meaningless to me. Oh, I was fed, at least. The tavern wench kept bringing me food. At one point the innkeeper stuck his head in, grinned, and said, "Keep at it, my lad! That's the ticket!" as if he was my best friend in the world. I managed a meager wave and realized that he was probably charging the women admission. He was making my money. It didn't seem fair, and if any part of me had been able to rise from the bed aside from the one part of me that appeared inexhaustible, I would have done something about it.

I tried to leave, several times. They wouldn't let me. Finally they tied me to the bed. There are worse ways to pass one's hours, but none come readily to mind.

* * *

I have no idea when Walker and his people showed up. It could have been a day later, a week later. I was floating in a haze of exhaustion and numbness. All I knew was that there was a thumping up the stairs, and the door burst open. For a moment I thought it was a mob of angry husbands, come either to chop me to bits or—for all I knew—have their way with me. Then I squinted as I recognized that improbably heroic face. I was nude from the waist down, obviously. I couldn't remember a time anymore when I'd worn breeches. He took one look, turned to others crowding in, and said firmly, "He has the ring."

There was certainly no use denying it. "You want it? Take it," I mumbled in exhaustion.

Walker stomped in, tossing a blanket over me. Producing a blade, he severed the bonds holding my hands to the bedframe. "It is not ours to take. I will not ask how you came by it; the past no longer matters. Thanks to the ring, you are now the possessor of the One Thing Which Rules Them All."

"The One Thing being . . ." and I pointed to my happy soldier.

"Yes." He nodded, and the others mimicked the nod. "That thing."

"And 'them all' would be . . . women."

"Yes," Walker said once more. "What you possess is a ring, forged in the—"

I held up my hands and rose from the bed, fumbling about for my breeches. "No. Don't tell me."

"But you should know," said Walker.

"Yes, it's a really good story," one of the dwarfs said, in a slightly whiny tone.

"I don't care!" I insisted. "It probably involves some powerful magic user somewhere, and dark forces, and evil hordes wanting it back. Right?"

"Well . . . essentially, yes," Walker admitted, looking a bit uncomfortable.

"Fine. Save it. And get them out of here." I pointed at the

cluster of women that was already assembling, seeming rather distressed over the prospect of my possible departure. "All I want to know is how to get rid of the thing."

"You must toss it," said Walker solemnly, "into the Flaming Nether Regions. Only there will it be melted, its threat ended for all time."

I knew the Flaming Nether Regions well enough. I had once been squire to a knight, Sir Umbrage, who hailed from thereabouts.

You may be wondering why I did not question the interest this mixed bag of meddlers might have had in the ring. I shall make it plain: Clearly they were heroes. Bubo, previous possessor of this lovely trinket, had probably been as much in demand as I was. Walker's people had obviously been serving to keep women away from him . . . or perhaps him away from women . . . while they escorted him to the Flaming Nether Regions. They were in the midst of some great quest, into which I had been unwillingly—and unwittingly—drawn. I like neither heroes nor quests, because becoming involved with either invariably gets people killed. I have no patience for adventures, even though I invariably seem to find myself in the middle of them, and the sooner I depart their vicinity, the better. Far from dauntless, I am easily daunted. I want nothing but to make money, have some fame, fortune, and fun, and survive to die of old age in my bed.

In short, I'm just like you. Look down your nose at me at your peril, for it is yourself you very likely judge.

So I had no interest in what had brought them to this point in time. I simply said, "Take me there."

We set off.

There was much trouble along the way.